CONFIDENCE

CONFIDENCE

*Rowland Manthorpe and
Kirstin Smith*

BLOOMSBURY
LONDON · OXFORD · NEW YORK · NEW DELHI · SYDNEY

Bloomsbury Publishing
An imprint of Bloomsbury Publishing Plc

50 Bedford Square　　　　1385 Broadway
London　　　　　　　　　New York
WC1B 3DP　　　　　　　　NY 10018
UK　　　　　　　　　　　USA

www.bloomsbury.com

BLOOMSBURY and the Diana logo are trademarks of Bloomsbury Publishing Plc

First published in Great Britain 2016

Extract appearing on page 2 from *Nietzsche: A Critical Life* by Ronald Hayman (1980)
29w p.340. Reprinted by permission of Oxford University Press.

Extract appearing on page 81 from *Nietzsche: A Philosophical Biography* by Rüdiger
Safranski. Copyright © Rüdiger Safranski 2002. Published by Granta Books, 2003.

Extract appearing on page 100 from *Nietzsche: A Philosophical Biography* by Julian
Young. Copyright © Cambridge University Press 2010.

This is a work of fiction. Names and characters are the product of the authors'
imagination and any resemblance to actual persons, living or dead, is entirely
coincidental.

British Library Cataloguing-in-Publication Data
A catalogue record for this book is available from the British Library.

Library of Congress Cataloguing-in-Publication data has been applied for.

ISBN: TPB: 978-1-4088-0254-0
ePub: 978-1-4088-3351-3

2 4 6 8 10 9 7 5 3 1

Typeset by Integra Software Services Pvt. Ltd.
Printed and bound in Great Britain by CPI Group (UK) Ltd, Croydon CR0 4YY

To find out more about our authors and books visit www.bloomsbury.com.
Here you will find extracts, author interviews, details of forthcoming events
and the option to sign up for our newsletters.

'The last thing I would promise would be to "improve" mankind. I erect no new idols; let the old idols learn what it means to have legs of clay.'

Friedrich Nietzsche, *Ecce Homo: How One Becomes What One Is*

Losing It

Before he died Nietzsche went mad. At the age of only forty-four he collapsed into insanity and never recovered. This is how it happened.

It began with a series of letters. At first these messages, written to friends and occasional correspondents, appeared to convey good news. For the first time in his adult life, Nietzsche was completely happy. His work was going wonderfully. His health was good – no, in fact, it was perfect. 'Everything comes easily to me,' he wrote. In the mirror he looked 'ten years younger'.

Gradually, this elation turned into a kind of megalomania. In reality, Nietzsche was an impoverished philosopher known to no one but a small circle of friends (among whom not a few believed he should stop embarrassing himself and do something respectable). In his letters, however, he was 'tremendously famous', a superstar. 'I exercise utter fascination on people,' he confessed to an old friend. To his mother he confided, 'They treat me like a little prince.' As his state of mind deteriorated, he took to signing himself 'Nietzsche Caesar'.

That was at the end of 1888. On the morning of 3 January 1889, Nietzsche saw a cabman beating a horse in the street. Tears streaming down his face, he ran over and threw his arms round the animal's neck, before collapsing on the ground. When he regained consciousness, Nietzsche was no longer himself; he sang and danced ecstatically and spoke in random bursts of thought. He continued to write letters, but now they were completely insane: 'I am flinging the Pope in jail,' he ranted. And it was these letters that caused his concerned correspondents to travel to see him, to find out if their friend really had lost his mind.

At first he showed signs of improvement. 'He recognised me immediately,' reported a friend, 'embraced and kissed me, was highly delighted to see me, and gave me his hand repeatedly as if unable to believe I was really there.' But over the next few years he shrank into lifelessness. 'Clearly he no longer suffers, no happiness or unhappiness,' wrote a visitor in 1894. 'In some terrible way he is "beyond" everything.'

Nietzsche's doctors diagnosed syphilis. Later scholars repeated this verdict – actually as a way of defending him against the accusation that his philosophy drove him mad – until it became part of the standard history. But aside from his headaches, which were most likely brought on by his bad eyesight, none of Nietzsche's symptoms are the ones you'd expect for someone with syphilis. (He did manage to contract an STI during a rare sexual encounter as a student, but there is nothing to suggest it was anything more than gonorrhoea.) From the perspective of the twenty-first century, syphilis looks like a default diagnosis, the kind of thing doctors surmise when they don't know what happened.

Here's what I think. Nietzsche's philosophy did drive him mad. He wanted to be his own ideal, and his ideal was a never-ending state of confidence, a perpetual high-on-oneself. Nietzsche was a philosopher of confidence, the first and the best. He didn't just write about confidence, he lived it too, through exhilarating highs and long, painful lows. In his determination to be confident, Nietzsche embraced his euphoria. Yet even as he shot up in his own estimation, the reality of his circumstances remained un-altered. The discrepancy between his ideals and his life became so great that his sanity could not sustain it.

Nietzsche told himself he could handle it. That's what confidence does: it tells you what you want to hear. *You can do more*, it whispers, and for a while it's true, because when you're confident, everything goes right. You've got a touch of magic. Risks seem less risky, and in a sense they are. You achieve, so naturally you believe – achieve, believe, achieve, believe, each time ratcheting up the level of risk, until belief exceeds the limits of achievement and the whole edifice comes crashing to the ground. It's the process that causes a financial crisis – and it happens in people just the same. Boom and bust economy; boom and bust personality.

Confidence lies to you. That is why you can't trust it.

The rain was stopping Ellie writing her dissertation. It dripped from the leak in the gutter onto the rotten wood of her window-sill: hard, heavy drips that sounded like someone knocking to come in. Ellie resolved to ignore it. She was lying in bed, laptop hot and wheezing on her chest like an asthmatic cat.

Today was the first day of the final semester of Ellie's final year of university. While everybody else went home over Easter, she had stayed at uni to finish her dissertation. Instead, her dissertation had finished her. She had . . . not a dissertation, but a mess, a disaster: thirty thousand words in infinitely nested folders, which at the beginning had been carefully filed with names like '1.5 (13 Feb 2008)' but now went under the titles of 'This shit' and 'The worst yet'.

Ellie took a deep breath to calm her rising panic. There was no getting away from it. She had to admit she was feeling 'down', 'really down', more or less 'desperate', and was showing all the 'symptoms' of 'depression'. She'd thought she'd be so much further on by the start of term. And she still had exams to revise for. But she couldn't think about that. 'Come on,' she murmured. 'Think. *What is important?*'

That bloody drip. Her best friend, Rose, had given it a name: 'Terence', after their useless landlord, who'd promised so often to come round and fix it, and the bathroom window, and the mushrooms in Rose's cupboard, it was as if he thought promising to do something was the same as actually doing it. Ellie opened up the email she had been mentally composing since the start of the year. 'Dear Terence. You arsehole.' Then she caught herself. She was wasting time – wasting time on something that she'd never send, that was sad and stupid anyway.

Rose shuffled sleepily into Ellie's room. Muttering darkly under her breath, she got into the bed, pulling the covers over her head.

Ellie typed a word – 'Nietzsche' – hoping that by some untapped instinct or muscle memory, it would transform itself into a sentence. After all, she'd done so much reading, she'd taken so many notes, she'd never worked as hard at anything in her life. But it was as if she began each day on the ocean bed. It took every scrap of mental effort to reach the surface and gasp some air. And when, the next day, she saw the two or three suggestive half-sentences this effort had produced, it astonished her. It sent her into shutdown. At times she felt really quite mad.

'Didn't Nietzsche go mad?' said Nadine, when she mentioned it.

No wonder. It made you think. If his philosophy drove *him* mad, fascistic old bastard, what chance did she have?

From under the covers came a muffled croak. 'That fucking drip.'

Ellie thought of things to say, but none of them seemed right. She wanted Rose to shut up, but at the same time she was glad of the company.

4

Rose lifted the cover to fix Ellie with a mascara-rimmed leer. 'It's Terence. He's lonely.' She spoke in time with the drip. '"Ellie, let me in. I'm wet for you."' She cackled.

'Ugh.'

'I told him. I said, "She's taken. Justin doesn't count, but there's this dead German guy she's been seeing. It's kind of complicated, but they've got a special bond."'

'Don't—'

'God, don't worry about Justin. He'll get over it.'

Ellie made a face – she had been worrying about Nietzsche. She was a truly rubbish girlfriend. She'd had a whole list of things to do over Easter – revise for exams, apply for jobs, read, jog, learn and then practise yoga, spend time with Justin – but it didn't make sense to focus on anything else until the dissertation was done. She'd make time for Justin later.

Rose wriggled her way up the bed, bones flashing just beneath her skin. Ellie saw, and then tried to forget, how thin she was. People – idiots – still said, 'It's just her build.' Right, the anorexic build. Strangely, it was often the same idiots who pulled Ellie to one side to whisper, 'You must be worried' and 'It's so sad.' It wasn't sad, it was bullshit – infuriating, but totally normal. Rose would grow out of it. In the meantime, all Ellie could do was try and keep her temper while Rose took half an hour to slice and dice herself a lettuce leaf and low-fat cream-cheese sandwich, no bread. (Though if Rose asked her again in that cooing tone of voice if she'd had anything to eat, Ellie wasn't sure she could be held responsible for her actions.)

'Lean forward.' Rose tugged at Ellie's pillow. 'And how is Friedrich this fine day?'

'I don't want to talk about it. Or maybe. I dunno.'

'I thought you had fifteen thousand words already,' said Rose doubtfully.

'I do. It's not.' Ellie swallowed a burst of irrational rage. 'It's not a problem of words, or number of words.' Rose didn't get it. She didn't think in paragraphs, or even in sentences. Her head was like a car boot sale: full of the thought equivalent of 'collectible' porcelain knick-knacks and cassette tapes, hidden masterpieces mixed in with weird old tat. 'I honestly feel like I'm not going to finish this dissertation. After three crappy years I'm going to fail and the whole thing will have been a waste of time. It's not like I care about having some amazing career, but, it's my *life*, you know . . .'

Spying something on the floor, Rose leapt up to grab a dust-filmed CD. 'I told you this was here!'

Rose didn't like other people's weaknesses. With a great effort of will, Ellie cracked a single laugh. 'Even my misery is a cliché!'

'Have you had anything to eat?'

There was a long, dark silence.

'Come on, let's do something. Cinema! We could go to the cinema.'

'I've got to work.' Ellie wasn't speaking right; her words were slurred. 'I'm gonna go to the library.' She made no move to get up: the thought of that desk in the library, her laptop wheezing away at her, the chaos of her thoughts countered only by the chasm of the internet, kept her pinned to the bed.

'Fuck you then.' Rose's voice boomed in the tiny bedroom. 'I've got to work myself anyway. But I will treat you to one drink at the Shackle first *if* you can spare the time.'

Ellie knew by now the Shackleton Arms's Cabernet Sickinyon didn't help. 'No. I should go straight there.'

'Okay, you're right.' Rose put her hands on her hips. In her pyjamas, she looked about eleven years old. 'Straight to the library *via* the Shackle.'

Ellie gave in and tried to muster a smile.

The drip dripped.

'Sorry I'm such a boring bitch these days,' said Ellie.

'You are,' nodded Rose. 'You are.'

Thinking about confidence is harder than it seems. Both in theory and in practice, it is hard to get a grip on. It's undeniable, yet impossible to define. There's something innately mysterious about it, more like magic than anything else.

You know it when you see it, that's for sure. Confidence is unmistakable: it comes off people like a smell (not necessarily a smell everybody likes). You know it when you feel it too. You're completely at ease, natural and right in yourself. Your movements are so sure they could be preordained, but at the same time they are free and relaxed; you are loose yet also alert. Nietzsche put it beautifully: 'A continual feeling that one is climbing stairs and at the same time resting on clouds.'

It doesn't matter whether you're dancing, running, speaking, writing or thinking, when you feel like that, it *is* magical. Those moments are like a gift from some higher power, but at the same time they're an expression of your true self, your best, most complete self. It's a perfect moment, extending seemingly for ever – a sense of infinite potential and possibility.

Maybe it's fear of losing confidence that stops us focusing on it: there's an almost superstitious belief that if you look confidence in the eye, it will disappear. I've wasted hours worrying about it – but I didn't *think*. What is confidence? Why is it so important?

Every aspect of life is conditioned by confidence: sex, work, socialising, sleep – everything from the way you dress to the way you stand. Even the economy is controlled by confidence: it's the invisible force that makes the whole thing go round, what John Maynard

Keynes called 'animal spirits'. But although everyone agrees it's indispensable, no one can say exactly what it is, or how to get it.

Self-help books don't help. They start with the assumption that confidence is the most precious thing in the world and everything in them follows from that premise. (It's like reading a business book to find out about the true nature of money.) When you speak to professional psychologists, you get the same thing. You can't even get a simple statement of what confidence is – it always turns out to be some version of: 'Everybody thinks it's important, so therefore it must be.' I'm not saying they're wrong, but it's frustrating. If I'd never read Nietzsche, I wouldn't have a clear idea of confidence at all.

'My dad's splitting up with his wife.' Ben rolled the ping-pong ball around his palm. 'So he kept wanting to take me out in Bristol and get shitfaced, which was incredibly depressing, and also annoying 'cause I was trying to do my dissertation.' He launched a looping topspin serve. 'Here's some life advice: don't become a single fifty-five-year-old who keeps making creepy remarks about Carol Vorderman.'

'The wanking man's think,' said Charlie.

'Exactly.' Ben narrowly missed Charlie's trickling dropshot. 'In other news, I had an actual recurring nightmare about my Quaternary Palaeoenvironments exam.' He shuddered. 'You serve.'

Charlie and Ben had followed a bunch of first years through the card-access doors of Paterson, their old halls. Despite its *Changing Rooms*-style makeover (seven years too late), the common room was still a perfect tragedy of the commons. A light snowfall of beanbag beans dusted the floor, the bags themselves piled in a corner, wrinkled and tired of life. Even so, Charlie felt strangely at home here. This was how he'd got to know Ben in first year: playing endless sets of table tennis, until they'd reached the point where they could just rally, passing the ball back and forth, with no end in sight.

'Mine was a nightmare too.' Charlie's backhand waft sailed over the end of the table. He fingered his bat distractedly. 'I've been thinking about breaking up with Sara – I mean I *am* breaking up with her. Now. As in, as soon as she gets back.'

'Shit.' Ben paused mid-serve. 'But I thought you guys sorted it out.'

'We did. I dunno!' Charlie threw up his arms. 'We had this big chat after Christmas about all our relationship problems, and it was good, and we agreed it was no one's fault—'

'You were all into each other at New Year—'

'It was such a relief I'd got it out there, you know? But then . . .' Charlie nodded for Ben to serve. 'You know when you get an essay back and it's got loads of feedback and you think, "Okay, I really see how to put this right"?'

'I always think that. Once I've stopped crying.'

'Then you start the next essay and realise you know how to make the *last* one better, but you still don't know how to write a good essay. You don't actually have a clue . . . Oh crap' – Charlie missed with a wild forehand. 'And then you start to think: maybe the problem isn't the essay, maybe the problem is the *person writing it.*'

Ben grimaced. 'Sounds serious. Luckily you've come to me with my dearth of experience.'

'Experience only confuses things as far as I can tell. I mean, when I think about Becky.' Charlie's first (and only other) girl-friend, Becky, had been second oboe to Charlie's third in the interschool youth orchestra. He had lost his virginity to her on an orchestra trip to Bordeaux in summer 2004. (Sometimes he still daydreamed about sitting through sunny rehearsals with a painful boner, miming along to the James Bond medley.) 'Maybe it isn't fair to compare, but when I think what that was like, it makes *this* feel kind of conscious and convenient and all about our little uni routines, you know? A bit like work. I mean, without the Commitment Craze – everyone suddenly in their little mini-marriages – I wonder if we would have got together at all. Christ, even *ending* it is work. Me and Becky split up 'cause she went to Aberystwyth – there wasn't all this torturous deciding.'

'Well . . .' Ben served an easy opener and they settled into a predictable to and fro. 'Maybe you're overthinking it.'

'This from Ben Redpath, who has to bring sandwiches because the lunchtime decision ruins his day.'

'Nobody sells cheese and crisp sandwiches – there's a business idea for you. All I'm saying is you like her. And I like her, for the record.'

'*Thanks.* What kind of advice column is this?'

'Well, I'm practically institutionalised,' Ben shrugged apologetically. 'I want everyone else to be in a relationship, so I can be sure they're having just as boring a time as I am. But what happened – did something change your mind?'

'Basically nothing.'

Ben caught the ball in one hand. 'Oh ho!'

'Seriously, nothing like that. Serve. I'll tell you but I warn you it's going to sound stupid. I bumped into Anita Wilkins in the George.'

'Who's that?'

'She was deputy head girl at St Stephen's, the girls' school nearest mine.'

'*Mmmm.*'

'Nothing happened. At all. The point is – I'm only saying this 'cause it's pertinent – everyone fancied Anita. Remember those

10

school parties where one minute it was incredibly awkward and the next you'd had three beers and were more or less unconscious?'

'Sadly, no.'

'Well, at those parties, she was the girl. I don't know how else to say it. Anyway, the point is, for what it's worth, she'd had a few drinks and she let it be known that in sixth form, she fancied me.'

'Wahay, seventeen-year-old Charlie!'

Charlie smiled sheepishly. 'She said I was "intriguing". Clearly, she hasn't spent a lot of time with me. I know this sounds totally pathetic, but—'

'It got you thinking you weren't such an ugly, boring bell-end after all.'

'You know me so well. I mean, whenever I saw Anita Wilkins, I was practically sweating with nerves and apparently I still managed to come off as "intriguing". I dunno . . .' Charlie shrugged, wide-eyed. 'Maybe I could be having an exciting relationship that I actually enjoy.'

'It's that kind of talk that endangers lives.'

Charlie's phone beeped in his pocket and he missed an easy backhand.

'Is that Sara?'

'Probably.' Feeling light-headed, Charlie leaned on the table. 'It's like an operation, right? There's no getting out of it. You've just got to be straight but not brutal, in and out, as kind as you can.'

'God knows.' Ben leaned back, fending off the question. 'I mean, that *sounds* right.' Charlie nodded mechanically. 'And I suppose . . .' Ben sidled towards the vending machines, doing keepie-uppies on his bat. 'I suppose if it doesn't work out, you can always get back together.'

2

What It Is

So confidence feels right – that's a bit like saying that happiness feels blissful, or love, lovely. This is the trouble with trying to get at confidence from the point of view of a confident moment: when you've got it, it's self-evident. It's obvious what it is and where it comes from, which is why there always seems to be more of it round the corner. (Like time: you've got loads of it, then suddenly you're running late.) I find it easier to think about confidence by thinking about what confidence is *not*.

What is the opposite of confidence? The opposite of happiness is sadness. The opposite of freedom is imprisonment. But is the opposite of confidence depression? When you're feeling down, you don't think, 'If only I could be confident.' You think, 'If only I could be all right' or 'If only this would stop.' Saying that the opposite of confidence is depression feels a bit like saying that the opposite of love is loneliness. If you were loved, you might not feel lonely, but that doesn't mean that if you weren't lonely you would be loved, the way you would be free if you left prison. Plus, you can be in love *and* feel lonely. (It doesn't make sense when it happens either.)

When I say 'what confidence is not', I don't mean opposites, not in that black and white way. I mean a less schematic but undeniable experiential difference, like when you're with someone and you appreciate their company and you respect them, and you don't fancy them at all. All of a sudden, it's lightning-clear what attraction is. This, you could say, is the theory of 'adjacent opposites'.

The adjacent opposite of confidence would be the feeling you get when you turn up to some event and you become aware that you don't feel as good as you expected to. You're not funny or lively; you're dull and at the same time, edgy. You can't get comfortable. You become horribly conscious of all your movements and thoughts, even the thought that you're horribly conscious, which as soon as you've had it, becomes the only thought in your head. It's as if you've been separated from yourself, for no good reason – it's just a party, for Christ's sake – but you're out of place, you don't work properly, and you probably never will.

It's not nerves, because nerves pass. Nerves can be settled with a drink, whereas drinking only makes this feeling worse. And, unlike nerves, this feeling can't be confronted. Trying to fight it is like trying to fight insomnia: the harder you fight, the worse it gets. You're overthinking, and you can't fight overthinking with thought.

Confidence, in a strange way, is acting without thought. It's not that we stop thinking when we're confident. Rather, we access a different part of our intelligence, one that is actually faster and more capable than the painstaking connection of cause and effect.

For want of a better word, I call the adjacent opposite of confidence: self-consciousness.

Nauseous with guilt, Charlie sat in Sara's room, waiting for her to get back from the loo. The rain hammered on the plastic roof of the kitchen extension. Charlie's task was overwhelming him. He trembled with intense, first-day-of-school nerves he'd almost forgotten he knew how to feel, recriminating himself for his careless handling of her feelings, for being, in uni terms, a 'bad bloke'.

Did he love Sara? Charlie wondered. How did you *know* when you were in love? Love was strange like that. The second you began to wonder, more than idly, whether you were in love or not, the game was up. Doubt killed it – or perhaps made it painfully obvious that it had never been alive to begin with.

Sock-muffled steps padded up the stairs. Charlie looked longingly at the first-floor window and dreamt of shimmying down the pipe, never to be seen again.

'Why are you sitting in the dark?' said Sara.

Charlie's thoughts raced in vital yet meaningless circles. To cover his confusion, he started for the light switch.

'No, no, stay there.' Sara climbed over her bed to turn on the fairy lights and Minnie Mouse clock lamp Charlie had bought her from Save The Children. Instinctively, he checked out her bum, then wished he hadn't. It was like seeing her from the perspective of the strange men who would soon be chatting her up. 'I think we should break up': the words rattled round his skull. 'I wish to break up'? 'Let's break up'? 'Do you ever think, maybe, about us breaking up some time'?

Over the Easter break, partly in order to mask his doubts, partly to deny them to himself, Charlie had attentively called Sara every day. Now he regretted it. He wished she already knew there was something wrong. He wished *she* would break up with *him*.

The photos on Sara's wall caught the light; bleached faces in uni clubs flashed in unison like a shoal of startled fish. Sara leaned over to give Charlie a kiss. 'Are you all right? You look a bit wild-eyed.'

It was the perfect opening, but all Charlie could do was stare mutely at the fairy lights. He got up and circled the room, watching his progress in the big mirror on the back of the door. The sight of himself was comforting – there he was, same as ever – yet also distracting. He needed to focus on the awful task at hand.

'Do you need a paracetamol?' Sara rummaged in her bedside drawer. She loved taking charge of people, not for herself, but for their own good. The combination of her desire to do things for others and his willingness to have things done for him was the central pillar of their relationship.

'I'm fine.'

'Taz was telling me' – Sara carried on rummaging – 'about this friend of his who's set up a business delivering drinks to . . . Well, anyone, but students, really. You can call up any time between five p.m. and five a.m. and they'll bring chilled drinks, snacks, skins, whatever you want to your door. Clever, isn't it?'

'Mm.' For a long time now, Charlie had wanted to be an entrepreneur. He knew that to be an entrepreneur, you simply had to get on with it. You appointed yourself – you appointed yourself boss. But somehow, in spite of Sara's cheerleading, he hadn't yet managed to translate his ideas into action. He had entrepreneur's block.

'They've already got like five hundred likes on Facebook.' Sara was on the floor now, sweeping an arm under the bed.

'I don't need paracetamol,' Charlie said, more snappily than he'd intended.

'I just want to know where it is. I told Taz he should put us in touch with them. It's quite similar to Social Tiger, don't you think?'

Social Tiger was Charlie's best business idea so far. Like all the best ideas, it was beautifully simple. He would offer queue jumps and free drinks to students via Facebook, then he'd get bars and clubs to pay to promote their nights. It would be an instant success and grow with incredible speed, until it was acquired by Google for $2 billion. Game over. He just had to set it up first.

When Charlie first had the idea, it had been incredible. It was like, those people who start successful businesses at uni, that was going to be him! It wasn't the money (he didn't care about money. As long as he could have nice clothes, good food and holidays three times a year, money wasn't important to him). It was the idea that he'd found his thing, the thing he was going to do with his life, and it was awesome. It was like discovering the girl you loved, the one you wanted to spend all your time with, the one you loved so much you didn't care what she looked like, and she was truly, objectively beautiful. You wouldn't have cared if she wasn't – but she was. He could have been an accountant – but he wasn't, he was an entrepreneur.

'I think we should break up' – the words were on the tip of his tongue, when from the room next door came the start-up chord of Meredith's computer. The walls in Sara's house were toilet-paper thin. There was always the sound of Meredith typing or breathing, or the window-rattling thump of Fergus walking about on top of your head. Charlie squatted down to put on some music.

What do you put on to break up with your girlfriend? Something sad? Something upbeat? Charlie had been watching a lot of old football documentaries on YouTube over the holidays. When Glenn Hoddle told Gazza he wasn't going to France '98, he remembered, he opted for Kenny G . . . This wasn't helping. In a panic, Charlie pressed play on whatever was in there: Lily Allen. But the first track was 'Smile'. That was about a break-up – he hammered at the eject button.

'What's wrong with Lily Allen?' said Sara. 'Or I know, put on that one with the whistling at the beginning.'

'Peter, Bjorn and thingy?'

'Yeah.'

Things were so much easier when Sara told him what to do. It was terrible for him, he knew, but he relied so much on her advice. Like: should he get a haircut? Should he leave it? (The possibilities were endless.)

'Leave it!'

Charlie looked up, startled.

Sara waved her hand under her chin. 'You'll make it worse.' He'd been picking at an ingrown hair on his throat, just above his Adam's apple. He hadn't even noticed. For the last year or so Charlie had been getting ingrown hairs a lot, little bumps under the skin that had to be operated on with a safety pin before they went septic. Normally Sara performed the surgery – and even claimed to enjoy it. 'Here.' She advanced on him. 'Let me.'

If only he wasn't so vain! Charlie was powerless in the face of her generosity. He was tilting his head back to let Sara get at his throat when all of a sudden he froze. 'Stop.'

'I don't mind.'

'I don't want you to!' Rather than waiting for Sara's reaction, Charlie turned away. Left hanging, she retreated in a hurt way.

As Meredith revved her hairdryer, Charlie snapped on the album with an unsteady hand. The CD chittered, then settled, and the chipper drumbeat filled the room with inappropriate optimism.

Charlie watched Sara until she sensed his agonised gaze.

'Do you ever think,' he began, 'about maybe us breaking up . . . some time?'

3

Instinct

Nietzsche said being confident was following your instinct: 'One acts perfectly only when one acts instinctively.' Exactly what Nietzsche meant by instinct is up for debate, but in essence, I think he's totally right. That is how confidence feels. When we act confidently, we are acting out some impulse truer and deeper than rational thought.

Nietzsche believed too much emphasis was placed on thought and self-control and not enough on instinct and self-expression. Like his great inspiration Darwin, he saw humans as part of nature. We are animals, he said, and the best thing we can do is to embrace our animal side. Being confident, for him, meant throwing aside the curse of self-consciousness and unleashing the potential beneath.

By acting on instinct, Nietzsche didn't mean going wild and letting it all hang out. As he put it: 'Every artist knows how far from the feeling of letting oneself go his "most natural" state is, the free ordering, placing, regulating, shaping in moments of "inspiration".' Unlike Rousseau, Nietzsche didn't believe in going back to some imagined Eden, where everyone would wander round naked and fruit would fall from the trees into our hands. The feeling was what mattered to him: he wanted us to *feel* natural. If we feel natural, he seems to say, we can combine the ingenuity of civilisation with the rightness and power of instinct.

That's Nietzsche; he liked to think big. I have more modest ambitions. When I say confidence, here's what I mean: the ability to do what you want without your thoughts getting in the way.

'I really loathe Nietzsche,' said Ellie.

Getting out helped her feel more like herself. She'd got dressed and everything, like a normal human being. Okay, so a normal human being wouldn't be sporting this particular combination of beige tracksuit bottoms, suede boots with fake fur trim (Ellie's only waterproof shoes, purchased, like most of her clothes, in a state of high stress at the Salvation Army) and Justin's XXL Slayer Death hoodie under a trench coat, but still. It was a start. Outside was better than it looked. The rain was easing off and it wasn't cold.

'Have you noticed,' said Rose, 'how it's always several degrees warmer outside than it is in the house?'

Under the same umbrella, they picked their three-legged way past a puddle. A group of schoolgirls were coming out of the school gate, black-lined eyes shining with some operatic drama. They glared at Ellie and Rose as if they were embarrassed to be sharing the same pavement.

'It's like,' said Ellie, 'here's this guy who barely spent ten minutes alone with a member of the opposite sex in his whole life—'

'Imagine that.'

'—and he's like, "Women shouldn't be trusted" and "Going to see a woman? Don't forget your whip." He genuinely believes there's this small group of "higher men" who are the only reason for existence and that everyone else should devote their lives to

19

helping them achieve greatness. And guess what, everyone in this group is *exactly like him*. You can really see why the Nazis thought he was the poster boy for the Third Reich. What a dick.'

'You should say that in your dissertation. You should say, "Nietzsche is a dick." Seriously. You should lay into him. Why not?'

'You can't. It's not like that. With the major philosophers, you're supposed to criticise them from the inside. You sort of trip them up by pointing out where they've contradicted themselves or—'

'You should cuss him out, rap style. "Your momma's so fat that she wore a blue dress and seagulls dived into it." Uh!' Rose started to rap. 'Yo Nietzsche. You've got problems. Did yo daddy beat ya? Did yo momma eat ya? Don't fuck with me or I'll be on you like Jack Reacher.'

Ellie laughed. This was why no one should feel sorry for Rose. Who could feel sorry for such an incredible bitch?

'Yo Friedrich.' On a roll, Rose started up some hip-hop hand waving. 'Do you like free dick? Don't make that face, Ellie. Do you like it up your arse? Do you . . .' She grimaced. 'You've put me off.'

'Don't look at me! Did Missy Elliot get where she is by listening to haters?' As they skirted another puddle, Ellie could feel the wisps of an idea ghost into her head. *Maybe I should criticise Nietzsche. I've been holding back. Maybe that's what's been inhibiting me.* She tried to let the thought come to her, keeping very still, as if it were an animal she might scare away.

'Neil!' bellowed Rose, making her jump. 'What are you doing?'

The Shackleton Arms was a mock Tudor bungalow in one corner of a blistered concrete car park, hung around with rotting Carlsberg bunting. A sign warned: 'Parking for ■ customers only.' Where the old name had been blacked out, someone had scratched

'DRUNK'. It was thoroughly off-putting, but for Ellie and Rose, that was the appeal. It wasn't a student venue. It didn't have TV screens advertising 'Your Letting Agent' and 'Your Student Nightclub'. No one was going to come in wearing a onesie or drop by for a hole on a round of pub golf.

In the shelter of a maroon trade refuse bin, a drooping emo kid with a purple streak in his dyed black hair sipped gingerly on a cigarette.

Rose marched towards him. 'Neil! Are you smoking?'

Neil flicked his cigarette into a drain below a 'classy touch', fake, hanging topiary ball. 'What's it to *you*?'

'Oh, Neil.' Rose put a barely-there arm round his shoulder. 'What are we going to do with you? Ellie, you've met Neil right? Neil's my main man, my partner in crime.' She waggled devil horns. 'Neil *rawks*, don't you Neil?'

Neil glared at his feet. 'When I'm not *working*.'

'Neil's my project, aren't you, Neil? He keeps me from going under when this job gets too depressing. So . . . most of the time.' Rose shook herself, like, *Let's not get into that now*. Inevitably, as soon as they had found this sanctuary, Rose had taken things too far, getting, losing and regaining a job working at the bar and embarking on fraught relationships with the owner, staff and regulars. 'Ellie, you're coming in for one, right? I'll give you my staff drink.'

Rose had taken the umbrella with her, leaving Ellie to shelter in the doorway of the pub. Her idea was gathering mass in her head. Why shouldn't she criticise Nietzsche? He certainly deserved it. She could almost grasp the first line. If she didn't spill it now . . . 'I'll come in for a bit.'

The Shackleton's bar was a square head in the middle of a male-pattern baldness carpet. Two oldie men sat on either side like a pair of sticky-out ears: Regular Steve and Regular Pete. Michael the Slovakian Giant loomed behind the bar.

'The girls!' he said. 'How are you today?'

Rose scowled. 'Michael, don't start. I'm not in the mood.'

'Hey, Michael,' said Ellie, going straight to the low table next to the game machine – her table. Paul, the owner of the Shackleton, had once told her that the electric blue leather armchair there was his 'signature piece'. She took out her laptop, then thought better of it. She should write this out longhand. Her bag was full of lint, scraps of paper and chewed pen tops, as if some large rodent had been nesting there. Eventually she found a biro and the back of a lecture handout.

And, yes, as soon as she had them, here it was: the blankness. It was so inevitable she could barely summon up the energy to panic. It wasn't worrying, it was boring, like the third day of a bad flu.

Ellie doodled, hoping to draw the ideas out.

'You won't be wanting this, I assume.' Rose placed a Slovakian-sized white wine in the middle of Ellie's pad. 'A goblet of inspiration for the Ellie,' she did her Michael. Ellie picked up the glass to move it. It seemed ungrateful not to take a sip. A glass of wine could be just the thing right now – it would stop her overthinking, keep her in this more positive frame of mind.

'That's my girl!' Rose perched on the arm of Ellie's armchair. 'You don't have a drinking problem. You've got problems. Therefore you drink.' Rose ducked suddenly behind the table. 'Hold up. We've got a trespasser.'

Ellie looked up. A dark-haired boy was ordering at the bar. He was wearing deck shoes, low-slung Jack Wills tracksuit bottoms and a green American Apparel hoodie. This weird imitation of American college style was the uniform of posh twats across uni.

In the Shackleton, he looked like a CBBC presenter doing a piece on the dangers of underage drinking.

'I feel violated. Didn't he see the sign? "No twats allowed."' Rose sipped her Diet Coke. At work, she used it like a drip, a constant supply of low-fat fuel. 'Shall I get Michael to turf him out?'

'Oh fuck.' Ellie paused her biro mid-swirl. 'Rose, it's today.'

'What's today?'

'It's the first day of semester. They'll all be back.'

Rose gave a shudder that turned into a shiver of cold. 'But why isn't he at the Mitre making racist jokes and saying, "Hahaha banter!"?'

The boy had paid for his drink and was standing at the bar, not sure what to do with himself.

'I blame *you*. He's probably one of your friends.' Rose did a plummy voice. '"Mummy, we were at halls together. He had the balcony next to mine."'

There were two universities in Rose and Ellie's uni town: Ellie's, founded some time in the 1800s, which required AAB at A-Level, and Rose's, founded some time in the 1960s, which required, well, less. Idiots at Ellie's uni called Rose's uni 'the Poly'. When, in a rash moment of early sociability, Ellie had gone to the Varsity football match between the two, the fans round her had chanted, 'Your dad works for my dad,' and the fans at the opposite end of the stadium had chanted back, 'I'd rather be a poly than a cunt.' It was the closest the two sides ever came to mixing. When Ellie had told her former housemates she was moving in with someone from the Poly, they'd reacted as if she'd announced she was marrying a horse.

Ellie looked more closely at the boy. He *did* look familiar.

'Oh ho! You *do* know him! What's he called? Tarquin! Yoo-hoo. Over here!'

'Don't,' hissed Ellie.

'You're old friends, you should catch up.'

The boy had turned and spotted them. He lolloped over with a surprised smile.

'I hate you,' Ellie told Rose.

'Was he one of your first-year mistakes?' yelled Rose.

'Hi,' said the boy, settling down with his pint. 'It's Ellie, isn't it?' He pointed at himself. 'Charlie. Haven't seen you for ages!'

The last time Ellie and Charlie had spoken, it was late one Wednesday in autumn of the second year. Nobody knew it, but everybody sensed it – this was the best, freest, most exciting time of university, the time that everybody would look back on with hazy satisfaction.

Charlie and Alistair were rounding another suburban corner.

'We're lost, aren't we?' Alistair shook his head.

'This must be it!' Charlie pointed at a bass-pumping terraced shack.

'Do you think we need a password or something?'

'It's a student squat party, not an Excel spreadsheet. Come on.'

Past the untamed hedges, a handful of people were smoking weed on the steps. The door was wedged open, framing a hallway crammed with bodies. Drum'n'bass boomed from the front room.

'Do you know *anyone*?' Alistair muttered.

'This is awesome. Let's get a drink!'

Ellie and Maggie pushed their way out of the dance room, sweaty and elated. They ducked down, wriggling a low path to the kitchen: a smoke-filled, fairy-lit cacophony, which spilled out to a garden, bonfire blazing. Edging through the mass, Maggie pulled a plastic bottle of White Russian from the fridge.

'So much milk.' She held her stomach. 'So much dancing!'

'But your bones are going to be like *iron*.' Ellie swigged from the bottle. 'You will basically *never die*.'

Charlie was suddenly disgorged from the crowd, and landed beside them on the cardboard-covered linoleum. 'Can I have some?' he asked, as Alistair followed. 'Also what is it?'

'It's all your dreams come true in a cool, calcium-packed drink.' Ellie passed it over. 'Didn't expect to see you here. Do you guys know Maggie?'

'Cool party,' Alistair greeted her.

'Ach, it wasn't really me,' Maggie smiled. 'Owen and Giles are the brains and brawn of this operation.'

'Is it true Justin made hooch?' Ellie pulled out a plastic pouch and began rolling a cigarette.

'Yeah! Jesus, it was so much fucking effort! And my God it smelt.'

'Yeah, my dad makes sloe gin sometimes,' said Alistair shyly. 'It's like his pet.'

'So you guys decided to give Rehab a skip tonight?'

'Yeah, just for a change. It's a real relief not to be there actually.' Charlie dug out beers for him and Alistair. 'Do you ever find clubs are like doing circuits? You don't really get to talk to anyone.' He opened his can. 'Like you two – I know you both, I know your names, I like you. But when do we ever actually get the chance to chat? Are we just going to leave after three years, never having got further than "Hello, how are you?"'

'I totally agree.' Ellie licked her cigarette paper. 'So how are you?'

'Yeah, fine. How are you?'

'Fine, yeah.' There was a pause. 'See you later, then.'

'*Exactly*. I'm done with this acquaintance crap. We're going to push through this barrier right now. Tell me something about yourself.'

'Can I have my cigarette at the same time?'

They squeezed over to the doorway, passing Owen carrying bags of ice on his shoulder. 'Maggie, wanna smash some of this?' Alistair hung back to help, Ellie and Charlie settled on the back doorstep.

'Something about myself . . .' Ellie lit the rollie. 'Okay, so this week is in fact my first week as a single person since I was fourteen.'

'Ah-ha! A serial monogamist.'

'Is instant judgement part of this game?'

'No, but statements of fact are allowed.'

'Fair play.'

'So. Bad break-up? If you don't mind my asking.'

'Not for me.'

'You did the breaking up, then?'

'So far, I've always done the breaking up.'

'That many times?'

'Mmm. I'm not massively proud of it.'

'So what are you going to do with your new-found freedom?'

'Well, obviously,' she laughed, 'get rid of it as soon as possible. There's kind of already a . . . thing.'

'Wow. You don't waste time.'

'Or I do – on like, an industrial scale. Anyway, what's your story?'

'Hmm . . . what's my story? I'm going to pick a new topic. Here's a little fact about me: I do Politics.'

'Oooh. Do you like it?'

'We-e-ell, I like *The West Wing*. You know, two a.m. negotiations, snappy dialogue walking down corridors. Politics at uni is more . . .' He gestured a level somewhere near the sky. 'Hard to reach. What do you do?'

'Philosophy.'

'Hmm, think-y. And?'

'I actually love it,' she shrugged. 'Genuinely just really like it.'

'That's all right – nothing to be embarrassed about. I wish I loved my degree.'

'No, I know. Anyway, I feel like my admission was loads more personal than yours. You've got to even this out.'

'Okay. So I've just started – what would you call it – seeing someone.'

'As in shagging but not going out?'

'Seeing someone. Exactly.'

'And do you like this unspecified person?'

'Um, so it's a she.' A guy clapped a hand on each of their shoulders to spring out into the garden. 'She's nice. Really good-looking, if that doesn't sound too boastful. Fun.'

'Sounds like a catch.'

'Yeah, I guess.'

'Are you thinking of taking the commitment plunge?'

'Well, that's second year. Everyone's doing it.'

'Is that so bad?'

'Not *bad*, but it makes everything a bit . . . Like the music's stopped and everyone's stuck with whoever's next to them.'

'Hopefully it's *slightly* less random than that.'

'Sure. I mean, you must like your new . . . prospect.'

'Yeah, he's a lovely guy.'

'Well, that's great. I mean . . . lovely.'

They broke eye contact, smiling at the muddy edge of the lawn. A couple of girls started doing a jig round the fire.

'So, if you had to give it a score out of ten—'

'If I *had* to,' Ellie laughed.

'Yeah. No choice, life or death.'

'Out of ten, how much do I like this person?'

'Yeah.'

'Are *you* playing this game?'

'I'll go next.'

'No way. If we're going to do it, we're got to go together.'

'All right, on three then.'

'As in, after three, on the fourth beat?'

'Yeah, exactly. One, two, three, then you say a number.'

'And you won't get confused and say four?'

'Is four your number?'

'No, no, I didn't say that. I'm just checking—'

'That I can count. You're right, it's important not to assume. Trust me, whatever number you say, I will be able to compute it.'

'Okay, fine.'

'So are you ready?' They looked at each other, fists clenched as if to play paper, scissors, stone.

'One.'

A neighbour leaned over the fence to ask who was in charge.

'Two.'

They didn't want to, they said, but they'd call the police if it came to it.

'Three.'

Charlie was feeling rather strange. Everything was too vivid: the fruit-machine lights, the twenty-four-hour news, the pint glass in his hand. He was hyper-aware of his new state of independence, as if he'd just realised for the first time that his heart was beating, and lungs breathing, and that those things were keeping him alive. He was on his own; he'd done it. It was hard to believe that he could make such an enormous change in his life, simply by saying so. It was frankly rather frightening.

'What are you doing in here?' asked Ellie. She looked quite odd. In fact, if Charlie was being completely honest, he'd say (not out loud of course) that she looked a little bit like a homeless person. He wondered what on earth had happened to her in the last year.

'She means,' said the dark-haired girl, 'why aren't you hanging round in the Union playing drinking games and discussing where you're going skiing?'

Charlie looked at her properly for the first time and almost gasped in shock. She was so thin. Seeing her was like watching a football leg-break in slow motion replay: Eduardo nicked the ball away from Martin Taylor, who caught him with his studs high up on the shin, and his leg simply snapped. Charlie tried to focus on the space around her. 'Actually, my . . . ex-girlfriend lives on this road.'

The black-haired girl barked a laugh. 'Bit of ex-sex?'

'Er—'

'Ignore Rose,' Ellie interjected. 'She can't help being a dick.'

'That's me,' snorted Rose. 'Predicted First in Dickishness from the University of Give A Shit.'

'She's going to be super-employable,' Ellie added brightly.

Rose, thought Charlie, did not look like a Rose. He was slowly starting to get used to her appearance. He could almost look at her without wincing.

Ellie pointed out a heap of loose sheets and a laptop. 'This is where I work. Not real work, uni work. Although Rose does actually work here.'

Charlie, whose parents paid for his fees and accommodation and gave him £100 a week in spending money (and who didn't know about his overdraft, let alone credit card), had never had a job at uni. He had never done paid work of any kind, except for the stuff he did for his dad as a summer pseudo-allowance. 'Cool.'

'So how are you?' said Ellie. 'You look a bit different.'

'Oh yeah.' Charlie ran his hands through his hair. Last term (during his second major Sara crisis) he'd made an effort to remodel his appearance, moving away from his non-style-style of checked shirts and jeans, and towards something more contemporary. Typically, he'd ended up looking to Sara for advice on the finer points, prompting his housemates to ask whether he also needed help with feeding himself.

'Did you two know each other before he joined the boy band then?' said Rose.

Charlie was finding her a bit much. Unable to think of a come-back, he went for an all-out admission. 'I'm kind of all over the place to be honest. I just split up with my girlfriend.'

'Oh.' Ellie's eyes widened. 'Right now?'

'Yeah.'

'Shit, sorry.'

'Cut to the nitty-gritty,' demanded Rose. 'Were you cheating on her? I can see that, Charles. You look like a ladeez man.'

'God, no. I wish.' Charlie felt a wave of guilt about Anita Wilkins, and had to take a moment to remind himself that no crime had been committed.

'What was it then?'

Charlie puffed out his breath. 'I'm not sure I can even explain.'

'Welcome to the blue leather suite of truth.' Ellie spread her arms mystically. 'Look around you. Nothing is too depressing for the Shackle.'

'Look who you're with.' Rose flourished her hands towards the bar. The massive bartender waved. 'Nothing is too disgusting for us.'

'I don't know.' Charlie shifted in his seat. Usually he never talked about Sara with anyone (apart from Ben, of course, who didn't count). It was strange to think that he didn't have to live by that rule any more. He could say whatever he liked. Charlie didn't even have to claim he was in love with Sara, or that he ever had been. He could simply stop pretending – it was both refreshing and disorientating. 'This might sound pretty awful, but I'm starting to wonder if I was ever really into her at all. Or if I just convinced myself I was.' Ellie and Rose nodded sagely; he *knew* they'd understand. 'That probably makes me a shit bloke.'

'Probably,' Rose agreed.

Charlie barely noticed; it was such a relief to speak the truth. 'It's like on day one, I knew deep down it was never really going to work. And instead of being honest, I got into a relationship with her, and stayed in it for most of uni. I'm not even sure why.'

Ellie sipped her wine. 'If it's any comfort, she probably did the same thing.'

'Strangely, that's no comfort whatsoever.'

'Sorry,' Ellie smiled. 'Anyway it sounds like the romance of the century. You should really make a film.'

Charlie managed a laugh. The joke helped: he had about fifteen years of experience in enforced banter, regardless of emotional capacity for it. 'Hang on, though.' A memory came to him just in time. 'I think we all remember the romance of the century. Broomfield Halls, Block B, two years ago? Lucas hasn't forgotten. That night with you changed him for ever.'

Ellie screwed up her nose. 'I doubt that.'

'That's not how *he* tells it. He's actually been trying to make a film about it, but he hasn't found the right lead yet.' It was rather satisfying to see Ellie's face reddening.

'Do you know Ellie's boyfriend Justin?' said Rose archly. 'Or is he too "little people" for you?'

Charlie bowed his head, letting Rose's jibe pass over him. He didn't know Justin, but at the same time he was pretty sure he could sketch him out. Justin would be exactly like the boyfriend-from-home that Ellie turned up with at freshers' week: some inexplicably unattractive nonentity, who wasn't funny, or good at sport, or even particularly nice. Lucas was incensed, Charlie remembered. It was the sheer inequality of it that appalled him – it made a mockery of the whole system. After he'd slept with Ellie, Lucas had referred to it as 'Equality Training'. ('Shame about the Trainer,' he'd said. 'He really ruined that session. It was so disappointing, I made an official complaint.') 'I don't actually,' said Charlie, before asking Ellie flippantly, 'Are you into him?'

'Of course she bloody is,' tutted Rose, as she drifted over to serve one of the old guys at the bar. 'They're in *love*.'

'Ah, love.' Charlie was surprised to find he had almost finished his pint. An unfamiliar feeling was rising in him, a streak of recklessness he'd forgotten was there. That was the problem with relationships – he'd been squashed into being 'Sara's Boyfriend' for so long, he'd lost his original shape. Now he could move freely, Charlie was beginning to stretch out the stiff limbs of his personality, wiggling his fingers and toes. *What would Lucas do?* Charlie wondered. Not quite sure of his intention, he ventured on. 'You never know with Ellie, she might just be passing the time.'

'What?' Ellie drew back.

'I mean,' shrugged Charlie (he couldn't quite believe he was saying this – he must be hysterical), 'everybody knows you tend to undervalue yourself.'

Ellie gave a surprised laugh. 'Did I put myself on *Antiques Roadshow*? "Got this from my great-uncle, maybe worth a tenner."'

'You know what I mean.'

'Mm, let me see.' Ellie's smile turned brittle. 'I'm not going out with one of your mates and therefore I couldn't possibly be happy? That's actually what you all think, isn't it? I'm basically, like, emotionally deformed, because I don't subscribe to the caste system.'

Charlie held up his hands. 'I'm trying to pay you a compliment here.'

'Wow,' she laughed. 'I'd hate to see what it's like when you insult people.'

'All right,' Charlie shook his head. He couldn't help it if she was oversensitive. 'I take it back. Sorry.'

A pause expanded into a silence. Ellie stared out of the window at the car park, shrinking into her chair. Charlie drained his pint and tried to think of something to say. Surely she could cut him some slack – he *had* just split up with his girlfriend after all. 'Well,' he attempted, 'it is actually nice to see you . . . even if I did manage to offend you.'

'Um, yeah.' Ellie looked up briefly, before her gaze dropped to the table. 'Good luck with single life.'

'I'll let you know what it's like.' Somehow his attempt to lighten the mood came out more like a jibe.

Ellie didn't respond. Rose walked over briskly and picked up Charlie's glass.

'Who wants to try a spirit I get free?' called the giant.

'No, thanks, mate,' said Charlie, standing up. 'I was leaving anyway. See you around.'

4

Nihilism

The word 'confidence' comes from the Latin: *confīděre*, to have full trust. Nowadays, the primary meaning of confidence is trust or belief in oneself, so this faith is largely internal. The original late Middle English meaning of confidence, however, implied trust in something external: a person, a thing or, most importantly, God.

Nietzsche was the first writer to see that confidence had a history. He didn't just explain why confidence was important, he explained why it was important *now*, in the period of modernity. The answer lay in religion. We need confidence, Nietzsche argued, to overcome the 'depression' caused by the death of God.

The most important event of Nietzsche's life was not an event at all, but a realisation: the realisation that God did not exist. He may have become an arch-atheist, but the author of *The Antichrist* grew up an enthusiastic Christian, the son and grandson of pastors on both sides of the family. Indeed, Nietzsche's youthful ambition was to follow his father into the priesthood. 'I have firmly resolved to devote myself forever to His service,' he vowed in a private note, aged thirteen.

By the time he was at boarding school, however, Nietzsche had begun to express religious doubts. For a rational person, he told his friends in their extra-curricular literature and music society, the

literal truth of the Bible was hard to take seriously. He was beginning to reach towards the thought that would lead to his famous
declaration: 'God is dead! God remains dead! And we have killed
him!'

No one had literally murdered God, nor even definitively
disproved His existence. Long-standing historical trends had simply
made Western society more secular. 'The ideal is not refuted – it
freezes,' Nietzsche wrote. We used to believe, but now we don't,
and it is hard for us to remember why we believed in the first
place.

Nietzsche wasn't certain enough of his religious doubts to
change his university subject. He committed to study theology,
because he thought it would please his mother. But it was too late.
The germ of doubt was in his system, and he had little interest in
finding a cure. Home from uni at Easter, Nietzsche abruptly
announced that he had given up theology and would not be
attending the Easter church service. He was making a scene, one
suspects, to prevent his mother from persuading him to recant.
After a tearful family row, Frau Nietzsche accepted his decision –
then never mentioned the subject again.

Renouncing God was like being let out of school for the last
time: release (God is dead! No one cares what we do!) followed by
disquiet (God is dead. No one cares what we do.). When we
believe in God, the meaning of life is clear. All the big questions
are settled. We don't need to spend time asking 'Why am I here?'
or 'Why is it worth getting up in the morning?' because Christianity
has provided the answers. Our sole purpose is to live a life of
Christian virtue so we can receive our reward in heaven.

When we stop believing in God, that overarching structure
stops making sense. The meaning of life is no longer self-evident.
Nietzsche called this loss of purpose 'nihilism'.

Nihilism, as Nietzsche describes it, is the quintessential modern condition. Of course, we don't call it that. Drifting, purposeless, without certainty or meaning, overcome by existential anxiety, forced to entertain yourself for hours on end, required to search for answers when before everything was spoon-fed . . .

Nowadays they even make you pay for it.

'I feel a bit bad now,' Ellie called over to Rose. She drained the last of her syrupy wine and studied her essay plan. She had to admit the result was disappointing. The swirly blue lines hadn't developed an argument and the cross-hatching totally lacked structure. Ellie checked the front – 'Nineteenth-Century Moralists: Handout 2' (had she even been in this lecture?) – and stuffed it back in her bag. Never know when it might come in handy. 'I said I feel a bit bad now!'

'Why?' Rose was up on a stool, wiping the optics. Ellie hoped she didn't black out up there. Recently, she'd been having dizzy spells: a distant look came over her and she had to crouch down to get her balance. On the other hand, there probably wasn't anyone worth swooning in front of here. 'He's a shallow, arrogant dickwad!'

'Yeah, I know.' Ellie shuffled over and dumped her stuff on the bar. She might be able to catch Rose from here if she had to. 'But he's just joining in.'

'That's what I love about the Nazis,' Rose told the upside-down Smirnoff. 'Big joiners-inners. Real team players.'

Regular Steve laughed. 'Look out, she's dropped the Hitler bomb!'

Regular Pete kept his gaze on the screen, where Alistair Darling was talking to camera. 'Hello, eyebrows,' he guffawed.

Ellie's phone rasped on the brass bar.

Rose squinted. 'Who is it?'

'Justin.'

Rose jumped down, suddenly eager. 'Do you want me to get it?'

It was horribly tempting. By letting Rose answer, Ellie could shortcut the conversation she'd been putting off since pretty much the first day of the Easter break. Ellie accepted the blame: it was her fault, she'd shut Justin out, and while she'd had her reasons, it was the wrong thing to do. She was happy to apologise. What she couldn't bear was the whole *conversation*, where they discussed *why* she did this and how it wasn't good for their *relationship*. Ellie wished they could skip over it and get back to experiencing the relationship, rather than debating it.

The phone blinked forlornly. Justin never accepted defeat. He rang all the way through to voicemail and left his name and number at the end of a five-minute message.

Rose shook her head at Pete. 'It's disgusting the way she treats him,' she said, doing her old Welsh woman. 'Croo-el.'

'She ought to put him out of his misery,' said Steve.

Bringing your relationship into the Shackle was basically kissing it goodbye. It was the one thing Ellie had said she'd never do. What did Steve think of your boyfriend, what was Michael's opinion on your sex life? Should you go out with Neil instead? Next thing she knew, Justin would be calling the pub like Steve's wife and Rose would be evading questions about her whereabouts.

'You can't blame her though,' sighed Rose. 'It's 'cause she under-values herself—'

Ellie snatched up the phone.

'Hello?' Why did she say it like that, as if she didn't know who it was?

There was a pause.

'Uh, hello, can I speak to Ellie, please? It's her boyfriend speak-ing? Justin? Justin Rufford?' The sound of Justin's voice made

Ellie think of resting her head on his chest and absorbing the vibrations. She would have loved to do that now, instead of having to talk. Why was it so hard to reach each other on the phone? It was exactly this feeling of painful separateness she'd been avoiding by not calling. She tried to push through Awkwardness and into Joke.

'Good afternoon, Mr Rufford, this is Ellie Taber speaking.'

That only made it worse.

'Justin!' Rose craned over the bar. 'Thank God you're back. She's been *so* difficult, a bloody nightmare! I can't wait to have her off my hands.'

Ellie gave Rose the finger, clambered into her coat and tried to start the conversation over. 'Hey. I'm just leaving the Shackle.' She waved to Michael and swung out into the car park, tugging at her hood. 'Are you back?'

'Nearly. I'm on the train.'

'Cool.' After a fractional pause, Ellie continued, 'God, why does anyone say "cool" any more? It's so Sixties and embarrassing, isn't it, so smug ageing hippie . . . Anyway, how are you?'

'I'm okay,' said Justin slowly. 'How are *you* doing? I feel as if—'

'I know, I'm a weirdo. Sorry. I keep on interrupting. I'll stop talking.' Ellie navigated a path around a press of uniformed kids by the newsagent, all waiting to be one of 'TWO SCHOOLCHILDREN ALLOWED AT ANY TIME'.

'I'm looking forward to seeing you,' Justin offered gamely.

'Me too.' Ellie was starting to remember how the adjustment process went. She offered something, and he offered something, and they kept going until they burst the membrane and made it through to the same place. It didn't matter what she said, she simply had to begin. 'This guy I used to know came into the pub, in first year or whatever—'

'Ah, yes, your glory year!'

'Oh yeah, God, best year of my life.' It was an old joke, but at least it was something.

'I'm surprised you remember anyone from that incredible, like, montage of football socials and back-to-school parties—'

'*One* football social.'

'Come on, Taber, I've seen the kit.'

'Stash. *Please*, it's called stash.' Ellie had reached the high street. The wine felt like it was corroding her insides; she should eat something before Justin got back. The last thing she wanted was to turn up on his doorstep – stressed, hungry, irrationally angry – and immediately collapse, demanding he look after her. At the very least, she wanted to pretend she'd been coping. Escaping the rain, Ellie wandered into the health-food shop.

'You must miss those guys.' Justin could keep a joke going for hours. 'They're really genuine people.'

'Well, I pretty much told him he was an arrogant twat.' Ellie picked up a falafel wrap. It looked disgusting, but so did everything else. She checked the label. £3.50? For dried-out chickpeas? 'I may have been a bit over the top.'

'That doesn't sound like you,' deadpanned Justin.

Ellie laughed. This was one of the things she forgot: she *liked* Justin. Their relationship didn't only consist of guilt, doubt and missed calls. 'I know. Unbelievable, isn't it?' It was a relief to express her qualms to someone. Looking back on the last few weeks, Ellie saw how much of an echo chamber the flat had become. No anxiety or conflict was put to rest: each one swelled and resonated until she was drowning in it.

'Is this why you haven't rung me or answered any of my calls?' said Justin, in the same easy tone. 'Too busy flirting with rugby players?'

'No.' Ellie leant against the fridge, throat contracting. She'd been waiting two weeks for this question and she still hadn't managed to prepare an answer. Whenever she'd imagined defending herself, it felt like the wrong approach. The point wasn't to 'be right' or 'get away with it'. She'd considered explaining how she'd been feeling, but that seemed unfair – she didn't want to dump on Justin, when she wasn't going through any more than he was. Justin had changed course twice, from Law to Engineering, then from Engineering to English, each time dropping down a year, without ever finding a subject he came close to enjoying. He was utterly unsuited to uni, but there was no escape; it was middle-class military service.

'No, it isn't,' Ellie repeated quietly, distracted by her jumbled reflection in the metal shelf. 'There isn't a reason, really. Not a good reason.'

'Okay . . .' An announcement went off in the background.

Ellie stared dumbly at the peanut butter display. It wasn't lack of effort (she tried to communicate by the power of thought alone); she simply couldn't find the words. 'I'm really sorry,' she struggled on. 'I've been working on my dissertation, or trying to.' It sounded unspeakably pathetic. 'I've missed you.'

'Have you?'

Justin hated this, when she went quiet. He thought she was being lazy and selfish, sloping off for mental naps instead of communicating. It was their standard row, endlessly repeated. This time, though, he was definitely in the right. Ellie couldn't figure out if that made everything worse or easier. She wished she could reassure him; she knew she ought to say some sort of soothing nothing, but she couldn't.

'I'll take that as a no, then,' said Justin, with ghastly false cheerfulness.

'I'm really sorry,' Ellie blurted out, barely convincing herself. 'It'll be all right when we see each other, I promise.'

'What does nihilism mean?' Nietzsche scribbled in his notebook in autumn 1887. 'The goal is lacking; "why?" finds no answer.'

Nihilism is best described as an extreme form of self-consciousness, brought about by the most dangerous question in the world: 'Why?' We are constantly asking this question – that, says Nietzsche, is what it means to be human – but when we believe in God there is always a ready answer. Without the comforting blanket of religion, we are forced to think for ourselves, to question our own identity and existence. We are forced, in other words, to become self-conscious.

Sociologists call this 'self-reflexivity' and agree with Nietzsche, at least in outline. Modern people *are* more self-conscious than people in previous eras. Once, identities were handed out at birth, like limbs – now they have to be constantly updated and cared for, a process with no end, prompted by a question with no final answer.

As secularism invaded every corner of the world, said Nietzsche, it brought nihilism in its wake, causing what he described as an epidemic of self-consciousness. We treat self-consciousness as a nagging personal 'issue', but for Nietzsche it was nothing less than the defining social question of the age, a historico-philosophical dilemma of world-changing proportions. This was what made confidence so important to modernity – the fact that self-consciousness threatened our very existence.

Not knowing where we're going drains our energy and makes us miserable. 'The old depression, heaviness and fatigue' was how Nietzsche described it. Worse, though, was the feeling of hope-lessness that nihilism brought about, the sense that 'trust in life is gone: life itself has become a problem.' A meaningless life is a worthless life, and if life is worthless, why not end it?

Nietzsche was one of the first philosophers to pose the classic question of existentialism. Nihilism, he believed, gave modernity a 'suicidal' tendency. It was this condition that he sought to cure, and his medicine was his philosophy.

Nietzsche's thought is an attempt to overcome nihilism and reinvigorate our faith in life. He intended to replace Christianity with an ideal of his own devising, spiritual medicine that would keep us alive after the death of God. We suffer from self-consciousness – he would teach us to act on instinct. In place of faith in God, we will have faith in ourselves: we will have confidence.

When Charlie had imagined how things would be after he'd split up with Sara, he had often pictured himself here: in the middle seat of Lucas's Fiesta, with the ladz, having banter, creating memories, taking uni for everything it had.

Leaving that horrible pub, Charlie had been sorely tempted to head home, crank up season seven of *Scrubs* and settle in for several hours of lonely moping. Lucas's call to adventure had saved him from this fate. What Charlie craved was uncomplicated distraction and what the ladz provided was twenty-four-hour tedium relief.

'Wot-sits,' Bradder sing-songed in time to five sets of clicking fingers.

'Walk-ers,' chimed Ben.

'Salt 'n' Shake,' Charlie took his turn.

'Prin-gles.'

'Mc-Coys.'

The ladz had double-parked outside the Chinese supermarket and were patiently waiting to splash Phil Logan. The scenario was simple: a huge puddle had built up on the road to the north of campus and they'd arranged to pick up Phil from the copy shop directly beside it. When he arrived, they would drive into it and soak him.

Why did they do it? They did it because they could. It was what made them ladz, ladz with a 'Z'. It was what ladz did.

Click click. 'Kettle chips.'

Click click. 'Squ-ares.'

Click click. 'Chip sticks.'

Click click. 'Monster Munch.'

Click click. 'Twig-lets—'

'Er,' Bradder interjected. 'Twiglets – a type of crisp? *Please.*'

'Well, what else are they?' asked Ben, on Big Derek's behalf. Derek was horribly hungover and quietly bracing himself on the front seat – not that it made any difference to his conversational style. Sober, drunk or hungover, Derek never said anything. It was central to his charm. He kept his thoughts to himself (if indeed he had thoughts), emitting an air that he was simply pleased to be there.

'Are they made of potatoes? That's got to be the question.'

'Nobody knows. They're not even food.'

'Vodka's made of potatoes. Doesn't make it crisps.'

'Oooh, write that down. The Tao of Bradder.'

From this position, they had a clear run to the puddle. It was a question of marrying the moments when P-Lo arrived and the traffic lights changed. Students ambled across the road as if they'd forgotten it was there. Miry and enormous, the puddle lapped invitingly at the kerb.

'Poor old P-Lo,' said Ben.

'We are such cunts,' cackled Bradder.

'But ask yourself,' said Charlie. 'What would P-Lo do?'

The traffic lights went green. 'Fuck,' muttered Lucas. The car behind them beeped repeatedly, and finally took over, the driver gesticulating as he passed.

43

In the pause, Charlie noted and resisted the urge to bring up the break-up. He'd have loved to unburden himself to Ben, but around these guys it would be conversational suicide. Quite why sensitive, normal-sized, geographer Ben lived with this group of reprobates was something of a mystery. Ben had been in the year above Bradder at school, and for Bradder that seemed to translate to undying loyalty. Despite this connection, in almost three years of uni Charlie and Bradder had never got beyond 'Hey, mate.' In fact, Bradder was often quite aggressive towards Charlie, not in the 'banterous' way, but the way that stemmed from straightforward dislike. If Charlie ever tried to moan about this to Ben, Ben told him Bradder was like that with everyone. (Charlie often suspected that Bradder's aggro attitude towards him was really his love for Ben finding expression.)

Bradder played for the uni rugby second team. He was a real lad, measured in the only ways that counted: the ability to drink and (same thing, really) to take abuse. Bradder didn't have relation-ships – 'Girlfriend's an oxymoron' – but he didn't seem to miss them. True laddishness was like becoming a monk or a marine; it took absolute commitment and a certain recklessness when it came to your own life. Whereas Charlie left his housemates to hang out with the ladz, Bradder left the ladz to hang out with *real* ladz, people with names like 'Unit', 'Machine' and 'Ferret'.

Charlie wasn't even a level-one lad. He didn't want to be. It was unpleasant, painful and degrading. That was why he didn't live with these guys: then he'd be Ben, who last term was kidnapped by twenty masked men, tied up, thrown in a boot and driven to Durham to be 'the gimp' on rugby tour. The ladz were awful and stupid, yet despite that Charlie couldn't help being drawn to them. There was something epic about them, something fearless and undeniable: they went beyond thinking, beyond dignity, beyond

social convention, beyond the constraints of self. They weren't like
the cool kids Sara was friends with, always playing some ironic,
self-conscious game. They were living for the moment, making the
most of their time at uni. Yes, it might be horrendous, but you'd
never forget the experiences. By the time you'd pissed yourselves
in public and been sick on each other's heads (it was disgusting, it
really was), you were bound in an eternal knot of pride and shame.

A bike caught the edge of the puddle, spinning up a wave of
spray.

'Oi!' Lucas yelled. 'That's my puddle!'

Lucas wasn't like Bradder either, but in him it didn't seem to be
a failing. He had this trick of being inside and outside at the same
time. Coming from London somehow meant he circumvented the
whole posh thing and could treat laddishness as a three-year-long
joke. He was laughing with them *and* at them, and they were all
laughing too. Charlie envied Lucas that freedom.

'There's P-Lo!'

Through the rain-flecked window, they scanned the edge of
campus. In regulation hoodie and joggers, P-Lo was picking his
way down the hill, a chubby chap sheltering under a ringbinder
and fiddling with his phone.

'To business.' Lucas gripped the wheel. Ben sucked his breath
through his teeth, as the light flicked from red to amber.

'T minus three.' Charlie had the puddle in his sights. 'Three,
two—'

'Argh!' growled Bradder.

A girl had crossed the road and was now trying to leap over the
puddle.

'Give it a minute,' said Ben. 'She'll move.'

'I hate girls!' shouted Bradder, letting out his inner
seven-year-old.

Once she scrabbled to the other side, for no apparent reason the girl stopped and stared into space, gazing at the ends of her hair.

Lucas wiped at the condensation.

'Oh, it's Ellie Taber,' said Charlie. 'I saw her earlier.'

'Who the fuck's she?' demanded Bradder.

'Just one of the select five hundred.' Ben was the group's collective memory and record keeper, like the team scorer in cricket.

'She's only human,' Lucas smouldered modestly. 'She used to be fit. What's happened to her?'

'This may shock you, but she actually thinks we're all pricks,' commented Charlie.

'Us?' Lucas pressed a palm to his chest. 'Pricks? Surely not.'

'Fucking do it then!' shouted Bradder, lifting out of his seat.

'She specifically mentioned that you were a selfish lover,' Charlie grinned. 'I could barely stop her. She seemed pretty scarred by—'

Ben's phone began to ring the Nokia theme tune. 'It's P-Lo. Fuck!'

'Now or never, gents,' said Lucas.

'I don't know,' mumbled Ben, holding his phone like a grenade about to go off.

'Come on!' shouted Bradder.

'Derek?' said Charlie. 'Speak up for the silent majority.'

'I've got to get out of this car,' groaned Derek, head in his hands.

'What was that?' Charlie cupped his ear, full of delicious naughtiness. 'We should . . . ?'

Derek mumbled inaudibly.

'Was that "choose life"?'

'Choose life!' Lucas shouted, putting his foot down. 'This is too good to waste.'

There was a moment's humid hush. They drove past the row of parked cars, a four-wheel drive, a group of Chinese girls in a flash of green umbrella. As they approached, P-Lo lifted his hand, his wave turning into a cringe as he realised what was happening. Lucas slammed his foot down. For a second they flew forward, and then, with a great angry *whirr*, drilled into the puddle, bombing up a wall of spume that crashed into P-Lo and Ellie. The surf splashed down on the streaming windows, turning the inside of the car a soft, wavery grey. The car kneed the kerb, bounced up, and everything fell silent.

'Derek, you lad,' said Lucas. 'Never knew you had it in you.'

As the windscreen cleared, a gaping, sopping P-Lo sucked himself in, trying to hold himself away from his clothes. Lucas leaned over to take a picture with his phone. Charlie saw Ellie reel backwards and shared a guilty look with Ben.

In the back, a door opened, letting in cold air and the sound of P-Lo's whimpers. Derek leaned out and was quietly sick into the churning water.

Ellie stretched out her arm and slowly, stupidly, studied her sodden sleeve. With a faltering step backward, she sat down abruptly on the wet pavement. Above her, someone was bent forward, wringing his hoodie out, and shouting something about 'fucking hell' and '*mate*'. As Ellie wiped the gritty water from her cheek, another guy rushed out of the car − '*So* sorry, we're such *dicks*' − and extended his arm to her. 'Lemme give you a hand.'

Ignoring the hand, Ellie peered up from behind her hood.

It was Charlie.

'Oh God, you're soaked,' he said, rubbing his forehead. 'I am really, really sorry. We planned it for P-Lo, and you were there and got caught in the crossfire. Seriously, I'm *so* sorry.'

Ellie surveyed the damage to her bag. Every time she looked up, Charlie was beaming an apparently apologetic expression at her, all crinkly eyes and pained smile.

If there was one thing Ellie couldn't stand, it was being lied to. 'I don't think you're sorry at all,' she said.

'I am! We are.' Charlie nodded earnestly. 'Aren't we, Ben?'

'Yeah, yeah, we are,' said Ben hurriedly. He'd been pulled from the car and was now scrambling around the puddle's edge, fleeing P-Lo's bear hug.

'You're full of bullshit!' said Ellie. 'When people are actually sorry, they feel terrible. You lot are having the time of your lives.'

'Oi oi!' Lucas piled out of the car, and was immediately dump-tackled by P-Lo.

Oh God, Ellie thought, *not him as well*. Her playground instinct was kicking in, a steely inner voice that told her to get up, just get the fuck up and tend her scraped knees elsewhere. She clambered to her feet and swung her rucksack over her shoulder.

Lucas dragged himself to standing. 'Sorry, Ellie!' he called, doing the bare minimum, before kicking the puddle at Charlie.

Ellie shook her head and turned to leave. A group of Chinese students had come out of the copy shop with their fresh module packs. They parted to let her through, watching this strange English custom in mild bewilderment.

'Wait!' called Charlie.

Ellie glanced back. P-Lo was holding on to Charlie's leg, trying to trip him up. Charlie was crouched forward, laughing and clutching his stomach, all the while still trying to make apologetic eyes in her direction. Short of physical violence, there didn't seem to be any way to make him drop this palliative nice-guy act. Ellie gave up and left them to it.

The thought of going back to the flat crossed Ellie's mind, but changing her plan now would feel like an unbearable defeat. It didn't matter what had happened, she was going to get to the library if it killed her.

Campus was hellish. Term had started with a vengeance: people were everywhere, swarming round the revolving doors screaming, 'Haven't seen you in *ages!*' and clumping by the vending machines. The security guard at the entrance to the library frowned over his desk, taking in Ellie's sopping clothes. 'My card won't let me in anywhere,' a girl complained loudly. People queuing for the lift turned their heads, one by one, as Ellie trooped across the foyer, her left boot making a loud squeal as it met the vinyl floor.

Ellie took the stairs. The library had been completely refurbished in her second year, turned from a shabby old sitting room full of comfortable nooks and crannies into a giant branch of Costa, all glass and hard surfaces and carpets the colour of static. As part of the renovation, the first and second floors were designated 'Quiet Zones', where talking and mobile use were permitted, which in practice meant that they went on all the time. As Ellie squelched past they squeaked and fuzzed with white noise, like a swimming pool. Only on the third floor, the 'Silent Zone', was there any semblance of genuine quiet. But when Ellie reached her desk she found it had been taken, staked out by some mystery bastard with a bumper packet of highlighters, two cans of Coke and a defensive line of Post-its. Aggressive notes and unfeasible piles of books had annexed all the desks on the floor. Her plan was descending into disaster.

Conscious of people staring at her, Ellie turned and trudged down a random aisle. At the end, she crouched against the wall. Motion-sensor fluorescent lights buzzed and flickered above her head.

She was soaking, she realised. There was no way she could sit down and work, even if she did find a seat. Her dissertation was a washout, and so was she. She couldn't even get to the library, let alone think of something coherent to say about Nietzsche. And why had she let those idiots do that? Why hadn't she told them how out of order they were?

That group: what a bunch of dickheads. They really thought they owned uni, that they were above everyone else, and whoever got in the way of their pathetic 'bants' was expendable – 'collateral damage'.

She couldn't believe she'd slept with Lucas. It was a horrible, confusing bind: on the one hand, she loathed the idea of them talking about her, of her being a tool in their moronic game; on the other, she defended her right to sleep with whomever she wanted. Regretting it went against her principles. So she didn't regret it – she just wished it had never happened. This lot weren't mature enough for principles. It didn't matter what you did. You couldn't win; you couldn't trust any of them.

Of course, Lucas was just an arsehole – he'd probably be like that in any context. The ones that really drove Ellie insane were the guys that, on an individual level, were all right. But you weren't allowed to relate to them as individuals, because they were too busy with their weird little boys' club and all its stupid rules. Take Charlie. He used to be a perfectly decent guy; someone who would talk to you like a human being. And now look at him. He was such a two-faced liar, doing stuff like that and then trying to make up for it with his let's-keep-things-amicable, don't-take-it-too-seriously bullshit. She *knew*, the minute she was gone, he'd be rolling his eyes and congratulating himself on smoothing things over. It was pathetic. It was really contemptible.

Ellie clenched her teeth and pulled out her laptop. It wasn't a good idea, but she couldn't face seeing anyone else. Stretching out on the ground, she propped the computer on her stomach, laying her head on the dry side of her rucksack. Ellie opened a new document and, for the millionth time, stared at the screen. She felt she had something to say, but this blank page sucked all her thoughts into it like a black hole. Signing into the library wifi, she logged into Facebook.

'Uni guys are a bunch of liars and fakers, who are under the impression they're "good blokes",' she wrote. 'Their only interest is homosocial status, and the only reason they want to have sex is so they can talk about it with their friends afterwards. They all think women want to be lied to and they truly believe that by lying, they're doing the right thing. This essay asks: where do they get these strange ideas? Why are they such dicks?'

Ellie wrote all evening, and not a word was about Nietzsche. About one, she fell asleep on the library floor.

At half past two, Ellie was woken by somebody kissing her face.

'Mwoah! Mwoah! Mwoah! Mwoah!' said Justin. His pale eyes and black hair and irrepressible grin were all she could see. She smelt his crisp, earthy smell, like dried leaves.

'Hello!' Ellie sang. She was *incredibly* happy to see him.

'Mwoah!' Justin kissed her neck. 'You smell terrible, Taber. Mwoah. You smell like a changing room.' Ellie laughed. Her jogging bottoms had dried against her leg like a mudpack. 'Mwoah. I love you. I missed you.'

'Aaaaah!' Ellie grabbed handfuls of his hair. 'I love you! Where have you been?'

5

Say Yes to Life

Nietzsche aimed at nothing less than a revolution in the way human beings behaved, thought and felt. Undaunted by the scale of his task, he compared himself to those other rebels, Socrates and Jesus. Both those figures succeeded in reversing what was commonly thought of as good. Seen from the perspective of today, it almost appears as if Nietzsche managed to do the same.

Nietzsche called his endeavour 'the revaluation of values'. Now that God was dead, Christian values weren't strong enough to keep nihilism at bay. New, more vital values were needed – and he, Nietzsche, would provide them. The ideals he battled for were confidence, creativity and self-expression. If this sounds slightly less than radical, that's because we are all Nietzscheans now.

Nietzsche was born in 1844 in Röcken, a small village in the Prussian province of Saxony. His upbringing was textbook nineteenth-century German conservatism: patriotic, Protestant and stiflingly conformist. The popular image of Nietzsche as a renegade mystic, cape whipping around him on a windswept mountain peak, is a dramatic exaggeration. This was a man who read the newspaper every day, a conscientious, straight-A student, who swore by moderate drinking and a good night's sleep.

Nevertheless, the basic insight is accurate: Nietzsche was an individual in a society in which individuality was less than welcome.

For Nietzsche, confidence was both a means and an end. It was the way he would break free of his conformist background, and it was also the eventual goal, the foundation of the society he wished to bring about. His books were written as guides for fellow nonconformists, the 'free spirits' struggling to escape the dead weight of nineteenth-century orthodoxy.

Nietzsche rarely used the word 'confidence' in the modern internal sense, preferring instead to describe this sensation through an array of slogans and metaphors. Sometimes he referred to it as a bearing, sometimes as a state of mind or an emotion, a flexible use which continues today. Nietzsche was not a precise or a systematic thinker, but in this case he was loose for a reason: because confidence for him was *everything*. It was a personal and psychological attribute, but it was also a worldview, a total philosophy of life, which, if understood correctly, would free us from despair and bring us into the bright world of un-self-consciousness.

The key to this mindset was what Nietzsche called 'world affirmation'. Broadly speaking, the idea was this: nihilism turns us against the world, so to escape it, we must embrace life in all its fullness. Yes, God was dead and, yes, suffering was meaningless – instead of despairing, we should celebrate our freedom. We should live: not because God tells us to, but because we want to, because we have things to do.

Nietzsche urged his readers to say 'Yes' to life, a sentiment which could be loosely translated as 'Feel the fear and do it anyway.' He celebrated 'growth' and 'the power of positive thinking'. To the modern ear, this sounds like so many platitudes, but if today Nietzsche's aphorisms have the air of self-help clichés, that only shows how successfully his thought has penetrated our collective consciousness. The reason it's so popular? Because it's so relevant. Whether he brought it about it or simply predicted it, Nietzsche defined a world in which confidence is the always-just-out-of-reach key to life itself.

But even if all the self-help advice in the world tells us it's a good thing, saying 'Yes' to life can be harder than it sounds.

It was three days since Charlie had split up with Sara, and at last he was beginning to feel more like himself. In the latter stages of their being together, Charlie had begun to wonder if this was it: this boring, unadventurous person, whose only desires in life were Sara and iPlayer – this was who he was now. He couldn't even be bothered to download a Torrent, that was how bad it had got. He was stuck with whatever crap came up under 'Entertainment' or 'Sport'. To discover that this wasn't him at all, but simply a side effect of their relationship, was an incredible relief.

It was as if, for a year and a half, he'd been plagued by a heinous, bulging spot. He'd prodded it, fingered it, worried it, making it ever redder and angrier. Finally, he'd accepted it as part of himself: a shit part but one he'd have to live with. Then one day, he'd got up and squeezed it – and now it was gone.

In a burst of vitality and decisiveness, Charlie forged three resolutions, three things he had to do before uni ended.

First – really last, but most inescapable – was uni work. Finals were in a month and a half, a month and three-quarters, if you didn't count Contemporary Italian Politics, which was so easy it didn't need revising. He had loads of time, and at least in exams, the task was clear. The job was not to fail. Not failing meant getting a 2:1.

There were only four possible grades at uni: First, 2:1, 2:2 and Third, roughly translated as Excellent, Average, Worse Than

Average and What Went Wrong? There was no Better Than Average, so the Better Than Average student could drift along taking in nothing and handing in shoddy work cobbled together from Google, Wikipedia and the set text. It was a stupid, inefficient system, but right now Charlie was grateful. If his calculations were correct (these days he needed a calculator to do times tables past two), the minimum result he needed from his next five modules to secure a 2:1 was 63 per cent. Surely, *surely*, he could manage that.

Charlie's second aim was to improve what he laughingly called his 'career prospects'. Not to find a job – there was no need to go overboard. Not to apply for a job – he had exams to do after all. If he had the time, Charlie supposed, it might be a good idea to find a summer internship or two to buff up the old CV – again, that was more than strictly necessary. All that was really required was to *clarify in some way his future direction*. Even with the bar set this low, Charlie had so far contrived to dip under it. But that was his old self – his new self, his real self, was much more active. Instead of daydreaming about being an entrepreneur, he was going to do something about it. This time next year, he would have his own start-up. He wrapped that promise to his heart with ten layers of mental sticky tape.

Third, and most important, Charlie intended to have an awesome time. This was the student's other task, in many ways the only task, because if you were having an awesome time, all your other failures were irrelevant. Spent your summers pissing around instead of doing internships? 'Yeah, but I had an awesome time.' Forgot to hand in your essay? 'It's okay, because I was having an awesome time.' And failing in this area was so much more humiliating. How could you fail to have an awesome time at uni, where everything was set up to enable that outcome? It was 'the university experience'. They even put it in the prospectus.

Charlie solemnly vowed to make up for the fun he'd missed when he was being boring with Sara. Of course, fun wasn't something you could put on a To Do list – you couldn't schedule it in, it didn't work like that. But what he could do was be more spontaneous, open to new things: he could say 'Yes' to life, instead of 'Do I have to?' That is, if life remembered he existed.

'You're just throwing money at the problem,' said Charlie, surveying Alistair's stationery binge. 'Have you got shares in Rymans or what?'

By way of reply, Alistair purposefully slotted highlighters into his desk tidy. He'd cleared the shelf above to make way for an absurd number of refill pads.

'You know they don't give marks based on number of trees used?

'You're not having any, if that's what you're getting at.'

'I can hardly buy more. Someone's got to offset your carbon footprint.'

Charlie had invested a lot of time and energy in making his resolutions, but so far putting them into action was proving a challenge. The only thing Alistair was saying 'yes' to was a revision schedule that doubled as an advanced torture technique. His three-part, colour-coded plan was pinned to the wall by his bed – the first thing he'd see in the morning, the last thing he'd see at night.

'Are you really going to work in here then?'

Alistair nodded. 'You know what the library's like.'

'Won't you go a bit stir crazy? There isn't even a window.'

Alistair raised an eyebrow. 'Where are you going to work?'

'Not sure yet.' Charlie considered. 'I've got to suss it out, get a feel for a place. Maybe a café?'

Alistair furrowed his brow doubtfully, focusing on his ringbinder labels.

'Hey.' In a flash of optimism, Charlie levered himself off the floor to poke Alistair with his foot. 'You don't fancy a final pre-revision Rehab Wednesday, for old time's sake?'

'Rehab? It'll be full of first years.'

'*Exactly.*'

Alistair made a face. 'It's practically grooming.'

After almost three years of living together, the question of who Alistair might be even slightly interested in having sex with was still a mystery to Charlie. For a long time he'd been sure Alistair had a thing for their housemate Romilly, but if he did, it clearly wasn't urgent enough for him to do anything about it. The same applied to his possible gayness (was he hiding it from himself or just from everyone else?). Until the mystery unravelled itself, the only sensible option was to assume that Alistair was completely void of sexuality, a slightly less human version of Kryten, the robot butler in *Red Dwarf*.

'A drink then.'

'I'm not drinking this semester.'

'All right, all right.' Charlie threw up his hands and made for the door. 'I'll leave you to your labelling.' He slouched down the stairs, rejected. 'See you in June.'

In the kitchen–living room, Katie and Romilly were sprawled on the sticky faux-leather sofa. Katie read aloud from a magazine: '. . . conjunction of Mars and Venus makes for an explosive outlook on the relationship front—'

'Oooh.'

'No, I think that's bad.' In her free hand, Katie held a soup spoon full of peanut butter, the tub clamped between her knees. 'Your energies may be pulled between the demands of home and career.'

'Career! LOL.'

Charlie threw himself into the spongy armchair. 'So. What are you guys doing tonight?'

Romilly was flattening her fringe with the heel of her hand. 'Josh is coming over and we're watching *The Apprentice*.'

Charlie sighed deeply.

'Oh, sor-*reee*. You weren't even invited.'

'Obviously I have nothing better to do.'

'Thought so.'

'Ben's with Clare. Lucas is out with the football team. Alistair's in with his stationery.' Charlie shook his head. 'To be honest, I've got no idea what I used to *do*. There's so much time in the day. The last thing I want to do is start revising, but that leaves about fourteen hours a day thinking about not revising.'

'You all right?' asked Katie, between licks of the spoon.

'I'm fine,' he said bravely. 'I suppose I just miss Sara, that's all.' Charlie was rather hoping they might suggest bowling, or a trip to the pub, or some kind of outing in Romilly's car to cheer him up.

'Well, if you want to know how she is' – Romilly jerked her head towards her laptop – 'Penny's doing live heartbreak coverage in Facebook statuses.' She frowned. 'Facebook stati?'

Charlie's stomach flipped. 'Like what? What's she's saying?'

Romilly rolled her eyes. 'Oh, you know.' She simpered: '"How do some people still look so gorgeous even when they're crying?" Here, I'll show you.'

'Oh God, no no no,' Charlie cringed. 'Keep it away.'

'Penny's bloody awful, isn't she?' said Katie.

'Yes.'

'Completely.'

Charlie had a horrible vision of Sara being dragged out, fed with shots, and persuaded to 'get back in the game'. 'Sara's not going to Rehab, is she? Actually, don't tell me, don't tell me.'

Romilly gave him a shrewd look. 'To be honest, I still don't get why you broke up—'

'*No*, we're not going through this again,' Charlie announced firmly. 'I can't take any more dissecting.' He slipped down in his chair, deflated. 'I can't even relax when I'm watching *The Apprentice* lately. I start worrying about my bloody "career".'

'Oh, I worry about that all the time,' said Katie. 'On the inside, I've got this constant, tiny scream.' She held her fingers to her cheeks in a miniaturised impression of the painting, letting out a high, thin 'Aaaaah!'

'Can you at least text Josh and get him to bring some beers?' Charlie moaned. 'To help me feel like less of a failure?'

'Fine. As a special concession to Charlie's pathetic state,' Romilly reached for her phone, 'I'll make Josh bring me white wine.'

From the second Justin rolled off the mattress and said, casually, 'Maybe we should fold the futon up today,' Ellie knew the holiday was over.

Since the institution of the Total Denial Policy about F****s and the d**********n, they'd been hiding out at Justin's, watching episodes of *Dexter*, smoking weed, having sex and eating various combinations of egg and toast. Ellie had never intended this to be a permanent state. What she'd really wanted was one of those calm interludes that happen just after the middle of an action film, when the hero takes sanctuary in a cool, tree-lined nunnery or a network of caves inhabited by friendly, wisdom-dispensing thieves. She'd wanted a moment of peace before charging into battle with renewed vigour and (possibly) a vital insight that would eventually save her life. Ellie had always known the respite would end, but now the end was nigh, she didn't feel up to donning her sword and galloping back out there. What she felt like doing was weeping quietly and having her hair stroked by a stern but kindly nun.

'It'll be like rolling over a rock.' Justin pulled on a Lou Reed 2006 Tour T-shirt. 'There'll be woodlice and everything.'

Justin's house was past Morrisons, over the railway bridge, beside the Iceland where hope went to die. (Hope, ever hopeful, wanted to be cryogenically frozen like Walt Disney and revived when technology caught up.) The area was so far off the uni map that, to the average undergrad, its existence was almost offensive. It implied what surely could not be true, that people their age, students at elite universities, grew up to be the sort of people who lived out here in ITV-land, in a semi-detached house down the road from the golf club with – if they were lucky – a little pebbled water feature in the front garden.

In the middle of this suburban chorus line, Justin's place stuck out like a toothless crone, its bricks blackened and crumbling, one top-floor window boarded up, the other rheumy and weeping. Once, way before Ellie arrived, the house had been a squat. Now there was some agreement with the owner, who lived in Peru with his much younger Peruvian wife, two-year-old boy and newborn baby. (Shafiq, the house organiser, got the updates on Facebook.) Even though it was inhabited, the house maintained an almost Victorian sense of abandonment. Inside, each door was like a portal to a parallel universe. Housemates had come and gone over the years, each one leaving their mark: a partially knocked-through wall, a spiralling purple and gold mural, a series of crusty scorch marks on the carpet by the bed. In one of the empty rooms upstairs (too damp to occupy), old computer parts were laid out in a twisting pattern on the floor, as if they were being used to summon a demon.

Justin headed downstairs – 'I've got a different way of poaching I want to try' – leaving Ellie alone, listening to Mattie take his midday shower and imagining his obscure postgraduate thoughts. Towards the end of last term he had declared, out of the blue, 'Speaking is writing – that's what my thesis is about! As well as sound engineering.' He was shy but fiercely independent, ever alert to the first hint of house bureaucracy, such as Shafiq's request that he sometimes bought loo roll. Most of the housemates had started uni with Justin, and were by now training to be psychiatric nurses or volunteering in co-op cafés. As far as Ellie could tell, the only thing they held in common was a total commitment to foraging from skips; if they got the call, they'd drop whatever they were doing, travel to a distant suburb and spend the afternoon carrying a wardrobe or a perfectly functional swing-top bin back to the house. They were like a squadron of superheroes whose shambolic daily lives were merely a cover for their incredible powers of furniture salvage.

Precedent had it that Ellie's next task was to get *Dexter* downloading so they could watch it as they ate breakfast, kicking off another beautiful day in three square metres of paradise. She turned on Justin's LINUX-operated laptop (hers had started death-rattling just from running Word) and went onto Pirate Bay. But some feeling, something she didn't want to name, had crept in, insinuating itself through the gaps in the floorboards. Ellie didn't draw the light-blocking curtain that Justin had found, washed in the bath and carefully pinned to the ceiling. (He was a bad sleeper.) She climbed resolutely back into bed.

Justin pushed open the door and stood with his back against it, holding the plates. 'Shit, sorry Shafiq, I haven't paid it yet. I completely forgot.'

Instinctively, Ellie curled up, retreating from the voice outside: the mere sight of Shafiq, or Ganna, or Luke, or Mattie, or Mattie's boyfriend Ed, would be enough to break the spell. Avoiding people was a crucial part of the Total Denial Policy, implemented with painstaking care. Showers were – naturally – out of the question. These last few days, Ellie had been waiting for absolute silence before she risked venturing out to the loo. Sometimes she'd found herself bemoaning how hard it was for women to pee in a bottle.

'Vinegar didn't seem to make any difference.' Justin closed the door, restoring the vital airlock, and Ellie pushed herself up to sit against the wall. He carefully handed her a plate and set his on the table he'd made last year from an old door. 'Aren't we watching *Dexter*?' He nodded at his laptop.

Justin was feeling it too, Ellie could tell. She felt a flash of irritation at his thought crime. 'What did you do to the eggs?'

Justin allowed himself a tiny, proud smile. 'Thyme.'

The kitchen downstairs had the look of a long-disputed territory, where a tenacious black mould fought with tacky nicotine-stain-coloured grease for sovereignty over all surfaces, cupboards and utilities. Bottles of chilli sauce and vinegar huddled against the wall, refugees displaced by the fray. The sole exception was Justin's section – a neatly wiped-down patch of blue, above a well-organised cupboard containing three types of lentils, rock salt and a tin of anchovies.

'Well, before we sink back into the life of a psychopathic cop, there's actually something I want to talk to you about.' Justin brushed his fingers through his hair. 'An idea I've had.'

'Oh, yeah,' said Ellie, guardedly. She burst the yolk of her egg and watched it ooze onto the bread. Even the word 'idea' was in danger of breaching the Total Denial Policy. Was Justin about to bring up some thought about Modernism or the Renaissance or exam technique? 'Nice eggs.'

'So it's about what to do after uni.' She looked up in surprise. Justin had put his plate aside and was rubbing his palms on his thighs, fingers trembling with nervous energy. 'I was thinking that what I'd like to do . . .' He anchored his gaze on a damp patch on the ceiling, as if reciting something learned by heart. 'I think what I'd really like to do is run my own café.'

'Oh wow!'

Justin flushed with relief. 'And,' he hurried on, 'I was thinking the best way to do that would be to stay here, and start working with Luke and maybe eventually I'd get somewhere of my own or we'd set up together or something like that.'

'Okay, yeah,' Ellie nodded. 'You're really good at this stuff.'

Justin pressed his lips together, turned up at the edges, like a toddler who had seen smiling on the TV and was trying to do it the grown-up way.

Ellie's phone chimed a text, a familiar sound she couldn't place at first. She started fumbling around the bed. 'And that sounds like a good plan. Do-able. I think it's brilliant!' Ever since they'd been going out – and long before – uni had been dragging Justin down, constantly demanding that he adapt himself to analysis and argument and referencing guidelines. Being the grafter he was, Justin had strived repeatedly and with all his might to become the thing they wanted, only to produce barely passable essays that managed to feel both plodding and baffling, even after Ellie had corrected them. She had never known it otherwise. All the useful things he was good at, like making stuff or feeding people, went for nothing, as if they were slightly embarrassing distractions from the real task of pointing out that such-and-such was a tautology or so-and-so contradicted herself. Ellie could *see* him doing this, and even being happy. For a moment she felt jealous.

'Oh, it's Nadine. I said I'd meet her tomorrow.' Ellie sniffed her own armpit. 'Wow. Maybe I should have a practice shower – get back into the swing of it.' She crammed an enormous forkful of eggy toast into her mouth and clambered out of bed.

'Before you do—' Justin held up a hand to stop Ellie in her tracks. 'I was wondering.' He met her eye. 'If you'd like to move in here. With me.'

'Orhm!' Ellie straightened up, preventing a bit of toast from escaping her mouth. On autopilot, she pulled off her Superman T-shirt and scouted round for a towel, before realising that the conversation wasn't over. Some sort of response was required. She felt . . . she couldn't work out what she felt. It was as if she'd been given an unexpected compliment by somebody she didn't know that well. It was pleasant, warming, nice, but she wasn't sure she actually agreed with it. She thought the person was probably wrong about her. She swallowed. 'Oh, right.'

Justin's eyes were trained on her face. There was a silence that lasted a little too long, before he stood up and said, 'Of course, you should think about it. It's a lot to decide all at once.'

'Yeah, exactly, it's . . .' Ellie could feel her brain shutting down: one by one, lights were turning off, occupants filing out, whole floors were closing, alarm codes being punched in. Knowing how much Justin would hate her silence, she tried to keep talking, to wedge a door open with words. 'The thing is, it's a big . . . I don't really know what I'm doing yet, do you know what I mean? Not us, I mean, more myself. I don't know what I'll end up . . . even what I want to try— or where, so I don't want to say—'

'It's okay, you don't have to tell me now.' Justin drew the curtain roughly. A few brass pins skittered down. 'I'm going to put up a rail,' he muttered.

Ellie took a step towards him, still holding her T-shirt. 'Sorry, I'm just trying to explain why I'm hesitating, because it's a great idea. I just—'

'I get it. Don't worry. It's all right.' Justin started picking up clothes and laying them over the back of his desk chair.

Ellie had a strong desire to go somewhere she could think, but to leave now would seem too much like a rejection. With a dim sense of failure, she returned to the bed and finished her eggs. A couple of minutes of silence passed as she bit and chewed and ruminated on exactly how and why she was cocking this up. Justin assembled a pile of dirty clothes next to the bin, then came to stand over his desk, shifting his laptop and a couple of used plates aside in order to stare at the piles of notes beneath.

'I suppose . . .' A look of miserable resignation settled on Justin's face. 'Maybe we should start to think about . . . the F-word.'

They looked at one another.

'Now you've done it. A SWAT team is going to come in here and take you out any second now,' said Ellie, glumly. At the sight of his wretched expression, she couldn't help feeling sorry for him. 'Before they do, I want to tell you I love you and it is a great idea and I'll think about it.' She got up, padded over in her pants, and held Justin's cheeks, pulling his face down to kiss him.

'Thanks.' Justin kissed her nose and they hugged. The sun had crept round the drooping curtain.

'I don't think I'm ready to resume life.' She shook her head. 'Honestly, I'm not sure I can cope with it. I'm made of the wrong stuff.'

'Lucky for you, it's not life you're resuming.' Justin brushed her greasy fringe to the side. 'It's revision – whole other thing.'

6

How to Get It

Nietzsche's philosophy was meant to be a guide to action, but it is hard to see how anyone would go about putting his advice into practice. Either it was extremely specific ('Tea is very detrimental and will sicken you for the whole day, if it's just a touch too weak') or so general as to be completely inapplicable. 'World affirmation' is not really the sort of thing you just can go off and do, and you only have to try telling someone to 'Say "Yes" to life' once to see how miserable *that* makes them. In any case, if the most important thing is to follow our own desires and no one else's, why should we listen to Nietzsche anyway?

There is a wealth of advice on how to become confident – some of it with a venerable philosophical history – but it all boils down to two basic approaches.

First, competence – that is, being good at things. The basic theory here: you become confident by gaining expertise. From a rational perspective, this makes perfect sense. You're good at something, so you feel good about yourself; the better you do, the better you will feel.

Unfortunately, it doesn't seem to work that way. Confidence is anti-meritocratic: it's what gets blaggers through on charm alone, while other people who are in many ways more expert struggle to achieve the same success, because they lack that spark of inspiration. If anything, being an expert can actually get in the way of confidence. You know too much; you're heavy, not light-footed, and if confidence is about anything, it is nimbleness and flexibility.

Nietzsche dismissed the competence approach out of hand. 'It is not works, but faith, that is decisive here,' he wrote. It is not *what* you do, but *how* you do it – or even, as Nietzsche claimed, *who* you are.

The second approach to gaining confidence is practice, in other words the idea that you can learn confidence as a skill. The most effective version of this method is summed up in a phrase that has become a battle cry for self-help books: 'Fake it till you make it.' At times, Nietzsche did appear to endorse this tactic, which derives from Aristotle's discussion of virtue in the *Nicomachean Ethics*. 'One must learn to love,' Nietzsche wrote. 'He who loves himself will also have learned it in this way.' Yet this technique never seemed to ignite his enthusiasm. Aside from a few brief mentions, he rarely returned it, and never with his usual vigour.

So what did Nietzsche suggest instead?

Rather than faking it, Nietzsche was more concerned with making it, as truly and fully as was humanly possible. Faking it, he says, is a normal part of growing up, one that can be helpful as a way of developing confidence. But when you fake it, when you pretend with your whole self, you have to be pretending to be *someone you are*. Like love: you have to work at it, but it has to be right, or all the work in the world will make no difference.

It's an irritating truth, but the thing about confidence is that there is no Step One, no easy way to start going after it. You begin, feeling awful, and you get absolutely nowhere, but you keep at it, always on the verge of giving up – and only after some time has passed do you realise that, actually, you don't feel as bad as you once did. Somehow, something has changed, and by the time you notice, it has already happened, like a sunrise or a room growing warm.

In a pub quiz, Charlie wasn't 'the knowledge'. He wasn't the go-to guy for film (Ben) or geography (Ben) or, if he was honest, very much at all. So he *studied* Politics. That didn't mean he knew what Nancy Astor was famous for or the name of the second President of the United States. Even football, his one truly specialist subject if you measured by time spent watching, was better handled by Alistair. All right, Charlie wasn't Lucas, who had managed to pick up literally *nothing* in his twenty years of life (quote: 'Is Moscow a Muslim country?'), but he wasn't that far off. And this lack of specialism – this knowing fuck all about fuck all – sometimes played on his mind, unsettling his hopes for the future. What could he actually *do*?

But last night, as Charlie had helped come up with the team name and provide the crucial banter that oiled the wheels of team DENSA, he had begun to wonder whether knowledge was really that important. After all, somebody needed to bring the best out of everyone with the right mixture of praise and mockery. And now that everything could be Googled, wasn't that more useful than being able to name five David Bowie albums from memory? It had even come up in the quiz. 'Who invented the first Apple computer?' Not Steve Jobs, who according to Alistair didn't even know how to write code. Jobs wasn't the inventor, he was the strategist, the man who saw opportunities and knew which way to head. And now Steve Jobs was Steve Jobs and that other guy was a trick question in a pub quiz.

Charlie had managed to drag Alistair to the pub, having spotted a momentary weakness in his Bran Flakes and revision routine. For the first hour Alistair had sat there with a guilty, shiftless look, as if the Revision Goddess were measuring his intake on her infallible golden scales. But before long, Alistair's cheeks had started to burn with deep spots of red, and he'd bought two rounds in a row with an air of slightly unhinged abandon. After that it had been back to Number 69 (the ladz' place, chosen because number 69 was banter) for a few hands of cards, some tongue-coating red wine, and the tin of pilchards in tomato sauce that was DENSA's prize for a highly respectable fourth place. By the time Charlie dragged himself away, it was past 2 a.m. It was only as he left that he remembered.

'Oh shit. I've got a group presentation on New Labour's immigration policy tomorrow – I mean, today.'

'Don't worry about it.' Lucas clapped his shoulder. 'You'll be in the perfect state. An empty mind is a clear mind.'

'Group presentation': a phrase for the process whereby everybody works separately and meets an hour beforehand to whack it together. After everyone arrived five minutes late, the next ten minutes had been spent trying to find a place to work. Now, at T minus 45, on the floor outside the library meeting room that no one had booked, Melanie Fisher had a pinched, nervous-verging-on-tearful look, and Sasha (Fit Sasha rather than Sasha Joyce) was rolling her eyes at every remark, as if she'd emptied the tank simply by turning up and not throttling somebody.

'In some ways you could see New Labour's immigration policy as a continuation of Conservative policy from the previous government,' Andrew Webster droned on. 'But not everyone agrees on that. I mean, thingy said . . . hold on, I've got it somewhere . . .' He lifted sheets of notes and scoured around. 'Um . . . You know the one that was on the reading list?'

'I was doing the conclusion,' Sasha announced into the silence. Kneeling on the floor, she propped herself up on her right arm, blue-black hair draped across one big, turquoise-rimmed eye like a Glaswegian Princess Jasmine. 'I think we should say that New Labour immigration policy was a failure. That's what everyone says. Even them.'

'But *what kind* of failure?' Melanie Fisher practically choked in exasperation. '*Why* a failure? *Who* thought it was a failure? *On what terms?*'

Unlike Melanie, Charlie felt quite calm. Lucas had been right – sometimes a hangover was a gift. Muffled throbs in the head, burning behind the eyes, stomach twinges – it gave the mind something to worry about, distracting it just enough to allow thought to flow clearly. 'Who says it was a success?' he asked.

'There's some good figures on that in this piece,' mumbled Andrew, lifting the same sheets of paper, as though the right pattern of paper-lifting might magically reveal the answer.

'We should start again from the beginning,' said Melanie. 'It doesn't make sense to do it this way. How can you write the conclusion when you don't know anything about the arguments? How is your evidence going to point to something if you don't know what it's pointing to? Christ.' She held her hands to her temples, shielding her eyes from the rest of the group. 'Why is this stupid presentation now? It's crazy having it when we're meant to be revising for other modules.'

Sasha was almost totally reclined by now. Her arm gave way beneath her. 'Helpful,' she muttered into the carpet.

'Here!' Andrew held up a photocopy. 'Will Somerville says "there is scant evidence that immigrants negatively affect native wages and unemployment levels or strain public resources, yet nearly half the population believe—" Oh, shit, no, that's for another section. Sorry.' He kept shaking his head long after it was necessary.

'Okay, let's not panic.' Charlie held up his hands. 'What about if we take it back a bit? Sasha, it sounded like you had a strong conclusion.'

Sasha raised a dubious eyebrow at him. Charlie had always fancied her, and now he was single he had the faint sense that he ought to do something about it – but at the same time, he knew his place. She was the kind of girl he'd get stuck having coffee with and 'being there' for while she had troubles with real men. Another time this thought might have got him down, but today it was an idle reflection. Once again, his hangover lent a thick, fuzzy layer of insulation to proceedings – his brain was like a Scandinavian holiday home.

'Melanie, you're right,' Charlie continued, giving everyone their due. 'The evidence needs to lead there. Andrew, it sounds like you've got a lot of the detail down.' Lying wasn't lying when it might become true. 'So maybe we should decide, what's our story?'

'What do *you* have, Charlie?' asked Sasha.

Charlie thought for a second. 'Everyone says it's a failure, right?'

'Like this presentation,' groaned Andrew.

'No, no, no! We're almost there. How long do we have? Thirty-five minutes – loads of time. Look, if everyone says it's a failure, maybe we should say it's a success. No. We should dispute the premise of the question. We should say—'

'But what about Sasha's conclusion?' interrupted Melanie. 'We can't just throw that away.'

Melanie, Charlie decided, was the group's Gordon Brown: furiously conscientious. 'You're right. We could turn that into the introduction. "New Labour immigration policy is generally regarded as a failure. For example" – what's his name? – "Somerville says". Sasha? Can you do that?'

Sasha looked amused. 'Then where will we go after that?'

'I could run through the history of the policy,' offered Andrew.

'Great, yeah! "This is what they've done, this is where we've got to." If we keep it simple, that'll take up a couple of minutes.'

Andrew burrowed into his notes. 'I think I've got a summary in here.'

'We can't *just* "keep it simple",' said Melanie. 'This is a massively complex topic. We have to acknowledge that.'

'Yes.' Charlie responded to the constructive comment Melanie had surely intended. 'That can be our third section. The "This is a very complex problem with lots of competing interpretations" bit. You know, the montage section.'

'Like in *The Lion King* where he grows up with Pumbaa and Timone,' Sasha smirked.

Melanie glared at her. 'And then?'

'I will conclude,' said Charlie. 'With a conclusion I will think of in the next . . . thirty minutes. Could be anything. But, I promise you all, it will be all right.'

And to Charlie's amazement, their presentation went off brilliantly. All right, so it was a bit sketchy in places – Andrew's idea of keeping things simple was to spend two minutes on the previous administration's legislation and then have half a minute left for the topic they were actually presenting on – but Melanie wrestled it back on course. His own conclusion was a minor masterpiece of smoke and mirrors. In the absence of knowledge, he'd gone for force, drawing the comment, 'Well argued,' from Dr Sanderson. That was good enough for him. If this presentation was 10 per cent of his overall mark, he needed the 6.3 per cent he would get for talking in English on something like the right topic. There wasn't anything in any of the other presentations that made him think he wasn't worthy of that.

'Great job.' He caught up with Sasha and Andrew in the corridor. 'And now we never have to do *that* again.'

'Yeah, cheers, Charlie.' Andrew was pink with relief.

'Yeah.' Sasha hitched her bag. 'Thanks for barging in and re-arranging the presentation even though you hadn't done any work yourself.'

'Any time.' Charlie smiled back at her. 'Your intro was actually the best bit.'

'Yeah, yeah.'

Charlie wondered if this counted as flirting. Years ago, he remembered, flirting was one of those things he used to spend a lot of time worrying about. He'd read blog posts about eye contact and squeezing upper arms, which in his experience made you come off like a creepy boss. Maybe all there was to flirting was being friendly, enthusiastic, nice . . . It was a curious thought. He wished he could travel back in time and share this insight with his fourteen-year-old self.

'See you both next week?' Andrew stepped back to let the next group by. 'Last seminar.'

'Oh yeah. You're coming, right?' Charlie asked Sasha.

She shrugged: *I guess so.* Her shrug vocabulary was wider than Charlie's verbal one.

'Well, I'll see you there. If not before.'

'Maybe.' Her friend was calling her. 'Anyway. See you whenever.'

'You look better than I thought!' Nadine greeted Ellie. Sprawling on the public art sculpture in the sun, Nadine looked like a bleary mosaic, all plastic jewellery and orange lips and stacks of afro hair.

'I'm going to wring the compliment out of that statement,' Ellie smiled back. 'Thanks very much.'

Nadine propped herself up, cocked her head to one side, and took in Ellie's puffy face, wet hair and trailing jeans. 'Rose called me up, said you're in a state. Like, you're gonna set yourself on fire smoking under the duvet. Then you went AWOL. She thought you were dead.'

'*Rose.*' Ellie rolled her eyes as she hauled Nadine up. Rose (Ellie strongly suspected) felt intimidated by her uni mates and liked to demonstrate the closeness of their friendship by calling Nadine up and making Ellie sound insane.

''S'it bad, then?' asked Nadine, cheerfully. 'One to ten.'

'One to ten, how bad?' They swung open the gleaming doors of the multiplex. 'What are we seeing by the way?'

'Everything,' declared Nadine. 'And we're talking through all of them. And you're telling me what's going on.'

Nadine had been on Ellie's Ancient Philosophy module in semester one of the second year. They didn't speak. Ellie always did that when she really liked a girl. She put a lot of energy into wishing uni girls were better, and was always complaining about their hair-straightening, pashmina-wearing ways. When she met one that was cool but still nice, funny without being mean, hot without being vain, it was off-the-scale intimidating.

They finally spoke at an Eighties-themed house party, up on the roof. Ellie had come in blue overalls, as Julia from *Nineteen Eighty-Four*. Way too highbrow – nobody got it. Nadine had pitched it about right, in a fluorescent visor and legwarmers. She was waving a toy welder around and pretending to tightrope-walk along the building's edge. *Bet she's having a good time*, Ellie thought, right before Nadine tripped on her peeptoes and tumbled – thankfully – towards the roof. Ellie ran over to help. It was the overalls, they gave her a sense of purpose.

'Yeah!' shouted Nadine, a heap of Lycra and tangled limbs. 'S'Ellie, s'Ellie's not a boring motherfucker, isn't it!'

Nadine was from London, which in temporal terms meant she was about five years older than everyone else. She had what Ellie's Ethics lecturer would call 'a healthy scepticism' about the uni system, keenly alive to the ways it constantly tried to persuade you that bullshit mattered.

The Chronicles of Narnia was terrible, but nobody else was in it. They took off their shoes and spread along the row.

Nadine had spent Easter temping as a receptionist in an ad agency.

'They were well old,' she said. 'Quite fit though. One of them was. They offered me a job when I finish. I don't want it but. I wanna travel. This is it, yeah, what you have to remember is, uni's practically over. And no one's gonna care anything about what you got in your dissertation. *No one.*'

Sex and the City was a parent and baby screening, but the half-dozen mothers and one lone dad didn't seem to mind them crashing.

'It's sort of embarrassing, eh.' Nadine didn't bother to whisper. 'Like watching your mum give someone a blowjob.'

'It was good though,' Ellie reflected. 'On the TV.'

'I remember it being good,' said Nadine, through a Minstrel mouthful. 'Miranda was all right. Samantha.'

'They were all all right apart from Carrie. What's fucked up is the way they all think they're Carrie's best mate. It's dysfunctional. I don't think the others even like each other.'

The strange thing was that nobody at uni seemed to appreciate how hot Nadine was. She perpetually complained that no one fancied her. Ellie found it unbelievable, unjust to the point of tragedy.

'Do you know what it is, though?' Ellie told her, as they wandered into *Iron Man* in their socks.

'I dunno.' Nadine threw her coat over the chairs in front. 'Do I wanna know exactly why I repel all men?'

'It's not *all* men, it's just the idiots here. I'll tell you what it is. Honestly.' They burrowed down into the seats. 'You're too sexy for uni.'

'Ha! You're *so* right. I'm also too sexy for this film, this VIP seat, these Minstrels—'

'No, listen, listen to me.' Ellie waved a hand. 'This is my new theory, yeah. Most uni guys are actually afraid of sex. You're too much for them. They like those safe, little blondy hair-straightened girls who wear leggings and Uggs, because they know they won't feel intimated by them. You're too sexy. It's like . . . It's not that they're truly asexual, right, but it's something about the place—'

'It's a sex vortex.' Nadine nodded glumly.

'Yeah! It's as if we all turned up at freshers' week, and to about seventy per cent of the students, they were like, "Hi, yeah, we'll take your five grand, thanks, and you're also going to need to hand over your genitals as a safety deposit. You'll get them back after finals."'

Nadine giggled. 'Hand over your genitals . . .'

It was good to feel funny. Who was she kidding, it was good to feel like a functioning member of the human race.

'*You* have sex, I used to have to listen to you.'

'Justin's not a uni guy though, is he. He's . . . "Other". Trust me, the minute you leave, it'll be a whole other story.' Ellie sucked the last, watery drops of Sprite through her straw.

'Are you gonna stay with Justin?' Nadine looked at her. 'Or is it like a uni thing?'

'Pfffff . . . Honestly, I don't know.' Ellie shook her head. 'He just asked me to move into his.'

Nadine inhaled through her teeth and raised her eyebrows. 'Maggie and Chris are getting a flat in York.'

'York?'

'She's doing a master's and he's gonna . . .' She shrugged. 'See.'

'It all depends what I end up doing.' Ellie pressed her feet against the seat in front and screwed up her face. 'And obviously I don't have a clue about that.'

'People who know what they want to do creep me out,' said Nadine, with passion. '"I want to be a doctor and I knew that in time to pick my GCSEs"? Like, who are you? This is the truth, yeah, if we haven't ended up in prison, or homeless, or dead in the next decade, that is a win as far as I'm concerned.'

'Massive win.' Ellie nodded gratefully. 'I'm going to stick that over my desk. With Justin, it's . . . I sometimes feel guilty that I'm not sure. Like I'm just hanging in, getting support, sucking him dry . . .' Nadine laughed. 'And then when finals are over I'll, like, chuck away the empty shell. What's *he* getting from it all?'

'He's getting *you*, you nutter. Are you joking me?'

Iron Man was all right. Ellie didn't like seeing Gwyneth Paltrow running round as someone's assistant, even an excellent and obviously underused one. It was beneath her.

After about five minutes of silent watching, Nadine gave Ellie a lengthy sidelong look. 'So you haven't seen it then?'

'This is the first one, isn't it?'

'*No*, I mean . . .' Nadine looked at her expectantly. Uncertainly, Ellie mirrored her expression. Nadine turned back to the screen, drumming her fingers on the drink holder.

'What?'

They watched.

'Honest to God you haven't seen it?' Nadine burst out, loudly.

'Seen *what?*' Ellie almost shouted. A man in the front row turned round to glare. Ellie raised a hand in apology. 'Could you *please* stop disturbing people who are busy trying to watch *Iron Man* at three p.m.?' she whispered.

'I thought you were like avoiding mentioning it 'cause it was such a stress.'

'Well.' Ellie frowned in confusion. 'I'm stressed about my impossible dissertation . . . What's going on? Have I been evicted or something and I don't even know?'

'No! Your rant. Your mad rant about uni guys.' Nadine turned to face her. 'It's an internet sensation. In, like, an insane-racist-comments-on-YouTube-crazy-trolling-of-women sort of way.'

'*What?*'

'So you posted it on Facebook, yeah—'

'I was just venting—'

'Then all these people started liking it and re-posting it. Then any dicks who could comment on your page started doing that, about how you don't understand banter and you're a miserable bitch. Then some other girl put it on her blog, saying how she loved it, then people started tweeting #uniguysaresexistdicks, giving like, examples. Then *they* got trolled, mad dark shit about women should stay in the kitchen or get raped and that . . . You honestly haven't seen any of it?'

Ellie shook her head. 'I've been . . . watching *Dexter.*'

'Well, in good news, you're sort of famous now. Not *really*, but you know what I mean. So.' She paused, like a seminar leader who knows the answer and is waiting for you to come out with it. 'What do you reckon?

'Shit.' Ellie was starting to feel slightly sick. 'I reckon I'm never going online again.'

'But you could do something about it!' Nadine exploded. The man in front twisted round and cleared his throat. 'Uni *is* fucking sexist, and loads of uni guys totally behave like dicks. Even the ones that aren't dicks. You could start a campaign! Like, an awareness thing.'

Ellie looked doubtful. 'But what would that even be?'

'A message—' Nadine corrected herself – 'a less ranty message. I mean, yesterday, yeah, I saw *this*.' Nadine pulled out her BlackBerry and scrolled through, digging out a blurry photograph of a woman in a g-string.

'What's that?'

'Okay.' Nadine sighed, reeling herself back to level one. 'So in Planet Uni there's a thing called the Safer Sex Ball. Remember? It's themed, as in, like girls-dress-as-pretend-prostitutes theme. And they hand out condoms. Like, for charity or whatever.' Ellie frowned. 'Maybe you went in the first year and dressed in a corset and felt kind of shit and sort of inexplicably angry but not sure why, so you got totally shitfaced and then you were that shitfaced girl wandering round in a corset feeling shit and maybe crying?'

'Nah.' Ellie shrugged. 'Don't get me wrong, I did do more or less that in a lot of very similar circumstances.'

'*Well*, it's happening in two weeks and the poster for it shows this ridiculously Photoshopped girl in a tiny g-string with a vag like a Barbie doll. They got some famous uni anorexic to pose for it, know what I mean? We could target those posters. For a start.'

Ellie stared at the screen. Gwyneth had just leaned in to Downey Junior for a kiss and been left hanging. It seemed unlikely, when you looked at that goatee. Ellie considered. On the one hand, the thought of putting herself up for a load of public abuse made her feel a deep, deep fatigue. From her attempts at revision, Ellie knew that feeling was actually fear, fear so strong the only way out was to fall asleep. On the other . . . she *did* complain that uni was sexist, all the time. She hated the stupid wannabe-frat-boy-meets-hip-hop-objectification-meets-same-sex-boarding-school-cluelessness-meets-playground-'girls are rubbish' culture, and it seemed as if other people did too.

'All right . . .' she said, at length.

'All right, let's do it?' Nadine perked up.

'All right, I don't know what I'm doing, and I'm kind of shitting it.' Ellie rubbed her brow. 'But let's do it.'

7

Become Yourself

Nietzsche understood the difficulty of pretending to be someone you're not. Of course he did: he'd been a first-year undergraduate. In his first year at university, Nietzsche tried to fit in – he joined a fraternity and took part in a duel, the nineteenth-century German equivalent of half-man–half-beer – but he didn't like drinking, which is most of what fitting in consists of, and he didn't relish banter or girls either. His fraternity brothers called him 'loony' because 'whenever he was not on campus, he could usually be found at home studying and playing music'. Nietzsche had the painful experience familiar to so many undergraduates: he did no work, spent too much money, got fat and felt shit about himself. 'My fitful, dejected diaries of that time, with their pointless self-accusations . . .' He was much happier when he changed subject and moved to the university of Leipzig, where he stopped trying to be a 'fast-living student' and worked and hung out with a small circle of close friends. He didn't know it, but it would be the happiest time of his life.

This is the other way of thinking about gaining confidence, the opposite of the 'fake it till you make it' school of self-improvement. The basic advice is simple: 'Be yourself.' Forget trying to improve yourself; work out a way to be happy and live in the moment.

In the most general terms, Nietzsche agreed with this advice, because he believed there was a self that we could be. For him, human beings were the product of nature rather than nurture. The drives that make up our souls, he believed, are as unalterable as our genes. We are born with a basic constitution that we are powerless to change. We can't decide who we are – that, he says, is 'the American conviction' – and the biggest mistake we can make is to try and be someone we're not.

But Nietzsche didn't like the injunction 'Be yourself'. In it, he saw a trap: by accepting ourselves, we cut ourselves off from growth. Instead of taking responsibility for our forward progress and striving to improve, we let ourselves off, saying, with a listless shrug, 'That's just who I am.'

Rather than 'being yourself', Nietzsche believed in 'becoming yourself'. 'Become who you are!' he proclaimed. This was his motto, one of the 'granite sentences' he laid down as command-ments. It's basically the equivalent of 'Become your best self,' which makes it sounds a bit cheesy, but when it comes to confidence, is probably just about right.

Self-improvement, for Nietzsche, was learning how to work with what you've got. We can't change our core selves, but we can learn what we are like, and how to work within our limits. That's what he was really getting at with his hyper-specific advice on topics such as the right way to drink tea. His elaborate directions were a means of emphasising that everybody has their own measure, and we should be careful to observe it. As he advised on digestion (always a Nietzschean fascination): 'You must know the size of your stomach.'

By learning our limits, we also learn what we can and can't change. Part of training is correcting – and if possible removing – unnecessary weaknesses. More important, though, is accepting the weaknesses that cannot be overcome, and working on them until they almost become strengths: 'One can control one's drives like a gardener and, though few are aware of it, cultivate the shoots of anger, sympathy, thoughtfulness and vanity as fruitfully and profitably as beautiful fruits on a trellis.'

There was no shortcut on this journey. 'To become what one is,' Nietzsche wrote, 'one must not have the faintest idea what one is.' He meant that we can't go looking for ourselves the way we look for an object. He intended his writing to be a guide, not in the sense of a user's manual, which tells you what to do step by step, but a travel book, which if it works at all, works by helping you discover what you were looking for at the right time and in the right way for you.

What we are looking for is not a thing but a sense of rightness. It will feel like finding what you sought all along, even though you couldn't have said beforehand exactly what that was.

'Charlie,' Ben called over the din. 'Would you say I "act first, then think" or "think first, then act"?'

Charlie scratched his chin. 'Is there an option for "overthink, then don't act, then cry myself to sleep"?'

The Barclays Wealth Multipurpose Sports Hall had been transformed into corridors of stalls, each with a glossy company banner. Trestle tables covered by branded cloths groaned with corporate USBs, pens and tote bags. By each table there was an eager-eyed rep, most of them barely older than Charlie, suited and poised for questions. The Careers Fair blurb had even suggested that attendees should wear a suit. Charlie owned one, of course, but the idea of putting it on to come to the Barclays Wealth Hall was bordering on the absurd, like dressing up in a white coat and turning up at a doctors' convention expecting to be offered a job.

Ben (who had actually worn one) had not so much persuaded as begged Charlie to come with him to the Careers Fair. 'My parents are giving me endless grief. If I just applied for something, it'd distract them for a bit.' Graduate schemes and law firms weren't that relevant for Charlie, but his schedule was pretty light – he could certainly squeeze it in. In order to make their brutally early timeslot, they'd had to set an alarm for half past nine. The whole thing had the feel of an excursion, as if they were off to Alton Towers. They'd tooled up with double-strength lattes and almond croissants while they queued.

'I hope you selected "Some people may see me as heartless, insensitive or uncaring",' said Ben. They were kicking off at the Career Suitability Test station: ten laptops displaying a Myers Briggs-type test that purported to tell you who you were and what you should do.

'Sorry, switched off there – must be 'cause I "prefer talking to listening". But I'm nonetheless a "mixer and a mingler". What an enigma.'

'Mixer and mingler? You've gone out once since you split up with Sara.'

'No one will come out with me!'

'Besides, wait till you *really* break up. Then we'll see.'

'We are really broken up—'

'Yeah, apart from the texts and calls and MSN.'

'That's part of the process.'

'When you really break up, you'll be full-time on Fantasy Football and celebrity biographies. I know you.'

'Ben, Ben, you're couldn't be more wrong.' Charlie tapped his screen. 'According to Science, I'm Extroverted, Intuitive, Feeling and Perceiving, and my abilities know no bounds.' Charlie scanned down his suitable careers and was relieved to find Entrepreneur among the options, nestled between Social Worker and Actor. (Social Worker! The lists seemed like they hadn't been updated since the Seventies.) Really Charlie thought these questionnaires were baseless, but it was like astrology – if you more or less believed what they told you already, why not take the encouragement?

'Yep, as I thought, we're exact opposites. I'm a "nurturer and defender". I'd be good as an Administrative Assistant or a member of the Clergy.' Ben had a large, squashy face. When he was worried, which was often, it puckered in the middle like a punched pillow. 'Fuck, this is depressing, I wish we hadn't done this.'

'Don't worry about it, it's bullshit anyway – it's just some crap you can read online any time. I'm telling you, you can do this. Let's go and find someone to talk to.' Charlie mimed a three-pointer, indicating the sign strung from a basketball hoop to the wall. '"Your career starts here!"'

Ben puffed out his cheeks and scanned the aisles of corporate cubicles. 'The one thing I did some research on was the Tesco Grad scheme.' Charlie thanked the god of enterprise that no such hell awaited him. 'So maybe we could look for them? Apparently it's brutally competitive.'

'Perfect. Let's look for Tesco and bump into your future on the way.'

The guys who had worn suits looked like footballers sitting in the audience of those Saturday night 'Evening With' shows. The girls looked uncomfortable and stressed, wearing clumpy heels and hugging clear plastic folders of printed CVs. Was this how they'd be in a few months' time? For a brief second, Charlie caught a glimpse of the future. The people still pouring into the hall were tiny and homogeneous, channelled into corridors that would convey them mechanically through the decades, building careers in HR or Project Management, inching their way up, only to retire in a bungalow at sixty-five, unrecognisable as the reasonably smart, funny, fit, sexy person they were at twenty-one.

Of course Ben was practically there already. He couldn't help it – his suit looked like he'd picked it out blindfold in the Debenhams January sale.

'This seems to be Law Firm Alley,' said Charlie. 'You into any of this? See yourself as a lawyer?'

'Well, I did like *Ally McBeal*. I'm not sure that counts.'

'Coming up for Management Consultancy Lane. Why not chat to someone here? It'll be good practice.'

They lingered on the edge of a conversation between a curly-haired blonde representative and a stubbly guy in a pinstriped suit. She was reassuring him that his degree subject was completely irrelevant. 'Listen, it doesn't matter what you've done at Undergraduate. Mine was in Biology – no use to anyone!'

The candidate laughed dutifully, while Ben and Charlie smiled along on the sidelines.

'What really matters,' the blonde woman went on, 'is leadership potential, an analytic mind and the desire to make a difference.'

Charlie pulled out his vibrating phone – Sara. He wasn't sure he had the energy to support two people at once, and ten-thirty was early enough to claim he was asleep . . . but policy was policy. Charlie's twenty-four-hour comfort line obeyed one simple rule: never initiate, always respond. It was a new service he was providing: victim support. (In this case, the victim was supported by the criminal but it didn't affect the quality of care.) 'Hey.'

'Where are you? It's loud!'

Pinstripe started in on his extra-curricular activities – articles for *The Badger* and charity fun runs. (*The Badger* was the inexplicably named uni paper, where future journalists practised fawning and rubbing people up the wrong way.) Charlie remembered Ben's

rugby tour gimp experience. That could definitely be dressed up –
sports team rep? A natural motivator? A selfless team player?

'Careers Fair.'

'Oh!'

Charlie moved off to the retail zone to observe Ben from a
distance. 'How are you doing?'

'Not great to be honest.'

'Oh dear.'

Miraculously, Ben seemed to have piped up, saving himself from
slinking away unacknowledged. Charlie gave him a thumbs up.

'I didn't sleep again. You're *really* at the Careers Fair?'

'Yeah.' Charlie tried not to sound too cheerful. At first, whenever they'd spoken, the sound of her voice had activated his latent
feelings of loss and sadness. Now though, it was getting more difficult to tune in to her downbeat mood. 'Ben wanted to come.'

'Hm.'

'What?'

'. . . Nothing.'

'Come on, I know that tone. Better out than in.' Charlie started
wandering up and down a corridor of big retailers, launching then
abandoning imaginary careers at ASOS and John Lewis, and
collecting USB sticks.

'It's just that I was always asking you to come to that kind of
thing with me and you said it was pointless. I actually saw it was
on and considered going and remembered what you'd said . . .
Anyway, it doesn't matter, I didn't call for an argument.'

Charlie didn't really see why he should be held responsible for
things Sara imagined him saying, but said, placatingly, 'Who cares
what I think anyway? You should do whatever you want.' He
peeped through the banners to see Ben taking an armful of freebies
from the management consultancy stall. Ben would make a great

employee, Charlie reflected – he was kind, he gave a shit, he was even quite hard-working when galvanised. It was strange that in order to find a Ben, companies had to put potential Bens through all this painful entrepreneurial stuff – all this flesh pressing and chat about innovating – when surely all they really wanted was someone who could do what they were told?

'Yeah, I know,' said Sara. 'Can I tell you my worry?'

'Of course.'

'I'm worried about whether or not to go to the Safer Sex Ball.'

'That's ages away, isn't it?'

'It's also Matt's birthday and everyone's going and they're buying tickets now.'

'Okay.' The question of if and when they would see each other had been hanging in the air for some time. Charlie thought he'd managed to skirt around Sara's proposals, neither rejecting them outright nor making any moves to make it happen. Of course he wanted to see her, but what good would it do? They'd get an hour of comfort before having to split up all over again. But they were bound to bump into each other sooner or later, and then they'd have to go through all that angst before a public audience. 'And do you want to go?'

'I don't know. I don't want to miss out because of all this.'

'Okay. Well . . . you should go if you want to.'

'You don't want me to go.'

'No . . .'

'I can tell by your voice!'

'Well, I just feel like—'

'You want the whole of uni to yourself so you can go round pulling other girls without feeling bad.'

Charlie just managed to stop himself swearing that wasn't true. He knew what would happen if he promised – he'd be bound by his 'good bloke' oath, and end up with neither the relationship, nor the fun he'd ended the relationship to have. He swallowed, suddenly nervous. 'I want to be honest with you, okay. And being honest, I can't promise that nothing will happen at SSB.'

'Oh *great.*'

'I'm sorry.'

'Right.'

'I am sorry, Sara.'

During the gaping pause that followed, Charlie walked further down the corridor, trying to collect his thoughts. He found himself in front of a poster tacked up on a piece of blue partition:

WANTED
DO-ERS, GO-GETTERS, MONEY-MAKERS

'Charlie?'

'I'm still here. Are you okay?'

'Not really, but I suppose I better go. I only called because I missed you. Bye.' Without waiting for a response, she hung up.

'Caught your interest?'

Charlie snapped out of his daze. An alert pair of eyes switched from a BlackBerry to him, with a look that declared: *You have my expert attention.*

'Um, sure,' said Charlie. 'Why, are you involved in it?'

The guy was young, but not so young as to make a conversation seem pointless. Short and broad-shouldered, he had slicked-back hair and a pink shirt with no jacket – a respectable middle ground on the suit question.

'Let me give you a bit of advice.' He tucked his phone into his breast pocket. 'Don't answer questions with "Sure". It doesn't sound professional.'

Charlie resisted the impulse to say 'Sure.' 'Understood,' he nodded. It was one of Charlie's strengths that he wasn't always itching to prove he was the alpha – if this guy wanted to sit at the head of the table and carve the beef, he could carve the beef. 'I'm Charlie.' He extended a hand.

'Arthur.' Arthur shook it like he meant it. 'What do you want to do, Charlie?'

'Well.' Charlie arranged his thoughts. 'I'm interested in setting up my own business, and according to this poster, there's a university seed-funding scheme. Are you involved?'

'I'm not, but I worked with a start-up that won a similar scheme when I first graduated. Do you have a co-founder?'

Co-founder? For a second, Charlie was derailed by quite how vague his plans were, but he managed to quell his doubts in time to reply, 'Not as yet. Is that a drawback?'

'I happen to know on that scheme they rejected individual applications in the first cut. So I'd recommend you find a co-founder. Do you want some advice?'

Charlie had the feeling he was going to get it. 'Certainly.'

Arthur leaned one hand on the table as if he were presenting the casual segment of the news. 'Think of the person that you'd least like as your competitor, and ask them.'

Instantly, Charlie thought of Taz. He was bound to be all over this competition – he'd have been masterminding his entry while Charlie was attending his first freshers' foam party. If Charlie were a real entrepreneur, of course, that thought wouldn't bother him – he'd tell himself he was unencumbered by business experience and the red tape of the Entrepreneurial Society and his fresh approach was in fact his greatest asset.

'Are you looking for part-time work?' Arthur asked confrontationally, practically winding Charlie with opportunity.

It was impossible to say no. Before he'd left the stall, Charlie had taken Arthur's card, described himself as 'innovative, decisive and passionate' in an application form for a post as a Student Brand Ambassador, and declared in writing his (non-existent) interest in taking part in flagship promotions before finals. He had to admit he was pretty impressed by Arthur. If Charlie could sell Social Tiger like that, there'd be no stopping him.

He found Ben standing at the back of a crowd watching an energetic, balding fifty-something wearing a headset mic. Behind him a banner proclaimed 'Talent Transitions' in off-looking red Times New Roman.

'Never use a font the average person could name,' Charlie murmured to Ben. 'Any idiot could tell you that.'

'It's about how you present yourself,' Mic boomed. 'If you ring up and sound like a piece of wet lettuce, you'll get a quick rejection. It's all about making rapport, influencing people.' He raised his eyebrows in a cunning aside to the front row. 'Do you know what can improve a woman's chances of getting a job fivefold and a man's threefold?'

The two girls immediately in front of him shared an embarrassed look.

'Where'd you go?' whispered Charlie.

'Assessment centre.' Ben's face was practically caving in with the multiple worries impressed upon it. 'God, this is bleak.'

'I'm asking, does anybody know?' Mic threw it out.

'It's a handshake,' muttered Ben.

'At the back. What's your name?'

Charlie glanced to his right and saw a tall girl in a trouser suit, hand raised. 'Is it a handshake?'

'Exactly! Well done.'

Charlie gave Ben a 'get you' nudge. 'You were right!'

Ben's eyes bored into him like lasers of despair.

Skit successfully completed, Mic got back to business. 'Now let's talk CVs. A CV is not a shopping list. Ask yourself, *What story am I telling?* You have to create a personal narrative.'

'Just kill me now.'

When political passions are roused, tedious administration is never far behind. They had spent an hour debating the exact wording of their vandalism. Then they had debated handwriting or printing (printing was more legible). Ellie had gone to Rymans, found stickers were pretty expensive, and instead bought some glue.

'It's bathos,' Maria had helpfully commented, when the printing system went down. 'The sublime to the ridiculous,' she explained before adding, 'I will have to revise pretty soon.'

'Don't talk about it,' Ellie burst out, clapping her hands over her ears. 'I'm asking you seriously, don't.'

'That's it.' Nadine slapped a hand on the printer table. 'I'm issuing a fatwa. Revision talk is banned – by order of the Prophet Muhammed, peace be upon him.'

Finally, armed to the teeth with stationery, they ventured out onto campus and began systematically pasting slogans onto Safer Sex Ball posters.

One of the things people rarely mention about politics is how embarrassing it is. You don't tend to read that Mrs Pankhurst felt like a twat every time she smashed a window or bombed a letter-box. Ellie couldn't quite decide who she feared meeting most: it could be her dissertation supervisor (though she wasn't sure Dr Longstaff would even recognise her), or one of several guys who had recently commented online that she was an insane bitch, or simply everyone she knew.

A group of girls streaming out of the Business faculty shot them looks that combined disgust and confusion in a perfect helix of contempt. A bunch of hockey team guys stopped in their tracks, weighed down by sporting equipment and bafflement.

'What are you doing?' one asked, as if she were urinating on the faculty steps.

Ellie felt a twang of irritation amid the drone of humiliation. She'd anticipated having to explain their actions (she'd even dreamed of bumping into Lucas and those guys and airing a few of her stronger opinions), but she hadn't quite realised how stupid it would make her feel. 'Protesting the objectification of women on campus,' she replied, hating the questioning intonation that crept into her voice.

'Obviously.' As they turned to go, he exhaled his disbelief at the lengths to which crazies would go.

One professor with huge round glasses and tufty purple hair stood and watched while they pasted up a sign outside the Union, recently transformed into a gastro-pub with standard lamps and five pieces of soggy vegetable tempura (all carrot) for £4.95. Eventually, she gave a one-sided smile and a single nod, before bobbing away, a dot of violet against the grey.

Maria wasn't completely getting it.

'What about that?' She pointed to a Domino's ad featuring a white-toothed gang of Americans tumbling artfully onto a sofa. 'That's annoying. They shouldn't even be allowed to monopolise advertising the way they do. Uni's sold out.'

Maria was the other reasonable girl in Ellie's second-year seminar group. She had bleach-blonde hair with a streak of blue, and big ambling shoulders that she shrugged a lot when she made a point. In their group, every question asked by the shy, quietly disappointed PhD student had met with brain-gnawing silence from ninety per cent of the participants. ('Why do they bother coming?' Ellie complained to Rose afterwards. 'How can they *stand* saying nothing week after week?') Maria could be relied upon to speak up and say something more or less coherent. But she wasn't getting it at all.

'*Single issue*,' groaned Nadine. 'You don't have a message if you're saying just anything, do you? Say one thing!'

Ellie tried to line up arguments in her head in case anyone else took issue, but as they headed through Library Square, no one paid them the slightest attention. The third years milling around the revolving door to the library had a ghostly air, taking up a fraction of their usual space – the rest of their person had floated off, pondering Locke or Laura Mulvey or . . . maths. All they were concerned about was hoovering up a packet of crisps or a white chocolate mocha and returning to the hive. Ellie couldn't help feeling slightly relieved.

'Yes, *but*.' Maria got her discussion voice on. 'If we say "Women Have Pubes", don't we ultimately end up looking like a bunch of pube fetishists who just want to see pubes?'

'I wouldn't mind seeing pubes,' Ellie countered. 'But I don't think *that*'s the single message. It's that campus culture is sexist and it makes it seem okay when uni posters objectify women like this.'

'Mm,' nodded Nadine. 'Nice and clear.'

'We want to say,' Ellie launched, not quite sure where she was going, 'You don't have to put up with this. Why is this happening? This is bullshit. Looking at this will probably make you feel shit—'

'It's not only those posters though,' Maria butted in. 'It's the whole commercialisation of uni. It's capitalism.'

'Single message!' cried Nadine. 'Pass me the glue. We're not going to take down the capitalist system and do our finals on the side.'

'It's true though.' Maria scraped her blue streak behind her ear. 'We're just attacking the symptom.'

Outside Arts Two, the posters were encased in glass. With some satisfaction, Ellie slapped a slogan on top and brushed glue over it, partly obscuring a poster for a burlesque version of *Waiting for Godot*. 'You know what I'd like to vandalise? The magazines in the campus shop, about who's fat and who's flashed their vag. And that fucking wannabe *Daily Mail* columnist in *The Badger*.'

'I won't say it again. Okay, I will – single issue.' Nadine added a final glue layer. 'But that could be a good phase two.'

'By Women Who Hate Women,' Ellie spelled out in the air.

'For Women Who Hate Themselves,' Nadine added. 'That's fucking good!'

'Let's not get victim-blamey though,' said Maria, meaningfully. 'Remember who the real enemy is.'

A few scattered trees and some regimented bushes marked the point where campus stopped and the real world began. Out here by the Philosophy Department, the quiet campus roads rarely saw a car, making their painted lines and intersections feel like some kind of road-safety display. The absence of a corporate sponsor or big-hearted investment banker to donate a shiny glass-fronted building meant Philosophy was still in its boxy, concrete-legged 1960s form. Ellie had had her single meeting with Dr Longstaff there, in the Philosophy–Classics café: a bench next to a tea and coffee vending machine. At the thought of that meeting, in which she had waxed lyrical about Nietzsche and seemed completely in control of her material, Ellie felt a wave of anxiety that threatened to topple her over. With a deep wheezy breath, she tried to tell herself . . . But what was she even telling herself now? She couldn't do the dissertation, it had been proven. That was that.

They stood on the paving below the faculty, next to one of the concrete pillars, and gazed up. Between two narrow windows that stretched right up to the floor above, there was a larger-than-life-sized SSB poster of the same girl, sprawled on her back with a danger sign Photoshopped behind her. Slightly twisted at the waist, she covered her breasts with one hand, and fingered her blonde hair with the other. Her skin was finished with a silky layer of correction, a strange combination of HD crispness and blurry erasure. Around her breasts and bikini bottoms, there were little blocks of peach, where the flesh colour hadn't blended. Any suggestion of a nipple had been misted over like the faces on *Crimewatch*.

Nadine craned her neck. 'How the fuck are we going to get up there?'

Shielding her eyes, Ellie sized it up. 'I s'pose someone could go up and lean out the window. Pretty far though.' There was a doubtful pause. 'I'm not saying I'll do it, but someone could climb the lamp post.' Their eyes travelled up, lingering on the uncomfortable distance between the tapering post and the faculty wall.

'Well, I guess that's it,' said Maria with some relief, as she checked the time on her phone.

'Could throw something at it.' Nadine twisted one of her rings around her finger. 'Bit mad though. We're trying to rebrand as less ranty.'

'Are we?' Ellie laughed.

Nadine winked at Ellie. 'Don't you worry your pretty little head about it.'

'Look, I might have to go.' Maria drew back, holding out the remaining printouts, her face suddenly sickly and twisted as a used tissue. 'I made this timetable, you see. If I don't stick to the timetable, I get a bit—'

'Stop talking.' Ellie grabbed the paper. 'You're stressing me out.'

96

'I'm actually stressing myself out. It's just hit me now.' Maria shivered. 'I've got to go. Good luck, okay. Don't die. We don't want any Emily Davisons here.'

'Thanks for the tip.'

Maria shuffled off, leaving Ellie and Nadine staring up. One of the people working at the window desks drew her blind.

'Maybe we should leave this one.' Ellie scanned left and right. Being this close to the philosophy department felt dangerous, as if she were revisiting a crime scene.

'So it's *you*.'

With a jump, they turned round. A tall guy with a shaggy, dark-blonde Mohican was standing right behind them.

'"Women have pubes". Cool.' He had a rangy, lean look. In his roughly cut off trousers and dirty vest, he might have spent the last few nights on the side of a motorway or living in a forest.

'Oh.' Ellie scratched her head. 'Thanks.'

He fixed his hooded brown eyes on her. 'I loved the mad online shit.'

'Ah, right,' she smiled. 'We're trying to sound a bit less ranty now.'

'Oh,' he said, apparently disappointed. 'Why?'

Ellie looked at Nadine, who was eyeing them both with a mischievous squint. 'So people don't think we're mad . . . I s'pose,' she trailed off.

'I'm anti-sanitisation. Why be reasonable?' He put his hands in his pockets, all elbows and shoulders and wiry limbs. 'I'm Oscar, by the way.'

Ellie shook her gaze from the freckles on Oscar's nose. 'Ellie.'

Nadine put her hands on her hips. 'How's your climbing, Oscar? 'Cos mine's not all that and we need someone to vandalise this abomination.' She pointed up at the poster.

Oscar gave a thin-lipped smile. 'Sounds dangerous.'

'Chivalry's not dead.' Ellie swung a stagey punch. 'It's just a lot less rewarding.'

'Someone should give it the final kick-in.' Oscar held out a hand. 'Let's see.' He took the sheets of paper and scanned them over.

Ellie felt strangely shy watching him read their slogans – 'AT UNI I LEARNED MY BODY WAS MY ONLY ASSET', 'WOMEN HAVE PUBES' and 'EDUCATION NOT OBJECTIFICATION'. Maybe they didn't capture it at all? Each one had #unisexism at the bottom, a testimony to Nadine's Easter work experience at the ad agency. ('You need somewhere for people to go, otherwise what's the point? How can you even measure it?') For a second, Ellie wanted to grab them and run away. She barely resisted the temptation to cover her eyes.

'All right,' nodded Oscar. 'May as well do them all.'

Ellie felt a crashing relief. With a final eyebrow-lift at Ellie's expression, Nadine ran upstairs to hand the paper and glue from the window. Ellie remained as lookout, not quite sure what to say now she was alone with Oscar. A couple of guys passed by, heading for the car park.

'Yeah, but mate, *mate*,' one was saying, 'the grad scheme at Goldy's stopped accepting applications ages ago.'

Ellie looked at Oscar and smiled awkwardly. 'You got yours in, right?'

'Fuck, missed it.' Oscar sucked air through his teeth. 'But I did send them a video of myself masturbating. Fingers crossed they might hire me anyway.'

With the coast clear, Oscar leaned his back against the lamp post and started to walk his feet inch by inch up one of the building's concrete legs, one spidery hand gripping the metal above his head.

His vest slipped off his slender shoulder and dropped down his arm. Blocking the sun from her eyes, Ellie took in his gradual, long-limbed ascent: carefully balanced, resting momentarily on the ball of each foot as if dancing, he had an easy concentration on his weathered face, his eyes glancing up every few seconds in a slow, syncopated rhythm.

The sudden appearance of Dr Longstaff between the concrete pillars made Ellie gasp with shock.

'Oh, hi, Ellie,' called her supervisor, both arms hugging a tower of essays. A wisp of hair flew into her mouth and she tried to blow it out as she passed by. 'Everything all right? Writing going well?'

No, Ellie thought, as she nodded fervently.

8

Style Your Character

Nietzsche did give one piece of advice to people trying to become themselves. To succeed in this project, he said, we have to reconcile ourselves with our past. True confidence, for Nietzsche, was being able to look back and say, 'I'd do it all again.'

Nietzsche called this way of thinking '*amor fati*', love of fate. It's basically 'no regrets' on a grand scale, not just 'oh well, never mind,' but 'thank goodness this happened to me, because if it hadn't, I wouldn't be the person I am today.' As Nietzsche described it: 'Now something you held as true or once loved strikes you as an error . . . But perhaps that error was necessary for you then, when you were another person.' One must, he wrote, be like those 'masters of musical improvisation' who can, with a nimble flick of the fingers, give each accident 'a beautiful meaning and soul'.

Nietzsche stayed on at university to do a PhD, but he was such a brilliant student that the University of Basel offered him a professorship based on the recommendation of his supervisor, and he was awarded his doctorate without having to complete his thesis. It was 1869; he was twenty-four. 'Why on earth,' he wrote later, 'does anyone become a university professor at twenty-four?' He had been at school since the age of six and he wanted to see the world and pursue his philosophical interests. His plan was to take a year out and go to Paris, the East London of the nineteenth century, to sample 'the divine can-can and the green absinthe'. But he needed the money – his father had died when he was six and his mother lived off her widow's pension – and he was ambitious and proud of his achievement. He left university lamenting the end of 'golden days of gloriously free activity'. 'Now,' he complained about his new job, 'I must be a philistine!'

His stint as an academic was one of the accidents of Nietzsche's life. Like everyone, he had his fair share: poor health, his father's early death, loneliness and lack of success as a writer. Taken in isolation, each of these experiences might seem senseless or regrettable. By seeing them as part of 'an artistic plan', Nietzsche was able to recognise the indispensable role each one played in forming the whole. Looking back in his philosophical autobiography *Ecce Homo*, he could declare, in all sincerity: 'I do not have the slightest wish that anything should be different to the way it is.'

The same holistic approach could also be applied to the good and bad parts of our personalities. Like good and bad experiences, isolated strengths and weaknesses were much less important than the overall character they produced. The secret to becoming yourself was not to try and remove the weaknesses, but to fit them into the overall plan, pulling all the different parts together 'until everything appears artistic and rational, and even the weaknesses enchant the eye'.

Nietzsche called this process '"giving style" to one's character'. Once again, he successfully forecast the shape of the modern world. Now, everyone has their own narrative, styled, crafted and curated, a constantly updated story of self. Nietzsche wrote: 'whether the taste is good or bad is less important than people think – enough that it's one taste!' Like a CV: it's not *the* story, but it's *a* story, and as long as you believe it, that's really all that matters.

Taz had his office in the Caffè Nero in the centre of town. In exam term, the competition for spaces was as bad here as it was in the library – he must have arrived at opening time, Charlie thought, to get the prized corner table. Every year, as the weeks of revision passed, the twitchy Nero regulars formed a disparate crew that managed to overcome ordinary social barriers. Revision was like that: you saw the same people day in, day out; you shared their boredom, hysteria, despair. The tedium and fear wore people down and eventually broke them – you couldn't help forming connections. That was how Charlie had first got to know Taz. He had revised here in first year, or more accurately, he had observed Rachel revising (Rachel was his hopeless first-year crush who had a boyfriend at Warwick, but still came to Charlie's room three times a week to watch films and platonically sleep over – thank God he'd finally cut that shit) and tried to win her over with a painstaking selection of YouTube videos. He'd spent somewhere in the region of £400 on grande lattes that semester.

In the long queue downstairs, the boy in front of Charlie was standing in stripy socks, musing over the pastries. As Charlie dug out his credit card, he positioned himself to block the view from the far corner. On the way in, he had clocked Sasha sprawled in one of the armchairs. Charlie wondered what Lucas would do in this situation – perhaps walk past without seeing her on the way out, just to remind her he existed and wasn't thinking about her. Or more likely, head straight over and make some joke about how he was only talking to her because he wanted to have sex with her. And by some perverse Lucas-logic, it would work.

Somehow, Charlie reflected, Lucas had managed to get it completely right – he'd gained trust by hiding his bad behaviour in plain sight. Meanwhile, Charlie had been working with a completely different brand strategy: 'Good Bloke'. Being a Good Bloke wasn't easy – it involved gradually building credit through small acts of decency, and recommendations from other users in the community. The acts couldn't be too ostentatious; on the other hand, you didn't want to go hiding your light under a bushel. Preventing a fight was classic. Helping some girl who had puked all over herself outside Rehab. Giving up your Sunday to help a girl move house.

The ideal result was that some unobtrusive, selfless favour you'd done came up in conversation between two fit girls and a guy. One of the fit girls would share your good deed and the guy would say, 'Yeah, he's a good bloke.' For some reason, Charlie had observed, girls tended to believe the statement more readily when it came from a guy, perhaps because it was clear that he wasn't the victim of a charm campaign designed to trick him into sex. But it was also crucial to have that endorsement from the other girl (in the ideal scenario, she would then say, 'He's fit as well'), because it gave her peers permission to fancy you. That was how you built trust in the brand and added value to your product. (Obviously, you had to be reasonably good-looking for this to work. Otherwise you were pursuing a different strategy again: either overcoming your deficiency by being a superhumanly good bloke, an 'Incredibly Lovely Guy', or alternatively becoming the kind of fucked-up, hilarious dickhead girls described as 'Ugly But'.) The Good-Looking Good Bloke theory was that trust would eventually come good in the form of casual sex with hot girls who were also nice people. Yes, it would be a long road, but creating a global brand wasn't easy (did you see Zuckerberg complaining?) and you could comfort yourself through the lonely nights with the fact that it was also making you a better person and improving the world.

Of course what had actually happened to Charlie was that he had got a girlfriend, because – as Lucas told him repeatedly – he was asking for it.

Well, nobody could accuse Charlie of not adapting to his environment. The board had instituted a major strategic shake-up. Lucas had been promoted to Best Friend, the position of Girlfriend had been made redundant, and Taz had shot from distant acquaintance to Career Accelerator.

When Charlie got back, Taz was finishing an email. 'Myup, send.' He tapped his laptop decisively. 'Sorry about that. I'm having this correspondence—'

'Nice beard,' interrupted Charlie. 'Very Craig David.'

Taz lifted a hand towards his jawline, stroking the fluffy crawl of hair he'd cultivated over the Easter break. Taz was deeply unstylish, not in the painful way of a true nerd, but in the manner of someone whose first-generation mum was still buying his clothes well into his teens. It wasn't what he wore exactly – Yale hoodie, jeans, loafers – it was how clean and snugly fitting it all was.

Seeing Taz's flicker of a frown, Charlie instantly regretted needling him. Taz wasn't a lad, he wasn't expecting abusive banter as a matter of course. Charlie was a little keyed-up, he realised – maybe it was because Taz was actually more 'Sara's friend' than his. Sara had worked for him, marketing a series of club nights he ran, a solid business idea, which (Charlie had noted at the time) had the happy side effect of Taz employing a small army of fit girls. 'Sorry, you were saying. Correspondence.'

'Oh yeah.' Taz shook his head wearily. 'The university wrote to me in February saying I was going to fail my course unless I spent more time on it. So I wrote back saying, "Look, this is ridiculous.

I haven't been wasting my time. I've done more for this university than ten people who contribute nothing and leave with bog-standard two:ones. Can't I get credit for one of the societies I've set up?" So they wrote back saying, "No way," and I was like, "Look, you're alienating someone who's potentially a major future donor here. Can't we come to some arrangement?" Long story short: we can't. Which is crazy, but now I'm motivated to see it as a challenge: can I do enough in my final four courses to scrape a two:one?'

'Oh.' Charlie never failed to be amazed by Taz's imperial sense of self-worth. This was the real reason, he remembered, why he needled him: to establish some sense of equality. 'So do you still want to—'

Taz flicked the worry away. 'Of course. That's just the uni game. Business is real life. So. How can I help you?'

'Well.' Charlie cleared himself a bit of space. 'I hope we can help each other. I've got this business idea that I think—'

'Have you got a business plan?'

'No. Not yet. That's what—'

'You should have come to Entrepreneurs' Night last week. Brian Miller gave a great talk on business plans.' Taz slipped back in his chair, evidently downgrading this meeting from Important to Low-Priority. 'Anyway, carry on.'

Charlie had prepared for this meeting using a technique he had christened 'anti-preparation'. As the name suggested, anti-preparation explicitly banned looking through notes or writing new ones. Such efforts were a) pointless, because what can you find out in the twenty minutes you've left yourself, and b) a positive drawback, because by preparing, you admitted you cared. That admission was the thing that made you nervous – and nerves were what made you perform badly.

Avoiding that pitfall, anti-preparation focused on getting mentally ready: long showers, the right clothes, intentionally running late to give yourself no time for reflection. It was this technique that had secured Charlie his AAB at A-Level (the rogue B − Biology, of all things − had almost scuppered his university entrance). Of course, at school he'd had all those lessons, a kind of deep leave-it-to-soak form of preparation. But hadn't he spent hours and hours discussing Social Tiger with Sara? Only, now, put on the spot, he felt an unexpected thrill, as if an invisible hand had strummed a chord right down his body. 'So, um, it's—'

'Start with the market. What market is it serving?'

The market was students − this, Charlie felt, was his central insight. He was amazed at how few people saw it. When he'd asked his dad why he didn't sell chocolates to students, he said, 'Students don't have jobs, Charlie. In business, I find, it's best to go for people with money.' (Charlie's parents had a chocolate company. Yes, they made and sold chocolates, and with malice aforethought they'd named him Charlie. Lucky for them he was so robust.) Students were just as bad. They might recognise their marketability, in a dull, cynical way − as Alistair said about their house, 'Obviously we're paying the "unlucky, you're students and you don't have a choice" premium' − but they failed to see the implications of that. Here was a captive audience, free from financial commitments, with nothing to do but spend. And who knew that market better than Charlie and Taz − students themselves, with first-hand experience? Somewhere in his bookmarks folder, Charlie had some stats: he couldn't remember them right now, so he made them up. 'The student market is worth something like eight billion.'

Taz nodded. 'And they're most likely high earners later. Huge opportunity for retailers and service providers to get them now and keep them for life.'

'Lots of people are in this space.' Charlie was back on track. He was even picking up the lingo. 'Like, the other day, I was head-hunted by this guy looking for student brand ambassadors.' He meant Arthur. This was another creative elaboration, but it was a construct-ive lie – as well as sounding vaguely impressive, it might encourage Charlie to reply to Arthur's officious follow-up, sent within minutes of meeting. 'But there's no one I know doing exactly this thing.'

'Which is?'

'We offer discounts and queue jumps to students by interesting companies in the potential of the student market. Then we sell advertising space on the website and eventually we collect user data and sell that too.'

Taz chewed the inside of his lip in silence. 'There must be other people doing it.'

'Maybe at other unis. But no one's cracked it so far, or we would have heard of them.'

'Of course, if it's a large market like this one, you don't need to be the first to do it.' Taz became suddenly animated. 'There was Pret, then there was Eat. Caffè Nero, then Costa – or the other way round.'

'Steve Jobs couldn't even code. He just took the ideas and—' Charlie twisted an invisible Rubik's Cube between his hands.

'Of course, I'm not into that sort of thing. Selling people things they don't need.'

'Oh, no, me neither,' agreed Charlie, who up to that point had never considered the question.

'A lot of people have that idea about me. After that arbitrage with the tickets to Rehab.' Taz's early forays into uni entrepre-neurialism had been pretty controversial. In his first term, Taz realised that people in the endless queue for Rehab Wednesday would pay far more than the £7 cover price to get in before it became one-in-one-out around 10 p.m. So he went early, bought lots of tickets in advance, and sold them for a sizeable profit. After a few of weeks of this, people were up in arms. *The Badger* included Taz in their wall of shame two weeks in a row, and the hockey boys stole his clothes from the dryer room and tried to auction them off on the lawn in front of the Walworth building. The level of vitriol had discouraged other students from similar interventions. But personally, Charlie didn't care. So maybe it was a bit crude, a bit rough and ready, but it showed serious initiative – the guy was providing a service. Taz pressed his palms together and gave Charlie an earnest look. 'I'm interested in disruptive innovations that will really overturn an industry.'

'Me too.' Charlie met his sincerity. 'As I see it, this is about opening up the market. Students are poorly served at the moment. There's so much expensive crap that only sells because it's not being challenged.'

'Mm. Are you going to do this on Facebook, because that can be tricky.'

'Well, I'm looking for your opinion on this.' Charlie wasn't above massaging Taz's self-importance. 'Either we use Facebook and start lean, or we set up a website—'

'With what money?'

'Here, do you mind if . . . ?' Charlie leaned across and opened a new tab to the seed-fund scheme. 'With this. It's a student-only competition, I reckon we'd stand a great chance. All we need is a business plan . . . CVs, branding design, market research, etc.—'

'Yeah, I know the guys who set this up.' Taz looked it over.

Leaning back, Charlie sipped his latte, trying not to crowd or look too eager. Rather than pressure Taz, he wanted to sneak up on the question of partnership, avoiding the possibility of a refusal.

Taz turned to him, scratching his beard. 'Listen, they won't go for you without a tech guy attached. Even if you start on Facebook, you're going to need a website soon, and one with additional functionality stored up for the future.'

A flash of inspiration hit Charlie. 'My housemate can code and I've broached it with him already,' he lied. The first part was true; the second could surely become so. 'Alistair Hayes? He built a website last year for his sister, a photographer – looks awesome.' Charlie reached for the keys again and brought up the site, fronted by a high-quality image of puffins nesting on a cliff. His heart beat a little faster. There was no way Alistair would want to make a website before finals – squeezing in meals seemed to be enough of a burden on his time – but maybe, possibly, if Charlie begged and pleaded and guilt-tripped and bribed, Alistair would consider mocking up a page, just for branding purposes. Charlie made a mental note to take Alistair a muffin.

As Taz broke off to reply to a text, a sense of momentum began to build in Charlie. The website, the brand values . . . it was all just detail. Social Tiger had been part of his imagined world for years: he'd pictured it, he knew it so intimately; everything was bound to fall into place.

Charlie headed out with a sketched-out business plan, a coffee-induced headache, and a lemon and poppyseed bribe to take away. Armed thus, almost on impulse, he stopped by Sasha's table. Pippa Lattimer was perched on the arm of the leather chair, wearing what looked like pyjama bottoms and a vest, brushing her cheek with the end of a long plait and staring at a photocopied article. Pippa was unbelievably dry, but her presence gave him the excuse he needed to keep it brief. 'Hey.'

'Hey.' Sasha looked up from her laptop without a hint of a smile. 'Are you taking your muffin for a walk?'

'It's a present for Alistair. I'm concerned he's crash dieting.' Charlie gave a wistful shrug. 'Shame, cause he's beautiful just as he is.'

A one-sided, feline smirk flashed across Sasha's face. 'I didn't know you were working here.'

'Oh, I wasn't revising.' Charlie opened the conversation out to Pippa, who was busy adjusting her hairband. It occurred to Charlie that it might not be a good idea to tell them about Social Tiger. After all, he and Taz hadn't won the scheme yet. But at this moment, with sugar and caffeine coursing through his veins, Charlie didn't care – it didn't matter if the business ultimately succeeded; all that counted was holding on to the feeling he had right now, this expansive sense of possibility.

'Picking on Shannon like that is just mean,' Becky Hamilton-Simm commented. Shannon Bond, it turned out, was the name of the model in the Safer Sex Ball posters. She was a really nice second-year Engineer who – according to Becky – was being victimised by an army of jealous bitches for being exceptionally good-looking.

Jane Thomas liked Becky's comment immediately. A second later, it got the thumbs up from Adam Matthias.

Ellie combed her fingers through the tangled clump of hair at the back of her neck.

'It's not personal,' she typed hurriedly. 'I've got nothing against her. It's a general thing about representacion.' She waited a few painful seconds, staring at the screen and absently yanking out a handful of long mousy strands. 'Representation,' she corrected.

'WTF!! Someone trashing pictures of you in your underwear!! – Not personal!?!!' Jane commented beneath.

Ellie swallowed.

'So were not allowed to talk about how girls are repsnted cos we'll offnd someone? Not just abt Shannon,' Tiffany Watson added quickly. Ellie thought she was in the year above – she must have stayed on to do a master's.

'Choice!?' Becky's thumbnail photo was a chip of tanned shoulder and a big brown eye. 'Feminism is choice.'

'Do whatever you want – that's femnsm?' Tiffany shot back.

'I can get a Brazilian and b a feminist!!!' yelled Jane.

Ellie's brain swam with thick, gloopy weeds, bloated with guilt, sleeplessness and inarticulacy. Nadine had insisted they set up the Facebook page: 'A place where people, like, debate and you post updates and targets and stuff.' Ellie thought Nadine was probably right (and God knows, *she* didn't have a clue), but every time she went on there and engaged in the 'debate' she'd gone out of her way to create, she found herself in a state of paralysing confusion.

'I saw those slogans and thought FUCK YEAH,' Caoimhe Louise Joyce pitched in. 'It's not about saying you can't do this, you can't do that, it's a culture – I'm not against porn, but I don't wanna be pornified all the time, I don't want to HAVE to see myself that way when I'm on my way to a lecture.' It was hard to express how grateful Ellie felt towards Caoimhe – a person she knew only as a small square of brick wall with a mural in Spanish – at that moment.

'Unis a zillion times more sxst thn my schl,' Tiffany Watson continued.

'Listen, I think we should talk,' said Justin.

Ellie tore herself away from the screen, heart pumping as if she'd spent the last hour in hand-to-hand combat.

Justin was staring at her, poised over a ringbinder, highlighter in hand. After the Agreement That Something Had To Be Done About The F-word, Justin had decided that he needed a change of scene. He stuffed his folders into reusable bags and carted them over to Ellie's on his bike. At 10 a.m. next day he began the arduous business of Getting Down To It. Even from her own state of hopeless, wilful inactivity, Ellie could see he had no idea how to revise. He spent hours making fair copies of notes he already had and furiously re-underlining the important parts. Sometimes he got into a frenzy of material gathering, printing PDF after PDF from the library website, as if having something on paper was the same as reading it. At the end of each grinding hour, he would reward himself with a cup of tea and exactly three Rich Tea biscuits. Justin didn't even like Rich Teas, but he thought they were a healthier option.

Ellie had considered giving him some advice, but the words 'glass house' and 'throw stones' came to mind. She was in no position to dole out revision tips – not *strictly* having started yet. Ellie totally agreed that Something Had To Be Done, but in practice she was hoping her continued denial would go unnoticed. If anyone wanted her, she'd be in her glass house, keeping still, quiet and as calm as possible while the temperature crept up and the oxygen dwindled.

A sudden worry struck her. 'Do you mean about next year?'

'Oh. No,' said Justin, surprised. 'I mean, we *could* chat about that . . . if you want.' He bowed his head and gazed uncomprehendingly at a printout, demonstrating his perfect ease as to whether or not they discussed that now.

'Um . . .' An email popped up in the corner of her screen – 'Interview Request: *The Badger* Hot Topic'. Ellie clicked on it with the speed of a reflex reaction. 'Hi Ellie! How would you like to write the "Pro" column for "Is Campus Sexist?"' asked a Melissa Gill, Senior Editor.

Ellie took a deep breath and slowly blew a raspberry.

'Do you want to close your lid?' Justin almost kept the edge of irritation out of his voice. 'If we're going to talk?'

Ellie slammed it down, and nodded earnestly. 'Sorry. This campaign thing is a bit intense. Kind of nerve-racking.' Since their vandalism spree, Ellie had spent roughly six hours a day in a frenzy of posting, emailing, tweeting and reading abuse about herself. She went from dizzying highs (a tweeted photo of a poster from another uni with 'EDUCATION NOT OBJECTIFICATION' scrawled across a poster for a RAG slave auction featuring two corseted women tied together) to dismal lows (the comments about her beneath a blog post entitled 'Why Students Should Grow Up and Get Over Themselves').

Justin arched back over his chair, revealing a few inches of white belly. In a quiet, unassuming way, he had been obsessing about his roll of stomach fat, subconsciously prodding it while he high-lighted. Ellie didn't think it'd be helpful to tell him it was the clearest example of anxiety displacement she'd ever witnessed. He heaved himself up. 'But I want to talk about something else first. Is it a good idea to be getting so involved with this campaign now?'

'Well, no, obviously.' Ellie scratched her head, watching dry flakes of skin rain onto her laptop lid. 'But it's exciting as well. It feels like people want to talk about it.'

Justin frowned at her.

'What?'

The 'seriously concerned' look kept coming. 'I don't want to be a pain in the arse,' he said, matter-of-factly, 'but what about your dissertation?'

With an almost inaudible groan, Ellie lowered her forehead to the table.

'I know you're stuck, but you're not going to hand in *nothing*, are you?'

The groan grew louder.

'That'd be such a waste.'

'I know! I do fucking know that.'

'So why don't you meet whatshername, your supervisor, and ask for some help?'

'It's pointless.'

'*No*, it's not,' said Justin sternly. 'It might make all the difference. Just do it, email her now.'

Ellie dragged herself up. 'But didn't you want to talk about next year?'

'Send. That. First.'

It took Ellie an hour and a half to draft an email to Dr Longstaff, which Justin took one look at and said, 'That's good, but she might think it's a little bit stalkerish.' With his help, Ellie managed a neutral, two-line request. Even that was eye-wateringly painful, but when she finally hit send, she did feel fractionally lighter.

'*Good.*' Justin's firm nod drifted into distraction. 'So.'

Ellie saw that he was nervous, and wondered how much he'd been stewing over the moving-in question since he'd asked. The decision had been preying upon her in the empty, static patches of each wakeful night. *What do I want?* she'd asked herself, and when only vertiginous blankness presented itself, *What's the right thing to do?* She'd imagined saying no and squandering the chance to be with somebody kind, someone who seemed to love her. Her dawn-light fantasies had deepened into morality tales in which Selfish Ellie Denied Love, and do you know, in the end, she died alone and miserable, because she didn't know a good thing when she saw it? Ellie saw herself in twenty years' time meeting Justin and his lovely wife and children, the natural and just result of his ability to love, and herself, withered and bent by the weight of her own pig-headedness. As she turned in bed once more – nose so close to the wall she could lick the woodchip paper – she became increasingly convinced of her own self-sabotaging disposition, her proven desire for what was bad for her. Look at last Christmas Eve's near-miss with that ridiculous idiot from school, and the subsequent day spent in chest-heaving misery in bed. There was good reason for Ellie not to trust her impulses. What if they were telling her *exactly* what she shouldn't do?

One thing she was sure about: Justin was *good*. Justin was a *nice person*, who deserved to be with another equally good and nice person. That was what she believed. Being grown up meant putting your own stupid destructive desires aside and focusing on somebody else for a change.

The idea was a powerful one. Becoming A Grown-up seemed to sneak past the element of choice and propose itself as a given, as a kind of destiny.

'Actually I have thought about next year,' Ellie told him, and at once a germ of gladness appeared inside her. She felt the abstract, arm's-length happiness of causing another's happiness, and it seemed to hold a promise for the better person she would be when all of her negative, mad shit was jettisoned, and she could be calm and good. She took a deep breath. 'I'd really like to live with you.'

Justin's eyes sprang open in surprise. 'Really? You're serious?'

She smiled and nodded. 'I'm deadly serious . . . if the offer's still open.'

'Don't be coy, Taber.' Justin shook his head, an enormous smile slowly taking over his face. 'As you're no doubt aware, I'm completely in love with you.'

9

How Nietzsche Wrote

'Now I know I need help, I feel so much better. Like, it's *okay* to need help, you know?' Ellie was sprawled on her bed, craning her neck to look at Justin's upside-down back, hunched over the desk.

'Hmm.'

'In a weird way I got *too* into it.' She hugged her knees into her chest. 'I thought the help would be distracting, get in the way. *Huuu*bris.'

'Nyup.'

'Usually I take whatever meagre help uni's handing out. I turn up, you know? I attend. But I got all . . .' She waggled a hand. 'Anyway, the point is, after Dr Longstaff's helped me, I might *actually* be able to do this, you know?'

There was a pause.

Ellie rolled up. 'You're trying to work, aren't you?'

Justin turned round. Over the past week, his stubbly face had slackened and drooped – he looked as if he'd just staggered out of bed at 2 a.m. to go to the loo, rather than slogged through four hours of revision and a litre of Coke. 'I'm sorry, it's just – I really can't mess this up again.'

'Sorry. I'm going. I've got to leave in ten minutes anyway.' Jumping off the bed, Ellie wrapped her arms round his waist and kissed the top of his head. His sides were a little softer and squishier than usual, she noticed. The observation made her feel protective, as if he'd told her something private or shameful, and she hugged him tighter. Ever since the moving-in decision had been taken, she'd been brimming with relief – at least *that* wasn't hanging over them. 'Keep it up.'

Rose was 'eating' breakfast and much more easily distracted.

'With help, I might *actually* be able to do this,' repeated Ellie, as she paced the sweaty kitchen linoleum.

'Hell, yes,' Rose hyped obligingly, adding a tiny splash of skimmed milk to her tea.

'I *can* do this.'

'Course you can!' Rose carefully watched the milk sink without trace. 'It's not like you're stupider than every other arsehole at uni. I mean, who *are* these punks? They hit every branch on the dimwit tree!'

'Yes. *Right*. I should get all my notes together.' Ellie leafed through a pile of newspapers. 'It's like, there's a certain stage of desperation where everything becomes very clear.'

'You've got a letter by the way.'

'Today's the day.' Ellie weeded out her scrawled notes. What did it matter if they didn't make sense? She was sorting it.

The letter had an official uni stamp – the kind Ellie had barely seen since she received an offer.

'Dear Ms. Taber,' she read. Rose snorted a laugh. 'This is a formal warning that if you do not desist from vandalising university property and inciting others to do so, the university will take legal action—'

'Shiiiiit,' Rose peered over her shoulder. Ellie swallowed and blinked hard, bringing the letter back into focus. 'Bastards!'

'. . . will also result in your expulsion from—'

'They fucking *live* for sending this kind of letter!'

'. . . ban from taking any examinations . . . graduating . . .' Ellie skimmed over the rest, squeezing the thick, ridged paper between hot thumb and fingers. Even under normal circumstances, uni's official communications made you feel like a half-citizen in some strange country, under suspicion for a crime you didn't know you'd committed. But this was something else. At the thought of phoning her mum and telling her she wasn't graduating, Ellie let out a dry croak.

'Fucking uni fascists! At *my* uni, one girl—'

'Right. I've got to go.' Ellie shoved the letter back in the envelope, ripping the plastic window. 'Do you know what we're doing with this?'

'Scanning it and posting it online!' cried Rose, excitedly. 'Or I know, shitting on it and sending it back!'

Ellie opened the fridge and stuffed the letter into the small, lift-up box on the inside of the door. 'It's going in the miscellaneous compartment. We aren't mentioning it until I've finished this dissertation.'

'You should get legal advice.'

'Ssshhhh.' Ellie closed the fridge and put her finger to her lips. 'Now I'm going to pick up my rucksack and walk out that door and we're never going to speak of this again.'

Dr Longstaff's room was right at the bottom of Humanities Two, a fluorescent-stripped warren of corridors lined with identical doors: B.31a, B.2.3, B.f. By the time she'd hunted the office down, Ellie was five minutes late and sweating.

At Dr Longstaff's call, she stepped into a tiny, coffee-scented cupboard. Piles of books and essays were heaped haphazardly on the floor. Computer cables snaked across the carpet, coiling ivy-like around the legs of the desk and chairs. Two other people – Chris from Ellie's course, and a wispy, pale girl she'd never met before – were wedged between Dr Longstaff's desk and the bookshelves, hunched over as if sheltering from rain.

'Things have got a bit end-of-yearish in this office.' Dr Longstaff held out her arms. 'Here, Chris, pass me those.'

Giving Ellie an 'all right' nod, Chris handed over a pile of essays, and Ellie sat down. Her heart was thumping. She knew it was an office hour, but somehow she hadn't imagined other people being there – it was like going to the doctor (a real doctor, not a PhD doctor) with an embarrassingly situated sore you'd been denying for weeks, and finding yourself ushered into a group session.

Dr Longstaff turned back with a cracked-lipped smile. 'My office hours have been getting rather busy and there's likely some crossover between you three, so I've put you together.'

Ellie nodded stiffly.

'You wanted to talk about . . . ?'

'My dissertation,' Ellie half-whispered.

'Ah-ha,' Dr Longstaff's eyes narrowed. 'But you are aware that we're not allowed to discussion your dissertation at this stage? S'cuse me.' She pulled a tissue from her sleeve and blew her nose.

'Sorry?' Ellie managed to say.

Dr Longstaff blinked away a sneeze. 'The module pack clearly states that fifth April was the cut-off date for dissertation super-vision. You didn't hand in a draft or arrange a meeting, so . . .' She shrugged, not cruelly, but not encouragingly either.

'Oh,' Ellie croaked. 'You . . . can't help at all?'

'Well . . .' Dr Longstaff sighed, scanning her desk for inspiration. 'We could talk *very* briefly in a *very* general sense. You have a draft?'

119

The last time Ellie had opened the dissertation folder on her desktop, over a week ago now, she'd seen four documents arranged horizontally, their single-letter names spelling out F – U – C – K. Slowly, she shook her head.

'You must have something *approaching* a draft though, because the deadline is . . .'

'Friday,' Chris chipped in.

A pause mushroomed into a silence. For a second, Ellie felt she might black out with anxiety.

Dr Longstaff locked eyes with her. 'I may be stating the obvious, but at this point, the most important thing is to hand in *something*.'

Ellie had an overpowering urge to explain that this *wasn't* her – she was a natural shower-upper and hander-inner. She used to be a student with First potential, not one who didn't read the module pack. But what was the point? Any explanation would sound feeble now.

Dr Longstaff's eyes bobbed up to the clock on the wall. 'Am I right in saying that your dissertation is about Nietzsche?'

Ellie nodded dumbly, still clinging to the hope that help was forthcoming.

'Because Chris wants to discuss Paper Five, late nineteenth- and early twentieth-century political thought. Nietzsche's certainly relevant to that. So why don't we discuss Nietzsche *in the context of* Paper Five.'

It wasn't a question. Dutifully, pointlessly, Ellie reached into her bag for a pen and paper, catching sight of all those useless notes.

'So.' Dr Longstaff closed her eyes. 'What is the connection between Nietzsche and twentieth-century political philosophy?'

Ellie knew this was going to be irrelevant, but going through the motions was strangely reassuring. She wanted to write something down. *Oh dear*, she jotted.

'Why is Nietzsche, who many people believe doesn't even *have* a political philosophy, on the paper at all? Hmm.' Dr Longstaff put her finger to her lips. Having posed the question, she seemed surprised, almost captivated by it.

Frowny face, Ellie wrote neatly, and then, automatically, *Ellie*.

'How about this? Forget about *political* philosophy, *all* of twentieth-century philosophy is a post-Nietzschean project.'

Nietzsche, Ellie added beneath her own name. She drew a love heart around them and then an arrow, carefully adding vanes to the feather.

'Not explicitly. Nietzsche was ignored by the philosophical establishment for— Of course,' Dr Longstaff interrupted herself. 'This is all in the Nietzsche lecture notes on Blackboard.'

At Dr Longstaff's pivot, Heather saw her chance. 'Can I ask a question about Paper Two?'

That was it, Ellie realised, as Dr Longstaff began to talk about Rousseau. That was all the help she was going to get. Unable to think of some kind of social conjunctive to say before she stood up, Ellie stood up anyway.

'Oh.' Dr Longstaff stopped mid-flow to fix her bloodshot gaze on Ellie. 'Are you leaving? Well, remember – *something*, yes?'

Ellie yanked the door over the wrinkled carpet, and lurched out. In the smothering silence of the corridor, she leaned both palms against the wall. She had thought she was afraid before – she hadn't known what fear was. *This* fear was so overpowering it was like being high. Adrenalin surged through her legs; her breath came short and constricted. She started walking, then running, down the corridor, not knowing where she was heading or what she would do when she got there.

Nietzsche wrote on the move. Movement was the essential principle of his writing, so much so that in the second half of his life he arranged his entire existence around it. In 1886, a typical year, he wintered in Nice, moved to Switzerland for the summer, then stayed for a month in the Gulf of Genoa before travelling back to Nice for the winter. He had no home and very few possessions, and he travelled from hotel to boarding house carrying clothes and writing materials, and little else besides.

For the act of writing, Nietzsche's preferred motion was walking. After suitable weather, the first requirement for him in any new place was a plentiful supply of hikes. He was quite capable of walking eight hours or more in a single day. Spending summer in the Swiss Alps in 1881, his daily routine included three or four hours' walking in the morning, followed by a similar stint in the afternoon. (After an early dinner he would sit quietly in the dark for two hours, conserving his 'spiritual powers', before retiring to bed at 9 p.m.) While he walked he thought and wrote, scribbling his reflections in pocket-sized notebooks. He walked alone, and as he moved, he talked to himself. His books, you might say, are a record of these conversations, the many parts of Nietzsche in constant dialogue.

Nietzsche wanted his thoughts to romp, to caper, to frolic. Such 'light-footed intellect' could never be achieved sitting down. Walking served as a practical substitute, but dancing was the purest expression of free-spiritedness, of breaking free of inhibitions and affirming life – 'the rapture of the Dionysian state, with its annihilation of the ordinary bounds and limits of existence'. 'Thinking must be learned as dancing must be learned, as a type of dancing,' Nietzsche wrote. 'One must be able to dance with the pen!'

The key to such writing was flow, although in many ways that word is too mild for what Nietzsche intended. The word he used was *Rausch* – 'intoxication' or 'rush' ('a feeling of higher power . . . strength as mastery over the muscles, as suppleness and pleasure in movement, as dance, as lightness and *presto*'). Nietzsche wanted the words to pour out of him in a kind of musical ecstasy. At many points in his life he was able to attain this creative high, although he had a tendency to overestimate his powers of production and underestimate the boring work of drafting and editing. The book Nietzsche passed off as 'the work of so few days that I cannot, with decency, reveal their number' actually took at least two months to write; hardly sluggish, so why did he feel obliged to exaggerate? He wanted his readers to believe there was no work involved for him in writing, that his books were uncrafted extensions of his life and personality.

The form of Nietzsche's writing reflects its mode of preparation. Eschewing complicated structures, he wrote in aphorisms, short chunks of prose ranging from a few sentences to a few pages. Nietzsche recommended that his books were read in the same fragmentary way, preferably on the move. 'A book like this is not for reading straight through or aloud,' he wrote of *Daybreak*, 'but for dipping into when walking or on a journey.'

For Nietzsche, mobile writing was less a personal preference than a moral–physical ideal. Sitting was bad not only for your health – 'Pinched intestines betray themselves, you can bet on that' – but also for your spirit: it was nihilistic, because it promoted thought over instinct. Even the greatest writers could be caught in this trap. Nietzsche's 1888 book *Twilight of the Idols* contains a characteristically kamikaze assault on the writing habits of Gustave Flaubert, who in a letter to a friend had made the apparently inoffensive statement: 'One cannot think and write except when seated.' For Nietzsche, this was a shameful admission of decadence. 'There I have you, nihilist!' he spat. 'The sedentary life [*das Sitzfleisch* – literally 'sitting meat'] is the very sin against the Holy Spirit. Only thoughts reached by moving have value.'

At its most basic level, writing is self-conscious work. Self-doubt is part of the process: to make your writing good, you need to be self-critical. Nietzsche wrote, when in truth he wanted to dance. He walked and talked, because by walking and talking he could get out of his head and into the realm of movement and feeling.

After the initial panic, after the paralysis, after the night in which she lost consciousness for no more than ten seconds and yet thought nothing, nothing at all, a lifetime of nothing, Ellie climbed out of bed with a single realisation, an epiphany that dawned with the morning: *she had to get out.*

In first year, Ellie used to do her best work in the library computer room, often late at night. She found the constant chatter a useful distraction – she could bounce off it. Around midnight, when the room was mostly empty, she liked to print her essay and spread it sheet by sheet over a large table. Her fondest memories were of dramatic structural alterations that struck her about 2 a.m. If she hadn't stayed up all night, she felt she hadn't done the essay properly.

Later, Ellie decided that was a sign of indiscipline. As her appetite for campus socialising dwindled, she took to working on her laptop in her room. Sometimes, when she was really on fire, she would put a beer in the fridge at the beginning of the day, knowing that it would be ready for her at 7 or 8 p.m., after she'd sent her essay off.

But now, home had got weird. There was no way she would be able to break the pattern there. And the other methods she normally used – music, earplugs, sitting in Waterstones, smoking, not smoking, working in other faculties, talking to herself, running – they hadn't worked either. Instead, they'd become their own independent, intricately constructed forms of weirdness.

Before 7 a.m., Ellie trooped out of the house carrying every-thing she'd ever written or read about Nietzsche. Fuelled by fear, she was in the library computer room in under fifteen minutes, hoping that the ghosts of essays past would be on her side. As the automatic lights flickered on, she laid claim to a corner station.

The trouble was how to begin. Ellie was keen on an arresting first line, something she could spring off and refer back to and question. It needed to be smart and compelling, but not clever-clever or irrelevant, not pointless wordplay. Perhaps she had a quote that would do . . . As the last computer station was snapped up and the smell of crisps and coffee filled the air, she started scouring through her primary material.

That was day one. Only at 4 p.m. did it hit her that she had squandered one of four available days, crafting and deleting count-less single-sentence openers. The airless room was suddenly unbearably hot.

'Oh, hi, Ellie,' said Chris, plonking himself in the neighbouring seat, which someone had clearly just vacated to go to the loo. 'Dissertation?'

Ellie grunted. Her eyes flicked from the note-spattered Word document to Chris's monitor. He signed onto Facebook. 'Aren't you doing yours?' she couldn't help but ask.

'Finished it,' shrugged Chris.

'Fuck.'

'To be honest,' Chris lowered his voice. 'I've actually finished my revision too. I'm kind of at a loss now.' He clenched his teeth in an 'eek'.

Ellie had no idea how to respond to this baffling statement. At least she knew how little she knew – she knew nothing, in fact, but at least she knew that. It only occurred to her after Chris Liked a video of a man falling over, logged off and ambled away: some of the people handing in dissertations were like Chris. *One* of them definitely was. She didn't need a work of art, for God's sake – she needed 15,000 words.

Ellie determined to start in the middle. Until late that night, and from 7 the next morning, she began bashing it out. It didn't feel like creating something, it felt like smashing down a building. 'Nietzsche thought,' she launched sentence after sentence, each one landing on the page with a squelch, like toast dropped jam side down. 'I would argue . . .' she squeezed out the others, followed by some strained, clunky, nonsensical non-argument. She brought into the world some of the ugliest, most fractured phrases she'd ever read.

This dissertation will go on to have argued that Nietzsche's philosophy clearly demonstrated and explores a definite, yet conflicted, conception of individuality, as both socially situated in society and radically autonomous from his or her environment. It will do so first by analysing three of Nietzsche's works of philosophy before going on to do a literature review of the secondary criticism in more detail, and finally end by concluding the argument.

Grimly resolved not to look back, Ellie staggered onward with her galumphing prose, scrawling out words like a two-year-old with crayons.

Early in the evening of the second day, she realised that she'd written 10,000 words – a new record in verbiage. She decided to print it out, assess what she had, and begin the uphill struggle of honing it. The computer-room regulars were winding down, the low-level chitchat crescendoing to loud laughter, and the tinny sound of music played through computer speakers. As she began to read, revisers were vacating for dinner and a group of second-year boys colonised her half of the computer room, all taking part in some kind of online role-playing game.

Some of her stuff was plain gibberish, it all needed to be rewritten, and there were loads of gaps where she'd put '[EXAMPLE]' or '[THAT QUOTE ABOUT . . .]'. And yet, hiding between the circumlocution and lacunae, there *was* some decent material. What she needed was to get out of this room so she could think. She left the warlords to it.

And, like a fool, she dropped in at the library café for a cup of tea and a sandwich. Maggie waved from a corner, barely recognisable in thick glasses and some kind of headband, beckoning Ellie over. Maggie was one of those people Ellie had lost touch with this year, not because she didn't like them, but because . . . Well, she wasn't sure why, and now wasn't the moment to find out. Ellie waved her printout apologetically and made a panicked face.

Social embarrassment drove her through the library barriers and outside. She began an aimless, yet super-fast, march around campus, taking the narrow, bush-lined path towards the business faculty at the top of the hill. *Ten thousand words*, she repeated, mantra-like, *I've got ten thousand words*. As she walked, the better elements of her argument whipped round her mind, making her face pulse and squirm – she must have looked like a madwoman. But the movement helped; she was forging connections, weaving arguments; she had a couple of decent linking ideas, and began to craft more elegant versions of existing points.

Before she even knew what was happening, Ellie began to hope that her dissertation might not be such a piece of shit after all. Straying ever further from the draft in hand, the material in her mind began to look substantial, rather good, potentially . . . excellent.

Ambition is a survivor. When the environment's hostile, you can pretend it's extinct, that you've outgrown dreams and are toughing it out on the coalface of reality. But one day, long before the conditions are right, you turn over a rock and find it's lived on under there, a gnarly little shrub that will shoot up at the first touch of sunshine.

Ellie found a cold, glassy corner of the business faculty lobby and furiously rewrote the first few pages of her work. She filleted the fatty prose; one by one, paragraphs became smoother, clearer, easier to swallow. At some point a man vacuumed, the wheezing buzz gradually homing in on her corner. With an apologetic smile, Ellie shifted to the opposite side, realising how sore her back was. She felt frantic, but also effective: moulding and cutting and rearranging – this was something she could really do. Ellie collapsed into bed that night safe in the knowledge that progress had been made.

At the crack of dawn next day, she woke to a nightmare: her dissertation was due tomorrow. Fingers mauling the laptop before her eyes were fully open, she read through what she had (9,500 – a net loss). After two pages of decent prose, it fell apart. Unnecessarily drawn-out, self-explanatory points that might as well have read '[PLACE PADDING HERE]' sat alongside long cut-and-pastes from primary and secondary works, and half-baked, ellipses-peppered brain farts:

- *Dionysus – TRAGIC SUBJECTIVITY*???? . . . . . .
- Nietzsche's later works i.e. [. . .] propose diff. idea individ. e.g. [QUOTE HERE]
- WHAT ABOUT *morality?*

This was it. These were the 9,500 'words' she 'had'. And she was exhausted already. She'd forgotten to factor in her own diminishing energy, like leaving out the friction in a physics equation.

On the brink of sinking back into sleep, she jolted into a state of wired alertness. The problem crystallised into the urgent question of where she would work. She couldn't face the library again, couldn't work on the business faculty carpet, she had to leave her house, but where could she go? The question was impossible to answer, because whenever she tried to think, her brain screamed, *YOU'RE WASTING TIME! YOU'RE WASTING TIME!* Not bothering to change her pants, she pulled on yesterday's clothes and trudged out.

Ellie trekked round campus in a panic-stricken search for some quiet, forgotten corner of an unknown faculty, a utopic place where she'd meet nobody and not have to be anyone. She was simultaneously nauseous and hungry, and her eyes felt like picked scabs. As she marched by a huge window, Ellie was stopped in her tracks by a chalk sign inside. It was propped against a hamper of bananas and it read 'FREE FRUIT'. Around it, the massive table was completely covered in waxy oranges and shiny Granny Smiths, like the surface of a children's ball pit.

Ellie dashed in, planning to take an armful of bananas and continue her hopeless search. The room seemed to be some kind of mental health initiative: a carefully staged calm environment in which handwritten signs encouraged her to 'LET IT ALL GO' and 'STOP! BREATHE'. Some well-meaning souls had Blu-tacked printouts of William Morris patterns onto the wall-panels, strung up hand-sewn, stuffed letters spelling 'TIME OUT', and scattered beanbags in calm shades of blue and grey. Ellie dropped onto one, opposite a sign that assured her: 'You're not alone :)'. But she *was* alone: gloriously, unbelievably alone.

This heavenly place was where she lived, worked and napped for the next day and a half. Every so often, an odd-looking boy with a halo of fluffy curls (who Ellie began to suspect was from the

Christian Union) arrived with more fruit. The Fruit Angel gave Ellie a quick, shy smile, and then scuttled off, obviously not wanting to disturb her vital Time Out. Otherwise the peace was punctuated only by an occasional sock-shod Biology reviser, ducking in furtively to swipe a banana. Best of all, this life-saving sanctuary didn't even get decent wifi.

Ellie didn't know she could operate at the speed at which she worked that day. But it felt dreadful. Every decision, every rewrite and addition, was a disappointing compromise, a form of shoddy damage limitation. The only priority she could afford was handing in the right number of words. As the afternoon dwindled, her word count stubbornly plateaued at 11,000. Even assuming they couldn't penalise you for being 10 per cent under (a rule she wasn't completely sure about), she still needed 2,500 more. She had to come up with a whole new section to her argument, whipping up statements as wispy and unwholesome as candyfloss.

As darkness finally settled over the biology faculty, and Ellie finished her sixth vending-machine coffee, she had the thoroughly novel experience of having quite a good idea, a point that made sense. Aware even at the time that it contradicted most of the things she'd already said, she furiously hammered it out. Now she needed a concluding section, but as the sun came up, she was losing the power to think – her brain whizzed and spun, chasing its own tail. What mattered most was Nietzsche's religious context – but what mattered most was the influence of Darwin – but what mattered most was the concept of individuality – that was the main theme of the essay – or *was* it, because what actually mattered more than that . . .

Dawn broke on a bitter countdown to the line, a marathon in which every step jarred painfully. With fours hours to go before the noonday deadline, Ellie forced herself to stop and write footnotes, spreading articles and books across the floor in a mandala of panic. Halfway through the referencing, she realised she was already six hundred words over the limit. Having filled the dissertation with guff, she had no perspective whatsoever on what she should cut. Desperately scanning the pages, she felt so ashamed she could have cried, and so tired she could have dropped dead. For a brief, luxurious moment, she heard the siren song that always played just before the finish line: *It's okay*, it said, *you're nearly there. Just. Slow. Down . . .*

But she forced herself on, knowing all she could hope for now – all she could feasibly achieve – was to hand in *something*, even if it was littered with typos and referencing errors and bullshit. She slashed sentences, invented page numbers for footnotes, and desperately tried to make the jumble of reflections make some sense. At 11.37, as she rewrote the last, disappointing sentence of an utterly inconclusive conclusion, she was hit by a new and horrible thought.

Binding.

That needless expense, that mysterious, last, symbolic hurdle, that strange test of organisational, stationery-based ability.

A bystander watching Ellie sprint to the library would have assumed a life-or-death medical emergency. While the automatic gates took several years to open, Ellie caught sight of a queue of more than twenty anxious students, waiting to have their dissertations bound. The sight chilled her to the core. Beside the desk, a large sign read: 'ATTENTION! BINDING TAKES **60 MINUTES. YOU MUST SUBMIT IN TIME!**' Ellie scanned the line of tense, unfamiliar faces, but could find nobody she knew.

She discovered Chris online shopping in the computer room.

'Chris!' she shouted, panting. 'Where did you bind your dissertation?'

He pulled out his headphones. 'Sorry?'

'Bindingbinding – binding.'

'Er . . . we don't need to do that. Philosophy submits online. Want me to send you the link?'

'Oh, God, thankyouthankyouthankyou.' Relief flooding through her, Ellie dropped to the floor and flipped open her laptop.

All she needed was a title.

'Anything,' she jabbered to herself. 'Come on, anything!'

A couple of students paused their conversation to stare at her.

She typed 'Friedrich Nietzsche's . . .'

'Shit, shit!'

'Um, you all right?' muttered Chris.

She jabbed the keyboard: 'Philosophy of Self . . .'

'But I haven't written about self,' she groaned, through gritted teeth. 'I haven't mentioned the *word* self.'

It was 11.58.

'. . . and Philosophy of Individuality,' she added frantically. With shaking, sweaty hands, she fixed two typos in the first sentence that must have been sitting there for four days, and uploaded the file to the intranet.

For a long, throbbing moment, Ellie stared dumbly at the confirmation message. Then, slowly, carefully, she dragged her Dissertation folder to the Bin.

Yes, she clicked, she *was* sure she wanted to erase it permanently.

Fuck you, Friedrich, she thought, falling back on the carpet and staring in exhausted wonder at the waffle-like ceiling. *I am never, ever, going to think about you again as long as I live.*

Momentum

Nietzsche's obsession with movement was more than a personal peculiarity. He embraced movement because movement was indispensable for confidence. As he gave himself to confidence, he broke apart his life until it contained almost nothing but the potential for forward motion.

Nietzsche was a good teacher, despite his misgivings. His students liked him and his colleagues appreciated his intelligence and commitment. But he never felt comfortable as an academic and his real intellectual energies were always in his own philosophy. He longed to pursue his vocation and in 1879, aged thirty-five, he took the plunge, resigning his university post, his one proper job, in favour of a life of nomadic solitude. He was following his own passions and instincts, becoming himself and no one else. He was also devoting himself to confidence and its demand for constant movement.

For Nietzsche, it was not enough to say that confidence required forward motion. Confidence *was* momentum, that sense of purpose and activity which is at once the antithesis of, and the remedy to, self-consciousness. His approach was summed up by his attitude towards habit, a term which included routine, regularity, convention and permanence – 'all habituation and regulation, everything lasting and definitive'. Such strictures, he considered, made life as a free spirit impossible. 'All that is habitual,' he wrote, 'draws around us an ever tighter net of spider web; and before long we notice that the threads have become ropes and that we ourselves are the spider sitting in the middle of the web, which has caught itself here, and must drink its own blood.'

The constant desire for movement was how Nietzsche distinguished confidence from self-belief. Self-belief, in his definition, meant unquestioning faith in oneself – the personal equivalent of religious dogmatism. Nietzsche had no respect for rigidity in any form. His perfect person would 'take leave of all faith', for faith was always a 'wish for certainty'.

Nietzsche's commitment to movement was characteristically extreme. Nevertheless, his reasoning is faultless. We think that security aids confidence; in fact, it's the reverse. New conquests, new frontiers: only these make us feel powerful, limitless and free. No one gets a confidence boost from kissing their long-term boyfriend. By contrast, one passed-on compliment from a perfect stranger can fill you with an inner glow several days after the fact.

We have a bad habit of treating confidence as a neutral force, without any true identity of its own. Think of confidence and you think of yourself at your best – confidence is simply the conduit to that more perfect self. If confidence is a conduit, however, then it is one that channels us in very specific directions. Like a language, it comes with its own set of embedded priorities, chief among them the demand for constant novelty. Confidence cannot be captured, it can only be replenished. To replenish confidence we must constantly be searching out new challenges, new feats, new opportunities for self-expression.

Think of it this way: on a night out, if you're really committed to having a good time, you can't stand still: you have to keep moving, keep going forward. The second you slow down and start thinking – or worse saying – 'Why don't we just stay in this pub?', you've given up the night for good. The same goes for the people you're with. As Nietzsche put it: 'A person who strives for greatness looks on everyone he meets on his way as a means, a delay or an obstacle – or as a temporary resting place.' When you're chasing the dream, you have to be ruthless in order to advance.

If there was one thing that really committed a person to having a good time, that made it pretty much obligatory, it was agreeing to take part in a group mankini look. With only an internet-sourced strip of Lycra between you and total humiliation, surely the world would be forced to cave in and for once in your sorry life, reward you for the effort.

'Where's Ben?' said Charlie, carefully adjusting his ball coverage.

'Probably stuck in his mankini.' Lucas poured two shots of vodka into sticky-looking glasses, and clapped his hands. 'Right! To the last night out before the official death of fun.'

'Wasn't that a year and a half ago?'

'And to Charlie finally sticking a wad in some lucky bird.'

'It's a big step.' Charlie held up his hands. 'I'm just waiting for the right girl who respects me for who I am.'

'Chop that.'

The vodka scorched a path down Charlie's gullet.

'What's your strategy?' Lucas checked out his mankini from behind. 'I'd go for first years if I were you.'

'I'm thinking about texting Sasha.'

'Fit Sasha?'

'Yeah. I've been chatting to her a bit recently, and I don't know . . .' Charlie rubbed his chin. 'I feel like I might actually stand a chance.'

'Text what?'

'Maybe "See you there? I'll be wearing the green mankini"?'

'Far too keen. You want like: "Got corset fatigue already. Hope you're coming fully clothed."'

'Hm, okay.'

'You never know, it could happen. Panic week, baby.'

'Panic week?'

'Where the fuck have you been? Where all the girls start panicking they haven't slept with enough people at uni and lower their standards massively. Basically, the female version of you, you lad.' He shoulder-barged Charlie's chest.

Charlie shoved him away. 'Are we going to the Union dressed like this then?'

'Ben is.' Lucas poured another two shots and pointed towards a heap of clothes. 'You can borrow those if you like.'

Charlie pulled on a pair of denim shorts, checked his reflection and got a pleasant surprise. Combined with the neon green mankini, the shorts were almost a look, kind of Mr Motivator meets Eighties club kid. A tremor of anticipation shot through him – he couldn't remember the last time he'd felt excited to go out.

'All I'll say is' – Lucas was still giving him the benefit of his wisdom. 'Don't limit yourself. First years in their underwear, feeling vulnerable? Older, more experienced man? I'm telling you, SSB is an all-you-can-eat buffet.'

From outside on the pavement came a thin shout, 'You guys! Come on, it's not funny!' They looked down to see Ben in his mankini, hammering on the door, while behind him a woman with a pushchair tried to shield her screaming toddler from the sight.

Charlie leaned out. 'I've told you not to come round here! We're not interested in your services.'

'We're finished!' Ellie greeted Nadine. 'Mine's abysmal!'

'Mine's a car crash,' returned Nadine, with an orange-lipsticked grin. 'Let's get shitfaced.'

The Mitre was strangely empty.

'I thought there'd be loads of people celebrating,' said Ellie, as they paid for their gin and tonics and hauled themselves onto bar stools. 'Not my mates obviously – Rose is working, I called Justin, you're here, so . . . But where's, you know, everybody?'

Nadine turned to stare at her. 'Oh my days, how do you do it? Have you got a tiny airtight pod that you step into when I'm not there?'

'Well, somebody's got to take the matrix down from the inside.' Ellie poured the tonic. 'What?'

'It's SSB tonight.' Nadine shook her head, clacking turquoise earrings. 'They'll all be waxing and vajazzling.'

'Ooooh. Oh, I see.'

'Yup.' Nadine raised her eyebrows. 'Don't think it's escaped my notice that you've been doing sweet fuck all for your fellow ladies, Ms Taber.'

Since the dawn of fear proper, Ellie had completely neglected the campaign. She hadn't even logged on to Facebook, let alone read her emails.

'Yeah, but come on,' she smiled. 'Writing the world's shittest dissertation *and* running its most poorly organised campaign? There's only so much of me to go round.'

'Well *I* posted one comment last week, so shove that up your arse.'

'That's impressive.'

'Wittgenstein was being a dick as usual.'

A thought struck Ellie. 'Do you think we should we be doing something tonight?'

'Mmm.' Nadine bit into her lime wedge. 'Being totally honest and straight with you, I can't be bothered.'

Ellie laughed. 'You had me at "can't".'

'Anyway, this is a night off, isn't it? You can't fight the good fight every day.'

'The world can take care of itself for a change. *We* can get some cans and sit on the roof of the Scott building.'

'Plan.' Nadine pulled out her purse. 'One more round here first.'

The official SSB pre-lash was in the Union Bar. Human-sized condoms, superheroes, firemen and priests crammed between the standard lamps and against the feature wall. Second years were buzzing with excited preparations, strategising about getting on the buses early and organising booze in plastic bottles. Girls had covered up with fleece tops and 'boyfriend-style' shirts, stockings beneath signalling that they were taking part. The guys who had put in serious preparation were already debuting their freshly cut abs, making sure everyone would still remember them tomorrow. Charlie felt slightly nervous at the thought of taking off his shorts.

On arrival, he had done a quick tour of the room, but there was no sign of Sara or Matt's birthday crowd. In fact, third years were thin on the ground. The ladz were playing a drinking game in a circular booth, Tom Race's girlfriend Sarah Morris and the mini-Morrises hovering nearby. The medic lot had turned up as (semi-)

naked hikers, in bobble hats and boots, and were occupying the window area. Charlie *knew* them obviously – everyone knew everyone, because everyone was always there – but there came a point when chitchat only served to highlight the fact that you hadn't become mates.

Charlie and Ben were penned into a five-deep tussle for the bar.

'So no money was actually taken, but I think it was a bit upsetting.' Ben was narrating Clare's recent identity theft to Tim Fletcher and Christie, who were dressed as Popeye and Olive Oyl. Charlie scanned ahead for movement, cursing inwardly as someone ordered a round of cocktails.

'Weird, all these first years, isn't it?' said Tim, out of nowhere. 'It's like we've already left.'

'What's that about?' asked Charlie, nodding at a troupe of girls who had just marched into the other end of the room. He read their long white T-shirts. '"Women have pubes"?' Massive bush wigs stuck out beneath the hems.

'I think it's that uni sexism thing,' explained Christie. 'You must've seen the posters.'

'Oh yeah, Clare mentioned it,' said Ben.

'They're pro-bush or what?'

'Well, it's a bit wider than—'

'Derek loves bush, don't you, mate?' Bradder rammed his way through the queue, yelling back towards the ladz' booth. 'He went out with a French bird! Ladz, do we want two rounds?'

'Brazilian, ladies.' Tom Race strolled up the path Bradder had cleared. 'It's all about the Brazilian.'

Tim caught a sigh at the back of his throat and rolled his eyes at Charlie.

'Why are they pissing on our night with their fucking hairy-muffed protest anyway?' Bradder boomed. 'What's their problem?'

Charlie held up an imaginary mic. 'Let's turn to our female correspondent. Views on pubes?'

'It's pathetic,' said Christie, into the mic. 'Cringing about pubes – I mean, get over it.'

'I like 'em pre-pubes,' leered Bradder.

'Personally, I like to experiment,' said Charlie. 'Weaves, extensions – I've got a French pleat in tonight.'

'Oi.' Lucas arrived, shouldering aside a couple of second-year Vikings. Say what you like about the ladz, but at least they got things done. By falling in behind Bradder and Race, Charlie was almost at the bar.

'You seen Sasha?' he asked Lucas.

'No, but I have seen Estelle Mohammed's arse. Pint?'

'I'll take a vodka tonic,' said Charlie, thinking of his mankini silhouette.

'Pint it is.'

While Ben ferried a gin and tonic back to Clare, Charlie went on a lap of honour with Lucas, circling the room, dropping in on girls they knew – or rather, girls Lucas knew. Charlie found it slightly tricky to interact with a girl in suspenders: were you supposed to ignore it, mention it, say 'Phwoar'? Being shitfaced would have made things easier, but he was pacing himself; he didn't want to ruin his night. But then they bumped into Louise and Jess who'd lived on Charlie's landing – 'I'm Lucas's body double,' he joked, 'I do the scenes with clothes' – and by the time the buses arrived, Charlie realised he hadn't checked the door for a good half-hour.

On the roof of the Scott building, it was still warm. A few alternative-type first years had colonised the other end, perching on the railings, smoking and defiantly not attending SSB. Far below, in Mandela Square, students trailed from the Union to the road where the coaches were parked, a straggling procession of luminous pouches and fake tan, ruffled basques and thigh-high boots.

A cheer went up from the Square, as some rugby twat streaked across the grass. They watched a smurf with a homemade erection receive a round of applause for dry-humping a French maid on the lawn. Hanging over the Union entrance was an enormous version of the SSB poster, staring out with a sexy pout, inviting everyone to '*Come on in.*'

'Ugh.' Ellie stuck out her tongue.

'Yeah, I know.' Nadine lay back. 'People did suggest picketing and stuff. But I mean.' She gave an exasperated sigh. 'It's impossible, isn't it. I'm not going to stand down there watching a load of first years toddling in in their hold-ups saying "You're objectifying yourself." I'd feel like—'

'A fanny?'

'Yeah. Like Mary . . . What's her name who hated sex and TV?'

Ellie nodded. 'Plus there's all the guys in g-strings and what are we saying to them?' She delved into the plastic bag and opened another can. 'And it's not quite the same. It *looks* the same, but that's how they get you. "It's not sexist 'cause we're all doing it."'

'And then you feel like an arsehole 'cause it sounds like you don't think women can wear what they want or whatever.' Nadine shook her head blearily. 'There's this one girl in the group who honest to God wants to ban pictures of women like *full stop*. And tell you what else.' She raised a pointed, silver-ringed finger. 'Running a campaign is like having a *job*, like, a real one.'

'I know! They asked me to write a column for *The Badger*, "Is Campus Sexist?"'

'Yeah?' Nadine missed her mouth and poured beer down her top. 'Ah, shit the bed.'

'I thought about it loads. I mean, worried about it without doing anything. But I don't think I even replied to the email in the end. It's like, I do think this stuff is true, but the minute I say anything, put my name on it and put it in the world, it sounds wrong.' In a sudden burst of clarity, Ellie clapped her hands. 'Actually. Do you know what? Campaigning is *shit*. I *hate* campaigning.'

'Oh my God, me too!' cried Nadine, crunching herself up to face Ellie. 'It *is* shit! Plus so many of the people that do it are *dicks*.'

'Exactly! It's like—'

'Oh my . . .' Nadine pointed down. 'Look!'

They watched a group of girls clipping towards the buses in long, handmade T-shirts declaring in thick black letters 'Women Have Pubes'. A guy in a sheer body stocking held up a hand to high-five one of them.

'What the fuck?' Ellie frowned. There was a pause. 'They can't do that, can they? I mean, that's our campaign.'

Nadine burst into laughter. 'But we were just saying we're too lazy to do anything!'

'I know but—'

'Ellie Taber, Selfish Feminist.' Nadine shook her head. '"I like feminism, but only when *I'm* doing it."'

'But wouldn't you ask the people—'

'"I'm into women's rights, but I'm definitely the rightest woman."'

'Who started the bloody thing?'

'"All women are equal, but I'm the *most* equal."'

'It's just good manners—'

'That's awareness, isn't it?' Nadine spread her hands. 'That's what we want. It's great!'

'I s'pose.'

'You're outrageous.' Nadine lay back again. 'I'm going to have to report you to the campaign committee.'

'Not those twats!'

'Lucky for you, one of the members is totally corrupt. I'm not saying she's bribe-able, but her favourite cocktail at Frankie's is a Prohibition Black.'

Lucas was heavily involved in a plan to strip Bradder and throw his clothes out of the bus window, Ben was sitting next to Clare, and Charlie's housemates had decided to cut the bus and cab it. The seat in front of Ben had one occupant.

'Oh my God!' Penny Austin squealed her customary greeting, waving a blue pompom. 'I heard about you and Sara.' Her head dropped to the right, an expression of pain seizing her tiny face. 'That's so sad. You were *perfect* together.'

Charlie shivered under a blast of AC. 'Yeah, so perfect we split up,' he muttered to himself.

'Mmmm.' Penny brushed down her cheerleading outfit. 'So what *happened*?'

Penny was a vampire who fed on others' misery. Many were the poor souls that destroyed their nights by becoming embroiled in her blood-sucking heart-to-hearts. She batted empathetic eyes at him. 'If you ever need to talk . . .'

No chance, Charlie thought. *Not if we were the last two members of the human species.*

'Yeah, thanks.' Looking out of the window as the coach rolled through campus, Charlie sorely wished he was drunker – he knew from bitter experience that the journey to Court, a massive club on the edge of town, was surprisingly long.

'You must be feeling *terrible*.' Penny had several ways of wheedling information from you: extreme empathy, emotional flashing and statements about your life that were so misguided, you had to disagree. 'Sara's practically had a breakdown. The other day I found her sitting in the bath and crying.'

Charlie doubted this was true, but it stirred his guilt nonetheless.

'She's so beautiful, isn't she?' Penny went on. 'And *so* lovely.'

'Yeah, sure,' Charlie took the chance to reply to something sane. He shot an SOS back to Ben, but Ben was leaning his forehead against Clare's shoulder, deep-breathing his way through travel sickness.

'You must be missing her. It's so tough being on your own when you're used to someone being there, isn't it? I mean,' she gestured under her chin, 'I know you get those ingrowing hairs.'

Charlie blanched. What else had Sara decided to share – his medical records, bank balance, penis size?!

'I get them too.' Penny smiled confidentially. 'On my bikini line. They're terrible, aren't they? So itchy!'

Charlie shook his head. Intimate details about Sara were on the tip of his tongue, but he knew sharing them would only make him look like a dick. Instead, mustering all of his conversational energy, he launched into an in-depth analysis of ingrown hairs, a filibuster that lasted almost the entire journey (To Tweeze Or Not To Tweeze?; When Squeezing Becomes Gouging; When Infection Strikes), all the while composing an imaginary text to Sara that began: 'Um . . . you what?'

Charlie was so relieved to see the concrete walls of Court, he almost didn't mind the queue stretching right down to the industrial bins.

'Oscar's the one Ellie wants to bang!' Nadine shouted at Rose over 'Eternal Flame'. Rose had turned up at Frankie's dressed like they did back when they were trying to get into bars at fifteen, in a miniskirt and sparkly vest top. After two cocktails, they were taking full advantage of the Eighties hits and half-empty dance floor.

'What's wrong with him?' Rose yelled back. 'Drug addict? Uglier than sin? Gay? Catholic priest?'

Ellie's enthusiastic spin sent her tumbling into Rose. 'Sorry!'

'What a lightweight.' Rose righted Ellie, teetered, and wafted into Nadine. 'Alchies! She likes them too.'

'He's a sort of androgynous hippy-who-can-build-shit type.' Nadine paused for the chorus, hugging herself and swaying. 'Lives on a boat by the Hope and Anchor!'

'Perfect.' Rose gave a sardonic thumbs up. 'First boyfriend Craig – literally becoming a priest. Second, Dennis, the *ugliest* man I *ever*, I mean *ever*—' A man in a denim shirt approached Nadine, and Rose broke off to raise Carry On eyebrows at Ellie and blare, 'A grown-up!'

Ellie assessed this closely shaven, short-haired, über-straight individual. 'He looks like a policeman on the telly. How old d'you reckon?'

''Tween . . .' Rose gave him a thorough inspection. 'Twenty-five and forty.'

The policeman turned a questioning glance out to Ellie and Rose, and gestured a drink.

'Double gin and shimline tonic, if you're buying,' yelled Rose.

'Whatever you're having,' added Ellie. 'Thanks.'

As Kate Bush kicked in, Rose threw back her arms, nearly scratching someone's eye out. School disco lights refracted through the chandeliers, and a group of hipster second years crashed onto the dance floor, ruffling their hairstyles in faux-faux-passion. Way ahead of the music, Rose charged into her own rendition of the chorus; Ellie joined in anyway.

When Nadine returned, she brought three more police officers. One of them started grinding with Rose, eyes locked on the

ceiling as if he were undergoing a medical procedure. Ellie scruti-
nised him for any obvious sign of being a sex criminal (result:
indeterminate). A short black guy in a tight designer T-shirt tried
the same thing with Ellie.

'Sorry – boyfriend,' she shouted politely.

'Shame,' he said. 'Lucky man.'

'Thanks,' said Ellie, not sure what to say. She couldn't remember
the last time anybody had tried to chat her up. The uni method
entailed admiring and ignoring someone from a distance, maybe
stretching to a bit of irony-laden banter over some bureaucratic
procedure, then embarking on an almost imperceptible courtship
ritual that involved going to the same club you always went to,
drinking six Jägerbombs without so much as making eye contact,
staggering outside and eventually, as if by accident, getting it on in
an alley on the walk home.

'I just finished my dissertation,' she added, feeling she ought to
say something.

'Ah.' A pause. 'What was it about?'

'Psychokiller' rescued them both from her answer. They sang–
danced in a circle, the fourth man trying to insert himself between
Nadine and Rose.

'Have that!' Rose pushed a drink into Ellie's hand, and fell back
against the guy's shoulder, eyes closed. Nadine and her bloke
turned face to face, his hands on her waist. Ellie drained the glass
and let it fall, rolling between dancers' feet, spilling ice cubes onto
the floor. *Over, over, over,* her heart sang. She turned away from the
others, creating her own circle of movement. 'Blue Monday'
brought a whoop of recognition from the crowd and she raised her
hands above her head and clapped in rhythm, tapping out a message
of elation to anyone who would hear.

—

'Get in a photo with us!' Romilly called to Charlie. She was in red underwear and devil's horns, draped over Katie in stripy bikini and sailor cap. They pouted at the camera. Romilly stuck out her tongue and mimed licking Katie's face.

The lobby was a photo-op bottleneck, as everybody stripped off and revealed their outfits. Sexy angels posed with half-naked workmen, groups of cheerleaders shook their bums for the camera, goths in thigh-high boots clawed at the chests of vampires.

'Get in here!' Romilly dragged Charlie over and pushed him into the middle. 'Look hot!'

'Hold on.' The moment to strip off his shorts had arrived, but in this crowded, fluorescent foyer, and without any further encouragement, Charlie couldn't quite muster the energy to do it.

'What are we waiting for?' shouted Romilly.

'Oh . . . nothing. Just take it.'

Bradder charged past, naked apart from a purple helium balloon tied to his cock.

'Come on, mate!' Lucas beckoned Charlie. 'Let's get this night started.' They headed into the main arena. 'So remember, yeah, spread your net.'

As they passed the bucking bronco penis, the first competitor was getting up, a tall, brunette athlete with a cardboard medal round her neck, reading 'Number 1 Shag'. Two dancers in snakeskin body suits were up on a podium, waggling forked tongues. Way over in the far corner, beyond the dance pit, a drag queen was kicking off a stand-up show.

'Aftershock?' Charlie needed to get drunk.

'Ah, look who it is!' Lucas rounded on a firewoman in a rubber dress, standing at the bar. 'The girl who lives in my old room.'

'Not any more,' she replied. 'I've flown the nest – got my own flat now.'

'So actually it's lucky we met you.' Lucas kicked off his laddish skit. 'We're about to play "I have never".'

'Right.'

'I see you've got a drink.'

'Yeah, but me and Tina are going to watch the stand-up.'

'Come on, Natasha, this night is for AIDS. Show some respect, okay?' Lucas grinned, mocking himself. That was how this patter worked for him, Charlie thought – Lucas was good cop and bad cop at the same time. It didn't leave much room for collaboration. 'I'll kick off. I have never . . . dressed as a firewoman.' Natasha rolled her eyes and drank. 'I win. My turn again—'

'That is *not* the rules.'

'Didn't I specify before we began?'

Charlie scoured the dark, laser-lit arena for any sign of Sasha.

'Okay, let's start again then. I have never slept in the same room as Lucas.' Natasha reluctantly sipped her Bacardi Breezer. Lucas leaned closer, a parody of a leer. 'And I have *definitely* never considered doing it again.'

Tina arrived, a hot secretary with a dark bob, horn-rimmed glasses and fishnets. 'Aren't we going to the stand-up?'

'Yes,' said Natasha firmly.

'Ah.' Lucas held up a finger. 'The game's not over yet. My turn again.'

Charlie knew he ought to say something to Tina. Unable to summon anything amusing, he opted for, 'SSB's kind of weird, isn't it, everyone standing about in thongs? It's not really my thing.'

Tina's wide, green and utterly bored eyes alighted on Charlie, took in all he had to offer, then flitted back to Natasha.

Brilliant, Charlie thought – the only role Lucas left open was Sideline Hater, and nobody liked that. Charlie knew he should get the night going by changing out of his shorts, but couldn't help but be discouraged by the prospect of facing Tina with only a neon sheath cupping his balls.

'Hey, mate.' Ben laid a hand on his shoulder.

'Hey.' Charlie turned to him with immense relief.

'Thought you'd want to know – Sara's here.'

Charlie fought the temptation to spin round immediately and pinpoint her whereabouts. 'Who did she arrive—'

'Er, Charlie?' Lucas butted in. 'I think we both know you've thought about sucking my cock, so drink up, mate.'

'He seems a tee-e-eny bit sleazy.' Ellie held up a lobster claw of sleaziness.

Rose rolled her eyes, taking her whole upper body with her. Using Ellie's shoulder for support, she pushed herself up off the kerb. Once erect, she anchored her burning eyes somewhere on Ellie's face. ''Cause you've got a boyfriend doesn't make you the sex police!' she blared.

'I know, I'm jus' *saying*—' Ellie was cut off by a blundering slap to the face. Rose's open right palm caught her chin with an ineffectual thump rather than a smack, sending Ellie into a comedy, slow-motion fall into the gutter. Once down there, Ellie couldn't get up – she'd left her feet behind on the pavement, her legs were tangled in an unpickable granny knot. The whole thing was utterly ridiculous. She hiccuped, and started to laugh. Body shaking, she peered up through a horizontal curtain of hair – at a livid Rose, looming over her in her fifteen-year-old's outfit – at Nadine's ringed fingers feeling that grown-up policeman's arse – at Rose's gormless bloke peeing against the wall – and it all made her laugh more, and hiccup more, until she could barely breathe.

'Hello, lady.' Nadine grabbed her arms and pulled her up. 'Enjoying yourself down there?'

Ellie hiccuped painfully. 'Rose slapped me,' she giggled.

'No way!' Nadine set Ellie back on the kerb. 'She's so lairy!'

'She's jus' hungry. That's the thing, she's jus' unbelievably hungry.' Ellie shook her head. '*I'm* hungry. D'you wanna get chips?'

Nadine pushed Ellie's hair back and whispered, 'I think I'm going back to Mark's.'

'Oh!' Ellie mugged, winking and attempting to tap her nose. 'Well, be careful.'

Nadine smiled shyly. 'You gonna be all right?'

'Great!' She wafted the air. 'I feel great!'

'Get a taxi, yeah.'

'Yeah! Yeah. Go and bang that policeman.'

'Do you mind?' Nadine held up a palm. 'He does Internal Communications for BT.'

The reply came to Ellie about ten minutes later, still sitting on the kerb. *I bet he does*, she thought.

Wherever Charlie went, Sara was there in his peripheral vision, casting meaningful glances at him or having a laboriously *amazing* time.

On one of his aimless walks, which were sort of trips to the bar, but really increasingly hopeless searches for Sasha, he'd ended up bumping into Rachel, his crush from the first year, and had somehow got stuck in a chat. So far she'd told him she was 'almost enjoying' exam term and was 'thinking of bringing down her cello'. Oh yes, and there was her boyfriend, a brick casually dropped at every opportunity.

There was nothing actually wrong with Rachel, apart from the long-established fact that nothing was ever going to happen between them, which left every interaction dead on arrival. Lucas would be ruthless, Charlie thought. He'd cut it short. Instead,

Charlie felt compelled to stick in and prove he was a decent guy, not just some arsehole out on the pull. It was ridiculous – why did he even care what she thought? – but the Good Bloke within wouldn't pipe down.

Rachel had started telling him about her sister who was training to be a vet. He nodded along, painfully conscious of Sara on the fringes of the shot bar crowd. Next to her, Meredith was dressed as Mystique from X-Men, painted entirely blue, while Sara wore a black corset and pants. *Aw*, he imagined people thinking, *she's too heartbroken to manage the theme, but she was brave to come out anyway.*

Sara hugged a pissed-looking Matt, dressed as Magneto in a tinfoil helmet. Charlie felt a dull kick of jealousy.

'Would you like a cigarette?' he asked Rachel.

'Oh. Have you got any?'

'I thought you might have.'

She shook her head. That killed it. Rachel engineered a polite exit, wishing him the best of luck with finals, and leaving him lonelier than ever. Automatically, he scouted the arena for Sasha, and again wondered whether he should go and take off his shorts. Perhaps it was the shorts that were holding him back?

Charlie squeezed round the rim of the dance floor, taking the long route to the smoking area. Footage from a camera in the corner projected onto a screen above the DJ and couples were taking it in turns to kiss in front of it. A girl leaned in for a close-up, waggling her tongue stud. Through the smoke and lasers, Charlie made out Lucas leaning against the DJ booth, daring to be spanked by a dominatrix with a paddle, mankini a scream of green up his crack. *He* was managing to have a good time. Charlie wriggled towards him, checking out a group of playgirl bunnies on the way. He danced half-heartedly in their direction, but the circle closed on him. When he next looked round, Sara was making her way down to the dance floor, holding hands with Meredith and some guy in a surgeon's mask.

How could he enjoy himself with her there all the time? Cutting his losses, Charlie headed past the slave auction, where Siobhan Davies was strutting up and down in a coat and heels, mouthing along to 'Hey, Big Spender'. She flung the coat off, turned round and touched her toes.

'Oh-oh! She's flexible as well, gents. What do you say to that?'

Ben, with a hoodie tied round his waist, and sexy-nurse Clare were wincing at the back of the crowd.

'Nice outfit,' said Charlie politely.

'I feel like I've done a twelve-hour shift in A and E, to be honest,' said Clare. 'We were just saying we hope you're all right. It must be tough, being out, seeing each other but not being together.'

'I'm fine.' Charlie glanced back towards the dance pit. Sara and Fergus were grinding, his chest covered in ultraviolet handprints. It was utterly predictable. Fergus had been a major source of arguments since before their relationship even began. He was constantly hanging around Sara being 'such a good friend', Sara always insisting that he *didn't* fancy her, when it was blatant to all concerned that he definitely did.

Charlie gave himself a shake: he had to stay positive. 'Have either of you guys seen Sasha?'

Ben and Clare shrugged.

Downstairs, in the smoking area, Charlie found Romilly and Katie huddled on a bench. 'Can I have a drag?'

'Oh shut up, Charlie!' said Romilly scornfully. 'You don't smoke. It's bad for you.'

Charlie sat down with a groan.

'What?'

'How can I be out with so many girls in their underwear and still be having a shit time? It's like Rehab, but worse.'

'I know. It's making us feel like pensioners.' Katie exhaled smoke with a toss of the head.

'And everywhere I turn, Sara's there.'

'Well, that's what you get for being the idiot who dumped his lovely, hot girlfriend,' Romilly yawned.

'Why *did* you split up with her?' said Katie.

'I've *told* you. *No big reason.*'

Charlie almost asked if they'd seen Sasha – but if she hadn't arrived by now, he had to accept she wasn't coming. It was so disappointing. Even if he hadn't got with Sasha, a conversation with her would have lifted the whole night; it would have felt like some kind of *event*.

A truly annihilated girl in fluorescent underwear clattered past, her embarrassed boyfriend jogging after.

'You know what kind of guy you are, Charlie.' Romilly practically swallowed the fag. 'You're a good guy who thinks he's a dick. It's one of the worst types. Because your signalling is all over the place. It's never clear when your dickishness is going to strike. Then you're nice, out of nowhere. *So* confusing.'

'Is it true that you asked Sara not to come to SSB and told her all the people you want to sleep with?'

'What?' Charlie turned to Katie in shock.

'Like, actual names? Seems a bit harsh.'

'*What?*' He shook his head. 'That's just wrong. Of course I didn't. That's not true.'

'Don't get angry with *me*.'

'But it's bullshit!'

'That's what I told them!'

'I can't believe this.' Charlie raked his hair, looking around for someone to confirm his outrage. 'That's ridiculous!'

'You know what people are like.'

'I should go and have a word with her.'

'Are you sure that's a good idea?'

'Yeah. I'm going to. I mean, *really*.'

Charlie strode back up the stairs, past the slave auction ('Sold! To the ladies' pole-dancing squad!') and over to the dance floor. Incredulity burned in his chest; he silently mouthed his disbelief as he squeezed past a grinding couple. Lucas waved through the smoke – Charlie ignored him, sights trained on the main bar. His shock was beginning to give way to indignation: he didn't deserve to be lied about – he hadn't done anything wrong! In fact, he'd done nothing but support her since they split up. The half-empty bar already looked like the morning after, strewn with plastic cups and sticky spillages. Sara was at a circular table, Fergus's arm drooped lazily round her bare shoulders. Matt was half-asleep, cradling his head on his arms. Charlie stood there, breathing steadily, as one by one, their eyes turned to him.

'Sara,' he practically growled. 'Can I talk to you, please.'

Ellie tottered along to Capel's for chips and cheese. In the queue, she tried to write a text to Justin, but it was hard to type, so it ended up as a basic 'xxxyxz'. Holding onto her chips for dear life, Ellie started out on her way home.

But somehow, she wasn't ready for the night to be over. She considered going to Justin's, but doubted he'd appreciate being woken by someone stinking of chips and booze. Instead of walking down the high street and either waiting for a mythical night bus or setting out on the long trudge to hers (with the potential welcome home of the sound of Rose and PC Whatisname doing it), Ellie found herself wandering down towards the canal. With a plodding, uneven gait, she made her way to the Hope and Anchor, its windows dark, picnic benches empty but for a few stray pint glasses. Opposite the pub, shrouded in shadow, were three canal boats.

Nobody was around.

Ellie tiptoed over to the central boat, and tried to peer into the window. It was further away than she thought — she fell forward and her purse dropped from her pocket onto the concrete edge.

'Bollocks.' Ellie heaved herself back up and stooped to pick up the purse. She knocked it into the water. 'Shhhhit.' Kneeling on the rough bank, she plunged her hand beneath the sludgy surface. 'Urgh.'

A head popped out of the next boat's window. 'All right?' someone said, in the darkness.

'Yeah, sorry,' Ellie slurred.

'Who's that?' said the shadowed man.

'Nobody, nobody.'

'Is that Ellie?'

'Mmmmm . . . Maybe?'

'It's Oscar.'

'Ah.' Using the boat, Ellie levered herself up and headed towards the voice, slimy hand outstretched. Oscar's head was framed in the square window, like a newsreader. 'Oh, hello,' she said, nonchalantly.

'Hi,' replied Oscar. 'What are you up to?'

'This and that,' Ellie shrugged, wiping her hand on her top. 'Ack-chally I just handed in my dissertation. Listen.' She crouched down, homing in on Oscar's flickering face. 'Listen.'

He smiled. 'I'm listening.'

'Listen. Why don't we have sex?'

II

Beyond Good and Evil

Nietzsche challenged his readers to go 'beyond good and evil'. He made this 'dangerous motto' the title of one of his books, a work he considered 'totally terrible and repellent', 'a terrifying book . . . very black, like a squid'. Elsewhere he described himself as an 'immoralist' and spoke of the need to 'overcome morality'. All this seems to imply that going beyond good and evil involves something ugly and depraved, an impression Nietzsche did little to dispel when he muttered darkly of the 'crisis' that 'one day my name will recall': 'the most profound clash of consciences, a decision that was invoked against everything that had hitherto been believed'.

Although he called himself an immoralist, Nietzsche did not actually propose to discard morality altogether. 'I do not deny,' he wrote, 'provided I am not a fool, that many actions that are called immoral are to be avoided and resisted; likewise, many that are called moral, should be done and encouraged.' Instead, he sought to introduce a different kind of morality, to replace 'Good and Evil' with 'Good and Bad'.

Strictly speaking, this was not an introduction but a comeback. Nietzsche's idea of Good and Bad derived from the ancient world, where for centuries it had been the dominant model of morality.

The move towards Good and Evil was brought about by Christianity, with its vision of life based on abstract extremes of salvation and damnation. It was this 'catastrophe of the highest order' that Nietzsche set himself to reverse.

Nietzsche called Christianity 'slave morality', an insult he meant quite literally. Originating among the slaves of the Roman Empire, Christianity began as a way of making victimisation bearable. To find hope in their oppression, the early Christians told themselves that powerlessness was not the punishment it seemed, because, contrary to appearances, weakness lay at the heart of goodness.

The aristocratic morality of Greece and Rome saw weakness in very straightforward terms, as a failed and contemptible version of strength. With Christianity, the slaves turned this notion on its head. They literally made a virtue of necessity by reinventing their enforced behaviours as signs of personal rectitude. Timidity became humility; self-consciousness was turned into thoughtfulness; submission to people one hates was rebranded as obedience; 'standing at the door' was given 'fine names such as patience'.

At the same time, Nietzsche argued, the Christians spun the best qualities of their masters – taking charge unthinkingly, never reflecting or self-questioning, letting their inner beast run free – to make them look like vices. Strength became brutishness; healthy aggression was portrayed as bullying; acting on instinct was made to look like lack of consideration. The raw confidence of the ruling elite was redefined as unChristian arrogance.

It might sound like an ode to brute power, but with the story of the masters and the slaves Nietzsche was presenting a psychological parable. Within each of us, he said, the same conflict between strength and weakness takes place every day. To allow confidence to triumph, we have to give up our inherited assumptions about the nature of good and bad. Above all, we have to give up our assumptions about guilt. This, said Nietzsche, was Christianity's most devilish invention: the idea that when you'd done something wrong (even if you were provoked, and you didn't mean it, and who said it was so bad anyway), your first reaction should be to hate yourself for it.

A blazing rectangle of light shone through the curtains, turning the whole room red. The Minnie Mouse clock read twenty past one.

In his first few moments of consciousness, Charlie was hit by a painful burst of fragmented memories – he was pepper-sprayed by his past.

In a dark, ultraviolet corner of the bar, he machine-gunned accusations at Sara's glowing eyes and teeth – what had she been telling people, why was she lying about him, why was she intentionally ruining his night?

In the car park, apologising for losing his temper, for shouting at her and making her cry, but at the same time, surely she had to understand – 'Why do I have to understand?' shrieked Sara.

In the toilets, trying to rescue the evening from this stupid row, finally wriggling out of Lucas's shorts and heading back out, arse exposed, to find that, out of the three hundred people there, absolutely nobody gave a shit.

On the dance floor, shuffling side to side next to a couple of frosty geishas, raising a hand to the DJ like he'd just come for the music . . .

That was the point he regretted most bitterly. If only he'd carried on having a terrible time, and not tried to go back and sort things out.

In the cab outside Sara's house, feebly insisting it should go on to his – 'You can't, you can't leave me like this,' she sobbed, the taxi driver casting a wide eye over his shoulder.

After that, it had actually got worse. The endless circular argument in Sara's room. They were torturing each other, but couldn't seem to stop. Fergus fancied her – why couldn't she be honest and admit that? Charlie was being deliberately mean, he just couldn't stand seeing her having a good time without him. She was making a drama over nothing – the truth was their relationship wasn't that important – he'd *never* fucking liked her.

The instant he said it, Charlie was sorry. At the look on her face, he began to cry too. They held each other, rocking back and forth. He loved her, he really did, he didn't want to be nasty like this – hadn't he been looking after her, hadn't he been there for her, why was she saying these things about him? And just like that, they were right back at the beginning.

In the end, tiredness won. At dawn, when Minnie Mouse said quarter to five, Sara began a new kind of crying: quiet tears of sheer exhaustion slipped down her grey, wrung-out cheeks. 'I have to sleep,' she repeated, dredging up the words. 'Please.' And he was tired too: too tired to carry on with this awful conversation, too tired to leave.

Charlie was in Sara's bed. That was the fact – the reality around which everything else arranged itself. Sara's elbow was digging into the back of his ribs, her thighs pressed against his, her right hand settled in the dip of his waist. Charlie stared blankly at the Kate Moss poster above the laundry basket, looking for an answer in the gap between her eyes. Kate stared back: there was no solution to this riddle. Sara snuggled up to him with a hum of satisfaction. Charlie submitted, relaxing into the contact, letting it happen.

God, he was sorry. The feeling possessed him, it was impossible to get beyond it: he was sorry, he was sorry, he was sorry. Charlie shifted, bringing Sara closer to him, as if he could communicate his regret through maximum skin-to-skin contact. Sara's cheek leant against his back, soft and warm. He heard her breath deepen.

A kind of stupid cunning began to mingle with Charlie's remorse; he reached a hand back and brushed Sara's lips. She stirred. This was idiotic, it was the worst idea, it would only complicate things further. But Charlie had to do something with this feeling – he couldn't bear it on his own. Sara's hand crept over his hip. With quick breath, Charlie heaved round to face her, hand on her waist – all of a sudden they were holding one another.

Afterwards, Charlie felt immediately, appallingly, overwhelmingly guilty. Regret weighed on his ribcage, pinning him to the bed. He wanted to stand up, find his clothes, leave, think, but moving was physically impossible.

Sara propped herself on one elbow and stroked his hair. 'You look tired.'

He screwed his eyes shut. 'It was awful, wasn't it? I'm sorry.'

'It's okay,' she laid a hand on his chest. 'It was awful for both of us.'

Next door, Meredith launched her hairdryer. She must have heard every syllable of last night's conversation. Sara yanked the covers up and they hid underneath.

'I've missed you,' she whispered, with a tiny smile.

Oh no, thought Charlie. He knew he had to speak now, clarify the situation before it got out of hand. Yes, it was confusing and difficult and heart-rending (it was for him too) – yes, they had just made impressively passionate love, but nothing had actually changed. 'Sara—'

'Hey there.' Somebody thumped on the door.

They both jumped. Sara peeked over the duvet edge. 'Hello?'

The door swung open. 'I've made you some tea.'

'Fergus! Um . . . not now.'

Charlie stayed hidden, curled into a foetal position, hoping it would all go away.

'Just wanted to check you're all right.' Fergus strode in, setting the mug on Sara's pile of *Vogues*.

'Um, yeah, I'm okay.'

'Tough night?' Was he *really* going to pretend that Charlie wasn't there? 'Well, just so you know, we're about to start *Rocky*. "Eat lightning and crap thunder!"'

'All right. I'll be down in a bit, okay?'

'I'll save you some eggs.'

Beneath the duvet, Charlie was running out of air. If only he'd crept out in the middle of the night, he reflected bitterly, it might have been a salvageable fuck-up – 'one of those', as the football commentators said. Charlie imagined going downstairs and sitting in the living room making fake chit-chat with Fergus and Meredith, all the while pretending they didn't have great thought-Zeppelins popping out of their heads saying 'What's this prick doing here?' and 'Are they back together or what?'

Charlie had to escape. He stretched out a foot to scout for his mankini, heart sinking at the thought of the ball-chafing walk of shame home.

'Hey,' Sara returned to the airlock. 'There you are.'

'Here I am.' Charlie's toes curled round Lycra.

'Do you want some breakfast?'

'Um . . .' Monkey-like, he transferred mankini from foot to hand. 'I'm actually feeling a little bit sick.'

By reinstating Good and Bad in place of Good and Evil, Nietzsche hoped to tilt the balance away from guilt and back towards confidence.

So what's the difference? First, while Good and Evil are absolutes, Good and Bad are on a sliding scale, more like Better and Worse, with a lot of allowance made for the particular circumstance and context. Second, Good and Evil are always tipped towards Evil, like a seesaw with a weight on the end. Evil is so much *more* evil than Good is good, whereas Good and Bad have a rough equality.

Good and Bad is the morality of confidence. Think of the way confidence helps you avoid taking things personally. When you're feeling confident, you don't mind criticism, because you know it's not *you* that's being criticised, but the thing you've done. (One reason why confidence is such a valued trait in the workplace: because, of course, at work, no one ever 'criticises' anyone – there's only feedback, which is always constructive, and should never be taken personally.) Good and Evil pins actions on people. There's this whole list of things that are evil, and if you do one of them, you're evil too. That's what sin is, and that's why, according to Christianity, we need forgiveness. Good and Bad, by contrast, lets you make the distinction between yourself and your actions. You're not an awful person because you forgot to log out or didn't code the invoice correctly. You did something 'worse'; it's not the end of the world.

Which raises the question: what is so dangerous and squidlike about that? How you answer that question depends in large part on how important it is to you that people take responsibility for their actions. So you've done something bad: you've hurt someone you love, even though when you did so you were only expressing your instinct. Should you feel guilty about it, the worming moral guilt of Christianity's slave-bred conscience? Or should you say to yourself, 'Well this happened, but there's no point beating myself up about it'?

Nietzsche would take this further still, by arguing that it is not *what* we do that matters, but how it is done, and, most importantly, *who* does it. Having done something bad, the true master would respond: 'I am the only context for my actions. If I did this, it must be right.'

Ellie didn't feel guilty. Nauseous and slightly manic, yes. Guilty, no. Perhaps it lay in wait for her, planning to pounce unexpectedly as soon as she relaxed. She sat on the tiny, hard bench at the back of the chemist's, waiting for her pharmaceutical inquisition.

'Why is it,' she texted Nadine, 'that the sexual mores of Victorian Britain live on in the procedure for getting the morning-after pill?'

'Two for one on any of our organic or hypoallergenic range . . .' the radio wittered on.

Nadine replied instantly: 'U no ur a finalist when . . . even ur humble brags about doing it turn into an essay question.'

Ellie smirked, pleasantly embarrassed. '2chez.'

She'd already told Nadine. (The verdict on PC Mark: 'pretty nice – a bit spitty'.) But if possible, she wasn't going to tell Rose, who had texted a demi-semi-apology around midday: 'Spect you're feeling utterly ashamed of your disgusting behaviour yesterday, Miss. violence is never the answer ps. Didn't pork. Vommed instead.' Telling Justin, she had decided, was unnecessarily cruel.

This embryonic lie – a lie she hadn't yet told – had already opened up a whole new dimension for Ellie. Until now, it had never struck her that she *could* simply lie and that it might not matter. For the first time, Ellie was consciously creating a disjuncture between the truth and the story she told her most intimate friends – perhaps, in time, herself. This dizzying rupture made her feel as if she had ascended to the next layer, where she could look down from a great height on the things she used to believe were important or real, and see them for the naïve, immature constructs they were.

Ellie was ushered into a tiny white room by a middle-aged Asian man. She told him her age, and when asked, assured him there was no chance of her being pregnant before last night (though the second he suggested it, she began to fear she was).

'And how long has it been since you had intercourse?' He averted his eyes politely.

'Um . . . eight hours-ish?' They had actually had sex twice, but presumably he didn't need a blow by blow. Afterwards, they'd taken an early walk along the canal, kissed under a bridge, eaten some instant noodles, and chatted about a few of the things that Oscar didn't believe in (exams, institutions, monogamy and borders, for a start).

'Did you use any protection?'

'Nope.' Ellie resisted the impulse to make an apologetic face. She had been on the pill, but came off it over Easter, complaining that she felt bad enough already. Since then her and Justin had been using condoms combined with the 'revision method' – a cycle of worry and boredom that precluded all sexual desire.

Only after they ran through allergies and side effects and headed out to the till did Ellie realise that she didn't have her purse. She was hit by a vivid memory of the gloopy sound it made as it slipped into the water, and the smell of the canal on her hand. A frantic search of her jeans pockets uncovered £2.43.

'Um . . .' she stood frozen at the till.

'That's £25, please.'

'Oh, God, I'm really sorry.' Ellie looked around, mentally running through the seemingly endless steps of going home, finding her passport (if it was even at uni), taking it to the bank and returning. 'I'll . . .'

At that moment, a pale-looking boy stepped through the automatic doors, dressed like a stray, rejected member of Village People. Without stopping to think, Ellie approached him. 'Charlie, hi. This is going to sound mad, but could I possibly borrow £25? Well, £23.56.'

'Erm . . .' Charlie came to a halt by the perfume stand, pulling himself out of an all-consuming meditation.

Ellie gave him a bright smile. 'I lost my purse last night, and I really need to buy something.'

'Oh, right, er . . .' He patted absently at his chest and pockets. (He *seemed* to be wearing a swimsuit.)

'Basically – I don't know why I'm being so coy – I need to buy the morning-after pill, and it costs £25. Do you mind?'

'Oh, um . . . I mean, of course, yeah.'

'I've done the interrogation and everything.'

'Right,' he frowned in confusion.

'But we might have to rejoin the queue.'

'Yeah, I mean, no problem at all.' Charlie obligingly stepped into the queue with her, taking it all in his slightly baffled stride. That was the beautiful thing about manners, she reflected, they could be adapted to almost any situation.

His politeness was catching. 'Thanks so much for this,' Ellie smiled again. 'Oh sorry, did *you* want to buy something?'

'Just some gum.' Charlie shook his head. 'I think it's at the till.'

'And I should've asked: how are you?'

'Oh.' Charlie raised his eyebrows in an expression of dazed shock. 'Well. As we're being honest . . . I think I did something fucking stupid last night.'

You slept with Sara, Ellie thought. 'Oh really? Well, that makes two of us.'

'Yeah, I . . .' Charlie rubbed his neck and winced. 'I slept with Sara.'

'Oh!' she tried to sound surprised. 'Oh, no.'

'Yeah . . .' He scratched his chin for a while. 'Not my smartest move.'

'Hard not to?' she asked encouragingly.

'Yeah, I mean . . .' He stared intensely at a moisturiser display. 'Just fucking stupid really.' With her newfound perspective, Ellie felt rather sorry for him. It's not easy breaking up, she thought hazily. At the end of the day, we're all people trying to get by.

165

'Me again,' she greeted the pharmacist. 'I've managed to find a sponsor.'

'Oh, yes,' Charlie came to. He chose some gum and at length, pulled a credit card from his shorts. '*Should* go through . . .'

The precious paper bag was handed over and with a courtly grace, Charlie also offered Ellie some gum. By this stage, he was warming up. As they left, he quipped, with an avuncular air, 'I hope you and Justin are more careful in future.'

'Oh,' Ellie laughed flippantly. 'Well, maybe one of us needs to be more careful than the other.' She knew she shouldn't have said it, but somehow she didn't care. Part of her wanted Charlie to know that she wasn't staying in with Justin, a condom-splitting drama providing a flare of excitement in their otherwise boring lives. 'But maybe also don't mention that to anyone,' she added quickly.

'Right. *Oh*. Oh, I get it. Of course.'

'And email me your bank details.'

'Don't worry about it.' Charlie batted a hand. 'I mean, it's—'

'All in a good cause?' smiled Ellie.

'Right,' Charlie nodded. 'Listen, also, I'm really sorry about that whole car thing.' A surprisingly pained look flickered across his face.

'Oh God, forget it—'

'No, I mean it—'

'Honestly.' Standing on the street, Ellie felt a rush of random affection: towards uni, Oscar, Charlie, the town itself . . . 'And thank you. Thanks a lot.' She stopped just short of giving him a hug.

'All in a day's work.'

'See you around then?'

'Sure thing.' Charlie raised a hand, walking backwards past the skater shop. 'Any time.'

12

Repression

For Nietzsche, the worst thing about guilt was the way it encouraged repression. Through his influence on Freud (who reported that he had to stop reading Nietzsche because he feared he would find he had nothing left to add), Nietzsche's views on the dangers of this condition ended up becoming part of both psychological and popular culture. However, whereas Freud pinpointed the origins of repression in the development of the child in infancy, for Nietzsche, repression was caused first and foremost by Christianity.

Repression was what happened when the instinct was blocked or stifled. 'All instincts which are not discharged outwardly *turn inwards,*' Nietzsche wrote. By restricting natural drives such as selfishness and aggression, Christianity had prevented them from flowing freely into action. People were forced to vent their drives against themselves, like a caged animal gnawing on its foot.

Nietzsche depicted Christianity as a kind of spiritual anorexia. Often, people think of anorexia as a disease of the weak-willed: if only you'd just get a grip, they say, then you could stop this nonsense in a second. But the last thing an anorexic needs to do is get a grip — on the contrary, what they need is for their grip to loosen. The problem with anorexics isn't that they're weak-willed, but that they're *too* strong-willed, and this crushing will – what Nietzsche would call 'the will to power' – has been directed inwards, onto themselves.

Nietzsche's ideal was affirmation of self and life: 'Saying "Yes" to life even in its strangest and hardest problems.' From the monks and celibate priests of Catholicism, from the sombre suits and bare halls of Protestantism, from the emaciated, virgin Jesus hanging on the cross and the sanctification of monogamy in marriage, he diagnosed the central doctrine of Christianity as a continual, controlling No. 'The ascetic ideal', he called this attitude, which he said could be found in every aspect of Christian belief and ritual. Even the idea of heaven was a kind of No. By setting up a vision of pure, unchanging perfection, it denied everything that was messy, animal and unsettled about life – in other words, life itself. 'A green and bitter gaze is turned against physiological growth, especially against its expression, beauty, joy; while pleasure is sought in failure, withering, pain, misfortune, ugliness, arbitrary atonement, self-flagellation, self-sacrifice.'

Nietzsche's focus on repression may seem dated to modern ears. Not only do we live in a post-Christian world, or so the theory goes, we also feel, post-Sixties, as if we have moved on from repression, and freed ourselves of the hang-ups of previous generations. But as Nietzsche emphasised, acting on instinct was never that straightforward: 'Who can know what happens within himself, what conversations take place within the sacred darkness of his soul?' Even if we were able to grow up in complete freedom, it still wouldn't be clear what we really wanted or how we should go about getting it.

For the next day or two, Ellie went around with a burning in her belly, a feeling she remembered from school on Monday mornings after she'd kissed somebody on Saturday. Somebody nice. She remembered, in particular, under the canal bridge, a sheer, thoughtless pleasure she almost hadn't recognised. The memory kept rebounding, never seeming to lose its force. Could it be, she began to wonder, that she actually *liked* Oscar?

On reflection, though, Ellie had to admit that she didn't miss him or want to see him. Rather than lacking somebody, she was full and easy, untroubled by either solitude or company (if anything this made other people more interested in her – they seemed to register a change, as if she smelled different). Ellie took quiet satisfaction from her secret – it cordoned off her actions and made them hers. She had done something unexpected, and in doing so, discovered a private, internal world, a reservoir of will, still to be mapped out.

After a while of this, it was almost a relief to feel guilty. That was in character; she was used to that. What exactly made her actions so fascinating, she asked herself – having a tawdry one-night stand? Lying? Being a bit of an arsehole? When the molten feeling subsided, there didn't seem much to be proud of.

And of course, she didn't want to *be with* Oscar. Yes, he was sexy, interesting, unusually free. But how could you be with Oscar anyway? It would be like trying to take in an urban fox.

What she wanted was to be with someone calm and honest and kind. Someone like Justin – Justin, in fact. Perhaps, she began to reason, sleeping with Oscar was what she needed to do *in order* to stay with Justin. She'd had a miserable couple of months, several when she thought about it. She'd gone a little crazy and got it out of her system, expelled the bad energy, been reborn . . . Whatever. The end result was that she and Justin were getting along much better. They'd started the second series of *The Sopranos* and Justin was experimenting with edible seaweed. Now the madness was over, she could settle down, be nice to her boyfriend, and revise.

'Revising is like being waterboarded.' Maggie rubbed her eyes. 'How can you concentrate for so long? Is it coffee time yet?'

'Nope, sorry.'

'I'm living from one shortbread biscuit to the next. That's my unit of time now – the shortbread.'

Ellie was working at the desk next to Maggie, on the mezzanine level of the airport-like history faculty. It had happened just like that. One minute she was awkwardly ignoring her former friends, blocked up with accreted social anxiety, like limescale in a kettle. The next she plonked herself by Maggie with a cheerful, 'Hello, stranger! Great to see you!'

Someone – neither her nor decisively not her – had flicked a switch. The impossible had come to look not merely achievable, but easy, almost enjoyable.

Rather than a form of torture, Ellie had decided to approach revision as a long, luxurious mull, a slow-motion consideration of questions that happened upon her. What is, say, duty? What *is* the relation of speech to action, when it comes down to it? What is reality? She felt she was peeling back layers in order to sift at a geological level, a place where time was measured in millennia rather than months, minutes or shortbreads, and existence was made up of giant, universal concepts that slotted together like the bricks in a game of Tetris.

'Duty = categorical imperative = reason' she printed carefully on a Post-it, which she stuck to the partition.

'Can I interest you in a Caramac?' Adébayo appeared behind her shoulder.

'Um . . .' She turned to look at him in surprise.

'I've bitten off more caramel-flavoured substance than I can chew.' Adé was a broad-shouldered, rugby-playing type, the type she'd discovered she was allergic to about two weeks into uni. She had a searing memory of him at Rehab in first year, doing a row of flaming sambucas while a group of 'ladz' who should know better chanted, 'Get it down, Zulu warrior!' If he'd approached her this time last year (unlikely – he'd have had to track her down to Justin's living room first, and he was almost certainly exclusively shagging lacrosse players at the time), she'd probably have made some unnecessarily withering remark. She thought Adé was up himself, and on a deep level, scared of girls, and a fucking idiot.

Now, such harsh judgements felt out of tune with her mood. Did *she* want to be forever pigeonholed according to her own first-year errors? Hadn't they all grown up since then? Perhaps, at this new moment, on the cusp of adulthood, everybody deserved a bit more respect.

'The sell-by date is July.' Adé nudged her shoulder. 'I will need to press you for a decision.'

'Sorry, I was off! Give us a square then.'

One thing you had to admit about Adé was that – to use her gran's words – he was a *very* handsome young man. Being nice to handsome men was new territory for Ellie, who tended to believe that dickishness and handsomeness were directly proportionate, and went by the rule that you couldn't trust a good-looking man as far as you could throw his pleasingly sculpted face. (A strange contradiction: the same view expressed of women would take her from 0 to 60 on the outrage scale before she'd pulled out the drive.) Thinking about it, she had to admit that Oscar was quite good-looking, but in the skewed, lateral way to which she was accustomed, unlike Adé's no-doubts-about-it hotness.

'So how's things?' offered Adé. 'Busy?'

'Oh, extremely.'

'Thinking?'

'Exactly. Thinking away, thinking very hard.' Oh God, was she flirting with Adé now? What exactly was going on?

'Not to mention.' Maggie's head popped over the partition. 'Vandalising university property.'

'It wasn't me, guv.' Ellie put her hands up. 'I swear.'

There had been a fresh wave of feminist vandalism, targeting posters for the new hockey team charity calendar. 'OBJECTIFICATION' someone had scrawled in marker pen, before abandoning the slogans and cutting to the chase: 'THIS IS SEXIST SHIT'. Outside the engineering building, the same vandal, or perhaps another, had scored '*BORING*' into the glass display case, scratching over the team, pictured with hockey shirts draped over their breasts.

'Tell it to the judge,' smiled Adé. 'Is that what you're planning this summer then, short stint in the slammer?'

'Oh Christ, who knows? I feel like the world ends when May does. What about you?'

'Well, I've got one thing I'm definitely doing, which makes me feel slightly better about life.'

You're going to work for Goldman's, thought Ellie.

'I'm doing summer work for this charity based where I'm from in Birmingham – like a children's literacy thing.'

'Oh.'

'It's usually pretty fun.'

'Yeah. Sounds . . .'

'Anyway, want a beverage?'

'Oh! Is it coffee time yet?' Maggie brightened.

'Definitely feels like mocha o'clock.' Adé looked at Ellie. 'I'll get you one.'

'I've just got to finish this plan . . .' Ellie murmured apologetically.

'No worries – hate to disturb that thinking.'

As Adé walked by, Maggie shot Ellie a 'get you' look, and whispered, 'Are you having a vending-machine-based frisson?'

'I don't think so,' murmured Ellie. 'I mean, no. *No.*'

'I wouldn't blame you. Can I ask you something?' Maggie looked over her shoulder and lowered her voice further, clamping her teeth ventriloquist-style. 'When was the last time you had sex?'

'Erm,' Ellie stalled.

''Cause for me and Chris, it's like . . .' Maggie counted on her fingers. 'Eighteen days. Nineteen including today. I mean, I'm starting to feel like I'm wasting my youth here, you know? Like my organs are going to shrivel up and—'

'Look out.'

Chris was on his way over. He couldn't seem to go more than an hour without coming over to be close to Maggie – she was his life source. With a touch of relief, Ellie turned to Kant, sinking back into the grand, abstract world of theoretical cause and theoretical effect. She wasn't in the frame of mind for cosy relationship moans.

'Is it coffee time yet?'

'Nearly.' Chris leaned on Maggie's head. 'Twenty minutes.'

Ellie's phone flashed a text. Hoping for Justin and a sense of normality, she got a punctuation-happy Rose. 'U got letter!!! shd i open??!'

Unwilling to abandon her train of thought, Ellie replied, 'S'ok. I'll get it at home x'.

Rose had recently turned into a kind of unofficial housekeeper. She was treating Justin like a household pet, to be overfed, cooed over and occasionally kicked, no doubt with a liberal helping of knowing remarks about how 'difficult' and 'distant' Ellie had been recently. It was bloody annoying. Mind you, Ellie realised, perhaps she wasn't best placed to complain about people treating Justin badly.

'You at the Shackle today? X' added Ellie, not really caring about the answer. She tried to refocus, pushing her phone to the far corner of her desk.

'I'm having a shortbread,' announced Maggie. 'Screw the schedule, it's time to partay!'

'opnd it,' Rose shot back. 'SHIIIIIIITTT!!! Ur xPelld!!!'

Fearful of a recriminatory call from Sara, Charlie allowed his phone to die, its dwindling bar a painful symbol of his own depletion. His SSB hangover wouldn't leave him alone. Unable to stomach his customary double-cheeseburger antidote, he lay in bed watching clip after clip of massive NFL hits, each one giving less satisfaction.

Three days slipped by in this manner, sodden with revision guilt and the exhaustion of inactivity. Only when Charlie finally plugged in and found a reassuringly breezy message from Sara did he recover some of his natural optimism. He put aside the nagging sense that *surely* she couldn't be that cool about it and dragged himself from his pit.

During his forty-minute mid-morning shower, Charlie came to a regretful decision. Having an awesome time was ruining him: he would have to put it on hold – temporarily – and concentrate on exams.

Half an hour into executing this plan, Charlie was already feeling more wholesome. It was lucky, he thought, he was so resilient.

Charlie's revision motto was, 'Don't work hard, work smart.' His revision method was to look for the answers on the internet. Today he was looking for the answers to that low-hanging fruit, Contemporary Italian Politics. He had downloaded ten past papers and scanned them for questions that came up year after year. The paper was actually less predictable than he remembered, but sure enough he'd spotted some patterns.

Now Charlie was on the hunt for a lecture from the University of Alabama, or Calcutta, or Adelaide, anywhere they spoke English, which went through this exact question in a five-point plan. He'd fill in the gaps with other people's essays and his smartwork would be done in barely half a day.

'What?'

Alistair had spun round in his chair to glare at Charlie. 'You're jiggling.'

Charlie looked down to see his leg pumping up an invisible airbed. 'I'm honestly not doing that.'

'Well, stop not doing it.' Alistair swivelled back to hunch over his desk.

Charlie was working in Alistair's room. 'You can't outsource your concentration,' Alistair had grumbled, but in the end he'd had to relent. Charlie *needed* someone else in the room. On his own, he didn't stand a chance against all the porn on the internet. He even found his *own* body too distracting (his ingrown hairs were bad again). Plus the whole thing felt sad, like Saturday nights in when you were fifteen. Charlie could have gone to the library, but he was no fool – he knew he'd leave five hours later, coffee-dazzled and sugar-high, exhausted from a long series of catch-ups and inquisitions about the state of play between him and Sara. In her absence, his only possible work companion was trusty, musty Alistair in his dingy monk's cell.

Google was being difficult. Charlie had gone through to page seven on all sorts of question variations and still nothing was coming up. It was slightly concerning, but that was revision for you. Like start-up success, it wasn't a linear process: for a long time you had nothing and then – BAM! You'd struck gold.

Charlie was chasing a link on a weird website that wanted him to pay for 'guaranteed first class essays', when without warning he found himself searching for 'how to write a business plan'. He still needed to bash one out for Social Tiger, and draft some brand values, plus there were a few other tasks he couldn't quite remember. He started googling the competition to check the deadline, which he had a feeling was close, and that somehow turned into flicking through photos of SSB on Facebook to see if anything new had come up since this morning. That second year secretary was in the back of one (sudden and unwarranted shame surged in Charlie). He hurried on to Halloween Rehab last year.

'Boop,' Sara surfaced on Facebook chat. Boop was her invented word meaning 'Hello', 'How are you?', 'I miss you' and various other shades of affection that Charlie preferred to filter out.

'Yo,' he replied, still flicking through photos. He was deep in friends-of-friends territory now, on holiday with a group of girls, somewhere equivalent to Magaluf.

'What you doing?'

'Revising.'

'Oh well I'll leave you to it' – smiley face.

'Cool yeah.' Sara seemed to take his dismissal so well, he felt obliged to add, 'Everything ok?'

'Fine, yeah. Just checking in. Keep going!'

'Will do.' By now he almost wanted her to stay on the line. Sara really was a genius at pushing his buttons.

'xxxxxxxxx'

'Bye xxxxx.' Charlie carefully kept his kiss-trail half the length of Sara's – one of many lines in the sand – and crossed off his Facebook tab. He needed to focus on finding the answer to 'How would you account for the dramatic political breakthrough of Berlusconi and his Forza Italia! Party?' quickly, so he could go to the gym before supper.

But God, revision was boring. Stray thoughts flashed up in his head like pop-up ads. Berlusconi – did he really put an exclamation mark in his party's name? That guy, seriously: What a lad. Charlie chuckled and looked round the room for a response. A tub of E45, the dusty hair gel that Alistair would never admit to using, hatched pairs of contact lens cases sitting neatly in a row . . .

'Hey.'

Alistair didn't reply.

'Al. Al-lis-tair.'

'I'm doing a timed essay.'

'Stop the clock. I've got something to ask you.'

Alistair made a grinding noise at the back of his throat, paused his stopwatch and wheeled round to face Charlie.

'What do you think I should do? With my life.'

Clearly, this wasn't the question Alistair had been expecting. His expression suggested he'd been asked to study Charlie's vomit and describe its distinctive characteristics.

'So I've got this Social Tiger pitch coming up.'

'You want to be an entrepreneur then?'

'I don't know! That's what I'm asking.'

Alistair sighed. 'Don't you have enough on your plate right now?'

Charlie was remembering why he didn't talk to Alistair about this sort of thing. 'What – exams? I'll be fine.'

'If you're sure. How many marks do you need to get in them?'

'Must be about . . . sixty-three-ish? Give or take. I've had a couple of essays back since then, but—'

'You don't know?'

'It's not that I don't *know* . . .' Charlie's 2:1 target was something he had a feel for. It wasn't as if you could aim for a particular mark in the exam, so he preferred to be guided by instinct. In his opinion, Alistair's obsession with figures was unhealthy, an offshoot of the way he couldn't walk past a vacant plug socket without making sure the switch was turned off.

Alistair was suddenly urgent. 'You've got to know exactly.'

Gratified to have drawn something out of him, Charlie sat up. 'I'll check now. Can you do the percentages?'

'You're a dick, you know that?'

'But I'm your dick. I can give you so much pleasure, so easily.' Grinning, Charlie navigated onto the My Account section of Blackboard, not expecting to see anything new. As far as he could see, lecturers at university had about half as much to do as teachers at school, but they took twice as long to get your marks up. To his surprise, there were new numbers in the box – and those numbers made his blood run cold.

'Well?' asked Alistair, after a lengthy pause.

'Fifty-six in Genocide. Fifty-four in New Labour.'

The marks were actually 54 and 51. Charlie had no idea why he'd told this tiny, pointless lie.

Alistair cleared his throat nervously.

'I can't believe it. I'm *screwed*.' Charlie sprang up, nearly hitting his head on the sloping ceiling. 'Genocide – that was my failsafe! New Labour? I don't get it. I nailed that presentation!'

Alistair made a noise that said *Clearly you didn't*.

Charlie was too disturbed to argue. 'Oh my God. I'm going to get a two:two. No one will ever hire me.'

'I thought you wanted to be an entrepreneur.'

Charlie fixed Alistair with a stare that mingled hatred and desperation.

'Hang on. Don't panic. What mark . . . Are you going to get that?'

Charlie's phone was ringing with a number he didn't recognise. 'No. Yes.' His brain had frozen. 'Hello?'

'Is that Charlie Naughton?'

'Speaking.'

'Arthur Collins from Flagship Promotions. I'm calling to let you know that your application was successful. You have the opportunity to be part of the Flagship promotional team.'

'Ah.' Charlie had forgotten all about the application. Into the pause he added, 'Excellent.'

'We'd like you to be a Team Member for Stop and Search this Friday.'

'Stop and Search?'

Alistair eyed him warily, as though concerned he might have had a run-in with the police. *Right*, Charlie projected furiously, *who knows what a 2:2 candidate is capable of? Prick.*

'An exciting new scent. We're looking to build long-term relationships with promising individuals. Depending on performance, you could rise to Team Member Star and, if you show leadership potential, Team Innovator.'

'Okay.' Charlie's mind fast-tracked to Innovator and then jumped directly to running his own, better, version of the same company. He was sipping a latte in a spaceship-style meeting pod, while Fergus pleaded with him for a job.

'We'll convene in the Union at eight-thirty a.m. Be presentable.' Charlie held a finger up to Alistair, who was attempting to return to his essay. 'Black jeans or trousers, no flip-flops.'

'Sure – I mean, of course.' Charlie wanted to ask how much he would be paid, but it seemed rude somehow, the sort of thing that someone who didn't want it enough might say.

'See you then.' Arthur hung up.

'What a day.' Charlie released a pent-up breath. 'I've got a job! Just a small one – but something for the CV.'

Alistair tucked his chin, barely suppressing his disapproval.

'I know, I know, I've got to revise, but . . .' Charlie shook his head distractedly. 'I need experience more than ever now. Besides, if Social Tiger takes off, I won't need a two:one—'

'But you still *want* one. You said—'

'Of course I do. The thing is. . .' Charlie tried to figure out how he could explain it to Alistair. 'It's the way I work. If the world is riding on this one set of exams, it's too much, you know? I'm actually being strategic.'

'*Right.*' Alistair didn't seem to appreciate this peek at the back-stage machinery. But then, Charlie thought, Alistair had no vision; that had always been his problem.

'Don't worry. It's under control.'

'But why waste your time doing—'

'It's fine!' snapped Charlie. 'I can make my own decisions, okay?'

'Can you?' said Alistair sarcastically. 'Brilliant. Do that then.'

Alistair started scribbling at his stationery. Charlie rolled his eyes and looked back at the screen. The seventh page of Google echoed like the lost cavern of the damned. Charlie tried to think of a new search term, but agitated as he was, there was no chance of getting back to work.

'Screw this.' He slammed his laptop lid. 'I'm going to the ladz'.'

13

Will to Power

Every animal, Nietzsche argued, instinctively strives to feel as powerful as possible. 'What is good?' he asked. 'All that heightens the feeling of power, the will to power, power itself in man.'

Perhaps this is a good time to explain what happened with Nietzsche and the Nazis.

Nietzsche died in 1900, so he could never have been a Nazi in the historical sense, but his name is indelibly associated with the horrors of the Third Reich. The blame lies with his sister Elisabeth. She was the real Nazi in the family, a toxic anti-Semite with an obsessive love for her elder brother. Nietzsche despised her. But after his collapse in 1889, she was left with responsibility for his legacy.

Elisabeth took control of Nietzsche's works, rearranging them piece by piece and using them (as well as forged letters, altered to remove derisory references to her) to promote herself as their true heir and representative. It was Elisabeth's cut-and-paste version of his philosophy that appealed to the Nazis, who used it to give their regime intellectual credibility. Nietzsche's public and private writing makes it absolutely clear that he had no sympathy for Nazism – 'These accursed anti-Semite deformities shall not sully my ideal!!' he protested when he saw the use to which Elisabeth was putting his works, even in his lifetime. But in his insane state he was powerless to resist her twisted supervision. When Elisabeth died, in 1935, Hitler attended her funeral. On her instructions, Nietzsche's grave, which had been placed next to his mother and father's, was moved one space to the left, so she could occupy pride of place between her parents and her famous brother.

Nietzsche cannot be absolved of all responsibility for the way his works were interpreted. He set out to cause a stir. He enjoyed being seen as wicked. (Or rather, he *thought* he enjoyed being seen as wicked. Having thrown out the challenge, 'I am not a man, I am dynamite,' he was initially delighted to see a rare review of *Beyond Good and Evil* pick up on the phrase. Soon, however, he was worrying that 'danger' had been stressed too much and he would have 'all sorts of police' onto him.) He was a sucker for a nice turn of phrase and he went all out to grab his readers' attention. This, in a sense, was what happened with the will to power.

'Will to power' is one of those Nietzschean catchphrases which sounds distinctly fascistic, but means almost the exact opposite of what it appears to mean. The confusion is created by Nietzsche's use of 'will' and his use of 'power'.

When Nietzsche says 'will' what he means is 'instinct'. The phrase seems to imply a desire for power, a deliberate choice akin to political ambition. For Nietzsche, the opposite is true. We don't decide to pursue power. We have no choice – our instinct for power demands it.

Nietzsche's use of 'power' is equally perverse. Rather than the political sense of power over other people, he used 'power' to refer to a quality of personal strength. There was no need to exercise actual power to achieve this inner authority. If anything, that kind of striving revealed a needy desire for admiration, the exact opposite of the serene self-assurance Nietzsche hoped to exhibit: 'The desire to rule has often appeared to me a sign of weakness.' The will to power wasn't *being* powerful, but *feeling* powerful – in other words, feeling confident.

But Nietzsche used the phrase 'will to power' quite deliberately. He wanted to make the connection between confidence and power – a connection that is very often overlooked.

Part of the appeal of confidence is that it's apolitical. It's good for everyone, like sunshine. Your good feeling about yourself doesn't take away from mine – if anything it adds to it. So we don't tend to associate confidence with power, at least not directly. It's a feeling, we tell ourselves, not a nasty, cold fact.

But put it this way: when you're losing power, do you feel less or more confident? When you're being bullied, and someone is wielding power over you, do you grow or shrink in stature? When you're weak, do you wish you were weaker? When you *are* power-ful, how much easier is it to *feel* powerful?

As soon as Charlie arrived at the ladz', he realised he didn't want to be there. He hesitated before ringing the bell. Even though he'd only been up for five hours, he already felt drained. On the walk over, an insidious whisper had been growing in volume: *You could go round to Sara's.* Charlie longed to slip under her covers, close his eyes and make it all stop. But the torment of the last few days was too fresh in his mind. Sara wasn't a source of sympathy; she was something else he needed to be soothed about.

At least Ben would be around. Charlie's mood rallied at the thought of sitting on Ben's floor and dumping all of his troubles.

After a long wait, Bradder opened the door. 'Ben's gone home.'

Charlie felt strangely exposed. 'How did you know I was looking for Ben?'

'Weren't you?'

'No. Well, yeah, but—'

'So what's your point?'

Now Charlie felt he had go in, if only to prove to Bradder that Ben wasn't his only friend. Squeezing past the mounds of fetid sports gear in the hall, he wondered why Ben hadn't let him know he was leaving; he'd just abandoned him without warning. When you were going out with someone, Charlie reflected, friends seemed so dependable and fun and available. The second you were on your own, it became clear you couldn't expect dick from anyone.

In the living room, Race was revising with one eye on *The Weakest Link*. Lucas lay on his back on the floor throwing a mini-American football up in the air. The girls had gone back to their houses – you could tell somehow from the smell. The place had a vacant feel, like a café where the staff were stacking chairs and wiping surfaces around you.

Race ignored Charlie. 'There, was that so hard?'

'Next time you get it,' snapped Bradder.

'I'm bo-o-ored,' Lucas moaned. 'Charlie, entertain me.'

Charlie couldn't have felt less entertaining. 'I could tell you about my revision.'

'Bo-o-o-oring.'

With an evil grin, Race picked up a half-empty packet of Monster Munch. He held it out to Bradder and said deliberately, 'This is a finish.'

Bradder glared at him, but replied, 'A what?'

'A finish.'

'Ah, a finish.' Bradder snatched the pack. 'This' – he turned to Lucas – 'is a finish.'

'A what?' asked Lucas.

'A what?' Bradder turned back to Race.

'A finish,' Race informed Bradder gravely.

'A finish,' Bradder told Lucas.

'Aaaah.' Lucas cradled the pack in both hands. 'A finish!'

And so it went on. It was a drinking game that had been turned into an everything game. You made a chain of questions and everyone had to remember where they were, until someone fucked up and had to finish . . . it really could be anything. Charlie had seen bottles of chilli oil, mugs of lard, entire tubs of dry whey choked down (and in the case of the chilli oil, vomited back up) by unfortunate losers.

Charlie knew if the crisps came to him, he would lose. He simply couldn't focus: stray reflections on genocide and New Labour streaked across his brain. But although the game did turn his way once or twice, Race and Lucas were more interested in picking on Bradder. Weirdly, Bradder was actually some kind of maths genius, but he couldn't keep it up with Race trash-talking in his ear the whole time.

As soon as Bradder succumbed, Charlie took the opportunity to escape to Ben's room, taking out his phone as if he were off to make a call. As he left, he heard Lucas say, 'Bradder, when you're ready, *this* is a finish.'

Charlie headed up the stairs and down the corridor, pursued by rising finalist's fear. If he got 51 in New Labour, what did that mean he had to get in Political Economy of New Europe? Or worse, the Idea of Liberty: 70? Jesus. The nagging omni-sense that he should be revising and wasn't rose from a dull drone to an unpleasant squeal. Charlie calculated and recalculated the days until exams: ten, including weekends – nine, if you subtracted the day handing out flyers. He couldn't tell which was worse: the realisation that he shouldn't have taken that job, or the thought of Alistair's smug expression if he bailed on it.

Ben's room had the quiet air of grandparents' houses and days off from school. Long strips of dust blew across the fake wood lino.

Charlie wondered whether he should go home too. He could get on the train this afternoon, take his folders in a bin bag, and still be back in time for supper. His sister wouldn't be home and Mum and Dad would be at the factory during the day, so he'd have the place to himself. But the idea made Charlie feel even lonelier; trying to revise on his own, there'd be no escape from the thought that was looping his mind on Scalextric tracks – his future was drifting out of his reach and there didn't seem to be anything he could do to wrest it back.

Downstairs, Bradder was embarking on the fifth of a six-pack of apples. 'I'm not eating the cores,' he said mushily.

Lucas shook his head sadly. 'You're only cheating yourself.'

Charlie slumped onto the sofa. *The Weakest Link* was over and *Eggheads* just beginning. He knew he should leave, but couldn't face confronting his revision. As long as *Eggheads* was on, he could still claim to be taking a break.

'B-o-o-ored,' Lucas groaned.

'We need someone else to bully,' announced Race. 'Charlie, you'll do. Where's my lunch money?'

Charlie knew the answer to that one. 'I gave it to your mum last night as a tip.'

'See?' Race told Bradder. 'Even Charlie's funnier than you.'

'Even Charlie?' said Charlie.

'Don't get too pleased. It's not much of an honour being funnier than Bradder.'

Bradder finished his final apple and threw the core, hard, at Race. It splattered against the wall. 'There.' He stood unsteadily. 'That is a fucking finish.'

Lucas levered himself up. 'We'll need some adjudication on that. I'm not sure if it counts without the cores.'

'I am a massive lad.' Bradder puffed out his chest and trundled towards the kitchen.

186

'Hey, Bladder!' called Race.

Despite himself, Bradder looked back. 'What?'

'Shut the fuck up.'

Charlie snorted.

'*You* can shut up,' Bradder snapped at Charlie. 'Dickwad.' He stormed out, pulling a right hook past the doorframe.

'What did *I* do?' Charlie asked the room.

From the kitchen came sounds of pots clattering.

'Did he just say, "Mwa ha ha, I'll show them all"?' said Race.

'He's losing it,' agreed Lucas. 'Must be the 'roids.'

On TV, the challengers were putting up a decent fight against the Eggheads. Charlie wished one of the girls were here. Without them and Ben, the ladz just abused each other: that was 'banter'. If they could only give themselves a break and agree not to care about banter for ten minutes, Charlie thought, they would all be a lot happier.

Heavy steps clumped down the corridor, as Bradder returned. In the crook of his arm he held a ceramic jar of Stilton, like the one Aunt Margery gave Charlie's family at Christmas. 'This,' Bradder said, with a greedy grin, handing the jar to Race, 'is a finish.'

'Fuck off, Bradder,' said Lucas.

'I'm sorry? Is this or is this not a finish?'

Race's face read *You're a twat*, but he said, with a nonchalant air, 'A what?'

'Oh God,' muttered Charlie, wishing he could make a run for it. He took out his phone in a vain attempt to look busy. Quickly he texted Sara: 'U ok? Miss u.'

'A finish!' cried Bradder gleefully.

'Ah, a finish.' Race accepted the jar. 'This,' he said wearily to Lucas, 'is a finish.'

The damp cellar smell of Stilton wafted across the room.

'A what?' Lucas enquired.

'A what?' Race asked Bradder.

'A finish,' Bradder told Race.

'A finish,' Race told Lucas.

'This,' Lucas turned to Charlie. 'Is—'

'No, not a chance.' Charlie pushed the jar away. 'Count me out.'

'Come on, Charlie,' cajoled Lucas, smiling. 'What is it?'

'What is it, Charlie?' Bradder babytalked.

'Is it a bird?' Lucas waggled the jar under Charlie's nose. 'Is it a plane? Nyeeeaaooow. Come on, Charlie, why don't you want to play with us?'

Charlie shook his head. Lucas chucked him under the chin.

'Was that a little smile? Was that an ickle smile?' cooed Lucas. 'Is Charlie coming out to play?'

'This is the gayest thing I've ever seen,' said Race.

'Thi-i-i-i-is is a . . .' Lucas tickled Charlie's armpit. 'Finish!'

Charlie wriggled, breaking into laughter. 'A what?' he capitulated, rolling his eyes.

'Wahay!' Lucas raised his arms in victory. 'A what?'

'A what?'

'A what?'

'A finish.'

'A finish.'

'A finish.'

Charlie passed it on to Race, who was surveying the scene like a Victorian father at Christmas. Without Race harassing him, Bradder followed each move with furious attention. Lucas rolled around the floor, delighted by even this much distraction. The chain became ever longer and more complex, but Charlie kept track. If only, he thought, he had brought this sort of focus to his genocide essay. Was it now too late for his 2:1 ambitions? Could he turn it around if he really knuckled down to revision over the next nine days (nine days was ages, after all – people took holidays for nine days)? It might be tough, but Charlie wasn't one for undue negativity. A few inspired points about Italian politics could bring him right back on track.

'Charlie!'

'What?'

'Finish it!' Bradder jumped to his feet. 'It's a finish!'

The jar of Stilton was shoved into Charlie's hands. He looked up at Lucas, who shrugged as if to say, *You came here*.

'Bradder, where are your manners?' sighed Race. 'Get Charlie a spoon.'

Bradder skipped out to the kitchen, cackling to himself.

'I'm not going to have all of this,' Charlie muttered to Lucas.

'You certainly are.' Race looked down at his essay.

'Win some, lose some.' Lucas stared at the TV.

'The city of Palma is the capital of which island group?' read Jeremy Vine.

'For you!' Bradder stabbed the Stilton with the handle of a soup spoon.

Charlie plucked it gingerly from the sweaty white cheese, studying the blue-green veins and clumps of mould. Why had he been stupid enough to join in? Ordinarily he maintained a kind of dishonourable exemption from this torture. He knew the ladz wouldn't even acknowledge not-eating-the-cheese as a possible outcome of this situation. 'Finish' was unambiguous: they meant what they said, and they didn't care what pain it entailed. Not doing it would be some kind of shameful admission about himself. He'd have ruined the game – not this game, but the constant, behind-the-scenes, intimate, painful game that the ladz were always playing.

189

'I'm bored,' moaned Lucas, lying back down on the floor.

'Chop chop, Charlie,' said Race.

'Where does it even say you're expelled?' Nadine sat on the swing, a sheet of paper in each hand.

'It doesn't. That was just Rose – I don't think people even get expelled from uni.' Ellie squatted on the playground tarmac. 'It says I can't take my exams and as of today my access card has been revoked and I have to appear before the disciplinary committee and depending on their decision, which I'll receive in eight weeks, I may be able to sit them next year.'

'This is *ridiculous*,' said Nadine, not for the first time. 'And why's it only you?'

'It's to do with the group. It's my Facebook account. I instigated.'

'And what's this they're saying about how they've already given you a formal warning? Bullshit!'

'No, I got a letter before. Did I not tell you?'

'No.'

'Oh, right . . . Yeah.'

Nadine sighed. 'Eleanor Taber, what am I going to do with you?'

A pair of parents advanced on the swings, buggies like tanks, a red-faced, squealing toddler in the vanguard.

'Ugh,' murmured Nadine, as they picked their way over to a park bench. 'Do you want a cherry? I keep buying about a stone of them and giving myself the shits.'

'Sure, I need the strength.' Ellie put two in her mouth, puncturing the tight skin and working the flesh off with her tongue.

Nadine spat a stone towards a bin, pitching just short.

'But it wasn't actually me this time, right?' Ellie brushed a crisp packet off the bench and plonked herself down. 'So surely I can just write back or go and see them and explain that it wasn't me and they might revoke it.'

Nadine chewed her lip doubtfully.

'You don't think?'

'You could try. I mean, definitely try. Have you emailed your adviser?'

'She's on research leave. But I emailed the person it said to email while she's away. He's not got back to me yet. I mean, it was only an hour ago. The normal turnaround time is about three weeks.' Ellie picked at the cracked green paint on the bench, pressing the pips into the roof of her mouth. 'I mean, *surely,*' she slurred, 'if I just speak to the right person, someone who actually knows who I am . . .'

Nadine squinted at her with the same dubious expression.

'No, I know.' Ellie rubbed her eyes. 'I couldn't think of anyone either.'

'Did you call home?'

'Mm, not yet.' Ellie hadn't called home for some time now, nor had she seen her parents since Christmas. She wasn't sure why she was avoiding it. In many ways their relationship hung far more on being in the vicinity of one another than conversing. Since she'd turned twelve or so, Ellie had exercised what she thought of as benevolent deceit towards her parents. Who wanted to know, for example, that last night their thirteen-year-old drank straight vodka by the river at the bottom of the graveyard, then puked up, and then proceeded to kiss an unconventionally attractive fourteen-year-old by the war memorial? Ellie felt she owed it to her parents not to bother them with that sort of thing, not for fear of reprisal, but simply to avoid embarrassing them.

Sometimes this reverse paternalism could take odd turns. Take, for instance, cycling. Ellie had bought a bike when she came to uni (the gears had packed in this January and its repair had fallen victim to a combination of Justin's determined self-sufficiency and forget-fulness). 'I hope you're wearing a helmet,' both of her parents had said, repeatedly. Ellie didn't wear a helmet, because she couldn't be arsed carrying it around, but whenever her mum asked if she wore one, she'd reply (compensating for the lie with forcefulness), '*Of course* I do. I'm not an *idiot*.' The act went so far that when her parents visited last year, Ellie had borrowed one of Justin's house-mates' helmets and carted it around with her as a prop. When she couldn't even tell her own parents (who'd never beaten her or locked her in a cupboard or insisted she'd amount to nothing) that she didn't wear a cycling helmet, how was she going to explain that she'd jeopardised her entire degree by committing (admittedly ideologically fuelled) vandalism?

'The way I see it,' said Nadine, as they walked round and round the park perimeter, 'you got two options. One: submit yourself to the uni system, hoping to God that if you manage to talk to your stand-in adviser and people on the committee and explain what's happened, someone will make it all go away before exams.'

'Yeah, that's what I reckon. I'll just have to swallow my pride and talk to everyone. Like, find out their names, find out where their offices are, and then camp outside them with a book, and be super-remorseful—'

'*Or*.' Nadine offered the bag of cherries. 'Option two: attract as much attention as possible, at the risk of pissing uni off, hoping that public pressure will persuade them to rethink.'

'Terrifying.'

''Course, you could do a combination. Throw everything at it.'

Ellie looked at Nadine with fresh respect. 'You're good at this, do you know?'

'Focus, Ellie, focus.'

'So what would two involve?'

'Go to the uni paper – that's step one, obviously. Then maybe go to the local press? "Feminist Banned From Sitting Exams", "Punished for Legitimate Protest"? Whatever. Then—'

'Would I have to have my photo taken outside a university building, looking sad?'

'Definitely, yeah. Like, holding a folder and a pencil – desperate to learn, but barred from the temple of learning.'

'With the caption. "Eleanor Taber: Sad feminist".'

'"Eleanor Taber: Learning the hard way".'

Ellie spat a pip at a lamp post. 'Maybe I should quickly make a calendar to fund my legal fees.'

'Totally, that'll be your only choice. "May" will be, like, your breasts with a sad face painted onto them, and a speech bubble that says, "I have been silenced".'

'"December" will be *you* with curly grey muffs over your boobs, a Santa beard and a sack full of feminist classics.'

'"June" will be you, naked, in the committee room, with only the uni letter concealing your va-j-j.'

They laughed, until Nadine started choking on a cherry.

'Oh, shit.' Ellie wiped her eye. 'I hope this is going to be all right.'

'Me too.' Nadine sat up from her coughing fit and gave Ellie's arm a squeeze. 'I'm really sorry, I feel responsible.'

'Oh God, it's not your fault.'

They sat on a bench in silence, listening to the 'weeeeeeeee' of parents pushing swings.

'Do you know what's weird?' said Ellie.

'What?'

'I'm actually a lot happier when I've got something to push against. Adversity is simpler. Know what I mean?'

Nadine nodded. 'Like when people have "allergies" and then they're given some other bug and their "allergies" go away.'

'So I'm full of bullshit, is that what you're saying?'

'Meh.' Nadine waggled her hand. 'Fifty:fifty.'

Ellie laughed. 'I'd go sixty:forty. Hey, you don't think it's worth trying to find out who did it?'

'Hmm, not sure they're gonna wanna step into your shoes. But enough public attention might guilt-trip them into coming forward.'

'To be honest, I support their actions anyway. The calendar *is* sexist shit. They only did what we did.'

'Yeah, I know.' Nadine frowned. 'This is going to be a tricky message to get across.'

'Well. Suppose I better start hunting out the committee members. Can I borrow your uni card?'

'Sure. I'll check out *The Badger* and see who's the best person to ring.'

'Cheers. Please if they have to take a photo, can you be in it with me please?'

'All right, just . . .' Nadine looked Ellie up and down, tried to find a place to start, and settled for, 'Do yourself a favour and wash your hair.'

14

Selfishness

Confidence is selfish. For Nietzsche, who believed that people were innately self-interested, this was simply a statement of fact. He was a full-blown anti-altruist, the sort of person who thinks that selfishness explains everything, that even when we believe we are acting altruistically, we are in fact motivated by self-interest. We give gifts with an expectation of return. We tell ourselves we are being caring, when in reality we are making ourselves feel effective, or keeping the other person dependent on our kindness.

One thing about Nietzsche: he followed through on his arguments. Having announced that selfishness is inevitable, he went on to declare his support for this state of affairs, on the grounds that selfishness is better for your health. Feeling sorry for people drags you down: 'It has a depressive effect . . . One loses force when one pities.' (Like when you listen to someone's problems until you start to believe that, actually, life *is* hopeless, and really, there's no point in trying.) Our vain attempts to pretend we're less selfish than we are usually end up making life worse for everybody.

As so often, Nietzsche saw the root of the problem in Christianity, and its repressive regime of 'life-denying' instinct suppression. In Christianity, he said, 'man worships a part of himself as God and for that he needs to demonise the other part.' In his version of self-love, we would treat our nasty side with the same affection as our more presentable nice side, recognising good and bad as inextricably intertwined.

Far from encouraging unpleasantness, Nietzsche believed this robust self-acceptance would actually improve people's behaviour towards one another. In his work, we find the origin of the now widespread idea that when people are spiteful or mean, it's not because of any character fault, but because they're 'insecure'. Nietzsche believed that nastiness was really an expression of self-hatred, which was itself a reaction to one's own weakness. And it's true: when we feel under attack or 'defensive', we *are* less warm-spirited and open to others, more likely to snap or avoid listening. Nietzsche's answer was to embrace ourselves, good and bad, and in doing so, become more generous to others. 'The noble man,' he wrote, 'helps the unfortunate, not from pity, but rather from an urge produced by the abundance of power.' In Nietzsche's conception, there would be no charity for the sake of appearance; no one would ever say something they didn't mean, just to make someone else feel better. It's a vision of a dynamic but unforgiving world, in which some people flourish and others fall by the wayside.

In his later writings, Nietzsche softened his view on selfishness, rowing back from the claim that all actions are unavoidably self-interested. His ethical ideal was still selfishness, but an enlightened, creative selfishness: 'gift-giving', he called it, rather than the kind that 'is hollow and wants to be full'. His model for interaction was a dialogue where the participants satisfied each other by pursuing their individual desires. Like sex: 'the one person, by doing what pleases him, gives pleasure to another.' The heart of confidence was not selfishness, but self-expression.

But, of course, self-expression *is* selfish – it's just a bigger word for it, one that implies adventure and deep personal fulfilment. Our desires don't have to be nastily selfish, but they can't help being self-centred, if only because when we express our desires, we give them priority over other people's. Although, as Nietzsche observed, when it comes to our deepest desires, we don't really have a choice. When we are on the verge of self-expression, it feels like a compulsion: uncomfortable, exciting and overwhelming, all at the same time.

The air on the boat was cool and clammy. Ellie walked her fingers from under the unzipped sleeping bag and traced a pattern in the dark mould that speckled the wooden wall. The wood brought to mind some other, bigger, non-human time, making her present circumstances reassuringly tiny and meaningless in comparison. *If I don't sit my exams*, she thought, *trees will still grow.* Those were the sort of reflections you could have on the boat, on the water, where time moved at a different speed. Also, the weed. The weed helped.

Beside the narrow bunk, Oscar was hunched over a gas camping stove. Ellie watched him twist his sandy hair, making it stick up in long, greasy clumps. He bit the end of his tongue as he stared at the water, now beginning to foam almost imperceptibly at the edges. Wearing nothing, Oscar stood to almost full height – living on the boat was giving him a slight stoop – and took two packs of instant noodles from a shelf. He crouched back down, ripping the flimsy wrapping.

It wasn't exactly comfortable, being at Oscar's. (But then, was there ever a casual sexual encounter that didn't feel awkward?) Oscar wasn't one for small talk, and whenever they spoke about politics or the environment or some other important thing, Ellie found herself worrying obscurely about putting an ideological foot in it. Instead, she preferred to settle into the silence, to enjoy being around Oscar the way one might enjoy being around a horse or a garden. In many ways, sex was the simplest part of whatever was going on. In the moments when she'd climbed off the barely lit canal path and onto the boat, it was completely clear what they were meant to be doing and why.

'You have a boyfriend, right?'

A steaming plateful of instant noodles was right next to her ear. Ellie craned round and stared at it for a moment, before slowly twisting over onto her side.

'Um . . .' She took the plate. 'Yeah.'

'Okay, cool. Thought you did.' Looking completely relaxed, Oscar passed her a bottle of soy sauce.

Ellie sat up and shook the bottle ponderously, listening to it sloshing around. 'Is that . . . okay?'

'Yeah.' He grinned quizzically, joining her to sit cross-legged on the bed. 'Course. Because you're in charge of yourself.'

'Right,' Ellie nodded, feeling slightly stupid. She blew on her plate and looked at Oscar through the steam. 'Just while I'm checking though, how do you feel about me coming round here? Because, you know, if it's an inconvenience . . .'

Oscar grinned, as though she were joking, and sucked up some noodles.

'For God's sake slow down!' shouted somebody on the path outside. 'People have to *walk* here!'

Ellie felt as if the conversation had died prematurely. 'You don't really believe in that, do you? Boyfriends. Relationships.' *Talking*, she added, mentally.

'You seem a bit unsure yourself,' he replied amenably.

'Well . . .'

They chewed for a while. A cyclist shot by, bell pinging.

'Nobody wants to die alone, I suppose,' she shrugged. 'And *don't* say we all die alone.'

Another few seconds of silence passed.

'No, you're right.' He nodded earnestly. 'We definitely don't all die alone.'

She smiled. 'You're annoying.'

They finished their noodles. Then they had sex.

About twenty minutes later, at midday, Ellie was on the canal path, wondering how long it would take to get from here to normality. It was surprisingly hot, and she was dressed for last night in hoodie and jeans. She drifted along the canal towards the park, unable to decide where to go next. After a few minutes she gave up and sat by a tree in the shade, watching the leaves jostle sleepily in the breeze.

What am I doing? she wondered. It was a treacherous question, but she felt strangely calm about it – if anything, she was quite curious to know what would happen next. Looking back, Ellie could see that she'd been quietly preparing for this whatever-it-was: she'd started back on the pill (they'd told her to wait seven days, but they probably tripled the time frame just to shit you up), she'd stayed a night at Nadine's in order to normalise being away, she'd gone to the big Sainsbury's near the canal where they sold the kind of Greek yoghurt she liked – the yoghurt, she remembered, that was sitting by Oscar's sink.

Feeling thirsty, Ellie pushed herself up and texted Nadine to ask if she could have stayed at hers last night.

'cd have,' Nadine returned. 'U dirty stop out.'

Ellie got up and rubbed the fine dirt from her back and legs. She decided to walk back to hers along the canal path – she'd never done it before, but there was a path that passed under a bridge only a few streets behind the flat, and she was sure it connected to this towpath. In fact she was certain of it.

Setting out, Ellie was immediately enlivened – she shivered with a feeling akin to happiness and excitement, but with no direction or object: a rush of sentience that was about nothing more than finding herself alive.

It was amazingly hot. She tied her hoodie round her waist. Her long-sleeved top was clinging unpleasantly to her sweaty skin. Rolling up her sleeves, she looked longingly at the canal; the water was green-tea-coloured, pearlescent and barely moving. Still, she wished she could throw herself into it, or lean back from the bank and let her hair fall into the cool liquid. Whenever she tried to think about things (Justin, exams, being a bad person), the thoughts weren't compelling enough to distract her more than momentarily from being hot and thirsty. Aside from those two problems, in fact, she was light, elated – if someone gave her a glass of water right now, she was sure she could die not only happy, but ecstatic.

As she walked, she thought about walking. It was a strange mode of locomotion, both awkward and flowing. Who was it who said that each step was allowing yourself to fall for a moment? It was strange what Nietzsche had done to walking; he'd reframed it as an intellectual pastime instead of a physical one. And didn't Rousseau write something about a walker too? Perhaps they were trying to figure out the relationship between philosophy and the everyday. She'd write that in an exam if she got the chance – if her notes on office doors, and trail of emails, and embarrassing newspaper interviews took effect. In this moment, for no reason, she had a superstitious sense the universe would help her out.

Ellie passed warehouses and mesh fences and houseboats strung with faded bunting, but the familiar bridge didn't materialise. Her phone rang with an unknown number. By the time she'd decided to pick up, she only had time to say 'Hello' before the battery died.

Finally, Ellie sat down on the bank, wondering if she should ask for directions, and if so, who to ask. She was out of the town centre now – she must have been walking more than an hour, maybe two – and there was nobody around. After brief consideration, Ellie lay down, flat on her back in the middle of the towpath. Bathing in the sunlight, she luxuriated in this glorious moment of not giving a fuck. There was nothing she had to do. She was doing this, and it was fine, wonderful even. The baked concrete and sun's heat lifted and dissolved her. She might have fallen asleep.

'Ellie,' someone said.

She squinted up to see a scrawny shadow peering over her.

'Oh. Mattie,' she said. 'Hi. What are you up to?'

'Picking wild garlic.' He waved a reusable bag. Mattie was wearing a collarless shirt, shorts and those shoes with moulded toes used by renegades for running from the man. 'What about you?'

'I'm out for a walk. You don't happen to know where we are, do you?'

Ellie arrived back at hers with an exhausted Mattie, who had heroically insisted on giving her a backie all the way up the hill. Justin and Rose were on the sofa, watching one of Rose's food-porn programmes: mountains of gleaming pasta set among luscious rivers of creamy sauce.

'She's not got you roped into this,' Ellie greeted them. They looked like the kind of domestic scene you saw on adverts: cups of tea on the coffee table, Rose's legs extending across Justin's lap, Justin yawning and dopily rubbing his eyes.

'Home at last.' He turned and saw Mattie. 'Ah, hello stranger!'

'What time do you call this?' demanded Rose. 'Your beau and I were about to send out the search party. You may have your picture in the uni paper, miss, but that doesn't mean you can treat this place like a hotel.'

Mattie held up his bag like a shield. 'Wild garlic.'

'Have you two been running?' Rose frowned, ever on the alert for other people's calorie consumption.

'Just a walk. It's *so* hot!' Ellie walked straight to the bathroom, opened the shower door and knelt down, black spots clouding her vision. A European-style charger was plugged into the shaver socket. Ellie turned her phone on and let the message play on loudspeaker, half listening as she stripped off her sweat-damp clothes.

'. . . Gareth Walker, Producer . . . breakfast show . . . picked up your story in the local paper . . . *love* you to come in for an interview with . . .'

Ellie got in, suppressing a gasp. The water felt incredible – she could feel her skin expanding like a dehydrated berry. She opened her mouth and drank.

'Can I come in?' Justin called, after a minute. He opened the bathroom door, slipped inside, and pressed his palm flat against the shower wall. 'Hello. I feel like I've not seen you in *ages.*'

'I know. I'm sorry.' She pushed her palm against his. 'How are you?'

'All ri–i–i–i–ight.' He circled his eyes.

'You been working?'

'We–e–e–ll . . .'

'Is Rose driving you crazy?'

'Oh, no, she's okay. I think she's keeping me sane to be honest – worryingly. But never mind about Rose.' He clapped his hands. 'What . . . are you doing tonight?'

Ellie considered. 'Nothing.' It was true. 'Nothing at all.'

'Well then, if you don't mind, I have decided to cook for you.'

'Have you?' Ellie gurgled, swallowing some more water. 'You don't need to work?'

'No, I need to see you. You need to talk to me about everything that's going on. I mean, apart from what I've read in *The Badger*. And more importantly, we both need to relax and have a night that doesn't feel like a state of emergency.'

Ellie pushed her hair back, reality creeping back in with the cold. It wasn't such a bad reality. Justin opened the shower door and kissed her cheek. 'Okay?'

'Okay,' she nodded, smiling.

'Who was on the phone?'

'I think it might be someone from the radio.'

His eyebrows shot up. 'Oh my God, you better call them back.'

'Yeah, I will.' He was getting wet. Drops of water spattered his T-shirt and pinpricked his hairy arms. 'Justin.'

'Yeah?'

'You're very nice, do you know that?'

'Oh really?' he beamed. 'Good.'

Charlie's marketing debut started with some unpleasant surprises. First, he had to wear a neon blue T-shirt with 'Stop and Search' scrawled across the front and 'Detain me' on the back, in graffiti font. Charlie had the dim sense that this might be offensive. The outfit was topped off by a flimsy matching baseball cap, which – Arthur had insisted – was to be worn with the brim completely flat, in a manner you basically had to be Jay-Z to pull off. (Arthur was so straight he didn't even understand the brand aesthetic.)

Second, Charlie wasn't out on the high street approaching strangers; he was in Library Square, where Arthur had instructed him to 'use his existing networks'. Charlie had thought he'd escape uni people for a day; instead, those very people had become his target demographic.

Being a Stop and Search Brand Ambassador was even more pointless than he'd envisioned. Charlie was essentially face-to-face spamming, handing out sample sticks (which looked remarkably like applicator tampons) of a scent he had privately christened 'Lynx Funeral' in return for email addresses. Charlie didn't even have USBs to offer: he had nothing to sell but himself.

Two girls in headscarves passed by the stall, sipping on ice pops.

'Can I interest you in an exciting new scent?' Charlie sprang towards them. Their eyes glazed over; benign but implacable, they padded past.

'You'd think we were trying to mace people, not give them free perfume,' commented Ginger Jacob. Jacob was Charlie's 'buddy' for the day – according to Arthur, they were supposed to buoy each other up when the going got tough, and offer honest, constructive feedback on interpersonal style. Charlie had been horrified to discover that Jacob was in first year. It made him feel suddenly ancient – Jacob was already racing ahead of him, getting experience he hadn't even known he needed back then. Charlie felt like one of those sad thirty-year-olds starting out on a new career because they'd cocked up the first one.

He tried to emit what Arthur called 'selling energy' as a group of second years approached. 'How about some useless plastic in return for your email address? You can use a fake one.'

A skinny hipster type laughed – but somehow the joke was on Charlie even though he'd been the one to make it.

'It's kind of like being homeless, isn't it?' remarked Jacob, as another swathe of revisers filed past. 'It's true what they say – the worst part is being ignored. When *I* see a beggar, I look them straight in the eye and say, "Sorry mate, no change." That's because

I'm saving my change for the fruit machine. But how much better do they feel having had that bit of human contact?'

'Oh, no, not them,' groaned Charlie, as Penny and Meredith wafted into the Square. Penny stopped to unwrap her sandwich, carefully pull out tomatoes and drop them one by one into the bin.

'What's wrong with them?'

'They're my ex's lynch mob.'

Behind them came Tom Race, swaggering towards the law faculty. Charlie quickly looked away. The cheese-finishing incident ('Stiltongate', Charlie would have called it, if the whole thing didn't make him feel so awful) had ended with Charlie refusing to go on – not because he didn't want to, but because he simply couldn't handle it. 'Pussy,' Bradder had spat delightedly, shortly before Charlie trudged out of the house. Race had rolled his eyes as if to say, *You've only just noticed?*

Afterwards, back at home and in bed in the middle of the afternoon, Charlie was forced to admit to himself he'd been nursing a secret hope that he wasn't just 'Ben's mate'; that he too might enter into the ladz' post-shame bond. Well, it wasn't to be. As it turned out, all the shame would be Charlie's, seeing as nobody else was using theirs.

With a regal smirk, Race passed by, as if the path was his personal red carpet and Charlie the second under-butler.

'How's progress here?' Without warning, Arthur was upon them, clocking the pitiful list of emails and stacks of remaining flyers.

'Um . . .' Charlie did his best to muster a self-motivated air. 'We were just saying, it's difficult to distract people from revision, so—'

'Distract students from revision? You can do better than that. Look. How about I watch and give you some feedback?'

Arthur gestured for Charlie to take the floor, while he cupped his chin in a parody of observation. Charlie assessed his options.

There was an Amnesty International stand, two first-year girls sitting on the wall (one of whom seemed to be crying) and – Charlie's heart sank – Penny and Meredith.

'Hi, guys, how's it going?' he opened, attempting to usher them out of Arthur's immediate radius.

Meredith looked at him in open hostility. 'What is this – racial drag?'

'Hi Charlie,' smiled Penny, flashing her eyes as if she'd finally found somebody who could truly understand her (God, she gave Charlie the creeps). 'I'm good, fine, well, you know, *terrible*, but . . .'

'Oh, tell me about it,' he parroted, as Arthur sidestepped over and lingered at an awkward distance. 'Revision's a nightmare.'

'No, it's my house – we've got *rats*.' She pulled a disgusted face. 'So I'm taking refuge at Sara and Meredith's. I'm actually sleeping in Sara's bed with her!' Penny smiled, as though Charlie would be especially tickled by this snippet.

'Ah,' said Charlie. Judging by Meredith's expression, she was finding this conversational tack as weird as he was. 'Well, what I wanted to ask . . .' He tried to ignore a new and insistent gnawing in his gut. Surely he couldn't be jealous of *Penny*? That was absurd. Arthur had edged closer and was hovering behind Charlie's shoulder. 'I wanted to ask—'

'The only problem is we keep distracting each other from working. I should be doing ten hours a day by now. But you know what it's like – Fergus suggests a tea break, then it's a beer break and . . .' Penny rolled her eyes at herself, like, *My problem is that when the party starts, I just can't help being the life and soul.*

Charlie didn't even feel strong enough to defend himself against Penny's usual guff. He loathed himself for being bothered by her. 'Right, well.' Behind Charlie, Arthur cleared his throat and made a note on his BlackBerry. 'I'm actually promoting a new scent today. Would you like to try a sample and sign our mailing list?'

Meredith was already moving towards the library. 'No.'

'I suppose I could.' Penny looked after her distractedly.

'Great, thanks!' Charlie handed Penny the clipboard and offered to hold her sandwich. Feeling he ought to do more, he used his teeth to pull off the lid from a plastic stick and wafted it in Penny's direction. Painfully, he managed to squeeze out, 'It's a fresh scent.'

'There. Will that do?' Penny handed back the clipboard, ignoring the stick. In loopy handwriting, she'd printed 'pennyandsara@ hotmail.com'. Charlie stared at the paper, momentarily stupefied.

'Nice to see you, Charlie.' Taking her sandwich, Penny weaved towards the library's automatic doors.

The last remains of a brittle smile fell from Charlie's eyes. His head dropped back and he stared up at the cloud-streaked sky. 'Take me away,' he thought. '*Please* just take me away.'

'Take away what?' boomed Arthur. 'Right. Feedback from me. Feedback from your buddy. Self feedback. Then we'll go again. Ready?'

15

Greatness

Nietzsche detested the notion of 'well-being', because it implied an affinity between confidence and happiness. For him, even if such an affinity existed, it should not be condoned or in any way encouraged. His philosophy aimed not at happiness or content-ment, but at great deeds and glorious achievements.

For Nietzsche, all that was bad about well-being could be summed up by the phrase '*English* happiness'. England was the birthplace of utilitarianism, the philosophy which measured the accomplish-ment of a society by how successfully it achieved the greatest happiness for the greatest number – as if, sneered Nietzsche, human achievement could be measured by an *average*. Greatness for him was defined by its highest peaks, not by its lowest common denom-inator. Besides, going in search of greatness often *involved* unhappiness, since without being hard on yourself, how could you ever hope to attain true excellence?

As ever, Nietzsche was speaking from personal experience. No stranger to self-discipline, he learnt as a schoolboy to immerse his foot in a bowl of freezing water to keep himself awake while study-ing. (His attack on self-denial stemmed from intimate knowledge of the ascetic temperament.) As an adult, he suffered from terrible migraines, yet even these, he believed, were an aid to creativity, as he claimed in *Ecce Homo*: 'In the midst of the agony of a headache which lasted three days, accompanied by violent nausea, I was possessed of a most singular dialectical clearness, and in absolutely cold blood I then thought through matters, for which, in my healthier moments, I am not enough of a climber, not sufficiently supple, not sufficiently cold.'

Nietzsche's commitment to self-discipline even led him to praise Christianity. It might be a 'curse', a 'depravity', but by making us hate ourselves, it gave us the incentive to strive for something bigger. Nietzsche praised Christian architecture for its depth and meaning; it 'referred to a higher order of things', unlike modern architecture, which simply aspired to look good. Christianity agitated; it poked and prodded. In its absence, Nietzsche feared, we would retreat into apathy and passivity. 'Are we not,' he fretted, 'with this tremendous objective of obliterating all the sharp edges of life, well on the way to turning mankind into *sand*?'

In this complaint there is a note of anxiety not usually found in Nietzsche's works. The worry stemmed from the close link between confidence and a dangerously easy-going sense of security. What if this was the flaw in his project? What if, instead of committing people to an endless quest for self-improvement, confidence became a source of complacency, even laziness?

Nietzsche presented this possibility as a very real threat, declaring in *Thus Spoke Zarathustra* that it was 'the greatest danger to the whole human future'. But when Zarathustra, Nietzsche's mouthpiece in that tale, warns a crowd waiting in a market square that they need to stop being happy and recover their contempt for themselves, instead of listening raptly, the people laugh at him. Of course they do. Why wouldn't they want to be happy? The very notion seems ridiculous.

Now that we live in a culture obsessed with confidence, has Nietzsche's vision of complacency come to pass? Strangely, it has not. Confidence has become a far more significant factor in people's lives, but that has not encouraged people to sit back and feel good about themselves. Instead, both confidence *and* well-being are valued as aids to productivity.

Take mindfulness: intended to bring inner peace, but popularised by apps that deliver it in minutes, like a double espresso for the soul, and cited by Silicon Valley entrepreneurs as an essential pick-me-up in their world-conquering schedules. Nietzsche feared life would become easy and placid, and people would work 'only as a pastime'. Instead, the line between work and leisure has blurred in work's favour, and the pressure to perform has crept into every area of life. Far from being eliminated, change is now a requirement: it's so all-encompassing, the only option is to be 'good in change'. Nietzsche complained that people were turning to sand; we, his descendants, live on shifting sand.

The alternately husky and booming voices of Jemima and Dave played out into the waiting room. Every few minutes, the same thirty-second montage of Jemima's throaty laugh and Dave's stock phrases ('You don't have to be crazy – but it helps!') cycled by. Now they were chatting Prince Philip's Gaffe of the Week, next up was The Biscuit You Couldn't Live Without – it was that sort of local breakfast show.

It was 7.20 a.m. and Ellie and Nadine were scheduled for 7.30. They'd been picked up in a taxi at 6.30, by which time Ellie had already come close to vomiting with nerves. 'It's like, I feel fine in my head,' Ellie told Rose, who had got up to wave them off. 'But my body—'

'Your body, your body's telling you no?' Rose had grinned.

'What it's telling me can only be expressed in expletives.'

Now Ellie was feeling it in her jaw, as if her back teeth had been clamped together. The waiting room was a shabby, windowless box with a water cooler and a few magazines. She picked one up and stared at it uncomprehendingly.

'You sleep?' Nadine asked.

'Not at all. Did you?'

'A tiny bit. I had the exam dream.'

'Oh yeah.'

'I'm at school, always, and late and I try and get a taxi, and then things get all David Lynch.'

'I was basically just lying in bed talking to myself. I don't think I've felt this nervous since A-Levels. Or maybe my Grade Five Trumpet.'

'You practised again, yeah?'

Ellie nodded numbly. 'I got Justin to listen to me.'

'What the pros reckon is: say one thing, one thing only, and keep repeating it. Like with a magazine, you know the big quotes embedded in the article that people see first? You wanna plan what those are in advance.' Nadine had been a godsend at the *Badger* interview, stepping in and summarising Ellie's waffling at the end of each answer. 'Wanna practise now?'

'No, I'll jinx it. Are *you* nervous?'

'Mainly tired.'

'I still can't believe they're letting us on the radio. We could say anything for God's sake. It's ridiculous, really.'

'Oooooh, I *love* a Mint Club!' Dave growled passionately. 'And so does Gabe on his way to work. I'm with you all the way, Gabe!'

'I want to step in and speak up,' husked Jemima. 'For the humble Digestive.'

'Digestive?! You're having a laugh!'

'Okay, ladies, are we ready?' Gareth, a skinny, tanned producer, sprang into the waiting room. 'It's about that time. How are you feeling?'

'Yeah, yeah.' Ellie shivered.

'Can we leave our stuff?' said Nadine.

'Oh, totally. Just leave it there. Becky sees everyone that comes in and out.' He held the door open, sparkling with what seemed to be genuine enthusiasm. 'Here we go!'

They shuffled out, exchanging a wide-eyed look.

'Now you get the whole backstage tour!' Gareth led the way down the uncarpeted stairs and along a bunker-like corridor. '"Glamorous", eh?'

'Huh,' Ellie tried a polite laugh.

They turned into a small, cramped room, with a glass wall. Beyond it were a reassuringly scruffy Jemima and Dave, who gave a cheery wave.

'So you're going to head in in one minute, okay? Do you need any water?'

They shook their heads. Ellie turned and gave Nadine an undoubtedly mad-looking smile.

'Oh God,' said Nadine, through her nose.

'I know. Why did we agree to this?'

'Okay, you're going to head in with this jingle.' Gareth seized the door handle. 'Knock 'em dead, ladies! You'll be great!'

They stepped into the soft, brightly lit cupboard, taking their places at one side of a wooden table.

'Welcome to the madhouse!' Dave boomed.

'Don't mind him!' Jemima gave a crinkly grin.

Gareth helped them into their headphones, and they gathered round a single mic. Ellie stared at the table, jaw clenched as though it were the vital pin preventing her body from exploding.

'We've been joined by two local students this morning,' Dave teed off. 'Sorry to wake you so early, girls! Or I say two students, but one of them's been banned from sitting her exams, is that right, Eleanor?'

'Yes, that's right,' said Ellie brightly.

'What have you done?'

'Well, I began a protest about sexism on campus, along with my friend Nadine here.'

Ellie looked at Nadine, who waited a fraction too long to speak. 'Hi—'

'Sexism on campus?' Jemima dived in. 'Are girls getting worse marks than boys?'

'No, actually, this was about the way that girls are represented. It was a protest against objectification and casual sexism, sparked by a poster for a uni event featuring an FHM-style picture of a girl in a g-string. We saw it and thought, "We're sick of that kind of tedious sexism."'

'Feel like we've time-travelled back to the Seventies here,' said Jemima. 'Hasn't this all been said before?'

'Yes, you're totally right,' replied Ellie. 'It's a good question. Given that we're in this age of supposed equality and girls can do anything they want, why is it that in our universities, the way a lot of students represent and talk about women feels like we've stepped back in time? How has that happened? This campaign was about drawing attention to that fact, and telling people that they don't have to accept it.'

'I mean, I didn't go to university,' shrugged Jemima. 'But when I first started in radio there were a lot of, shall we say, "blue" jokes around backstage. At the end of the day, though, it was harmless. Is there a danger you're taking it all a bit too seriously?'

'Well, I think that's part of the trap.' Ellie met Jemima's gaze. 'It's ironic, it's a big joke, and so we're supposed to be cool about it. In fact, if we're not cool about it, we're joyless and we hate fun or we hate sex. But actually we don't.'

'We-e-ell,' Dave guffawed. 'Who does?'

'Steady on, Dave!' hammed Jemima.

'And why should we be cool about it? At what point does this stop being a joke and start being the standard way of talking and thinking about women? I don't want to live and study in a place where we're supposed to accept that. I want to feel like our generation is moving forward, not backward.'

'So tell us what you did,' said Dave.

'We put slogans on posters that we thought perpetuated this attitude. Slogans like "At Uni I Learned My Body Was My Only Asset"—'

'"Women Have Pubes",' Nadine chipped in.

Dave reeled. 'Bit early for that!'

'And the campaign got a *lot* of support,' Ellie pressed on.

'Though haven't you been criticised by other girls at your university?' Jemima looked at her notes. 'I understand some think you're not respecting their choices.'

'Well.' Ellie took a breath. 'Everybody has free choice. I'm not trying to tell other women what to do. But I do take issue with a kind of diluted, commercial version of feminism, which tells people: feeling good about yourself, that's feminism. Or having great hair, that's being strong. Proponents of that kind of "strong hair" feminism tend to react badly whenever anyone brings up anything vaguely political. Because it's not very feel-good. I'm not saying I want people to feel bad or have bad hair, I'm just saying we can get sucked into the idea that what really matters is an individual sense of being on top, which very often boils down to being attractive. I don't want to be told that the only way I can be powerful is to be sexy. I can be sexy on my own time – or not, you know. The point is: that isn't all that we're here to do. Especially at uni.'

'So stickers on posters – that's why you've been banned from exams?'

'A display case got scratched—'

'Now it's coming out!'

'But basically yes. Because of a legitimate protest, I'm now not allowed to sit my exams. And—'

'So you— Sorry, go on.'

'The actual piece of "vandalism" that got me banned – it happens that I didn't do it, and I don't know who did. Though naturally, I agree with their point.'

'But what do you say to people' – Dave got investigative, leaning back in his chair – 'who say, "You broke the law. You did the crime, you should do the time"?'

'I suppose I'd say . . . Isn't university supposed to teach you to think for yourself and stand up for what you believe in? If so, it's succeeded. We're doing it.'

'Well, what do *you* think?' Jemima took it out to the slumbering dozens. 'Does this make you want to burn your bra in support or roll your eyes and go back to sleep? And what about your desert island biscuit? You've got five more minutes to decide.'

'If it's not a Mint Club, I'm staging a walkout.'

The jingle cranked up.

'Lovely, girls!' Jemima was already turning to Gareth. 'Who's up next?'

'Next it's the charity fashion show, I've got Becky bringing the Dogs' Hospice . . .' He read his clipboard. 'Event Coordinator, Keisha. Coming up now.'

'Thanks!' Ellie stood up suddenly, her head surprisingly light. She took Nadine's hand and led her out of the glass bubble, giving a final smile and wave to Dave and Jemima. Dave was massaging his eyeballs, while Gareth checked if Jemima had anything in her teeth.

The corridor was dark and dreamlike. Nadine shook her head, smiling to herself.

'Well done! They're lovely, aren't they?' Gareth ushered them up the stairs. 'And you're okay to find your way back yourselves?'

'Yeah, fine.' Ellie nodded, with no real notion of where they were.

'I'll leave you here then, ladies. Have a great day!' He skipped away.

When they reached the waiting room, Nadine thumped herself down on a chair. 'Oh my God. I just went on the radio and managed to say nothing at all!'

'Oh sorry, was I hogging it?'

'No—'

'You didn't say nothing, did you?'

'It's worse than that.' Nadine stared at the water cooler in disbelief. 'The only thing I said was "Women have pubes"!'

'Oh no!' laughed Ellie. 'I mean, that *is* very important.' She pulled Nadine up and grabbed their bags. 'Plus you're the brain of this outfit. You engineered this whole thing. I'd never have been able to do that if I hadn't heard you with the *Badger* guy. Honestly. I'd have been screwed.'

They pushed out of the heavy door and into a shockingly sunny morning. It felt like tumbling from a club at dawn, bleary-eyed and aching.

'You did ace.' Nadine looked around. They seemed to be somewhere near the bypass. A steep grassy slope led down to a major road. 'It was a fully sane performance.'

'Thanks. I can't believe that's it.'

'I know.'

'I mean, that's *it*. It's, what, seven-forty? We spent all yesterday preparing and it lasted about *one* minute!'

'I know. And the only thing I said was, "Women have pubes".'

'How many people do you think heard it?'

'No idea. Rose, Justin, Maggie – that's three.'

'And now today's ruined. It's a write-off.'

'I know. Shall we try walking along the hard shoulder?'

'I'm knackered *and* completely hyper. The only thing I'm fit for is the multiplex.'

'I need to get shitfaced after that,' said Nadine. 'From now on, my anxiety dreams are going to be about *that* experience.'

'And I know I should revise—'

Nadine groaned, as they sidestepped down the slope.

'But how can I, knowing I might not have to sit my exams? It's the worst thing ever, but it's also this massive get out of jail free card. You know when you're going to an exam and you think, "I could not go. I could just run away"?'

'Yeah.'

'Well, that's happened. But it's someone else saying, "We won't let you go."'

'I'm almost jealous. Where shall we go? Seriously, I can't go to the library, I'll do something drastic.'

'Rose opens the Shackle at eleven. We could try and walk there and then sit outside.'

'A lockout?'

'Exactly.'

'Charlie', Taz's email began. No 'Dear', no 'Hi', not even a comma at the end: the epistolary equivalent of a slap in the face.

'Pitch. Tomorrow 9am. ETA on:

1) pitch?
2) market research?

TW?'

'Who waits till the night before to send this?' Charlie fumed at Alistair. 'Where's the, like, friendly, timely reminder? The "Shit, mate, this is coming up, have you realised?" We're meant to be business partners here – business *partners*. I'm not his *slave.*'

'Yeah, how unreasonable,' Alistair replied sarcastically, as he took down the blue bowl he'd been using for every meal since May. 'You've only known about it for a month.'

'Could you give the "disappointed dad" shit a rest?' In revenge, Charlie swiped one of Alistair's beers from the fridge (he never drank them anyway). 'At least I'm *doing* something, instead of sniping from the sidelines.'

'Wow, what are you taking on next?' said Alistair. 'World peace?'

'Fuck off.'

Alistair carefully stirred his baked beans.

In the silence, Charlie eyed him hopefully. 'What are you doing tonight?'

Alistair gave a heroic sigh. 'I suppose I'm helping you with this pitch.'

'Really?' Charlie brightened. 'Awesome!'

'No, you fucking dick, of course not really! I'm revising for the exam I'm sitting in *four days.*'

'Right.' Charlie thudded out of the kitchen. 'Cheers, *mate.*'

Everybody was letting him down.

The night that followed was relentless. Charlie delved blindly into the internet in an endurance form of digital apple ducking. A list of his search terms between 9 p.m. and 7 a.m. would have read something like: business parter, business partner, business partner relationship, business partner contract, business partner verbal contract, business partner betrayal, business partner betrayal facebook, fantasyfootball, market research, market research students, market research students free, stats students, stats student spending, who invented pie chart?, fantastfootb, pitch how to, pitch template free, pitch top ten, pitch video, Dragon's Den top ten, worst Dragon's Den, top rejections Dragon Den, wheelbarrow, wheelbarrow accessories, fantasyfoo, student spending Powerpoint, student spending Powerpoint free, student loan, how much student loan, student loan how much year, moneysupermarket student loan investment, student stock market investment loan legal?, student number, how many student Uk, ingrown hairs infected?, ingrown hairs scratch, ingrown hairs symptom of other, scratching ingrown hairs?, ingrown hairs shaving, beard, top ten beard, nhs direct, folliculistus, keratosis pilaris, molluscum contagiosum, howmanywords 5 mins, howmanywords 5 mins fast talker, how talk slower, student images, student image free, business plan, what is business plan?, top ten business plan free, logo, logo design, logo top ten, logo free, fantasyfo, student money video, student spending video, how rip YouTube, rip YouTube free, edit software free, how split audio video, insert video PowerPoint, how stop PowerPoint put everything in Calibri?, PowerPoint template, PowerPoint crash when save, PowerPoint keep crashing, why people dicks on PowerPoint forums, Mark Zuckerb, how many dollars in £, entrepreneur, entrepreneur advice, seed-funding, seed-funding how to, entrepreneur personality, are priests celibate?, Myers-Briggs, Myers-Briggs extrovert, Myers-Briggs extrovert entrepreneur, best Myers-Briggs type entrepreneur, laptop fan loud, how stop laptop fan loud, how long Toshiba?, fat cheese, cheese protein, best protein, whey, whey makes sick, whey alternatives, break up fat, break up, break up advice, top ten break up, Jennifer Aniston break up, Jennifer Aniston John Mayer reason break up, Friends highlights, Gunther actor, baldness, baldness early onset, average number relationship, average number people sex, average number people sex 21, average number people sex uni, faceb, asos men swimwe, Hugo Boss Tuna Swim Shorts Black small, Hugo Boss Tuna Swim Shorts Black small sale, natwest, sperm count, sperm count how do you know, sperm count should worry?, iPlayer, piratebay, True Blood seeson 2, True Blood season 2 torrent, youporn, cuckold, cuckold amateur, cuckold amateur compilation, girlsgonewild, girlsgonewild compilation, what to do when graduate, how many coffee, how many coffee safe, student spend, student spend report, Parkins & Esther UK 18-24 Consumer Spending Patterns 2006 pdf, Parkins & Esther UK 18-24 Consumer Spending Patterns 2006 pdf free, finals, finals advice, finals stress, low, feeling low, how know depression?, depression symptons, not depression similar, ingrown hairs depression, folliculistus depression, keratosas pillaris depression, PowerPoint alternative, PowerPoint alternative free, facebook business plan, facebook business plan, facebook business plan pdf free, how many hours sleep, should sleep?, should sleep if can't 4 hours?, should eat if can't sleep?, effect no sleep, no sleep insanity, no sleep depression, no sleep ingrown hairs, anyone else hate Calibri?, HP Laserjet 2470, HP Laserjet 2470 install, HP Laserjet 2470 troubleshoot, dicks on HP forums, Toshiba recognise printer, what is wrong with HP Laserjet 2470 won't recognise my computer Toshiba?, what is wrong

Charlie wished Sara were there. She'd have brought him toast and Dairylea when he was losing the will. Hunted out statistics he could slot into the yawning emptiness of his slides. Smuggled slivers of design advice into artful compliments. Charlie could have got unreasonably annoyed at her, instead of the makers of

PowerPoint, the makers of Toshiba, and himself. As if to seal her absence, Sara didn't reply to his 10 p.m. text. Carefully, deliberately, Charlie squashed the mental image of her and some dickhead in a trilby, sniffing coke off whatever you sniffed coke off – probably the toned stomachs of other dickheads in other trilbies.

By the end of the night, Charlie felt several years older and sadder. Yet somehow, when 8 a.m. rumbled around, he had done it: he'd written a presentation and fabricated some market research and woken Alistair up by barging in to use his printer (Alistair deserved it).

Standing under a hot shower, Charlie finally allowed himself a mental break. As the steam rose around him, his thoughts billowed and broke free. Charlie imagined that the pitch was over – and somehow, he'd nailed it. 'The Comeback Kid,' he football-commentated to himself. 'From nowhere, Naughton has pulled it out the bag.' It had been a shaky start, but Charlie had turned it around. At a certain point, guided by intuition, he'd ditched the script and looked each audience member in the eye, speaking from the heart. They'd seen through his nerves and recognised his potential. Charlie couldn't quite believe it, but later that same day, they'd offered them the seed-funding. And in spite of all the excitement and distraction, afterwards he'd suddenly found he was able to focus on revision. Knowing everything wasn't riding on his exams, he'd gone in and done his absolute best.

As he helped himself to Romilly's shower gel, Charlie's future unfurled and laid itself out before him. By the time news of his 2:1 had reached him, it was barely relevant any more, because the business was taking off – its growth was remarkable. Lucas wanted to work for him, and Alistair had to admit that Charlie had been right to take the risk, and apologise for not believing in him. Within five years, Charlie was living between apartments in New York and London and a beach house in California; he'd paid off his parents' mortgage and set them up for retirement, earning their eternal gratitude and respect; even his sister Rachel looked up to him – she pretty much had to, because he was so much richer than her.

When he got out of the shower, Charlie realised he was running late. At ten past nine, he ran into the Barclays Wealth hall, sweating heavily, clutching his USB and printouts, hating himself for being a childish, incompetent, arrogant idiot.

About twenty people sat at the far end of the room. Three judges were behind a trestle table – an older man who looked like an academic, and two young guys that definitely didn't – with the pitchers standing just in front of them. Taz was sprawled at the back, hands in his hoodie pockets, next to one of his entrepreneur society mates, a bearded postgrad Charlie didn't know.

Charlie squeezed along the row to sit next to him, and quietly handed over the material, telling himself to wait until the show was over before he let Taz feel the full brunt of his irritation.

'Morning.' Taz leafed nonchalantly through the pitch script, a chief exec skimming his business section digest.

'I've been up all night.' Charlie's eye twitched, and he resisted the urge to scratch it. Despite his shower, he already felt dirty, as though fear were seeping out of his pores.

The nerdish odd couple at the front were drawing their pitch to a close. They were PhD students, selling something to do with biology or seeds – Charlie had missed the vital layman's section.

'Intro's a bit weak,' murmured Taz.

Piss off, Charlie thought, saying only, 'I've split it up so we can present alternately. Yours is in blue.'

Taz looked at Charlie, and pointed at his own chest. 'Me present?'

Two girls in front turned shut-up glares on them. Charlie raised a hand in apology. 'Yeah,' he whispered. 'We should both talk, as partners. It'll look weird otherwise.'

Taz's eyes narrowed. 'But as a consultant,' he said, a bit too loudly, 'it wouldn't be appropriate.'

'What?'

Taz sank further in his chair and looked up at Charlie, pursing his lips. 'We're not partners, I'm a consultant. I advised you. I thought that was clear?'

'What do you mean?' Charlie edged down to be level with Taz. 'In Nero's, I told you the idea, and you were into it.'

'But you didn't ask me to be *partner*. That's a massive commitment. If I was partner, I'd have been involved at every stage. Josh can tell you, as a partner, I'm a *nightmare*.'

Josh smirked, pleased with his shout-out.

'But you told me—'

'I didn't. No offence, Charlie, but I'd never put my name to something without working on it properly. I mean, I'll take a look now, but . . .' Taz pouted and rubbed his beard: *I doubt I can do much with this.*

A thin round of applause bounced around the hall, as the biologists shared a relieved smile. Mechanically, Charlie joined in, and found himself clapping after everybody had stopped.

So we're not partners? Charlie almost said again, but he managed to stop himself before any further debasement could take place. The humiliation tapped into an ancient, familiar feeling. He was that guy at school who thought a girl was going out with him, only to be told, two weeks later, with an embarrassed, train-tracked smile, that not only were they not going out now, they never had been. The milkshake, and the muffin, and the long walks home when he'd helped her scale the fences round the tennis courts and

223

they'd chucked a tennis ball back and forth, sometimes for over an hour – none of that had meant a thing.

'I actually consulted for several groups,' added Taz, as if the conversation were being recorded.

'Hm, I see.' Charlie did his best professional nod.

The next group was called forward – two computer science finalists in suits, with some kind of software idea. As Charlie watched one of them dance from foot to foot, he began to comprehend something. He looked down at his script, reading snatches of sentences he'd written about assessing the student market and leveraging social networks and building a national brand. And he saw that it was so many ways of saying he would impress himself upon the world, that people would be buoyed and moved by *him* – not by him doing or affecting anything, simply by him whipping up a sufficient amount of energy to give an impression of movement.

It wasn't that the concept was intrinsically bad, or that somebody out there couldn't make it work. But Charlie saw clearly and finally the irrevocable distance between that person and himself. He'd had a good idea for some other student, someone with more energy and better networks and a good work ethic, someone without nagging doubts. The thought of promising this plan, and then having to deliver it, made Charlie feel inexpressibly leaden, totally incapable of galvanising himself or others. Right now, if someone gave him a company to run – a company that ran on him – he would probably sit down and weep. He *couldn't* do it. He certainly couldn't do it alone. He wasn't sure he could do it at all.

Charlie stared at the printouts and tried to figure out what this meant, and what he should do. He wanted simply to stop, to put the paper on the floor and walk out of the room. Beside him, Taz drew a pen from his breast pocket and drew wavy lines under a large paragraph of Charlie's business plan. *Don't bother,* Charlie wanted to say. *It's just a load of words.*

A smattering of applause signalled the end of the pitch, and Charlie wrenched his eyes from the clockwork motion of the speaker's sway.

'Social Tiger?' one of the young judges called. 'Social Tiger's next up.'

As Charlie stood up, the room seemed to move under his feet. *It's a performance,* he tried to tell himself. *Just do it.* A hand reached over and took his USB from him. Charlie smiled inanely over the judges' heads. *I'm not your guy,* he wanted to say. *It isn't me – sorry.* Instead he filled the silence by miming a shot at the basketball hoop hanging above them. It was something that his more confident self might have tried – except that he would have brought it off somehow, or judged the situation better. As it was, the judges looked bemused. *Just force it out,* Charlie thought, as he turned towards the quiet but utterly inattentive audience. *Just start and then you'll be able to keep going.*

'Students,' he started. *I've started,* he thought. 'Are poor.' *But I could stop.* 'Right?' *I can still stop.*

It was impossible. It was impossible to pitch when you knew the whole project was hopeless. Charlie sounded like an imbecilic TV presenter. Like a person raving on a street corner. Like his own dad, holding forth. He sounded like the star of a *Dragon's Den* disaster video, sweating and smirking with nerves, hands trembling, tongue clacking in a dry, stripped mouth.

The pitch ground on and on. Charlie was so far outside himself, his words and gestures were in another universe – a twanging, jolting place where the air was thick and pressing, and there was a constant, insistent ring.

16

Overconfidence

Overconfidence is what happens when confidence goes bad. By definition, therefore, there is no such thing as bad confidence – there is only overconfidence. As a way of thinking, this is not especially helpful.

Overconfidence makes it very hard to discuss the reality of confidence, especially its inbuilt tendency to self-destruct, because if confidence is always good, then logically there can be no such tendency. As soon as confidence becomes undeserved, or nasty, or tips over into recklessness, it has turned into something categorically different: *over*confidence. It's like the idea that the market is always right – because, if the market went wrong, that can only mean it wasn't functioning efficiently enough. Somehow, in both cases, the anomaly serves as confirmation of the theory.

You can see the same circular reasoning in the way overconfidence is only ever defined retrospectively. Think of any parable of overconfidence: Lance Armstrong, the Iraq War, the financial crisis. It's only *after* everything has gone wrong that it suddenly becomes obvious to everyone that we were dealing with a raging case of hubris. Beforehand, when things seem to be fine . . . well, we may have had our suspicions, but as long as the enterprise was succeeding, any accusation of overconfidence was just that, an accusation. And if, by some miracle, things work out – if Lance never gets caught, if the Iraq War creates a stable Middle Eastern democracy, if the banks catch their mistakes and dump the evidence in the river? In that case, it wasn't overconfidence at all, but something else, something admirable and impressive. There would still be a plaque in Nike headquarters praising Armstrong's 'fearlessness and confidence'. George W. Bush would be known by his self-appointed nickname, 'the decider'.

Nietzsche would have disliked the notion of overconfidence, although not primarily for its lack of logic. The phrase 'too much of a good thing' meant nothing to him. In many ways, overconfidence was exactly what he desired and wished to inculcate: a 'triumphant abundance of life' wielded by individuals 'far above and beyond the average'. Our separation of overconfidence from confidence would have appeared to him as a way of 'levelling down' the boldest and strongest spirits in favour of 'the herd'.

So went the theory. But when Nietzsche encountered someone who truly seemed to live at the pitch he sought, the practice was far more complicated and painful. That someone was Richard Wagner, the greatest composer of the age, who Nietzsche first met when he was a young professor at the University of Basel.

It was love at first sight, at least on the part of Nietzsche, who after only his second meeting with Wagner was signing his thank-you notes 'your truest and most devoted disciple and admirer' and addressing the older man as 'master'. For the next three years, Nietzsche was a dedicated member of the Wagner family, a pseudo-son and functionary who could be relied on to shop for Wagner's silk underwear and pen blistering attacks on Wagner's critics. Even his philosophy was an elaboration of Wagnerian theory. *The Birth of Tragedy*, his first book, begins with a sickly dedication, in which Nietzsche assures Wagner that as he wrote it he 'communed with you as with one present and could thus write only what befitted your presence'.

Nietzsche's relationship with Wagner followed a similar path to his relationship with God. By the 1880s, the former disciple had become his master's most acid critic, denouncing him at book length (twice) in typically no-holds-barred style. 'Wagner's art is diseased,' runs one assault. 'He has made music ill.' For Nietzsche, the controversy aroused by attacking such a famous figure was all part of the appeal. The name 'Wagner' was enough to give his books a much-needed sales boost.

What changed? The first hint of difficulty came in a letter to a mutual friend in February of 1873. 'I can't conceive how anyone can be, in fundamental matters, more truly and deeply committed than I am,' Nietzsche protested. 'But in little, subordinate side-issues . . . I must grant myself a freedom, really only to preserve my loyalty in a higher sense.' Quite simply, Nietzsche needed to take back his life. Wagner's 'tyrannical nature' left no room for anyone else to breathe. To become himself – to be his own man – Nietzsche had to escape the composer's oppressive presence.

Did Nietzsche like the idea of his ideal man more than the dominating reality? Perhaps. But that is not what he claimed. Far from criticising Wagner for going too far, Nietzsche condemned him for not going far enough. The ideal was perfect – it was Wagner who could not live up to it. He courted popularity and did things for money; he gave people 'shows' when he should have been giving them art. He stuck to what he knew would be popular, rather than continually seeking to develop. Wagner was not *too* confident; in Nietzsche's terms, he was not confident enough.

Whatever the contradictory emotions that lay behind his utterances, in his published writings, Nietzsche stuck to his theoretical guns. He did not believe in overconfidence, because overconfidence did not exist – it was simply the extension of confidence, the place confidence goes when it is pursued to its logical end point. That is the reason we can only identify it after it has taken effect: overconfidence is not a phenomenon in its own right, but simply a more complete version of the confident mindset.

For most people, this might be read as a warning, the danger of a situation that feels so right, but goes so wrong. For Nietzsche, it was a challenge. More, always more, he commanded his readers: 'Live dangerously! Build your cities on the slope of Vesuvius! Send your ships into unexplored seas!'

Barred from the library, Ellie was revising on a bench in the scrubby parkland between Tesco's and the canal path. It wasn't ideal. She'd brought along a photocopied article on Hegel's dialectics, which was disturbingly good. After the first paragraph, she had to stand up and walk round the bench, thoughts branching chaotically in every direction. Immediately, she began applying the concept to the campaign, half-murmuring phrases she might say in an interview or write in an exam essay in which she successfully wove her own political experience with Hegel's philosophy in a sophisticated exploration of dialectics in the contemporary media.

Catching herself in this triumphalist fantasy, Ellie looked around, fearing the topless man lying on the grass might be able to read her thoughts. He was engrossed in *The Sun* – she'd got away with it. Ellie settled down to beginning the paragraph all over again.

This was the problem with revision. She knew she should do it, because she might (or might not) be able to sit her exams when they began (with or without her) in five days. But highly associative reflections on Hegel seemed like a waste of time when she could be taking some action to lift her ban. Surely she should be practising for interviews, emailing journalists, or knocking on the doors of empty offices and explaining to obstructive administration staff that she was (and yet wasn't) a vandal, in an effort to meet someone on the interdepartmental disciplinary committee.

What she needed, Ellie decided firmly, was some water. She left the bench (fearing that someone else would steal her sweet spot) and headed toward Tesco's. Purpose already waning, she browsed the potted plants outside, considering how she would respond to an interviewer's question about Shannon, the girl in the SSB poster, and whether it was feminist to single out—

'Looking for anything in particular?'

It was Oscar, swinging a plastic bag, looking both sexy and unwashed.

'Oh,' she said.

'Oh?'

'I mean, hello.' She fingered the leaf of a nearby nasturtium. 'Here you are.'

''Fraid so,' he smiled broadly.

'How come you're not on your boat?'

'Where I belong?'

'Yeah, exactly. You're all out of context.'

'I had to buy some toothpaste. Sorry about that.'

'It's confusing of you.'

'I know you hate being confused.'

'I mean, where do we go from here?'

'I've got my toothpaste so I'm ready for anything.'

'What are the rules? What's the etiquette?'

'There are no rules. I hate etiquette.'

'What a nightmare.'

Oscar tipped onto the balls of his feet. 'I suppose we could get a drink. Isn't that what people do when they meet by chance?'

'I have heard that,' Ellie nodded.

'What can go wrong?'

'Okay,' she agreed dubiously. 'It's your funeral.'

By now, it felt like it had been hot for ever, and would never be cool again. In the balmy late afternoon sun, the picnic tables by the canal were full of civilians and second-year students, blissfully free of finals. It occurred to Ellie that they should probably go to some dark, ill-attended dive, maybe the horrible St George near the station. But she was practically a grown-up, and it was sunny, and so what if people saw her and Oscar having a pint together? Who were these 'people' anyway and why was it any of their business? If anyone had something to say to her, they could join her for a cider, rammed between an earnest postgraduate reading group and some French tourists who had somehow been duped into thinking this would be a good place for a holiday.

'What are you doing come summer?' she asked Oscar.

'I'm trying to fix the boat.' Oscar rolled a cigarette. 'Do you want one?'

'Yeah, thanks.'

'I want to take it on a trip, coast to coast.'

'Oooh, nice.'

'But it'll probably take me to the end of the summer just to get it running. And then it might not be running. I don't mind if I get stuck though, it's a good town when we're not here. What about you?'

'Um.' She wondered how to approach this question. 'Have you by any chance heard about the exam ban thing?'

'I have. Which is saying something. I saw it in the local paper. "Girl Vandal's Exam Ban".'

'Yeah, it's blown up a bit.'

'S'pose that's what you want, isn't it?'

Ellie frowned – she'd never quite expressed it to herself that way before. 'I suppose. Anyway, if they don't let me take them, I can't go home. I'll have to run away. Maybe cycle coast to coast if I manage to fix my bike. I'll meet you in John O'Groats.'

'I was thinking east to west – I'll never get the boat that far. Do you want another drink?'

'Oh, decision time?'

'Looks like it.'

'I suppose it's gone pretty well so far.'

'I've no complaints.'

'Let me get these ones then.'

'Actually . . .' Oscar swapped his rollie to the other hand and reached deep into his pocket. 'Here's another decision for you.'

'You're not going to propose, are you? I thought you didn't believe in monogamy.'

'Do you want some mandy?'

Ellie paused. 'Serious?'

Oscar nodded.

'Oh.'

'Back to "Oh"?'

'Now you've thrown a spanner in the works.'

'I've had it kicking around for ages. If I keep it much longer, I'm going to end up putting it through the wash.'

'Oscar, you don't need to pretend you wash your clothes. I've been in your boat.'

'There's a system. It's all part of the system. Anyway, do you want this or what?'

'Yeah. Yeah, of course I do.'

'At least there'll be no more decisions to make.'

'I suppose so. Do you want some money?'

'No, no.'

'Okay.' Ellie hovered over the bench. 'Shall I still get pints?'

'Why not?'

Squeezing into the bar, she waited behind a group of office workers clutching their 5 p.m. drinks. Under the air conditioner, she felt a shiver of cold and excitement. Searching for the right word, she decided that she felt *voracious* – she wanted everything, she wanted the whole world. The pursuit of pleasure was beginning to make sense to her in a way it never had before. Previously it had always seemed shallow and rather stupid, a kind of non-philosophy for people who enjoyed drinking more than thinking. Now she wondered how anything could be wrong with feeling this way. Ellie was sick of checking herself, bored of keeping her eyes down and not being rude or flirtatious, done with pre-emptively hedging against having any effect on others.

'London Pride and Amstel, please.' She smiled at the woman behind the bar. As well as indiscriminate, Ellie's voracious feeling was also inclusive – she wanted everyone else to feel voracious too. Maybe this was what the Sixties were like, she thought. Maybe this was what everybody in the Sixties wished the Sixties were like.

By the time she was back outside, she'd whipped herself into a high state without even taking the stimulants. But she took them anyway, washing down the rank chemical tang with half a pint of Amstel, and worrying briefly about quite how much it would poison her. There was no point in dwelling on it – it was in her body and would take whatever course it chose. Ellie enjoyed the edgy, in-between period in the emotional waiting room, chatting to Oscar about the perils of going back home.

When her phone rang with an unknown number, she thought twice about answering.

'You're fine,' Oscar told her. 'It's probably some cold caller anyway.'

In fact, it was Kristen from BBC News who wanted to interview her for a TV segment about the 'death of student politics' (she inflected upwards, as though it were a question). As she responded, Ellie heard her own 'professional voice': bright and capable and extra-clear. Oscar's smirk drove her away towards the canal as she listened to Kristen's instructions on where she'd be picked up, what she should wear, what sorts of questions she could expect from Gita, the presenter. 'You were so articulate on the radio,' Kristen gushed, brisk and encouraging. 'And what an interesting insight into contemporary university life. Our viewers will just want to know the facts – why you did what you did.' Ellie had the presence of mind to ask if Nadine could accompany her.

Having hung up, she inwardly let go – the string slipped from her grasp, and the balloon rose up into the sky.

'I want to walk,' she decided, finding her glass empty. 'Let's go for a walk in town.'

Oscar drained his remaining pint and joined her. As they stepped away from the pub (leaving the Hegel essay on the bench), she reached out and took his hand. The sun was still warm as they walked towards the market square.

'It's not such a bad place, is it?' She looked with fresh eyes at the bank that had been converted into a Wetherspoons, the two opticians positioned side by side, and the sagging Save The Children window display. 'I feel like every time I'm here I'm swearing under my breath in the queue at Rymans or Tesco Metro. Do you ever feel like uni separates you from life? I mean, only being with people your own age, it's not really natural, is it? I swear the other day, I was on campus, and I caught out of the corner of my eye a child and my first thought was that it must be a dwarf, or little person, is that the right word? Anyway, basically I'm saying, that's how far off my radar children are, you know? It doesn't seem like that's normal.'

'One of my friends has a kid. She's wicked.'

'You're really not at uni at all, are you?'

Ellie took a deep breath as they passed the group of homeless people who gathered near the cathedral. She pressed her hand into Oscar's lower back. It was *lovely*, it was unbelievably beautiful, how his lower back felt. She slid across to the side of his waist, which was both muscular and soft, like a perfect fruit, and then back to the bony base of his spine.

Oscar hummed in response. Ellie turned him round to face her, and kissed him, leaning against the cathedral fence. His lips were dry and chapped, his tongue soft.

'You smell like a tyre,' she sighed happily. He laughed. 'In a great way! I love it.'

Out of the corner of her eye, Ellie caught sight of Maggie and Giles, wheeling their bikes past a fruit stall. She couldn't believe it. Taking Oscar's hand in both of hers, Ellie led him over, calling their names.

'HI!' She spread her arms like a visitation. 'I'm so happy to see you both! This is amazing.'

'Hi, Ellie.' Giles grinned, with a sideways glance at Maggie. 'How are *you* doing?'

'You seem *very* well.' Maggie nodded, eyebrows raised.

'Yeah, we just took a load of drugs, I feel excellent. This is Oscar,' Ellie told them, putting her arm around his waist.

'Hi.' A strange half-grin twisted Oscar's face.

'It's so brilliant that you can all meet. You would love each other.' Ellie traced a triangle connecting them, before asking, in fascination, 'What are you doing?'

235

'We're taking a break and buying some fruit,' explained Maggie, as if to a child.

'It's okay,' Ellie reassured her, understanding completely. 'I know I seem ridiculous, but I'm fine.'

'Sure, you're great. Would you like some mango?'

'No, no thanks.' Ellie brushed mangoes aside. 'I need . . .' she looked at the cathedral tower, trying to conjure what she needed with her hands.

'Music?' Oscar suggested.

'Yes!' She was so relieved to know just what it was. 'Yes, that's it.'

'Okay, well, we've got to get back to the library.' Giles hitched a tote bag of oranges over his shoulder. 'But you guys have a lovely time with the music.'

Ellie shook her head and smiled at him. She hadn't seen Giles for *so* long and he was *amazing*, he was the one of the nicest people she'd ever known. And Maggie – Maggie had been such an incredible friend to her, even when she'd been antisocial and difficult, Maggie didn't care because she was *awesome* and *beautiful*. Ellie didn't want to leave them. Perhaps she should go to the library too. She could lie under a quiet table, thinking . . . but a claustrophobic feeling warned her it would be too hectic, too crowded, it might ruin everything.

Before Ellie could express her thoughts, Maggie and Giles had wheeled away their bicycles. Bicycles were amazing, with their two wheels and their chain, the way they merged with your body and became something else, they were almost alive, you could almost think that a bicycle had a soul, the way this town had a soul, the way every single person they passed had a soul, and their own complete world, it could almost make you cry, it made you want to reach out to them and tell them that you *saw*, you *knew*, you *knew exactly how it felt* – they were alive, and you were alive too, and it was overwhelming that that could be the case, it made you want to stop and run your hands over the stones of buildings and wonder, *were they alive*, did they *feel* when you touched the surface of the sandstone, ridged and rough, and pressed your cheek against it, did the *stone know* that you were feeling the stone, and the stone – could it be – how could it not be – feeling you?

For a while, they watched a dog tied up outside a shop, tiny body quivering, sentient and incredible.

Before or after that, they sat back to back on the cathedral wall, watching all the people pass by, taking turns to hum and feel the vibrations.

At the same time, Ellie laid her head on Oscar's lap and stared at the sky.

'I forgot the music,' she told him, dreamily. 'I forgot.'

'The music,' murmured Oscar. He looked down at her, his face funny and heartrending and perfect.

As Ellie inhaled, she was struck by a wonderful idea. 'The Shackle. There's a jukebox.'

There must have been a period between that thought and being in the Shackle's car park, hit by the exceptional colours of cars and the sticky look that tarmac got in the heat. They were lying on the ground getting a better sense of where the tarmac was at when Ellie spotted Charlie beyond the bunting. He leaned against the wall, expression somehow bent in on itself. Ellie froze for a second, worried that talking to Charlie might steer them into turbulence, when what she wanted was serene, microscopic calm. But he looked so lost, scratching at the lichen on the wall, trying to untangle himself, and she felt certain that her tidal wave of happiness could wash any worries away.

'Charlie,' she whispered, grinning, as she crawled on her belly across the tarmac. 'Chaa-a-ar-lie.'

—

The enormous eyes that unexpectedly popped over the Shackle wall looked *insane*. It took a moment for Charlie to realise that they belonged to Ellie. She seemed to be conjuring with his name, and some bloke with a Mohican was sprawled on the ground behind her.

'Um—' Charlie stuttered.

'Hi!' She beamed. 'Charlie! Amazing.'

'Are you on drugs?' he asked, and immediately wanted to punch himself in the face.

'Yes,' she said happily.

Charlie's surprise quickly turned to bitterness. Literally everyone at uni was having a better time than him. Even the poster girl for hating on uni was having a more authentic university experience than Charlie had ever had.

'Come in to the Shackle and listen to music.' She reached through the fence and nipped at his elbow.

'I'm kind of on my way . . .' Charlie tailed off, looking down the street towards Sara's house.

'I really want to talk to you,' said Ellie, eyes like planets.

'Really?' he asked suspiciously.

'I have to tell you. You started it all. You splashed me, then I wrote about what an arsehole you were, and it started everything!'

'Right,' said Charlie dubiously. He wasn't really in the mood to be humouring fucked people while they made incomprehensible but obscurely cutting remarks at him. On the other hand, further lingering on the street in a state of emotional paralysis didn't appeal either.

'Come on!' She was already up, pulling Oscar to his feet. They nuzzled at each other's necks and shoulders until Charlie had to avert his eyes. *Honestly*, he thought, *get a room*.

'It's okay, Charlie.' Suddenly, Ellie was stroking his cheek, face almost touching his. He looked into her eyes for a moment, then

238

stepped back awkwardly, casting a confused glance at Oscar, who watched hazily, betraying no sign of discomfort. 'Don't worry, everything's great.'

The pair of them were making Charlie paranoid. Maybe they'd offer him drugs – a prospect both worrying and appealing.

Before he could take a firm stand against it, Ellie had led him into the Shackle. The same massive guy was behind the bar, this time wearing a wife-beater. One of the old-man regulars was perched on his stool. He greeted the new arrivals with a bemused nod.

'Rose!' Ellie hugged Rose like an armful of pick-a-sticks. 'I love you! I know I'm ridiculous but it's true, you know, and I should tell you more often.'

Oscar began prodding at the jukebox, oblivious to anything but its red and yellow lights. He was probably the kind of person that hung round the DJ at parties, Charlie thought, suggesting tracks and making inaudible technical adjustments.

'Hello, gentlemen.' Rose eyed Oscar and Charlie, apparently unable to decide which she disliked most. 'What is this – double-act date rape? Has she been Rohypnoled?'

'I've got no part in this,' Charlie told Rose. 'Can I have a pint?'

'Aren't you barred?'

'Oy oy,' the regular chipped in.

'Please, no bars,' said Michael wearily. 'Be friendly to customers, Rosie. Show them smile.'

Prince's 'Kiss' leapt into the empty room. Ellie threw up her hands and circled the blue chair, tapping it and jerking arrhythmically.

'So how's it going in the boy band, Charles?' Rose poured a Fosters. If possible, Charlie thought, she looked even paler and more rake-like than she had a few weeks ago; so terrible, in fact, that it would be offensive for him to put up a good face.

'To be honest,' he admitted, 'badly.'

'Album sales down?' Rose sat the pint in front of him. He stared at it glumly. An encouraging nod from Michael prompted Rose to continue, 'What's the problem then?'

Even this frosty invitation was enough for Charlie to unburden himself. Surely Rose of all people could understand misery. 'Everything. I'm cocking everything up. I've ruined my chance to have a business. My marks are terrible. I'm even starting to wonder if I did the right thing about Sara.'

'She work here?' said the regular.

'Shut up, Steve!' snapped Rose. 'The one you ditched? I thought you didn't like her.' She caught sight of Ellie and Oscar, who were entwined in the corner by the jukebox, kissing each other's faces. 'Oh my Christ. What the fuck?'

'No, I—' Charlie broke off at Rose's shocked expression. 'What is it? Is she still with . . . Justin?'

'Technically, yes.'

Steve tutted and shook his head.

'You're one to talk, you cheating bastard.' Rose shut him down with sudden venom.

'I'm so confused.' Charlie was anxious to steer them back to the subject at hand. 'I just don't know what to do.'

Michael leaned across the bar gravely. 'You have to follow heart.'

Charlie nodded in agreement. 'But it's complicated. I didn't think it would be like this. I miss Sara.'

'No one told you?' Rose yanked open the steaming dishwasher.

'What?'

'Being single's shit.'

'Don't know about *that*.' Steve puffed out his lips and rolled his eyes, vaguely invoking the ol' ball and chain.

Rose shot him a disgusted look.

'Ro-sie,' he sang, mock-romantically. 'Ro-sie. Give me your answer do-o-o-o-o-o.'

'But is it right to commit?' Charlie focused on Michael. 'Is that fair on her? Is it fair on me?'

'I'm half cra-a-azy.' Steve jumped up, sidestepping with surprising lightness. Rose rolled her eyes, half smiling. 'Over the love of yo-o-o-ou.'

'You love her?' asked Michael.

'Yes. No. I don't know.' Charlie rubbed his eyes. 'I just thought . . . I thought I was someone else. Someone better.'

Steve had waltzed his way behind the bar. 'It won't be a *sty*-lish marriage—'

Suddenly irritated, Rose shoved Steve back towards his stool. 'Michael, don't you have to do the stocktake?'

'Ah.' Michael nodded and headed for the back door, pausing to impart sagely to Charlie: 'Remember, follow heart.'

'Thanks, mate.'

'Look, Charles.' Rose picked up her Diet Coke. 'It's not your fault you thought you were better. That's the burden of poshhood. They tell you you can do everything, regardless of your actual talent or ability.'

'Oh, not this again,' Charlie sighed. 'I'm not even that posh. I mean, seriously. You should see some of the people who were at my school.'

'Great argument.'

Limbs untangled, Ellie and Oscar were shuffling their way towards the bar, vaguely in time to Bob Marley.

'Okay,' Charlie conceded. 'But honestly, I bet there's almost no difference between my parents and yours. Neither of mine went to uni. The only books they have are by Delia Smith.'

'All right. Pop quiz. What do you call a body warmer?'

'A body warmer?' Charlie frowned in confusion. 'I give up.'

'You call it fucking gilet, don't you.'

Charlie rolled his eyes.

'What do you call your evening meal?'

Charlie waited.

'You call it fucking supper, don't you.'

'But what's your point? You can't hate for me knowing the word "gilet".'

'I don't hate you, Charles.' Rose started fishing out glasses and stacking them on the shelves. 'I prefer you in a crisis actually. Being deeply troubled really brings out the best in you.'

'*Great.*' Charlie ran his hands through his hair. This advice session was giving him problems he wasn't even aware he had. He longed to go home and sink into a *Scrubs* stupor.

'Rose.' Ellie steadied herself on Charlie's shoulder, as Oscar edged onto a stool. 'Are you giving him a hard time? Remember, Charlie's *sensitive.*'

'No, I'm not.'

'You are,' Ellie corrected Charlie. 'But don't mind Rose, she doesn't mean it.'

Rose snorted.

'The thing with Rose is, let me tell you something, do you know what it is?' Ellie leaned very close to whisper to Charlie, crazy-eyed and compelling. 'Do you know what's she done?'

'What?' Rose cocked an ear.

'All her amazingness and talent.' Ellie stretched out her fingers, leaning back. 'It's going *in*. Like an X-woman who hasn't figured out her power yet and keeps setting fire to people.'

'Okay.' Charlie frowned, confused.

'Except she's setting *herself* on fire.' With a delighted smile, Ellie concluded, 'See! That's why she's *anorexic!*'

In the awkward pause that followed, Oscar tapped along to 'Is This Love', rolling his shoulders luxuriously.

Charlie stared down into his pint, wishing he could disappear.

Rose turned to face the spirits, patting the worktop in search of some activity. Even Steve seemed to realise something had gone wrong. He got up and stepped behind the bar, reaching an arm round Rose's shoulders.

Ellie folded her arms and laid her head on the bar, smiling blissfully. 'How are you doing?' she asked Oscar.

Charlie couldn't see the response. He tried to drink but the sip sat in his mouth, refusing to go down. The Shackle was too horrible. It felt like a dream in which he'd done something awful and couldn't quite pin down what it was.

'Me too,' murmured Ellie. 'Mmmmmmmm.'

17

Higher Men

Greatness, for Nietzsche, was defined on a personal level, by great people and their great works. 'Higher men', he called these heroes, describing them as 'philosophers of the future' and 'adventurers and circumnavigators of that inner world called "man"'. (Although not as *Übermensch*, sometimes translated as 'superman'. This term was taken up by the Nazis, but, one brief mention aside, it only appears in Nietzsche's highly poetic *Thus Spoke Zarathustra*.)

The higher men were the people Nietzsche wrote for and wished to herald, but identifying them wasn't always simple. Nietzsche cites Goethe and Beethoven, Napoleon until power corrupted him, plus of course himself; after that the list peters out, leaving the higher men as a nameless elite, like saints or legends in their inhuman vagueness.

Nevertheless, Nietzsche tended to depict these legends as members of some earnest, self-important club (a boys' club, naturally). He was imagining himself with friends, equals, although even if he knew their names and addresses he wouldn't be able to invite them round, because higher men were, like him, solitary by nature. Other features of these 'strong, imperious' individuals include their creativity, judgement and robust good health, again like Nietzsche, who spent almost his entire adult life afflicted by one ailment or another, yet considered himself 'intrinsically sound'. Most importantly, the higher men are supremely confident, with all that entails. They are a glorified self-portrait, Nietzsche as he wished to be and, in his final madness, how he believed he was.

What, then, of the lower men, the not-quite-confident-enough who fail in some way to match up to this standard? 'Good-natured herd animals,' sneered Nietzsche. For 'mediocre' public opinion he had nothing but disdain: 'Books for the general reader are always ill-smelling books, the odour of paltry people clings to them.'

Nietzsche was that rare thing, an unabashed elitist. He simply did not believe that equality was a good thing, because such 'levelling down' interfered with the development of higher men. In higher education, for instance, 'democratisation' prevented the truly exceptional from realising their potential, and gave the 'lower types' expectations they could never hope to fulfil. As always, Nietzsche put it in the strongest terms: 'If one wants slaves, one is a fool if one educates them to be masters.'

Nietzsche's two-tier vision of society is one of the most difficult parts of his philosophy for modern readers to come to terms with. But you could say that, when it comes to confidence, this is exactly what we've ended up with: a select cadre of confident individuals at the top, with a larger mass of extras making up the crowd. For all the democratic talk that surrounds it, confidence maps disconcertingly well onto traditional class and gender divisions. You can see it in any conversation: some people are happier to speak and more willing to believe they will be listened to, and invariably, they are the people with more power. In public-speaking training, they talk about 'the right to voice' – the theory that you'll never speak well unless you believe you *should* be speaking. So is the answer just to believe? Maybe – but that kind of positive thinking ignores the fact that, most of the time, there's a *reason* some people believe their voice should be the one being heard, while others never do.

Yet confidence is persistently difficult to systematise. It might be the gift of privilege, but it's also the unruly force which enables less entitled people to break away from a typical trajectory and excel. It's hierarchical, yet also 'aspirational'. And it was in this spirit of aspiration that Nietzsche wrote, at a time when confidence was more subversive, less familiar than it is today. Nietzsche was never on the side of the establishment. His version of confidence was wild, ungovernable and free.

Nietzsche advocated inequality more as an attitude than a political policy. A sense of superiority, of being the best, was for him a necessary part of greatness, especially the kind of creative greatness he admired the most. It sounds plausible, harmless even, until you consider the real-life implications of such an attitude. There were two kinds of people in the world, Nietzsche told his readers: you, in pursuit of your vision, and everyone else, whom you should treat as tools for your use.

Charlie left the Shackle like Scrooge after a vision of Christmas Future. What on earth had he been thinking asking for advice from that bunch of fruit loops? Ellie was all over the place (who took drugs right before exams?) and Rose was clearly hanging on to sanity by her fingernails.

Charlie had to decide one way or the other about Sara. He considered calling a friend, but he knew in advance what they'd say. Ben: 'Get back together.' Lucas: 'Don't.' Alistair: 'Fuck off and stop bothering me.' There was nothing for it: he had to figure it out for himself. He browsed the newsagents, hoping it would aid his process.

As Charlie stared at the tins of fruit, two inalienable truths became apparent. First, he needed Sara. He was miserable, lonely and desperately unproductive without her. Second, when exams were over, there was no way he'd still want to be with her (although she would be incredibly helpful when he was looking for jobs). In spite of all that had gone wrong, Charlie wasn't willing to give up his vision of the person he might become. He'd simply realised that he couldn't be that person until finals were taken care of and he'd escaped this town for ever.

What he had to do, Charlie realised, was be completely honest with her about how he felt. That was always the answer in the end. He picked up a Curly-Wurly (Sara's nostalgic comfort food) and jelly sweets in the shape of rings: a gesture, a joke really.

Charlie hadn't been prepared for Penny Austin answering the door.

'Charlie!' she called loudly, evidently warning everyone in the house that the incarnation of evil was about to cross the threshold. She was wearing some sort of onesie sleep suit (it was repellent). Charlie pictured Penny eavesdropping on the upcoming conversation, dragging the juicy details to her lair and feeding on them for days to come.

'Penny, I forgot you were staying here. I was hoping to see Sara.'

'I don't think she's expecting you, is she?'

'Are you running her diary?'

Both smiled, almost as if they were joking.

'It has been very tough on her, you know.' Penny crinkled reproachfully. 'You don't see how upset she is after you leave. We're all worried about her, she's barely been eating.'

'Well, I brought her a Curly-Wurly.'

Penny frowned – this wasn't an appropriate moment for Curly-Wurlies.

'So are you going to let me in or is there some kind of application process?'

Penny sighed, shrugged – it was out of her hands unfortunately – and opened the door just enough for Charlie to squeeze through. 'I'll call her down.'

'It's fine. I know the way.'

Penny raised her eyebrows – *all too well!* – and lingered downstairs, pretending she didn't have front-row seats in Meredith's room.

Charlie knocked and, receiving no reply, pushed open the bedroom door. Sara was on her bed listening to headphones. (This struck Charlie as suspicious, but he tried not to let paranoia overwhelm him.) She gave a cheerful wave, pulled the headphones off and jumped up to give him a hug. Sara looked extremely well; if anything, better than when they were going out.

'This is a nice surprise!' she smiled.

'I brought you a present.' Charlie handed over the chocolate bar.

'Ooh, did you make it yourself?'

'Just for you. What are you up to?'

'Oh, you know, "revising".' Sara sat back down on the bed, hugging her knees to her chest. 'How's yours going?'

Charlie shook his head – *badly*.

'Oh, *Charlie*. I knew you'd find it hard to get organised.'

'I know. You predicted it.' He laid a friendly hand on her bare foot. 'It's been a bit of a washout to be honest.'

'When do you start?'

'In five days.'

Sara made an 'eek' face. 'Mine are late. Everyone will be finished before me. To be honest I just want to get them over with.'

Charlie instantly thought of the period after exams when he had finished and Sara hadn't. That would be a drag if they got back together.

'I was sort of wondering if I could come and revise here with you.'

'Oh.' Sara's eyebrows lifted quizzically, but she said, 'Of course you can. I hate working on my own.'

'Me too. And Alistair's a terrible work buddy compared to you.'

'No pink-wafer breaks.'

'Exactly, and he doesn't like it when I try and kiss his neck.'

A question hung in the air between them, filling the silence.

'Have you tried the library?'

Charlie groaned. 'Not with all those arseholes.'

Sara giggled. 'You like lots of people.'

'I like you.'

By this point, the question was doing a high-wire act on a string held taut between them. The moment to speak had arrived: he had to tell her the truth.

'I miss you, Sara,' he whispered.

She held his gaze, neither responding nor dissuading him. He leaned over her curled-up knees and kissed her.

Closing her eyes, Sara took a long, deliberate breath.

'And I got you something else. Keep your eyes closed.' Charlie reached into his hoodie pocket, and pulled out the paper bag of jelly rings. He held one up in front of Sara's face; she opened her eyes and blinked, focusing. She smiled and laughed, and he popped the sweet into her mouth.

'You idiot.' Sara shook her head. For a moment, she chewed in silence, and then he kissed her again, licking the sugar grains from her lips.

'Hi,' she breathed.

'Hi.'

'I can't believe this,' she said slowly, smile fixed on her face. 'For ages I thought you would come round, but then time passed and you didn't, and I started to think you really meant it.'

Charlie sighed. Nothing but blazing honesty would do; he wanted to open his soul to her. 'I did really mean it,' he explained gently, causing her forehead to pucker. 'But then I missed you so much. I need you, Sara. You're lovely, you're amazing, you really are.' She brimmed with satisfaction. 'I want to be completely open, I don't want to hide anything from you.' Sara nodded. 'I've learned a lot about myself over the past few weeks. And I don't want to stop doing that. I don't want to restrict myself – or you, you know?'

She nodded again – Charlie felt he was expressing this well.

'I've thought about it and thought about it. I've *agonised* over it.' He took a deep breath and held both her hands in his. 'Is there a way for us to *be* together, but not "get back together"?'

Her eyes narrowed in confusion.

'I know I want to be with you more than anything. But I also know if we get back together, I'll end up hurting you again. That's the last thing I want to do.' He held out open palms, presenting the insoluble paradox in his heart. 'What if.' He brushed her cheek. 'What if we were together but we still stayed open to other people, to what life brings? I mean we both know uni will end soon, we'll go our separate ways – or not, you know? But why make future plans? Why worry about it, when we can just enjoy being together without putting a label on it?'

Sara's frown gradually deepened.

'It could be the best of both worlds – we get to be together, but we don't have to tie each other down. We can be ourselves: no false promises; complete honesty.'

'Hm.'

'What do you think? Take your time, don't rush. I know it's a lot to take in.'

'Mm-hm.'

'You look so beautiful.' She did look pretty, her hair loose and curly – it had been ages since he'd seen her properly. He kissed her hand.

Sara leaned her forehead on her knees, speaking into her thighs. 'Can I just get it completely straight in my mind, what it is you're saying?'

She looked up and Charlie nodded.

'You're saying: let's get back together, but not commit to one another. So we could pull other people, sleep with other people. We could do whatever we liked. And this arrangement would only last until the end of uni.'

'That makes it sound a bit joyless. It's not like—'

'But basically . . .'

'It's not how I'd put it. The important thing for me is that I want to be totally honest. I don't want to string you along.'

Sara swallowed, making Charlie worry she was going to cry. Perhaps what he had in mind was too delicate to discuss: they should have found it in the doing rather than running through the terms and conditions.

'Are you worried what other people will think? I was too. But at the end of the day it's our lives. Screw them – who cares what the world says we should do?'

The Minnie Mouse alarm suddenly exploded with a loud, tinny rattle.

'Oh shit.' Sara leaned across to slap it, twice. 'I've started setting it every hour 'cause I keep falling asleep.'

'I hope we'll still have nap breaks.' Charlie shifted closer to her as she returned to the middle of the bed. 'It's a crucial part of the process.'

251

'Charlie.' Sara stared at the duvet.

'Yes?'

'To be totally honest, I . . .' Her breath caught; she slowed it down. 'I want you to go away.'

'Sara—'

'I want you to go away and let me get on with my revision.'

'Okay.'

'Actually, I never want to speak to you again.'

'That's a bit much, isn't it?'

'I don't think it is a bit much.'

'But aren't you even going to think about it? We could talk about it some more.'

'No, I want you to go.'

'All right, I could call you later.'

'Don't call me. Get out my room, please. I mean it.'

'Okay, I'm going, Sara, just listen for a second—'

'*Please* leave.' Her voice was louder now.

Creaking on the balcony told him her backup was on its way.

'Sara, I—'

There was a knock at the door. Charlie jumped up and swung it open to find Penny and Fergus, a chorus of concerned passers-by. 'I'm just on my way.' He held up his hands.

'Are you all right, hon?' Penny wriggled past, ignoring him.

'I'll call you!' Charlie called back into the room. Penny already had Sara in her clutches; Sara was shaking her head, lips forming silent words.

Fergus waited to watch Charlie go down the stairs, ensuring he didn't try anything crazy as he stalked through the hall.

'Hope you enjoyed the show!' Charlie shouted over his shoulder. He breathed an awkward laugh before slamming the front door.

—

Justin had been out in the hallway for some time now. After Ellie told him, he'd said he needed a minute alone, and sat himself down by the piles of misaddressed mail in the dusty corridor, back against the wall, mouth clamped in deep, deep reflection. She asked him if he wanted her to stay; he shook his head, so instead she settled onto the sofa in the living room on the other side of the wall. At one point, he shouted, 'Jesus Christ!' (She'd never heard him shout, not in almost three years.) A subsequent series of bangs suggested he was hitting the wall.

Rose had woken Ellie at 2 p.m. by growling into her ear, 'If you don't tell him, I will.' She had used her old Welsh woman voice. It wasn't completely clear if she was joking or not.

'We were in the Shackle,' Ellie had murmured as she came to.

'You certainly were,' Rose had snorted. 'Bapped off your tits with some hippy in tow. Upsetting the customers. Talking out of your arse. I had a hell of a job persuading Michael not to bar you.'

Luckily Ellie retained only the blurriest memories of anything beyond the car park. One thing, however, was crystal-clear: she was openly cheating on Justin, a sin on the level of dropping your baby out of a third-floor window.

Ellie kept up a vigilant watch from the sofa, listening for every scuffle and creak from the other side. It was a bit like waiting off-stage while somebody played a tragic scene. She needed to pee, but couldn't leave. The inescapable knowledge that she was the worst person ever pinned her to the polyester. Ellie checked her expression in the mirror behind the telly – *See here*, she thought, *the face of the worst person ever.* She still looked a little wild, eyes deeply shadowed, hair thatched on one side. Stretching out, she lightly patted her arms and legs, checking they were in order. In spite of everything, she had somehow remained all of a piece.

It was a further half-hour before Justin re-entered and the next scene began. He leaned against the kitchen counter, staring up at the ceiling, fists clenched.

'Do you want to sit down?'

'No,' he told the light fitting firmly. 'I want you to know, Ellie, that I am really angry with you.'

'I know,' she nodded. 'I'm sorry.'

'I don't think I've ever been as angry at anyone in my life.'

'I'm so sorry.'

'Your timing is also . . .' He shook, anger rising.

'I know, I'm *so* sorry,' she agreed vehemently.

'I also want to know some things.'

'Okay.'

'Like, did this happen more than once? How long has it been going on?'

'There was one other time.' The lie was out before she had decided to lie. 'The night of SSB.'

'Ugh. And do you like this "Oscar"? I mean, do you love him?'

'No!'

Justin studied her face.

'No, no, definitely not. Of course I don't love him. I love *you*. And I'm so sorry for hurting you. Please, come and sit down.'

After a moment's hesitation, Justin sat at the other end of the sofa and put his head in his hands. 'I should be revising.'

Justin's undone revision topped up Ellie's cup of guilt, keeping it at 'overflowing'. *God*, she thought, *I am endless trouble for you.* She squirmed wretchedly, trying to think of something to say, but there was no way to fix the mess she'd created.

'I've thought about it very carefully,' Justin told Rose's *Closer*. (Jade Goody was dead, but they still found things to write about her.) 'And I've decided . . . that I forgive you.'

'Oh.' Ellie took in this unexpected statement. He was really going to forgive her just like that?

'I forgive you . . .' Justin turned his exhausted eyes to her. 'Because I love you, Ellie, and I still want to be with you.'

'I . . .' she began awkwardly. In a split second of clarity, she wondered where he got this sacrificial instinct. Why *was* he so ready to throw himself under the bus? 'Thank you.' After a moment, she added, 'I love you.'

'That's all I want.' Justin reached out his hand. 'It's the only thing that's important to me.'

As she touched his fingers, she was hit by a brand-new problem. 'What is it?'

'It's . . .' She rubbed her forehead, unwelcome comprehension gathering. 'I'm worried I'm not going to be able to do this.'

'Do what?'

'Be your girlfriend. I want to be with you, I really do.' Panic was rising in her chest. 'But I don't think I can put a check on myself.'

Justin's grip tightened.

'I'm just starting to figure out a lot of things about myself.' Ellie struggled to wrestle words from her inchoate thoughts. 'Sorry, I know that's wanky, but it's true. I feel as if I'm growing – I couldn't stop even if I wanted to.'

Justin rubbed his eyes despairingly. 'So where does that leave me? Outgrown?'

'No! If anything I'm catching up. You're much better than I am.'

He stared at the coffee table, blinking rapidly.

'Maybe we shouldn't be together,' she forced out. 'I'm bad for you. I'm only going to make you miserable.'

'No, no, no, don't say that.'

'But it's true, isn't it? I'll only hurt you again.'

'*No*. You're perfect, I love you, you're everything I want. Listen.' Justin's thoughts raced across his face. 'Whatever you're going through, I'll be here. Whatever you need to do, I'm not going anywhere.'

She stared at him. 'But that's horrible for you—'

'It's worth it, I know it is.'

'I make you so unhappy!'

'You don't, you don't. You make me *incredibly* happy. Listen, you might not be as certain as I am.' He was gathering strength. 'But I'm certain enough for us both. I *know* this is right.'

A bus rumbled by outside. Ellie stared blankly at Rose's 'Hot Priests' calendar. Perhaps, if Justin thought so, they *could* find a way through. Perhaps she needed to tune out the destructive voices and listen to the good one. 'Are you sure about this?'

'I've never been more sure of anything in my life.'

Justin's certainty was both comforting and constricting.

'Okay,' she said, at length. 'I trust you.'

'You *should* trust me. I love you.' Justin moved closer and hugged her tightly, taking a deep, shaky breath.

Slowly, she relaxed into his embrace. 'I love you.'

Exhausted, Ellie lay down with her head in his lap. Justin stroked her hair. She closed her eyes.

In the long, wrung-out silence, Ellie caught her mind wandering over to her wardrobe to seek out a TV-friendly top that wasn't red, black, white or patterned. Chastening herself for this disgusting selfishness, Ellie determined to do something for Justin, here and now. 'I could help you revise this afternoon, if you'd like?' she suggested, looking up at his pale face.

'I'm not sure you can help.' He gave a sad, brave smile. 'But we could work together maybe?'

'Okay. That'd be nice.'

Justin kissed her forehead. 'Everything's going to be all right, you know. I'll look after you.'

'Thank you. I might do some research for my interview.'

'And also maybe revise?' said Justin gently.

'Oh, yeah, also revise,' she nodded. 'Sorry.'

18

Boom and Bust

Nietzsche sought to live as a higher man. To achieve this goal, he set aside habit and structure and embraced a life of nomadic improvisation. He intended to channel an ecstatic, godly confidence. Instead, confidence channelled him.

The biggest impact of this was on his health. From his mid-twenties onwards, Nietzsche was almost constantly ill. 'Three-quarters blind', he suffered from almost permanent indigestion and migraines so severe they would leave him incapacitated for days. 'My existence is a fearful burden,' he confessed during one such attack. 'Consistent pain, something close to sea-sickness combined with semi-paralysis, which makes it difficult to talk, alternates with raging attacks (the last had me vomiting for three days and nights, I longed for death).' In 1879, he calculated that he had 118 days of headaches during the year. Wagner, ever sympathetic, put the condition down to compulsive masturbation.

One thing that was compulsive was Nietzsche's insistence on taking his treatment into his own hands. Diets, drugs, climate cures – he self-prescribed them all. One remedy he alighted on was the idea that he must live all year round in temperatures between 9 and 12 degrees Celsius. The fact that achieving this required him to travel constantly, often for days in very poor conditions, which always made him ill, was simply beside the point. He enjoyed moving, so he convinced himself that movement was good for him.

Nietzsche's maladies followed a familiar pattern. He would push himself to the limit, then, when the inevitable collapse had passed, he would proclaim himself cured and start the whole cycle again. His ups were stratospheric; his downs fathomless. He set up a pattern of boom and bust which ended up ruling his life.

Not that this pattern was unique to Nietzsche. It belonged, not to him, but to confidence, the force to which he had devoted himself. Quite simply, the basic pattern of confidence is boom and bust. There is no escaping it – in fact, our belief that we can escape it is precisely what causes it in the first place.

At this point, it is helpful to think of an economic cycle. In the beginning, the economy grows in tandem with confidence. They boost each other, the physical and mental sides of the growth equation. Economic growth makes us feel better about the economy, and because we feel better, we borrow, and so the economy grows. (In financial terms, confidence is debt, which is why every financial crisis is also a crisis of debt.) For a while, growth is real, and it is *good*. On it goes, until at some point – and it is impossible to know when – our belief in the economy starts to exceed its fundamental strengths and weaknesses. Genuine growth has turned into a bubble. Confidence has soared – *pop!* – out of the atmosphere of reality. And it takes a painful crash to bring the whole thing down to earth.

Nietzsche's last boom was the one that preceded his madness. He had never been afraid of self-aggrandisement, but in his final writings his boasting was off the scale. He signed off his last work, *Ecce Homo*, 'Dionysus versus the Crucified' – he was a Greek god in opposition to Jesus Christ. Nietzsche scholars debate the extent to which *Ecce Homo* was directly influenced by Nietzsche's madness. The contents certainly prefigure the letter-writing campaign which signalled his insanity's arrival.

Even in madness Nietzsche was living out his philosophy. A few years earlier he had suggested that for every true innovator, 'if they were not already mad, all that was left was to make themselves mad or to feign madness . . . "Madness so that I can finally believe in myself!"' Now, truly insane, he acted out fantasies he had previously only dared to write about. In his letters, he was an emperor. In the room of his boarding house in Turin, he danced naked, as if at a Dionysian orgy.

Although he was diagnosed with syphilis, it now appears that Nietzsche was suffering from a case of manic psychosis. (The other plausible diagnosis, a non-malignant brain tumour, does not quite match up with the details of Nietzsche's pathology.) Like his other ailments, this condition was exacerbated by his way of life. A few months before his breakdown, he had moved to Italy in search of suitable weather. Always isolated, now he was completely alone, adrift in an unfamiliar country where he spoke barely a word of the language. His financial situation, never very stable, was about to get worse – the University of Basel planned to cut his pension by a third the following year – and he had committed himself to extensive redrafts of works old and new. Psychologists studying these breakdowns talk about a patient's risk factors. In Nietzsche's case, his entire life was a risk factor.

What could have prevented Nietzsche's madness? Nothing can stop confidence overreaching itself, so the best way to handle it is to create structures that stop it doing too much damage. Friends, family, a job, lasting commitments – all these give you ballast in the good times and bad. This, however, was exactly the life Nietzsche rejected. His disdain for 'habit' and love of solitude made his mental state dependent on the ebbs and flows of his good feeling. Sadly, success, the one thing that might conceivably have connected him to the wider world, arrived six months too late.

Nietzsche never said we should be confident all the time. What he does say is in many ways more terrifying: even though it is impossible to be confident all the time, we must still maintain complete confidence as our goal. 'Everyone has his good days where he finds his higher self,' he writes, 'and true humanity demands that everyone be evaluated only in the light of this condition.' Our best days are the standard; everything else is underperformance. Ignoring the inevitable dip to come, we must be able to say with Nietzsche, 'Today I love myself as a god.'

And there you have it, the reason we can't wean ourselves off boom and bust and live in a steady state: because, like Nietzsche, we have set a standard for ourselves of complete and unfailing confidence. We know, deep down, that no one is confident all the time, that such a thing is impossible, but at the same time, there's always a voice whispering, *But if it were possible, wouldn't it be lovely?* It's the myth of the confident person – and philosophically, it traces back to Nietzsche.

'To be a human being with a single elevated feeling, the embodiment of one great mood – that has hitherto been merely a dream and a delightful possibility,' Nietzsche noted. 'As yet history offers us no certain examples.' Nevertheless, he could not but hope. This time, he told himself, this time is different.

It was the night before his first exam, and Charlie was in despair. Admitting this fact felt momentous. He experimented with saying it aloud: 'I am fucked. I am *fucked.*'

The earth-shattering statement didn't take effect – nothing stopped, nothing changed. When he went upstairs to tell Alistair,

Alistair shouted through the door that if Charlie had nothing to contribute on German Constitutional Law then he wasn't welcome.

Charlie stared at an essay plan on Berlusconi he'd cobbled together from part of a coursework essay and an article he'd sourced four hours ago on the intranet. Given that substance wasn't going to be his strong point, he knew his argument needed to be nothing short of field-changing, the sort of thing that would prompt the examiner to stop everything, jump on a train and travel to Italy to explain it to Berlusconi in person.

He was doing it again – imagining things going well instead of doing something to bring that outcome about. God, he was a waste of space.

Seeking human contact online, he found an email from Meredith, no subject heading: 'Don't contact Sara. She's gone home to revise.'

Charlie stared at the screen, reading the sentences over and over.

On the desk, his phone flashed 'Lucas'. Charlie felt a twinge of shame – he hadn't seen or spoken to Lucas since Stiltongate. He stared at the phone, hoping some instruction would emerge, and finally forced himself to pick up.

'Mate, come to the Mitre. Everyone's here.'

'I've got Italian Politics tomorrow.'

'So?'

'So I'm fucked!'

The solemnity of this situation passed Lucas by.

'Last-minute cramming's not going to help. Have you learned nothing? You've got to relax, keep supple, get in the zone.'

Charlie had the dim sense that this was poor advice but he was in no position to judge. 'I'm not drinking.'

'Sure, mate. Whatever you want.'

———

'You don't need much, you've got lovely skin,' Ashley the make-up artist said, liberally applying foundation to Ellie's forehead. Nadine perched on the dressing table between transparent plastic make-up cases, highlighting sections of her 'Topics in Epistemology: Knowledge and Justification' essay.

'Exams?' Ashley asked her brightly.

'Yeah, we got our first one tomorrow.' Nadine grimaced.

'I bet you'll be fine!'

'Doubt it. 'Course Ellie can't even sit hers.'

'Ridiculous, really,' murmured Kathryn, the National Student Union rep. When they'd been introduced earlier, Kathryn had seemed extremely focused and very political. The moment she excused herself to take a phone call, Ellie hustled Nadine off to the loos to replan their strategy.

'I'm going to focus on the censorship angle,' Ellie had brain-stormed. 'Censorship. And punishing protest.'

Nadine nodded, distractedly eyeing her ringbinder.

Now, Kathryn glanced through interview notes while Ashley's colleague, Derek, dabbed her left cheek. Ellie's quarter-sheet, torn from Nadine's notes on cognitive pluralism, hardly seemed worth the effort.

'How are you feeling?' Ashley brushed under Ellie's eyes. 'Bit nervous?'

Ellie smiled in vague agreement, but in fact, she didn't feel nervous. It was strange. She was basically unprepared, but she still felt ready for any question. Knowledge of the topic seemed irrele-vant when she knew herself. Ellie was even quietly excited at the prospect of discovering she was good at this.

Deep down in the miscellaneous compartment of her brain, wedged between near-forgotten humiliations and stubborn mem-ories of wrongdoing, was an email she had received that morning.

'Dear Eleanor,' it read:

I've just returned from paternity leave to find your emails and the various messages you left with Jonathan in the office, who kindly stayed late yesterday to pass them on. I'm sorry that you've had this experience. The disciplinary letter was issued automatically and should never have been sent without further discussion. These letters are reserved for cases of serious criminal damage or assault to other students, and such escalation was not appropriate in this case.

Naturally we do not condone vandalism to university property in any circumstance, political or otherwise. However I understand that you deny having carried out the subsequent vandalism and so the committee is content to let the matter rest.

Please accept this email as confirmation that you are authorised to sit your examinations as set out in your timetable. I wish you the best of luck with them and I hope that this has not caused undue disruption to your revision.

I understand you have contacted various media outlets to publicise these events. Although I appreciate your motivation, it is a matter of regret to me, the other committee members, and the university administration, that you did not feel able to resolve the matter internally. Were you aware, for example, that Dr Michelle Pritchard is responsible for all third-year pastoral matters and could have assisted you? (This information is in the handbook and on the intranet.) Your methods have had the unfortunate effect of tarnishing the university's reputation unnecessarily. (Please also see the handbook for our policy regarding protest.)

It remains for me to wish you all the best in your exams and the future.

Regards, Simeon.

'That's you!' Ashley smiled at Ellie. 'Do you want to head back to the green room?'

'Actually, we'll take them into the studio, please.' An absurdly attractive man stepped in with a walkie-talkie. 'We're close to time.'

There were a surprising number of people in the pub: a febrile, oddly attired group sipping on lime and soda or buckets of tea. Lucas kept trying to make Charlie have a pint, which was pretty annoying. All anyone else had to talk about was revision. If you weren't hysterical when you arrived, Charlie thought, you would be when you walked out the door.

'Haven't seen you in ages,' said a weary Romilly.

'Well, whose fault is that?' Charlie replied, more gruffly than he intended. Whatever part of his brain managed conversation was out of action.

'I know, I've been working at Josh's. If we don't revise together, we never see each other, because what else is going on? I feel like I have room for about two people in my life right now: Katie and Josh. We watch *Cash in the Attic* together. Pathetic. But it's our break. We're all doing about eleven hours a day, it's just crazy. Katie got up yesterday and fainted. It'd been that long since she'd stood up.'

Charlie stared glumly at the beer mat.

'So.' Romilly looked at him reproachfully. 'I heard about you and Sara.'

'Oh God,' Charlie couldn't help himself saying.

'Look.' Romilly put down her tea to do a demonstrative impression of Charlie. Katie and Josh smiled and drew closer, as though this were the beginning of a familiar skit, one they all took turns at as they watched *Cash in the Attic*. 'Look. I know you're broken-hearted 'cause I dumped you. Even though you're beautiful and lovely and I'm an idiot. So how about this? Let's shag every so often. Obviously I'll shag anyone else I can lay my hands on as well. Oh yeah, can you also stroke my forehead while I revise?'

'*And.*' Katie deepened her voice. 'When we leave, I never want to see you again. Obviously.'

'Yeah!' grinned Romilly. 'What do you say? I bet that makes you feel pretty special.'

'What a lucky lady,' Josh chipped in.

'It wasn't like that,' muttered Charlie.

'Do you know what your problem is, Charlie?' Romilly swayed in her seat, enjoying herself.

Charlie sighed. 'I'm a nice guy who thinks he's a dick?'

'No – well, yes, actually. But your other one. You don't take any responsibility for yourself. You . . . How can I put this? You're a *hopeless* shambles.'

Charlie was on the brink of straightforwardly agreeing (not even in a self-deprecating way), when Sasha and Pippa walked through the Mitre door. Catching Charlie's eye, Sasha gave a faintly ironic wave as she headed towards the bar – a wave in which Charlie saw his only hope for salvation.

The interview had gone brilliantly, even better than the radio one. Gita was primed to talk about how students were depressingly apolitical and didn't give a shit, but Kathryn and Ellie had success-fully challenged her view. Ellie mentally replayed a moment in which she had criticised previous generations for believing they had a monopoly on politics and accused them of blaming current students for the failure of their own ideals. 'Politics didn't end in the Seventies,' she'd said.

Ellie called Nadine over as the taxi arrived.

'Train station, please.' They swung out of the drive.

'Ugh, can't read in the car.' Nadine snapped her folder shut and swallowed queasily.

'So.' Ellie took a breath. 'I've got a bit of news.'

'You're pregnant.'

'No, thank God.'

'*I'm* pregnant?'

'Not as far as I'm aware.'

'Phew.'

'No. Uni's decided I can sit my exams.'

'Oh my God.' Nadine stared at her. 'Amazing! When did that happen?'

'I got an email from the committee this morning.'

'Wow. That's brilliant!'

'I know! It's kind of frustrating, because now I haven't done any revision. But at least this way I can finish uni. I'm relieved.'

'Me too.' Nadine looked at the passing streetlights for a second. 'This morning?'

'Yeah. I'm sorry I didn't tell you earlier.'

'Yeah, why didn't you tell me?'

'I just thought it would complicate everything. We still had the interview to do and I didn't want to ruin the story, you know? It seemed easier "not to see it" for a few hours.'

'Okay.' Nadine tapped her folder. 'But . . . did we need to do the interview if the ban was over?'

'That's four pounds eighty, please.'

Ellie pulled out a fiver. 'God, we could have walked.'

Nadine climbed out and slammed the taxi door.

'You all right?' Ellie reopened the door and stepped onto the pavement.

'Yeah, just feel a bit sick.'

They walked into the central waiting area and checked the departures board. 'One in twenty minutes,' Ellie narrated needlessly.

'So including the train home that'll be about eight hours travelling and preparing and hanging about.'

'Yeah.' Ellie rolled her eyes.

'For nothing.'

'Not for nothing. I mean, it's still awareness, isn't it?'

Nadine laughed incredulously. 'But you know that I – and you – have an exam tomorrow, yeah?'

'Yeah, I do *now*.'

Nadine flicked her thumb and fingernails, staring at the board. 'So I was totally willing to come given I'm responsible too and I want to support you.'

'Thanks.'

'But do you get the difference between *that* and me coming when there's actually no point and you've kind of lied to me?'

'I haven't *lied*.'

'Yeah. Well.' Nadine laughed again. 'Don't worry about it. It's good news.'

Ellie scouted round for a bench, suspecting this would all be easier if they could sit down.

'So, I mean, what about your revision?' Nadine strived, but failed, to change her tone. 'Done any?'

'Some.'

'Gonna work when you get back?'

'I said I might go to Oscar's.'

Nadine threw her eyes up to the domed glass ceiling.

'What?'

'I know this is none of my business, yeah, but are you being . . . fair on Justin?'

'I told Justin – he's okay with it.'

'*Is* he though?'

'Yes.'

'But is he.'

'Yes!'

268

An announcement rattled across the hall, scattering pigeons.

'Can I ask.' Nadine spread her silver-ringed fingers. 'What is it you're *doing*? I don't get it.'

'*This*. All the stuff you encouraged me to do. It's good!'

They held one another's gaze. Nadines eyes were wide and apparently expectant – Ellie couldn't figure out what she wanted.

'Well,' concluded Nadine, at length. 'I'm gonna get a chai latte and try a timed essay on the train.'

Charlie was hanging around by the *Who Wants To Be A Millionaire?* machine (picking up quite a crowd as they made it through to thirty-two thousand). He sipped the pint he hadn't asked for and watched Sasha chatting to Josh and fiddling with her necklace. She was wearing the girl revision uniform – low-slung joggers and a vest top, the hint of a belly-button ring under the fabric, an inch of flat, brown stomach beneath.

The problem with his singleness, Charlie reflected, was that he hadn't made the most of his opportunities: he hadn't pursued them doggedly, relentlessly, clinically. The thought would have filled him with the bitterest regret, sending him deeper into the pit of self-loathing – *would* have, except that now, in his darkest hour (perhaps in answer to his prayers?), an opportunity for redemption had presented itself.

'Which of these zodiac signs is *not* represented by an animal that grows horns?' shouted Lucas. 'Who knows animals?'

As Sasha stood up holding a cigarette and lighter, Charlie saw his opportunity. He moved away from the *Millionaire* frenzy – 'Aries! What the fuck is Aries? A deer?' – and sidled over to the door.

'Any chance I could scab a cigarette?'

Sasha considered, unenthusiastic. 'I sup*pose* I could give you a drag.'

'They are very bad for you.'

'Don't expect any thanks for saving my life.'

Outside, the Mitre's fairy lights glowed in the late dusk. In the cool air, away from all that group hysteria, Charlie felt a little calmer.

'Before we start.' He leaned on the windowsill. 'Let's get a few things straight. You've been doing . . . eleven hours of revision a day? Well, just so you know, I've been doing twelve.'

Sasha lit her fag. 'I've gone twenty-four/seven – not slept since April.'

'I hope not. I've not eaten since March. Had to be hooked up to a drip.' Charlie sipped his pint. 'I start tomorrow so I've still got a solid twelve hours.'

'Tomorrow? Shit.'

'Yeah . . .' Charlie gave a half-shrug, wondering if Sasha would find his recklessness sexy. 'However, we seem to have tricked ourselves into talking about revision.'

'Who started that?' Sasha passed him the cigarette. 'How's your business venture? Bust already?'

'Oh, it's taking off,' he lied seamlessly. 'In fact, are you looking for a job? Because we've got some great opportunities.'

'As it happens, I've got fuck all lined up for the rest of my life, so I guess you could say I'm available.'

'I'm sure we could find something for a candidate like you. What would you say was your biggest weakness?'

Sasha reclaimed the cigarette and took a drag. 'Impatience.'

A middle-aged couple came out of the pub, digging around in their pockets. 'Martin, I definitely had a pound coin somewhere.'

Charlie's next line didn't come to him and he was conscious of himself turning inward in the silence. He knew he had to make a move, but he couldn't just fling himself at her in an awkward pause. Perhaps he could catch her eye? (She was listlessly studying her fingernails.)

By the time Charlie had taken another sip of the pint, his internal monologue had conspired to bind this moment with his entire university experience. He *wasn't* going to leave university having kissed four girls and slept with two in three years – he wasn't going to be that passive loser any more – he just wasn't.

As the couple clip-clopped down the alley, Sasha stubbed out her cigarette and prepared to go inside.

Seizing the moment, Charlie took a step forward and went straight for the neck. He lunged at her, lips parted, eyelids closing—

'Ugh.' Sasha jerked her head sideways, leaning back. 'Christ!'

'Um—'

'Charlie, what are you doing?' Her flippant mask momentarily slipped, revealing surprise and embarrassment beneath.

'I . . .' He hung his head. 'Sorry.'

The middle-aged woman ran back towards the pub door, handbag flapping round her elbow.

'It's all right.' Sasha gathered herself. 'Pretend it never happened.'

'No, I want to explain.' Charlie stopped her heading back inside. 'I've been having the worst time. I'm all over the place. I keep getting it wrong, I'm sorry.'

'It's okay, Charlie, just forget it.'

'No, I owe you an explanation. This semester has been disaster on disaster. For one thing, I don't even have a business. I'm just full of bullshit as usual.'

'Charlie—'

'I fucked it up like everything—'

271

'Charlie!'

He looked up at her. In spite of it all, a brief, mad hope crossed his mind: that Sasha might kiss him then, moved by his tortured state.

'If possible,' said Sasha, 'this is even worse than being face-attacked. Do yourself a favour and go home.'

'Okay,' Charlie nodded hopelessly.

'Goodnight, Charlie.' As a cheer went up from the soon-to-be millionaires, Sasha slipped back into the pub.

She wouldn't tell everyone, Charlie knew; she'd just tell *one* person and make them promise not to tell anyone else. And somehow, inexorably, it would spread, sweeping through the population – social Black Death.

Leaving his pint on the windowsill, Charlie walked away.

Making her way back from Oscar's, Ellie felt so alert and percep-tive, she wished she could take her exam there and then. They had celebrated her imminent Final with a whisky on the roof of the boat. Now, Ellie intended to root out all of her Epistemology essays and notes, lay them over the living-room floor and meditate on them until dawn. *Does knowledge exist?* Ellie turned her thoughts into a continuity announcement. *Tune in at five a.m. to find out.*

As she rounded onto her street, an ambulance passed by, lights flashing. After a few steps, she realised the person must have come from their block – the front door was open and a middle-aged man hung around in the doorway staring after the ambulance as though he had nothing better to do. At the bottom of the path, she recog-nised Steve from the Shackle.

'Steve.' She hurrried towards him. 'What are you doing here? Are you all right?'

'Ellie, there you are.' He looked anxious, fingers rubbing busily against one another. 'Rosie's had a turn.'

'Shit, what's wrong?'

'She collapsed. Out cold on the floor. I couldn't get much of a pulse.'

'Oh my God.' Ellie looked down the street. 'Do you know where they went?'

'St Edmund's, they said. They asked if I wanted to go but I thought I'd better wait for you or your fella. The thing is, your door's going to need some attention.'

'My door?'

'The door to your flat. I had to break in, you see. Because Rosie was unconscious.'

'God, okay.' Ellie felt in her pockets. 'I mean . . . Steve, would you mind staying a bit longer while I get a cab to the hospital?'

'No, no.'

'You can sleep on the sofa if you want.'

Only after Ellie called a cab (Steve insisted on maintaining his doorstep position while she waited) did she think to ask. 'So Rose collapsed here. Not at the Shackle?'

'Yup,' nodded Steve, jowls shaking.

'And you found her?'

'I did. Got a hell of a shock.'

'Why was it you happened to be coming round?'

'Well . . .' With slow cunning, Steve's face fell into a blank, clue-less expression. His hand jangled loose change in his pocket.

Did she leave her phone or purse? was on the tip of Ellie's tongue, but something told her to hold back. She looked carefully at Steve's reddening cheeks. For a fleeting second he met her eye, before flicking back to the path.

'What?'

'Pff.' He shook his head. 'Don't know why I'm getting the third degree. Just as well I was here. You're supposed to be her mate.' A leaden weight settled in Ellie's stomach. 'That's your cab now.' Avoiding her gaze, Steve ushered Ellie down the path. 'Have you got cash?'

Ellie got in without reply, gripping the door handle for stability. 'St Edmund's, please.'

'Everything okay?' the driver asked, as they lurched away.

'Um . . .' Ellie caught the woman's eye in the mirror. 'I really don't know.'

Charlie couldn't prevent himself from taking a slightly longer route home in order to pass by Sara's house. It was perverse, he knew (she wasn't even there), but he felt compelled to revisit the scene of his most heinous mistakes. Perhaps it would offer some insight into where he had gone wrong.

As he slowed to a reflective pace, Charlie was shocked to see Sara struggling with her broken bedroom window. It was as though he had dreamt her, brought her into being – except that he was furious at her existence.

'Sara!' he shouted.

On seeing him, she forced the window down (making an unhealthy splintering noise) and disappeared.

'Sara!' He marched over to the window. 'I know you're there!'

He picked up a few pieces of gravel and threw them at the glass. 'Why did you lie?' Charlie headed up the path and rang the bell. 'Sara!' He hammered at the door. 'I want to talk to you. I just want to talk. I'm sorry, okay? I'm really, truly sorry.'

Just as he was about to ring the bell again, Fergus opened the door. 'Charlie.'

'Let me see Sara. I know she's home. In spite of your little conspiracy.'

'I'm asking you politely to leave.'

'What are you guys anyway? Bodyguards? Just let me see her.'

'I'm asking you.'

'We went out for almost two years, for Christ's sake. What do you think I'm going to do to her?'

'Don't make me chuck you out.'

Later, when he went back over it in his head, Charlie replied, 'Out of where, you prick? I'm already outside. That's the problem.' At the time, having made the instant calculation that Fergus probably *could* chuck him out, he chose instead to *look* deeply offended.

Fergus sighed. 'You're disturbing us all. We've got exams. And she's told you she doesn't want to see you.'

'It's so obvious, all this.'

Fergus didn't deign to ask.

'All this protective friend crap. Sara!' he shouted past Fergus. 'I'm sorry!'

Fergus slammed the door.

Charlie sat down on the step. 'I'll wait here! Sara, I'll wait all night if I have to!'

He hugged his knees, righteous anger burning in his chest.

About half an hour passed in this manner. Occasionally, Meredith came to the front window to check if he was still there. He was.

Charlie's anger cooled to keen, humiliated dejection. He wondered what he was doing but couldn't bring himself to leave. If he left, it would all become real. Tomorrow would arrive and this would be a thing that had actually happened – another notch on his bedpost of despair – and on top of it all, he'd have an exam to sit.

The thing that sent Charlie over the edge was the premonition that Berlusconi wasn't going to turn up in this year's Contemporary

Italian Politics paper. Suddenly, he knew unquestionably that it was going to be one of those joker papers, especially designed to ruin anyone who had thought, 'But Berlusconi *is* contemporary Italian politics' and failed to come equipped with a Plan B. He wouldn't be able to answer a single question. He would have to sit in silent agony for the minimum period of forty-five minutes and then take a walk of shame out of the hall, as everybody else cracked their knuckles and planned their second brilliant answer on the lesser-known aspects of the Italian judiciary.

'You can't keep away, can you?' Penny had scuttled up the path and was suddenly squatting beside him on the doorstep.

If anything could make this situation worse, Charlie thought, it was Penny. 'I'm waiting to see Sara.'

'But it was so painful last time,' said Penny, as though she and Sara were now so close, they shared one body.

Charlie sighed irritably.

'It must be hard for you, too,' she intuited. 'Losing her. I bet it's terrible.'

He wished she would go away and stop probing him for emotional fodder.

Just as he was about to tell her to go inside, Penny rolled up her sleeve and shoved a thin, raised scar under his eyes. 'I did this when me and Freddie split up,' she confided sadly.

'That's horrible.' Charlie winced. 'Don't do that.'

'I hardly ever do now,' she reassured him.

Traumatised by this insight, Charlie hugged his knees tighter.

'So what's the matter? Apart from the obvious?'

Charlie shrugged dismally.

'Is it Meredith?' she suggested sympathetically.

'What?' He was baffled.

'I always sensed something between you.'

'What?' He didn't know where to go from here.

'Maybe it's subconscious. You might not be aware of it. It wouldn't be *that* surprising if she fancied you.'

'I think it would be very surprising.'

'People often fancy their close friends' boyfriends. Besides,' she cajoled, 'you must know you're attractive.'

Charlie hated himself for feeling comforted. 'I don't feel it,' he deflected half-heartedly.

'Aw. You're just having a low day.'

'No, everything's gone wrong,' Charlie corrected her. 'It's not one day, it's my whole life. I've failed and I haven't even begun yet.'

'When I feel down, I get an HIV test.'

Charlie's bewilderment was quickly overtaken by depression. 'I haven't even slept with enough people to make an HIV test worthwhile.'

'Get one. I've only slept with one person but they can't refuse. They have to give you it if you ask. Honestly it'll cheer you up.'

'I wish I could go home.' Charlie laid his cheek on his knees. 'I could sleep for a month.'

He felt her hand stroking his hair, but was too despondent to prevent her.

'I've cocked it up,' he murmured.

An arm curled round his shoulders; Penny clung to his side, koala-like. 'Ssshhh,' she whispered. 'It's all right.'

'I only have myself to blame.'

'Ssssh . . .'

Rose was in and out of consciousness, lying on top of the bed sheets in a curtained compartment. Further blue curtains stretched in every direction, opening and closing like an intricate puzzle. The ward might have stretched into infinity.

To Ellie, Rose's treatment looked a lot like chaos. Someone had put her on a drip; someone had mentioned her liver; someone had told them to wait for someone else who would do something, a test perhaps. That was an hour ago. Ellie wondered whether she should ask. What was the right way to behave in hospital? Was it like Argos, where you thought they'd forgotten you until finally your number was called? Or was it like those other times in Argos when they'd actually forgotten you?

Ellie sat on the plastic chair beside Rose, gaze switching from her gaunt, bloodless face to the crack in the curtains, and back to her face. When did Rose slip from tediously skinny to this frightening, skeletal state, and how had Ellie failed to notice? Piecing together the last few months, Ellie realised that Rose hadn't been at uni at all – had she dropped out altogether then?

And *Steve*. Surely that was all in his mind – he'd been cracking on to Rose at work, chasing her, bothering her perhaps. But if it wasn't . . . (Ellie peeked down the corridor – stocky blue and green figures apparated and disapparated at random.) Had Rose truly been *that* lonely? Had Ellie left Rose so completely in the lurch she'd turned to Cheating Regular Steve for comfort?

Ellie buried her head in her lap. Guilt overpowered her. She was the worst friend, the most selfish bitch that had ever lived. It was incredible how solipsistic she'd been, unaware of anything but her own internal roundabout. Ellie wanted to drop to the floor, sink right through it; if somebody had produced a cat-o'-nine-tails, she'd have thanked them.

'Who's that?' Rose interrupted Ellie's crying.

'Me.' Ellie sat up, quickly wiping her face. 'How are you? How are you feeling?'

'Fine,' she tutted. 'Can we go?'

'You're not fine. I've called your mum.'

'What did you do that for?' Rose demanded irritably.

''Cause you're ill, Rose.'

Rose frowned deeply and turned her face away.

'I should've realised sooner. I'm sorry.'

'Don't know what you're crying about,' Rose muttered thickly.

'I should've been looking out for you. I've been a shit friend.'

'I'm *fine*. You're the mental case.'

Rose closed her eyes for a few minutes. Ellie thought she'd gone back to sleep until, without moving, she murmured, 'Can we go home soon?'

'I don't know, Rose,' said Ellie gently. 'You'll have to rest and see people and get better. You'll probably go home-home. To your mum's.'

Rose's face twisted. She spoke into the pillow. 'She's fat. And she wants to make me fat.'

Ellie had never heard Rose express a view like this, never heard her say words like 'fat', 'thin', or 'diet'. They were too crude to convey what Rose was doing; they made it sound so practical.

Ellie put an awkward hand on her upper arm. 'That kind of thought is trying to kill you, do you get that?'

Why hadn't they ever spoken before? Ellie could have tried harder, forced Rose to open up to her. Instead she'd taken the polite, easy path; she'd weaved around Rose's taboos until that perverse, winding circuit was the only possible route.

'Shut up, you turd bucket,' whispered Rose.

All right, Ellie thought, that was why. But she should have done it anyway.

The next time Rose fell asleep, Ellie checked her phone – it was half past two in the morning. Theories of Epistemology began in six and a half hours. She shouldn't go, Ellie decided instantly. She had practically killed Rose through neglect: she needed to stay right here and make up for it. Who cared if she failed her degree? It wasn't important. Frankly she deserved it.

As she stared at the crack in the curtain, Ellie imagined explaining this to her mum. 'I couldn't go,' she'd say, regretfully. 'We were stuck in the hospital and I needed to stay with Rose.' It sounded good, but Ellie had a feeling that her mum would not be pleased. So be it: her duty was clear.

What if Rose's mum arrived before the morning? (The thought of Pam sent Ellie into a wriggling dance of shame. Ellie could have phoned her during Easter, just to check in, told her Rose wasn't her best, invited her to visit . . .) In that circumstance, Ellie felt her presence might not be necessary. Would it be feasible to miss the exam then? After only two hours' sleep, it was barely worth doing it at all.

Hold on – what was she justifying here? Thoroughly confused, Ellie considered calling Justin, but she was beginning to grasp the fact that she had for some time now been treating him like shit: waking him at 3 a.m. to 'help her think' was reaching Stalinist levels of tyranny. And what about Nadine? Her mind slowly paced back over yesterday, the day before Nadine's first exam, spent chaperoning Ellie to unnecessary TV appearances. She winced.

As a thought experiment, Ellie decided she would go to the exam. A whole new raft of problems fell into her lap. In the fluorescent light of the ward, she saw several things very clearly. She was: a) completely unprepared, having done approximately three days of revision in the entire semester; and b) not even sure where the exam was taking place or what her exam number was. These observations led her to the highly credible prediction that she would do *very badly indeed*. In the best of all possibly scenarios, she would brush mediocrity with her fingertips. Crushing failure was a far more likely outcome.

Ellie settled her head on the edge of Rose's stiff bed sheet and closed her eyes.

Finalists milled outside Nicholson Hall like bees kept from the hive. The morning was unseasonably cold. Friends talked past one another; a boy mumbled Descartes quotes over and over; another counted pens in his pocket.

'My brain is empty,' someone said, shivering.

'The emptiness is good,' intoned her friend. 'The emptiness is awaiting a question.'

After an age, but still too soon, the hall doors opened. They streamed in, as invigilators called out directions, ushering them into sections according to paper. Invigilators were always wrong somehow, too short or too hairy; they couldn't live up to the momentousness of the occasion.

Charlie sat down at the edge of Italian Politics and cast his eyes up to the beamed ceiling.

'This is Politics Paper Sixteen: Contemporary Italian Politics,' the dude in his section announced. 'If you need extra paper . . .'

It was all exactly as he'd seen it; he knew what the page would say without even turning it over.

Ellie ran in and sat at the desk next to Charlie, immediately dropping her pens. She bent to pick them up, casting a jittery glance at him. *Charlie*, she thought. *I saw you somewhere.* An obscure feeling of shame blinked in her mind like a signal from another planet.

Charlie averted his eyes. For no reason, he was racked with guilt about splashing her. Even though it was only a stupid joke. Even though he had apologised and bought her abortion pills. Even though she was mental last time he saw her.

'This is Philosophy Paper Eight: Theories of Epistemology,' the woman in Ellie's section announced. 'If you need extra paper . . .'

Out of nowhere, Ellie remembered a conversation they'd had in the second year about how much she'd liked Justin.

You knew you didn't really like him, she scolded herself. *You knew it then.*

'You may now turn over your papers,' an invigilator said. 'And begin.'

19

All Nietzscheans Now

Nietzsche described the way confidence actually works, not the way we wish it did. He identified its difficulties, dangers and possibilities – and embraced them all. He lived his philosophy until, in the end, it proved unliveable.

We, his philosophical heirs, have made the same pact, with the same possible consequences. In our case, however, it is not a choice, but a destiny. We live in a world of enforced confidence, and we are obliged to love it as if we chose it. There is no escape, no opting out of confidence, not if you want to 'be all that you can be'. (And if you don't, what's wrong with you?) Either we have to be confident, or we have to be working on becoming confident. Whether we like it or not, we have to be Nietzscheans now.

How did this happen? Seeing the process as it was starting, Nietzsche named secularism as the driving force, but at best that is only one half of the equation. Greater responsibility must lie with our economic system, and the demands it places on us for flexibility and endless movement. Confidence is a capitalist virtue, and as we become more capitalist, so our dependence on it increases.

In his scattered remarks on economics, Nietzsche was consistently hostile towards capitalism. Seen from this perspective, however, he could rank among its most powerful advocates, because of the way in which he gives dynamism and change an almost transcendent quality. He even approved of inequality, for the familiar capitalist reason that it promoted striving and achievement.

Why might confidence and capitalism be particularly compatible? To understand, it helps to compare confidence with a rather more medieval virtue: honour. For much of the Middle Ages and beyond, honour was at least as important to people as confidence is now. You would pay on time, go to war, estrange yourself from family members, give up the person you loved and shun friends, all for the sake of this intangible quality and its system of social rewards and punishments.

Honour declined because it was incompatible with capitalism. It was the glue that held pre-modern society together, but its insistence on everyone knowing their place was too sticky for capitalism, which preferred mobile individuals maximising their competitive advantage. (This is one of those instances when it makes sense to speak of grand historical forces as if they had personalities.) Confidence, with its love of flexibility and shapeshifting, was far more appropriate to the new system.

The history of confidence makes the connection with capitalism clear. Emerging as a word in English in the fifteenth century, it was a Godly quality among the first capitalists, the Protestants of pre-Reformation Europe. Confidence first came to prominence in nineteenth-century America, during the era of mass urban migration. For writers in this confusing time, confidence was the quality that symbolised the death of small-town communities and their replacement by a society of strangers. Herman Melville wrote a book about it, *The Confidence-Man*, in which a man who is 'in the extremest sense of the word, a stranger' tours a riverboat asking passengers to trust him, then conning them out of their money. The popular obsession with 'confidence tricksters' in newspapers of the time warned of the deceptiveness of confidence, while at the same time illustrating its desirability: it was the trait of scammers and con men, but it was also the quality that could make you rich.

Fast-forward one hundred and fifty years, and confidence is not simply accepted, but held in the highest regard. This shift has been especially noticeable in the last thirty years; not coincidentally, in the same period, life has become correspondingly more capitalistic. The big corporations of fifty years ago have been broken up, downsized, delayered (the shift from bureaucracy, literally 'rule by desk', to hot-desking). Employment is less stable and 'careers' are a thing of the past. The market intrudes into every arena, not least education, so that if you go to university, you start off working life with tens of thousands of pounds' worth of debt to recover. And so the existence Nietzsche chose for himself – impoverished, itinerant, uncertain – becomes, simply, the way we live now.

When Charlie arrived, Ellie was already perched at the end of the bar with a goblet of red wine. In the split second before saying hello, he wondered how he should greet her. A high five seemed ridiculous; on the other hand, she didn't exactly scream *Hug me*. In the event, Ellie got up and pecked his cheek.

'I'm afraid I started without you.'

'That's all right.' Charlie took off his raincoat. 'I wasn't expecting you to wait in the freezing cold until I arrived.'

'No, I mean I had one before this.' She nodded at her wine.

'Ah. No problem. I'd better order then.'

As he turned towards the barman, Charlie acknowledged, but resisted, his impulse to institute some edgy, hyper-banterous style of conversation. He didn't want an exhausting evening of quipping past one another, uni-style. Charlie was completely convinced by the maturity and rightness of this approach; the only remaining problem was he wasn't sure how else to talk.

He'd bumped into Ellie on the Strand around 1 a.m., hood up, arms clamped against the wind. Charlie was on his way back to Lucas's, enjoying a solitary venture in the breathless city night, a fleeting sense of urbanity compounded by his knowledge of which bus to get. The meeting was brief – his bus arrived in about a minute – and felt unfinished. Not pleasant exactly, enervating in some ways, but nonetheless interesting. As Charlie jumped onto the bus, he'd suggested a beer next time he was down. Then, two weeks later, as part of his new regime of following things through (facilitated by his freshly emptied schedule), he'd arranged it.

'So how are you doing?' he began, consciously not minding that he didn't have some hilarious anecdote on hand to kick off.

'Do you know what? Not that bad actually.' Ellie was wearing an old leather coat and black eyeliner, a kind of messy glamour with an emphasis on the messy. 'I mean, hopeless on the work front obviously. I'm waitressing. And sometimes I temp in a hospital. At the end of the day I usually feel like downing half a bottle of vodka, and I think it's fair to say that I'm on the verge of having a drinking problem. On the up side, I have a financial crisis to blame, so that's great!'

'That's true.' Charlie nodded to the barman. 'Kronenbourg, please.' Ellie seemed a little keyed up, he thought, as though she'd been working up conversation pieces while she waited.

'How did we not notice it was happening?' Ellie shook her head. 'I certainly didn't. There we were, getting down to our finals. Everyone must have been thinking, "Best not tell them they're fucked – they'll find out soon enough." Although' – she shifted, crossing her legs – 'I quite like being termed the "lost generation", rather than like the "Facebook generation" or whatever. *Finally* I'm on trend. If I'm authentically lost then I must be doing it right.'

Charlie smiled, subtly deflecting her nervous energy.

She sipped her wine. 'Are you trying not to ask what I got?'

'What you got?' he said, surprised. 'No, I wasn't at all.'

'Well, I got a two:two.'

His expression lifted. 'As a matter of fact, so did I.'

'No!' She looked pleased. 'I thought I was the only one!'

'It's an elite group. Lucas is in. What was your average?'

She rolled her eyes. 'Fifty-nine.'

'Oooh, unlucky.'

'I know.'

'I wasn't even close. I don't know if that feels better or worse.'

Charlie's pint arrived and he handed a fiver to the barman, who was scattering charisma all over the place – probably an actor, Charlie thought.

'So, how are things with you then?' Ellie took a breath, settling a little. 'Is real life everything you'd hoped?'

'Well,' Charlie considered. 'I'm living at home.'

'I *thought* you looked sort of country-ish.'

'Yeah, there's not much call for mirrors in deepest Sussex.'

'I don't mean it badly.'

'No, I know. I've also got a job, in a manner of speaking: I'm working for my parents at the chocolate factory.'

'Ah, okay. That's great. I'm a committed apply-er. Applicant, I mean. It's like my hobby. I may as well drop them all down a drain. Still. I apply.'

'In my job you've got to be willing to accept bed and board as part payment.'

'A kind of feudal system.'

'Yeah. They got a bit . . . screwed in the crash.'

'Oh no.'

'Yeah, bit of a disaster.'

'Not many people know this.' Ellie leaned in. 'But the Chinese symbol for "disaster" *also* means "fucked up the arse".'

Charlie laughed. Ellie was funny – he caught the thought before it came out.

'I thought people bought chocolates during recessions though. Isn't that what they're always saying? Lipsticks and chocolate or something.'

'No, I've heard that. But they – my parents – were planning on expanding and they remortgaged. And then it turns out people don't buy as many chocolates as all that.'

'Ah.'

'That was the first thing I did. Redundancies.'

Ellie's eyes widened. 'Oh God.'

'Not choosing the people or telling them, thank God, but helping my mum sort out all the paperwork and share out the workload . . . mostly to myself. Yay. I do the day-to-day stuff that used to be done by about three people.'

'Oh. How's that going?'

'Mmmm.' Charlie rubbed his hair, making strands rise with static. 'It's a combination of stress and a weird amount of responsibility, and no real skills or experience to deal with it. And boring. It's also boring.'

'Ergh.' Ellie bit her lip sympathetically. 'At least you're getting some experience. I feel like even if there were any jobs, which there aren't, and I got an interview, which I won't, I'd go in and be like, "Don't give *me* a *job*! Are you crazy? I don't know *anything*!"'

'A few of the people who work in the factory I've known since I was a kid.' Charlie played with a beermat. 'And then I've sort of turned into their boss. But a boss who doesn't know anything. Can you imagine?'

Ellie winced.

'They *hate* me. They despise me. And I get it, I do.'

Ellie fingered the stem of her glass in the pause. 'Do you ever see anyone in Sussex then?'

'Well, I just split up with my girlfriend actually.'

'Oh sorry about that. Was it someone from school?'

'Um, no.' He sipped his beer. 'It was Penny.'

'Penny Penny? As in, uni Penny?'

'Yup.'

'Penny Austin?'

'Yes.'

'Right. Yeah.' He watched Ellie struggle to swallow her surprise. *Yes, that's right,* he felt like standing up and declaring to the pub. *I, Charlie Naughton, had a long-term relationship with Penny Austin.* He couldn't pretend that the admission wasn't humiliating, but Charlie was determined not to be a traitor. All right, Penny was nuts, but she was also extremely sweet and had been an incredible support during his summer of self-loathing, and his not-so-magical adventures in the chocolate factory.

'We started going out during exams,' he offered, hoping Ellie would read between the lines.

'Uh-huh.'

'I feel like it might have been more a product of that situation rather than anything else. And because she lives quite near me and I was having a shit time, it ended up lasting longer than it perhaps should have.'

'God, well, I know that feeling.'

'I've made a decision to stay single for a while and stop copping out. Try and get along by myself.'

289

'Good decision.'

'Don't tell me *you*'re single.'

Ellie's eyes meandered up to the soft yellow lights.

'Thought not.'

'I'm not exactly not-single, I'm just not exactly single either.'

'Do you like whoever it is?' asked Charlie bluntly, empowered by his new independent state.

'Did *you* like Penny?' she returned quickly.

He hesitated. 'No.'

Ellie gave a single nod. 'Well. I *quite* like him.'

'Like a four.'

'Like . . .' Ellie's head cocked to the side. 'A generous five. As opposed to what for you?' She stretched out her hands. 'How *do* you signify negative fingers?'

Charlie looked down at the tiled floor, irritated but not sure why. 'So who are you living with?'

Ellie drained her glass. 'With this guy, whose name is Dominic – he's in Nadine's room while she's in Ecuador. And with Rose.'

'Living together, eh?' Even Charlie could hear the edge in his voice.

'Yes, as it happens we live in the same house.' She raised her eyebrows. 'That all right with you, Charlie?'

'Of course.' He shook himself. 'Sorry. How's Rose?'

'A lot better. She was at home and an outpatient for a while, and just moved down this month. She's waitressing and applying for uni next year. Still as mad as anything but . . . better.'

'What's she going to study?'

'Philosophy,' said Ellie. 'Or French. She can't decide. It's funny – I never saw her write an essay all the time we lived together. But she's got pretty into it. How's Lucas?'

'Fine. Wants to go and work in the City.'

Ellie took a moment to process this news. 'Only Lucas could possibly look at what's happening and think, "Sounds like the game for me. Pass me the subprime mortgages." That's *insane*.'

'I kind of agree to be honest.' Charlie tracked the barman. 'What do you want to do, if you get the chance?'

'I don't know. The closest I came to doing a real job was even more bullshit than my bullshit jobs.'

'What was it?'

'I temped at a consultancy. They got us in late at night to call American second-hand car merchants and ask them all these in-depth questions about their business. Most of the time it was just being told to fuck off in a transatlantic context. Sometimes they would talk to me and I didn't understand half what they said. But I tried to plug it into the spreadsheet. Anyway while I was there, I was chatting to the guy next to me who was full-time, and I was like: "This isn't it, is it? I mean, consultants don't just phone people up and hope they'll get some information, right?" And he was like: "Basically, yeah." Then they dress it all up in a PowerPoint with a few made-up figures thrown in. It felt like uni group presentations all over again. I mean, I'm sure they're not all like that, but . . .'

'So what then?'

'I dunno.' She sagged. 'To be honest I don't really want to want anything in case I don't get it. It's a bit depressing.' She took a sip of his pint. 'What do *you* want? Are you in the chocolate business for life now?'

'Oh my God, I hope not.' Charlie rubbed at the edge of the polished wood with his sleeve. 'I'd like to do something where my main contact isn't with a tight group of middle-aged women who loathe me. I'd like to have a life. I'd like to actually be in love, not half pretending and lying.' He looked up. 'Sorry, is this more of a catch-up than you bargained for?'

'No, don't be daft.' After a moment, she asked, 'Why *did* you want to meet up?'

'I'm not sure. I was glad to see you.' Charlie finished his pint. 'It might sound strange but I always felt I could be honest with you.'

'Really?'

'Or not honest exactly. I was still bullshitting. But I felt like you knew that.'

'Yeah,' Ellie nodded. 'Yeah, pretty much.'

20

Confidence and Love

When Nietzsche collapsed he was handed over to his mother and sister. It was not what he would have wanted, but there was no one else who could care for him. He was a childless, unmarried man of forty-four, who had lived alone almost his entire adult life. Indeed, if it weren't for the STI he contracted as a young man, there would be doubt as to whether he'd ever had sex. Inevitably, speculative theories abound, but he was neither gay, nor a victim of abuse, nor a woman-hater, despite his best efforts to appear as one ('Are you going to see a woman? Do not forget your whip!'). His problem wasn't with women, but with the idea of lasting love.

For Nietzsche, love and confidence were opposing forces. Given the choice, he chose confidence every time.

In his twenties and thirties, Nietzsche often said he'd like to get married, but he was never able to find a 'convenient' wife. Even when he did alight on someone suitable, he seemed ambivalent about the whole affair. He proposed to one young woman, Mathilde Trampedach, via a third party (who was also her unofficial fiancé – such blunders are a feature of Nietzsche's courtships), having known her for less than a week. When she refused, startled, he seemed generally relieved. He wasn't sure whether getting married was worth the bother. He needed a 'reading machine', he wrote to a friend, because his eyesight was fading and his type-writer was on the blink, adding: 'I need a young person around who is intelligent and educated enough to work with me. I'd even agree to two years of marriage for this purpose – in this case, of course, a few other conditions would come into consideration.' One dreads to think. Perhaps one of the buttons had fallen off his shirt.

Relationships for Nietzsche were a one-way street. Any marriage he might enter into would work for him or not at all. He would be the employer, she the intern. His friendships were the same. He prized friendship and wrote powerfully in praise of it, yet he had few friends to speak of, and those he did have were more like supporters than true equals. (Peter Gast, in many ways his closest companion during his nomadic period, served as his copyist – a friend, but also a useful secretary.) He appreciated their help and encouragement, yet he had to be able to disengage himself at any time. He was unattached, and as a result, free.

During the early years of his self-imposed exile he was lonely and sometimes very low, to the point of questioning whether he had done the right thing by sacrificing intimacy for the sake of truth. 'Even now,' he wrote to Gast, 'my entire philosophy falters after just an hour's friendly conversation with total strangers. It seems so silly to insist on being right at the expense of love.' But – there was always a but. How awful it would be 'not to be able to disclose what is best in oneself for fear of losing sympathy'. Entering into a relationship would compromise not only his physical freedom, but also his ability to be himself, to pursue his thoughts and speak and act without fear of causing offence. Bearing someone else in mind, watching out for them, wondering what they would like, making allowances, thinking, anticipating and being considerate were all very well, but they would inevitably constrain freedom of spirit.

Despite his misgivings, Nietzsche longed for love. He wanted company in his mission: 'a free spirit and a free heart!' 'I lust after such a soul,' he told the long-suffering Gast, adding quickly: 'Marriage is another story – I could agree to a maximum of a two-year marriage.' He believed he had found such a person in Lou Salomé, a twenty-one-year-old Russian girl he was introduced to by his friend Paul Rée in the spring of 1882, when he was thirty-eight.

Salomé was bold, intense, independent-minded, his intellectual equal. In the photos she appears wasp-waisted and strong-jawed, someone who knows her own mind. For the first time in his life, Nietzsche was smitten. His opening words to her were: 'From which stars did we fall to meet one other here?'

The courtship was the usual mix of timidity and over-assertiveness. After only a few days Nietzsche issued one of his kamikaze third-person proposals, this time via Rée, who with stunning inevitability was already in love with Salomé himself. Salomé declined tactfully, but whereas on previous occasions rejection had come as a relief to Nietzsche, this time he was undeterred. There was definitely something between them. 'Talking with Nietzsche is uncommonly beautiful,' Salomé recorded in her notebook. On a romantic mountain walk – for him, 'the most exquisite dream of my life!' – they talked for hours, sharing their deepest philosophical thoughts in a kind of mutual creative epiphany.

He proposed again, earnestly and intently and, unusually for him, in person. Salomé told him she was not interested in marriage, with him or with anyone else, and that she wanted to live the life of an independent woman. She preferred an alterna-tive plan: why didn't she, Rée and Nietzsche move in together, to set up a house for free spirits where they could read and discuss philosophy? For a while, Nietzsche embraced the idea: it fulfilled his own ideal of love-without-ties. 'I have such high hopes for us living together,' he wrote encouragingly to Salomé. It couldn't last. With a helping hand from Nietzsche's jealous sister and the equally rivalrous Rée, the whole thing collapsed into a stew of bitterness and misunderstanding. To him she was: 'This scrawny dirty rank-smelling monkey with her fake breasts – a disaster!' (The letter remained unsent.) For her: 'Nietzsche's nature, like an old castle, contains within it dark dungeons and secret cellars, which are not apparent in fleeting acquaintance, yet perhaps contain his essence.'

Was she ever really into him? Probably not – or, at least, not in that way. Some commentators have accused her of leading on the lovestruck, unworldly philosopher. (Over 100 years later, empathetic middle-aged men still keenly feel the cruelty of Nietzsche's dismissal by a twenty-one-year-old.) Another school regards her as the victim of his voracious ego – it's a vital area of Nietzsche scholarship. But her confusion is completely understandable. Nietzsche was much older and, let's face it, not exactly a catch; even so, she could have loved him. Yet there was something about him that was cold and unloveable – a single-mindedness that repelled affection. He wanted, he told Salomé, to gain an heir in her. She worried that by 'heir' he meant 'secretary'. Not at all: 'It hadn't occurred to me that you should "read and write" for me; but I very much wish to be allowed to be your teacher.' Creepy overtones aside, the statements are revealing about Nietzsche's state of mind. He wanted a teacher–pupil relationship where she depended on him, not a lover–lover one where they depended on each other. Even *in extremis*, a part of him resisted love's true abandonment.

After Salomé, Nietzsche rejected love and the world altogether. During their affair he had confessed to her: 'I don't want to be lonely any more and I want to learn how to be human again. Ah, in this area, I have almost everything still to learn!' (The genuine sweetness of the remark is slightly undermined by the hint that in every other field, his knowledge is superior.) Afterwards he lived only for his project. 'It was as if,' reported a friend, 'he came from a land where no one else lives.' His disenchantment was accelerated by the failure of his love affair, yet it was also the culmination of a long-term trend. He had based his philosophy on confidence, and confidence is not the friend of love.

Neediness is the hidden side of love, love's necessary evil. Without it, we might desire other people, but we wouldn't *need* them – not in the way love requires. Nietzsche was scared of dependency in any form, yet without dependency love is impossible. Free spirits require constant novelty if they are to maintain confidence. The truly confident person can live without love, because the truly confident person needs no one but themselves.

Confidence and love both involve being open to other people – but the openness is different in kind and degree. Confidence wants to connect to others and go with the flow, but it always seeks to affirm itself. By contrast, love makes us open to the point of vulnerability. It demands that we change – not merely elaborate or extend ourselves, but rather change in essence, in a way that might feel like diminishing or destroying the self. In love, you can't take your pride with you, and you can't reserve yourself intact.

'So what did you do after you broke up with him?' asked Nadine. They were squished together in an armchair in the corner of the living room – *at* the party, but in practice sharing a bottle of wine and talking while the party washed around them.

'Changed all my passwords,' said Ellie.

'God, was Dominic a total shit? He seemed kind of awful, but was he worse than I realised?'

'I really don't know, I've lost all perspective. I went to a café, changed all my passwords, denied him access to my Google calendar, waited till he went out, bought some bin bags, went back to the flat, got his computer, searched it for any naked pictures of me, deleted the one I found, made sure I had any diaries or anything private I'd ever written, put all the rest of my stuff in the bags—'

'This is quite scary. How long were you planning this?'

'I considered logging onto his email and deleting all messages from me, but I held back.'

'Um, good. I'm not sure you get any sanity points for that.'

Squeezing around the edge of the room, a woman Ellie vaguely recognised just saved her glass of wine from tipping into Nadine's lap. 'Oooh, sorry!'

'No worries.'

'Then I went to Maggie's, deleted all record of our relationship on Facebook and where I couldn't delete it, I detagged it, and when I realised I couldn't detag it all, I left Facebook—'

'Then changed your name and got plastic surgery.'

'That's actually not a bad idea.' Ellie drained her plastic glass of wine. She was simultaneously exhausted and hyper-alert: survival mode had well and truly kicked in. Hunger and tiredness had lost their purpose; they cropped up occasionally at odd points in the day or night, but without any insistence, as if natural urges had been temporarily suspended.

'Look.' Nadine patted Ellie's knee in a worryingly parental fashion. 'Look, I mean this in the nicest possible way. And obviously this is all very fresh and you're doing well just by washing and eating and stuff. But do you think you maybe need to rethink your approach?'

'To breaking up?'

'More to getting together in the first place?'

'Yeah, I know, I know,' Ellie nodded earnestly. 'That's my next job. Do you fancy a cigarette?' Ellie was hoping to take some inspiration from Nadine, who managed a multi-layered but apparently low-angst love life. Most recently, Nadine had slept with a woman from the advertising agency where she worked, afterwards remarking only: 'Well, we'd just finished a big project and I felt like it, you know?'

'People don't let you smoke in their houses any more,' said Nadine regretfully.

'Obviously my main plan and number-one priority is to stay single.'

'Yes,' said Nadine patiently.

'Stop it.'

'I'm not doing anything!' Nadine sipped her wine and wrinkled her nose. 'When did it stop being okay to drink wine this disgusting?'

'Since we joined the twats to thirty-five age demographic.'

'Let's have this cigarette then.'

Nobody had quite whipped up the momentum to dance. Ellie hauled Nadine up and they made their way through the tightly packed, chatting groups.

'Can I say,' said Nadine, 'I'm not trying to peer pressure you at all, but what you should do next is just have a bit of a fuck about.'

'How do you mean?'

They headed downstairs, followed by a furtive group of last-tubers.

'As in, there must be loads of people you felt like having sex with and couldn't 'cause you were with someone,' said Nadine, as they pushed out of the front door into the humid evening. 'Well, now you're a free woman. Have a rifle through your Rolodex.'

'Is that a euphemism?'

Nadine laughed. 'Well, why not?'

They walked down the steps and leaned on the railings opposite a metal-shuttered Londis. Ellie pulled out a packet of tobacco. 'Maybe 'cause I'm still on a daily crying schedule and my bedroom consists of a bare mattress and a heap of bin bags?'

'So what? There's no requirement not to be a mess. Just do what you like without feeling guilty about it. It might be a refreshing change.'

'Hey.'

Ellie turned around to see Charlie approaching them, carrying tins of beer and wearing shorts and a baggy T-shirt. 'Oh, hi Charlie. Long time no see. How are you doing?'

'Yeah, all right thanks.' Charlie's hair was longish and unshaped, and he had some non-designer stubble.

'You know Nadine, right?'

'Um, sort of. Hi.'

'Yeah, I sort of know you too,' said Nadine. 'We're just having a cigarette if you'd like one.'

'Um, I'm okay. But I might stand out here for a minute anyway.'

'Raring to party?' Ellie licked her rollie.

'Mm,' Charlie smiled. 'I told Romilly I'd come and didn't want to bail but to be honest I'm pretty knackered.'

'Did you come down from Suu . . . ?'

'Sussex, yeah. Had to work today.'

'Charlie has a chocolate factory,' Ellie told Nadine.

'Amazing! What are the chances?'

'Yeah. I'm actually trying to break free of my destiny and get out of the chocolate game at the moment.'

'Did they call you back in to make one last case?'

'Ha. Sort of.' Charlie shifted his weight from foot to foot. 'I have to change job if I ever want to leave home and have some sort of . . . "life". But—' He frowned. 'Sorry, this is really boring, isn't it?'

'No, not at all.'

'Okay. But if I do leave, my parents will probably have to wind down the business, because they can't really afford to pay someone. I mean, they're not on my case – they want me to move on too. But it's a bit confusing. And also my mum's been ill—'

'Oh no. What's wrong?'

'They're not completely sure yet, but it's sort of zapped all her energy. Anyway.' He shook his head. 'This isn't really party chat.'

'What would you do if you weren't making chocolates?'

'That's my other problem. I don't know.'

'Don't worry,' Ellie wafted her cigarette. 'Nobody does.'

'I certainly don't,' Nadine agreed.

'What are you doing now?' Charlie asked Ellie. 'It must be a couple of years since I last saw you.'

'Well, I'm working reception for a GP so that I can volunteer at this refugee charity.'

'Sounds good.'

'Don't be fooled by the fancy titles. It doesn't mean I have a clue. Like, what if I spend years working for free for this charity and eventually get a job and it's shit pay and I don't even like it?'

'All the Single Ladies' spilled out of the open window above.

'They're playing your song,' Nadine grinned at Ellie.

'I take it that's ironic,' said Charlie.

'No. She is *actually* single. I know – it's hard to believe.'

'I'd give it to the end of the evening.'

'Come on, she might make the end of the week—'

'Fuck you both,' said Ellie.

'You've got to be quick off the mark,' Charlie continued, eyes brightening. 'It's like a game of musical statues. There's probably about ten guys who've been poised for the last however-many years, waiting for this twenty-four-hour window. Everyone's totally still. Then suddenly . . .' Charlie's arms flew in all directions. 'And – freeze!'

Nadine laughed. Ellie rolled her eyes.

'Do you know how long I've been single now?' said Charlie. 'Two and a half years.'

'Stop showing off.'

'Out of choice?' said Nadine.

'God, no – I meet nobody! I've reached depths of loneliness you can't even imagine! I'm practically a monk.'

'Order of the Fruit and Nut.'

'Maybe I should become a nun,' Ellie mused, seriously entertaining the notion. 'A quiet life. I like getting up early.'

'Shut up, you idiot!' said Nadine.

'Thanks.' Ellie came to. 'Good you were here.'

'Shall we go in then?' Nadine stubbed out her fag on the top of the railing.

'Do we have to?'

'S'pose I better say hello,' said Charlie. 'But then we could always hide in a corner and talk to each other.'

'Sounds good.'

Nadine led the way, her orange silk dress glowing up the stairs. Ellie walked just behind Charlie. As they reached the top of the stairs, she found herself looking at a point on his back, between and just below his shoulder blades. Nadine raised her hand to push the door open and at the same time, Ellie raised her hand, and placed it on the patch of green T-shirt she'd been staring at. Charlie turned around, his eyebrows raised a little in surprise, perhaps expecting her to explain she was removing an insect or tucking in a label. She looked at his face, tired and tanned and unguarded. Quite out of nowhere, she kissed him.

'Oh,' said Charlie.

'Don't worry,' she said quickly. 'I'm not starting a relationship with you. That's the last thing I need.'

'Okay,' he said. 'So . . .'

'I just kissed you,' she shrugged, 'Because I wanted to.' Ellie went to push open the door.

'Hang on!' He reached for her hand. 'Don't run away. I'm not – I'm just catching up.'

'It's fine if you don't—'

'Ellie, of—'

'I'm not trying to—'

'Ellie, of course I do—'

'And I know you've taken your vows of—'

'Look,' said Charlie. 'Please just wait a second so I can kiss you.'

21

A Philosophy of Confidence

'It sounds like you're in love,' said Ellie, as she tied the top of a bin bag.

Rose was upside down on the sofa, legs sprawled up the wall, head dangling awkwardly. She groaned.

It was now four years since Rose had collapsed. Glancing at her, Ellie thought she could legitimately be described as 'of slim to medium build'. It changed her completely. Rose no longer seemed to be half out of herself, a loud voice loosely tethered to a pale, brittle frame. This Rose was in every way weightier.

'People talk about love as if it'll feel pleasant,' Ellie went on. 'But when you're falling in love you actually feel, like, total panic. You're freaking out. The thought that you might care about the person makes you hyperventilate. You suspect you might die.' She dragged the bin bag through the kitchen, pausing to study the floor. 'That's definitely mouse droppings. We need to clean more.'

'How can I be in love with Len?' demanded Rose. 'He's called *Len*, for fuck's sake. He comes from Birmingham. He's a physicist and likes *trains*.'

Ellie pulled the bag along the corridor and out of the front door. She heaved it into the wheelie bin and dusted down her hands. 'I don't think you get a choice!' she shouted.

'I suppose . . .' called Rose, as Ellie thudded back into the kitchen. '*You* fell in love with a posh, arrogant twat.'

'By then he'd stopped being a twat. Or *as* arrogant.' Ellie shifted Rose's leg to sit next to her. 'But he was still a bit posh. I found that quite weird for a while. I kept thinking, "I never suspected it would be you. Of all the people I've ever known, it's you! How weird."'

'Arrogance will probably get beaten out of you. But liking trains? That's for life.' Rose closed her eyes and moaned. 'I'm dying. I'm waiting to hear from him for no reason and I don't even know what I want to hear. If he said, "I'm flying to Tanzania for ever," I'd be like, "Thank God. Just leave immediately before I do something stupid."'

'Yeah,' nodded Ellie. 'The first night I slept with Charlie I thought, "Oh no. This isn't some joker person. It's someone I might marry." It was terrifying.'

'Did you tell him that?'

'No! Not at the time. But I felt better about it because the second time we slept together he accidentally drunkenly proposed. Then he said' – she hung her head in shame – '"Sorry, sorry."'

'Ha ha! Did you kiss Charlie or did Charlie kiss you?'

'I kissed him.'

'Harlot.' Rose pushed her hands into the floor, arching her back.

'Good for me, that's what I say.'

'Len kissed me, although by that stage if he didn't do it, I was going to come straight out and tell him to.'

'That wasn't really the important bit though. We didn't get together for quite a while after that.'

'What was important then?' Rose heaved herself up, red-faced.

'Mmm,' Ellie cocked her head to one side, 'It was probably when Charlie told me not to get together with him.'

'Romantic.'

'It actually was. He was like, "I want to be with you. I'm waiting. I'm not going to see anyone else. Tell me when you're ready."'

'Big move.'

'Course, that's the other thing you've got to get your head around,' said Ellie. 'Len might love *you*.'

'Like a *fool*. I'm a *nightmare*. He hasn't the first idea what a loon I actually am.'

'You're great. Len's probably thinking about how great you are right now.'

'He's probably thinking, "I can't be in *love* with someone who studies philosophy and likes the Backstreet Boys. That's absurd. And I *always* thought I'd end up with a Brum."' Rose clambered up. 'I'm gonna make tea.'

'What you are doing today?'

'I am attempting to write my dissertation,' said Rose. 'On your old friend, bloody Nietzsche.'

'Bloody Nietzsche,' echoed Ellie. 'I don't know how you can hack it. I swore off him after mine.'

'I probably never would have picked him if you hadn't. He's like some tortured shit we've both been out with, isn't he?' Rose smiled, filling the kettle.

'I feel like I shagged him when I was about fifteen and you're gonna end up with him for life.'

'I definitely lost then – he's got some serious commitment problems.'

'What did you decide to focus on in the end?'

Rose considered, brushing her long hair across one shoulder. 'I'm going to write about Nietzsche's philosophy of confidence,' she said, frowning at the wall above the sofa. 'A critique.'

'Sounds a lot better than mine.'

'Don't jinx it. I haven't even started yet.' She threw her head back. 'When can I resume normal activity? I mean, this is a fucking piss-take. I hope Len knows how much time I've lost with this full-time mooning schedule.'

'It does pass. You will be able to do stuff again.'

'Maybe I'll be better as an "in love" person,' mused Rose. 'Maybe they're loads more productive.'

'Nah.' Ellie shook her head. 'If anything they're less productive.'

Rose sighed. 'Oh well. Luckily we're not in Maoist China. Nobody's checking – it's just my own life I'm frittering away.'

'Charlie's coming over tonight by the way. He's just had his last day.'

'Oh yeah. Does he know what he's doing next?'

'He's not sure yet. Rose . . .' Ellie tiptoed towards the question. 'Is there any chance Charlie could move in here for a little bit? He'd contribute to the rent.'

Rose looked around and shrugged. 'Have you told him we have mice?'

'No. But he learned to clean a few months ago and he's really taken it to heart.'

'Okay then, great. He's in.' Rose poured tea. 'I actually like Charlie, you know.'

'Good,' Ellie brightened. 'That's cheering.'

'Now he loves himself a bit less there's more room for other people to like him.'

'Yeah.' Yesterday Charlie had spent his last day at work making a short animated film about Ellie's latest trip to Sussex using his desk stationery. 'He's really nice.'

'Oh God, is that what my face looks like? How your face looks now?'

'Probably.'

'Ugh.' Rose dumped an enormous mug of tea on the table they'd constructed from their landlady's discarded belongings, found piled in the garage. 'Right! I've had it with this idiotic blabbering about Len. *If* that's even his real name.' She rolled her eyes, failing to mask her excitement. 'I'm starting my dissertation.'

'All right. Good luck.'

'I'll need it.' Rose hugged herself. 'To be honest, I'm actually losing my shit. It's all kicking off in here.'

'You're hiding it very well.'

'Piss off.'

By the time Nietzsche died, on 25th August 1900, aged only fifty-five, he was famous. He had been insane for eleven years, largely comatose for the last five – yet already his legend had taken on a life of its own. As if playing its part in a horribly well-structured tragedy, the world awoke to his brilliance at the very moment of his collapse. The first serious treatment of his philosophy appeared barely a month after his breakdown in Turin, to be followed by a flood of attacks and appreciations, which continues unabated to this day. With his sister energetically campaigning on his behalf (she would invite journalists and dignitaries up to see the 'mad philosopher' babble helplessly in bed), Nietzsche the man was already on his way to becoming Nietzsche the genius.

For someone who was so determined to become a higher man, it is a strangely fitting end. But, for me, Nietzsche's achievements as a philosopher cannot be separated from his life. (To write about confidence with no consideration of people as feeling, experiencing beings is to ignore what confidence is, the means by which it

308

exists.) It's not that Nietzsche's life was completely sad or pathetic, as some people like to suggest – Nietzsche made his own choices, and for the most part, seemed happy with them. It was, however, a lonely life, based on a lonely philosophy, and in any assessment, that loneliness must be taken into account.

Nietzsche's life and works reveal the internal logic of confidence: the way it guides us, whether we are aware of it or not. We tell ourselves that confidence is good for everyone, and that more of it is always a good thing. We want our children to be confident – which is just another way of saying we want them to thrive and be happy. But confidence is very particular, and when we devote ourselves to confidence, we also agree to a certain logic. That logic might not fit with the lives we want – indeed, it might actually work against them.

That is why we need a philosophy of confidence, which both draws on Nietzsche and learns from his lesson. Because whether we like it or not, confidence has a philosophy of us.

Acknowledgements

This book has been years in the making and we've relied on the help of a lot of people. Huge thanks to the whole team at Bloomsbury, particularly our editors Helen Garnons-Williams, Richard Atkinson, Alexa von Hirschberg and Oliver Holden-Rea; our patient agent, Charlie Viney; our readers, Ben Schiffer and Robert Rowland Smith; and all those who gave us inspiration, advice and encouragement along the way: Jonathan Yiangou, Jennifer Foy, Lucy, Sapphire and Bonnie Manthorpe, Richard Mann, Benji Stanley, Olivia Stewart, Laura Bunt, Alex Beard, Daisy Leitch and Liz Epstein. Special thanks, too, to The Society of Authors, for their advice in times of need, and for their generous assistance via The Authors' Foundation

A Note on the Authors

Rowland Manthorpe is an editor at *Wired* magazine. His writing has been published in the *Guardian, Observer, Sunday Telegraph, Atlantic* and *Spectator*. Rowland studied History at Cambridge and Political Theory at the London School of Economics, and has been awarded the Ben Pimlott Prize for Political Writing by the *Guardian* and The Fabian Society.

Kirstin Smith was born in Edinburgh and studied English at Cambridge. Having worked extensively as an actor in film, television and theatre, Kirstin completed a PhD in Theatre and Performance at Queen Mary, University of London. Her prize-winning research on the history of stunts has appeared in The Drama Review.

Rowland and Kirstin first met at university. They live and write together in south London.

@rowlsmanthorpe / @KirstinMSm

A Note on the Type

The text of this book is set in Bembo, which was first used in 1495 by the Venetian printer Aldus Manutius for Cardinal Bembo's *De Aetna*. The original types were cut for Manutius by Francesco Griffo. Bembo was one of the types used by Claude Garamond (1480–1561) as a model for his Romain de l'Université, and so it was a forerunner of what became the standard European type for the following two centuries. Its modern form follows the original types and was designed for Monotype in 1929.